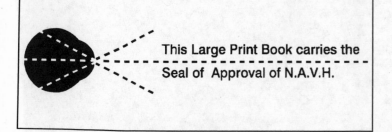

This Large Print Book carries the
Seal of Approval of N.A.V.H.

FULL STEAM AHEAD

FULL STEAM AHEAD

KAREN WITEMEYER

THORNDIKE PRESS
A part of Gale, Cengage Learning

GALE
CENGAGE Learning·

Farmington Hills, Mich • San Francisco • New York • Waterville, Maine
Meriden, Conn • Mason, Ohio • Chicago

GALE
CENGAGE Learning®

LIBRARY OF CONGRESS CATALOGING-IN-PUBLICATION DATA

Witemeyer, Karen.
    Full steam ahead / by Karen Witemeyer. — Large print edition.
        pages ; cm. — (Thorndike Press large print Christian romance)
        ISBN 978-1-4104-7055-3 (hardcover) — ISBN 1-4104-7055-5 (hardcover)
        1. Large type books. I. Title.
    PS3623.I864F85 2014b
    813'.6—dc23   2014015679

Published in 2014 by arrangement with Bethany House Publishers, a division of Baker Publishing Group

Printed in the United States of America
1 2 3 4 5 6 7 18 17 16 15 14

To Bethany
My own beautiful
female mathematician.
This heroine's for you!

There is therefore now no condemnation
to them which are in Christ Jesus.

Romans 8:1

PROLOGUE

New Orleans
November 15, 1849

Passengers jockeyed for position along the steamboat *Louisiana*'s railings, waving and calling merry farewells to the crowd lining the levee. Darius Thornton stalked determinedly across the deck in the opposite direction. He'd done all the smiling he cared to during the previous half hour while Captain Cannon gave him, and a handful of other investors, a tour of the vessel.

His brother, David, should have been the one mixing with the Caribbean coffee barons and southern cotton tycoons, not him. David was the diplomat of the family. Mingling with wealthy plantation owners and charming their wives came as naturally to him as adding a column of numbers came to Darius. But David's wife was expecting their first child and insisted her husband remain by her side in case the babe

9

chose to come early. Early? Darius snorted. The birth was months away. The little tyke wasn't scheduled to arrive until January.

Darius rested his forearms against the river-facing rails and stared into the dark water off the starboard side of the bow. New mothers. Always so jittery and anxious about everything. Tying their men to their apron strings and making their brothers-in-law suffer through torturous affairs when they could be at home in their office poring over ledgers and schematics — objects that didn't expect wit or charisma. Solid, dependable things that required a man's brain, not an ability to titter and chat about the weather. Stuff and nonsense, all of it.

But sharing the familial load was what brothers were for. David had stepped in for Darius on more than one occasion. It was only right that he return the favor. Too bad he had to be so formal while he did it. He much preferred working in his shirt sleeves behind closed doors to prancing around in a tightly tailored coat and beaver hat with a bunch of dandies who considered a man's fashion an accurate measure of his importance.

With a groan, he dug a finger beneath his collar, wishing he could rip the thing from his neck and fling it into the river's murky depths. The ridiculous starched points had been jabbing the underside of his jaw all afternoon.

"I thought King Star Shipping specialized in ocean vessels, Thornton. What's your interest in riverboats?"

Darius bit back an inhospitable retort as he turned to face one of the investors from the tour. *Drat.* What was the fellow's name? Something starting with a R. Or maybe an N? David would have remembered. He would have known the man's wife's name, the names of each of their twelve kids, and probably the monikers of the horses in his stable back home. All Darius could recall were the numbers. The man owned four Mississippi steamboats, each capable of hauling two hundred fifty passengers and five thousand bales of cotton.

"We're not against expansion," Darius drawled, hoping the man wouldn't notice his lack of proper address. "With the rate the Port of New Orleans is growing, one would be a fool not to consider investing in the steamboat trade."

The man nodded, his pea-green waistcoat not quite containing the rounded girth of his belly. "True. But riverboats are an entirely different animal from your ocean liners. Temperamental things, you know.

One cannot just assume he is fit to add one to his collection without first gaining a proper respect for the vessel."

The smug expression on the fellow's face combined with his superior tone snapped the last thread of Darius's tattered hold on civility. Straightening to his full height, he glowered down at the man. "King Star Shipping does not *collect* vessels, sir. We live and breathe them. Not one of our transatlantic liners has failed to reach its destination, and I daresay the same cannot be said of your riverboats. One has only to read the papers to learn how often they run aground on sandbars, get snared in debris, or catch fire due to negligent captains. Not to mention the boiler explosions that sink ships and take lives when greedy pilots push their engines to reckless speeds in order to race.

"If King Star does decide to expand into river transport, you can bet we will be enforcing higher standards than any who have come before. Respect the vessel, sir? You don't know the meaning of the word."

The mottled purple hue staining the man's face was the first clue he'd gone too far. The slap of the man's glove across Darius's face was the second.

"You high-and-mighty Thorntons think you're above the rest of us, don't you? Well,

12

one of these days disaster will knock on *your* door, and then we'll see just how far your lofty opinions take you." With an audible *humph,* the man pivoted and stormed off in the direction of the waving masses.

Darius sighed and turned back to the railing, searching the dark water below. Lofty opinions, indeed. He never should have opened his mouth. He should have just smiled at the little peacock and walked away. But no. He'd let his temper get the best of him and spouted off like a bull-headed idiot. The green-vested fellow could be a stellar boatman for all he knew. He had no right to accuse him of not respecting his vessels or his crew. This was why David handled the people and Darius handled the accounts. The minute one of them switched assignments, a mess was sure to follow.

If God were merciful, he'd eliminate any need for polite conversation for the length of the voyage.

Another steamboat came abreast of the *Louisiana.* The bright red lettering on the side declared it to be the *Bostona,* and its decks were equally full of passengers and goods. Darius frowned. Must the boats pack together so closely while in port? It was bad enough that the *Storm* anchored nearby having just returned from upriver, but now the *Bostona* was crowding in. Once the *Louisiana*'s captain shoved off, they'd have to do some fine maneuvering to get to open water.

Darius pulled his watch from his vest pocket and flipped open the brass case. Nearly five o'clock. Good. Time to depart.

He replaced his watch as the chimes rang the hour from the cathedral bell in Jackson Square. Then the *Louisiana*'s whistle blew its piercing call, and the steamboat eased away from the wharf.

All at once a deafening roar crashed over Darius. The deck shuddered and splintered as if besieged by cannon fire. Debris shot through the air. A metal object collided with Darius's head, sending him reeling. He grasped the railing and barely kept himself from toppling over the side.

Vision blurred and head throbbing, Darius closed his eyes against the chaos, trying to calm his rioting senses and decipher what was happening. Screams assailed his ears. The smells of scalded flesh, blood, and burning wood churned his stomach.

The boilers. A moan tore from Darius's throat as his eyes flew open in comprehension. The boilers must have exploded.

How? They were in port for pity's sake, not racing at top speed up the river. This

14

wasn't supposed to happen. Not with a capable captain at the helm.

But the *why*s didn't matter. Not when people were dying all around him.

The deck shifted, collapsing inward. Darius linked his arm around the railing. Heaven help them. The ship was going down!

Blinking away the blood dripping in his eyes, Darius peered out over the river. They were only a hundred yards or so from the wharf, thank God. Swimming to shore would be easily managed — for those who knew how to swim, at least. Having grown up in a shipping family, Darius was as at home in the water as on land, so he had no concerns for himself. But he needed to help the others. The masses trapped on the upper decks or in the boat's midsection would perish if they couldn't reach the rails before the sinking vessel dragged them under.

Recalling the ships around them, he jerked his head up. Surely the crews of the *Storm* and *Bostona* would aid in the rescue. However, the sight that met his eyes punctured his hopes. The *Storm* had been laid waste by the explosion, splintered and crumbling from side wheel to the stern. The *Bostona* hadn't fared much better. Her upper works were a mess, her pilothouse had been knocked off, and her wheelhouse was badly crushed.

Bodies littered the river between the three boats, some moving, others not. Bile rose in Darius's throat.

Then something hardened in the pit of his stomach. His fingernails dug into the railing. The ship was going down. No time for weeping over what couldn't be saved. Turning away from the watery scene, he braced his legs wide beneath him and catalogued what *could* be done.

Setting his jaw, he strode forward. Directly into the path of the man with the pea-green vest. The fellow lay crumpled on the deck, gripping his head, seemingly unaware that a deep gash in his arm bled profusely.

The fellow's name suddenly came to him. "Monroe!" Darius knelt at his side and yanked the wide silk tie free from his own collar as Monroe's sluggish gaze found Darius's face.

"Thornton?" he rasped.

Wrapping the impromptu bandage around the man's arm, Darius nodded. "Can you stand?" he asked brusquely.

"I-I think so." Monroe started to push himself up.

Darius grabbed the man's good arm and assisted. "Good. The boat's going down. We need to evacuate the passengers."

Monroe's eyes rounded as Darius's meaning sank in. "But the only way off is into the river."

"I know. The women will need something to keep them afloat, so their skirts don't drag them under." Darius scanned the deck for anything that might be suitable. "Wood," he declared, pointing to the debris scattered about them. "They can grab on to planks and kick their way to shore."

Monroe nodded, his shoulders straightening like a soldier receiving orders, no sign of lingering animosity. "I'll gather some men and see to the ladies' safety."

"Good. I'll see if I can reach the passengers on the upper deck." Darius pushed his way through the staggering masses, encouraging everyone to make their way to the railing. Yet the farther inside he went, the more grim the scene. Dead and dying passengers covered the floor, their skin scalded from the violent expulsion of steam, bodies fatally pierced by metal projectiles launched by the explosive force of the ruptured boilers.

The stench of blood and burned flesh clung to him as he picked his way through the horror. A woman lay to his right, moaning, her clothing shredded from the blast.

He ripped his coat from his shoulders and draped it over her torso, knowing even as he did so that she'd never survive her injuries. Moving on, he tunneled his vision to a narrow space directly in front of him and let his mind go numb. The people here were too far gone. He had to get to the upper deck. Had to find a way to get the passengers there to safety. But when he reached the staircase, fallen timbers barred his path. He grabbed the one closest to him and strained against the weight. It didn't budge.

"No!" Darius slammed his palm against the wedged beam. He hung his head — and noticed water seeping over his boots. Time was running out.

Darius rushed back outside and headed for the railing. There was more than one way to the upper deck. Ignoring the unsteady lurching of the boat as the river sucked it down, Darius scrabbled on top of the railing, using one of the connecting pillars as a support. He reached over his head and managed to grab hold of the bottom rung of the upper-deck balustrade. Now he just had to haul himself up.

Loud splashes echoed around him. Dark forms dove through his periphery as men and women alike started leaping from the upper deck. Darius hesitated. Should he continue?

Then a woman's voice cut through the panicked mass of screams. "Please, sir!" she cried. "Take my child. He can't swim."

Darius barely registered the woman hanging over the rail directly above him before a pair of child-sized shoes knocked against his nose. Without thought to his perilous position, Darius released his hold on the support pillar and clutched the lad's waist. In an instant he had the boy on the lower deck.

Catching sight of a pea-green waistcoat, he yelled, "Monroe! Take the child!"

Monroe turned and immediately scurried forward.

"Here!" the woman above Darius called again. And before he knew what had happened, a steady trail of children were dangled over the side into his waiting arms.

Sweat beaded his brow. The little ones were easy enough to handle despite their wailing, but the larger children kicked and screamed their terror, nearly sending both themselves and him over the side on more than one occasion.

Thanking God for his height and strength, Darius wrestled them to relative safety, though they'd still have to manage their way ashore. He prayed there'd be smaller boats on hand before the *Louisiana* submerged.

Darius reached for the next child, but instead he saw a girl holding fast to the outside of the rails, no adult in sight. She must have been twelve or thirteen, her eyes round, pleading with him to save her.

But she was too far down the railing for him to reach. "Easy, now." He held a hand out to her. "Let me come to you."

Taking hold of the pillar again, Darius carefully swung one leg around the post, then the other. "I'm coming. Just be still." Her legs batted the air so wildly, he feared she'd jar herself loose before he could get into position. Darius moved his hold to the upper railing and eased a step closer to her. "I won't let you fall."

He widened his stance on the railing and braced his legs to take her weight even as he reached up to grab hold of her waist. At the same moment, something below gave out a mighty groan and the *Louisiana* pitched violently.

The girl's hold broke. Darius lunged for her, but she slipped through his arm. Her scream rang in his ears as she plummeted past him into the dark water.

Darius leaned over the side, scanning the water for the girl. How could he have let her fall? He'd promised.

She sputtered to the surface, arms flailing in the panicked motions of one who'd never been taught to swim. Without hesitation, Darius dove in after her.

He kicked quickly to the surface, the water too dark for him to see anything below. Yet there was no sign of her above, either. He swiveled his neck from side to side, desperate. Where was she? She should have been right there.

Then a tiny splash to his left drew his attention. A limp hand was disappearing into the river a couple yards downstream, a hand edged with a pink sleeve.

Darius sucked in a lungful of air and dove underwater, kicking with powerful strokes to the place she should have been. But the currents were strong, and the girl wasn't. Darius slashed his arms through the water, hoping to collide with her torso and be able to drag her to him. He hit what seemed to be the wilted length of her arm and fumbled for a hold, but the currents tugged her out of his reach.

Darius swam after her, but the darkness hid her from him. Deeper and deeper he went. Searching. Praying. His lungs burned, but he refused to stop. He had to find her. He'd promised he wouldn't let her fall.

He swept his arms out again, and his right

arm hit something solid. He circled his arm around the girl's chest and kicked for the surface. They broke through. *Thank God!* Darius gasped for breath yet never stopped swimming. Angling the girl so her head remained above water, he made for the shore.

His legs finally found purchase on land, and Darius lifted the girl into his arms. Utterly depleted, he stumbled under her slight weight. Clenching his jaw, he righted himself and managed to get her to dry ground. Her body hung lifelessly from his arms. He dropped to one knee and rolled her over until she was draped across his thigh. Then he pounded her back with all the strength he had left.

"Please, sweetheart," he begged. "Please breathe."

Water pumped out of her mouth, but she remained limp. Lifeless.

Darius cradled her body and tenderly laid it out upon the sand. He bent his ear to her mouth, longing to hear the rasp of breath even as he knew it wouldn't be there.

"I'm sorry." Reality slammed into him, tearing a sob from his throat. The girl was gone. He'd failed her. He'd let her fall.

Darius pounded his fist into the sand and shouted his grief to the heavens.

CHAPTER 1

Galveston, Texas
April 1851

Nicole Renard gripped her mother's letter in her gloved hand as the carriage rattled down Bath Street, away from the docks. *Come at once,* her mother had written. *Your father is very ill. He might not survive to the end of your term.*

Nicole had packed her belongings the day the letter arrived and left Miss Rochester's Academy for Young Ladies the following morning.

The voyage that had seemed so swift and exhilarating last fall dragged out interminably on the return trip. Her stomach had been so knotted with worry that she rarely left her stateroom for anything other than meals. This behavior from the girl who used to cry inconsolably if her sea-captain father made her go belowdecks, where she couldn't feel the ocean spray against her face and smell the salty tang of the sea air. The briny air and windy spray on this journey, however, only intensified her distress as memories of the strong, vital man she remembered from childhood wilted beneath her mother's description of the decimation brought on by his illness.

"Dear Lord," she whispered for the hundredth time since leaving Boston. "Don't take him from us. Please. Strengthen him. Heal him. Give me back my papa."

Her hand trembled, crinkling the letter. She pressed both against her stomach and blinked back the tears that threatened to escape her lashes. Nicole bit down on the edge of her tongue. There'd be no crying today. Her papa hated tears, said they were a weakness, a woman's affliction. A man wouldn't cry. A man would set about fixing things. So that's what she'd do. Fix things.

She'd spell Mother in nursing him. She'd oversee the accounts and check in at the Renard Shipping offices every day to keep him apprised of his business interests. She'd prove herself as valuable to him as the son he'd always lamented not having.

The carriage turned a corner. Nicole braced her arm against the upholstered seat to aid her balance. Five more blocks and she'd be home. She looked out the window at the familiar landscape, her heart stirring as the marshy environ welcomed her.

Then she saw it — Renard House. Its white columns stood tall and proud, exactly as she remembered. Her gaze flicked to the second-story window on the far side, her bedroom. The light glowing within brought a smile to Nicole's face. All those times that she and Tommy Ackerman had stayed out too late at the bayou, fishing or playing pirate, her mother would light a lamp and set it on the table near her window so Nicole would have a beacon to guide her home when darkness began to fall. Now, years later, as dusk settled over the island again, that same lamp beckoned.

When the driver pulled the team to a halt, Nicole didn't wait for him to assist her. She unlatched the door and bounded out, grabbing a handful of her full skirts to ensure she didn't stumble. Heart pounding with a mixture of dread and longing, she dashed up the front walk. Before she reached the covered porch, her mother had both the door and her arms open wide.

"Maman!" Nicole raced up the steps and threw her arms around her mother's neck. In that instant, all the questions and concerns plaguing her flew out of her mind. She was home. Her *maman* was holding her.

Everything would be all right.

Together they swayed gently from side to side, her mother rubbing her back and humming softly, just as she used to do when Nicole had been small enough to curl up in her lap.

"It is so good to have you home, *ma petite.*" Her mother eased back, taking Nicole by the arms and studying her face as if afraid she had forgotten what her daughter looked like. "But what is all this dashing about?" A sparkle lit her lovely brown eyes as she lifted a well-manicured brow. "Your father and I paid good money for that finishing school, and here you are still running about the place, as much the hoyden as ever. Really, Nicole, John looked quite exasperated when you threw that carriage door open without waiting for him. The poor fellow was probably looking forward to welcoming you home with a gallant flourish, and you stole all his fun."

Following her mother's gaze, Nicole turned her head to see the coachman standing a few feet away, her steamer trunk balanced on his shoulder. The man's expression was as bland and bored as always. John had no fun to steal. Not that she hadn't tried over the years. It was a game she had played since childhood, trying to coax a smile out of the old curmudgeon. She'd yet to see one, but she believed they were there. The man was just too accomplished an adversary to let one slip free.

Trying to look contrite, Nicole dipped her chin in his direction. "I apologize for ruining your fun, John. I can only imagine what I missed by rushing out on my own. How grand was this flourish supposed to be?"

The coachman strode forward as if to move past her into the house without reply, then stopped when he reached her side. "I believe there were to be rose petals flung upon the ground, a trumpet anthem, and dancing horses, miss." His impassive voice recited the fanciful list as if he were ordering groceries at the mercantile.

Nicole choked on a giggle. "Dancing horses?"

The man's bored expression never wavered. "Been training the beasts for weeks. And all for naught." He gave a sad shake of his head and continued into the house.

Nicole met her mother's disbelieving glance, and the two immediately dissolved into laughter.

Her mother wiped at the moisture leaking from her eyes and smiled. "Oh, it feels good to laugh. There's been too little reason for merriment of late."

Nicole sobered. "How is Father? Has there been any improvement since your last letter?"

Her mother wrapped an arm around her shoulders and ushered her inside. "The doctors are offering little hope for recovery. They've discovered a . . . growth . . . in his abdomen."

Nicole gripped her mother's hand when she would have turned away to close the door. "What does that mean?"

"It's hard to know. He isn't in a lot of pain yet — thank the Lord — but he barely eats, has no energy, and is just . . . wasting away."

She sighed. And for the first time Nicole noticed the lines of fatigue marring her mother's usually flawless skin. "The doctor is loathe to operate. Says it would be too dangerous. But if the tumor continues to grow, there's a chance your father's condition will worsen and eventually end his life."

Nicole tightened her grip on her mother's hand. "But there's also a chance it won't grow. Right?"

Her mother cupped Nicole's cheek in her hand, a sad smile curving her lips. "Yes, there is a chance, *ma petite.* We will continue to pray and hope that God will give us the answer we desire. But we must also prepare to say good-bye. For your father's sake as well as our own. Your papa, he's just stubborn enough to refuse to die if he thinks his girls will not be all right without him. And I won't have him suffering pain needlessly."

A fierce light sparked in her eyes. Her *maman* could be just as stubborn as her father. "We will love him, we will nurse him, and we will give him peace so that he may leave when the Lord calls him home. Are we agreed?"

The challenge resonated in Nicole's breast. The child in her wanted to cling to her papa, to hold him fast and never let him go. Yet her woman's heart recognized the wisdom in her mother's words, the love that drove the sacrifice of letting go.

"Agreed."

Her mother squeezed her hand, smiled, and turned back to close the door.

"Pauline?" A deep voice rasped from behind them. "Thought I heard the carriage. Is our Nicki home?"

Nicole spun around, eager to greet her father, but as her beloved papa shuffled into the hall, a cry lodged in her throat. The man who had always been larger than life in her eyes emerged from the parlor a man so thin his clothes hung from his frame as if his shoulders were nothing more substantial than a pair of hooks in a wardrobe.

29

Determined to hide her distress, she pasted on a bright grin and strode forward. "I'm home, Papa. I'm home." Embracing him with a gentleness that broke her heart for its necessity, she kissed his cheek and then stepped back.

"Missed you, my girl. The place isn't the same without you." He patted the wall as he spoke, then left his hand braced there. Nicole didn't miss the way his body sagged as he let the house take on a portion of his weight. What little there was of it. "Your mother told me you took another first in mathematics last term."

His eyes sparkled, and Nicole relaxed. He was still there, inside that emaciated body. Her papa was still the same proud, stubborn, loving man she'd always adored.

"My mathematics instructor, Miss Brownstead, even managed to acquire a copy of the examination they administered at Harvard last year and let me take it after hours. She said my score would have placed me in the top quarter of the first-year gentlemen."

"Ha!" her father boomed, a hint of what she'd always thought of as his captain's voice returning. "That's my girl. Always knew you had it in you. The crewmen down at the docks still talk about how they could throw cargo numbers at you from the manifest and your totals would match the accounting every time."

Nicole chuckled over the memory of the game she and the men had played when her father took her down to his office with him. "Except for that time when I came up with a different tonnage, and the men insisted Mr. Bailey check his figures."

Papa nodded, his rich laugh filling the hall. "I remember. Gerald was in such a state. He insisted his numbers were correct and refused to recalculate, so I took the books from him and did it myself. When my answer matched yours, he was livid — until he checked the work himself and found his error. The men badgered him for weeks after that. Wouldn't let him hear the end of it." He shook his head. "He's double-checked his numbers every shipment since, though, and we've never had another discrepancy."

"You know I'll always do whatever I can to help Renard Shipping, Papa." Nicole smiled as she delivered the lighthearted statement, but the truth of it ran deep. Renard Shipping was in her blood. Now that her father was ailing, it was up to her to keep things running, and she aimed to do just that.

"Let's get you back to your chair, Anton,"

31

her mother said, coming forward to take his arm. "Nicole has had a long journey. I'm sure she would like time to rest a bit and change before dinner. Wouldn't you, dear?"

A denial rose to Nicole's lips. She wanted to stay with her father. To visit and reconnect after months away. But when she met her mother's gaze, she bit back the words. Papa was the one who needed the rest. He tried to hide it, yet on closer inspection, Nicole realized her mother supported much of his weight as he stepped away from the wall.

"Yes." Nicole let her shoulders slump a little. "I *am* weary. A short rest before dinner would be just the thing. Then I can tell you all about the coastal steamer I rode down from Boston. It had one of those new iron screw propeller systems, Papa."

His eyes lit with interest, and his posture straightened. "The screw propeller, huh? Did it have a paddle wheel, too, or —"

"At dinner, Anton," his wife scolded gently. "She'll tell you all about it at dinner." She pressed him into motion back toward the parlor. "Let the girl catch her breath. They'll be plenty of time to quiz her later."

And, of course, her mother was right. In fact, once she was closeted alone in her room, Nicole found that she truly *was* weary. The constant worry of the past weeks followed by the sad evidence of her father's deteriorated condition had left her exhausted.

She put on a bright face again for dinner and eagerly regaled her papa with what knowledge she'd managed to glean from Captain Sanders during her time aboard the *Starlight*. When Cook brought out dessert, however, Nicole failed to contain the yawn that stretched her jaw downward into a thoroughly unladylike position.

"Darling, go on up to bed." Her mother's smile said so much more than her words. *I love you. Take care of yourself. Don't worry about what you can't control.* All of those sentiments communicated silently through the tender curve of lips and the radiating warmth of a pair of brown eyes.

Nicole returned the smile, hoping her *maman* would recognize her own messages in return. *I love you, too. I'm here to help. Thank you for taking care of all of us.* Then she rose from the table, kissed her mother's cheek, and turned to face her father.

"Good night, Papa." His skin felt paper-thin beneath her lips as she softly bussed his cheek.

"Good night, scamp. It's good to have you home."

Nicole made her way upstairs and readied for bed, her yawns coming with increased frequency. When she finally stretched out upon her bed, sleep claimed her quickly.

Sometime later, a muffled crash below-stairs woke her. Disoriented at first, it took a moment to recognize her room as the one at home instead of her accommodations at the academy. Sitting up, she probed the silence for clues.

Another sound echoed from downstairs. A thud. *Papa!* Had he fallen?

Throwing back the blankets, Nicole rolled to her feet and grabbed her dressing gown from the end of her bed. Pushing her arms through the sleeves, she crossed the floor in urgent strides. She opened the door and sped down the hall to the stairway, her bare feet silent upon the floorboards.

Reverberations of angry voices stopped her descent. Male voices. Voices she didn't recognize.

Someone had broken into her house.

CHAPTER 2

Nicole gnawed on her lip as she pressed her back against the wall that sheltered the staircase from view. She had to find a way to get to her parents. They'd started sleeping in the room off the parlor when the stairs became too taxing for Papa, so they were directly in the path of the intruders.

John slept at the coach house. Unless the thieves had made a noise during their approach that awakened him, he'd still be sleeping soundly. Best not to expect any help from that quarter. Margie, the cook, was the only other servant who lived on the premises, and while she was handy with a knife when it came to butchering meat, live quarry was a bit beyond her experience. Besides, the woman's sense of self-preservation was far too strong to put her anywhere other than behind a solidly locked door. They'd not see her until the trouble passed.

That left Nicole.

The knife and garter sheath her father had given her for her fifteenth birthday lay at the bottom of her trunk. Going back for it would waste precious time. Better to assess the situation first, then decide whether or not to retrieve it.

Nicole eased down the stairs, holding her breath when the wall shielding her gave way to open space, exposing her feet and the white of her sleeping gown. No shouts of discovery sounded, so she continued downward, praying the boards wouldn't creak beneath her weight.

"Where is it, old man?" one of the intruders demanded. "Tell me, or I'll start snapping the bones in your fingers and work my way up your arm."

"Go ahead. I ain't good for much these days anyhow."

Papa! Stubborn, defiant man. He'd never give in to their threats. His body might be weak, but his will was as strong as ever. That's what scared her.

"Oh yeah?" a second voice sneered. "What if we break your lovely wife's fingers instead? Still want to play the hero? It'd be a shame if she couldn't play the spinet for you anymore, don't you think?"

"No!" Her father's shout echoed Nicole's

mental cry. "Lay a hand on my wife, and I'll kill you. I swear it."

"Big words from a man who can barely stand. Now, where's the dagger?"

The dagger? No. The situation was worse than she'd thought. Her father might swallow his pride enough to hand over money or other valuables to spare her mother, but the Lafitte Dagger? It was the Renard family legacy. He'd die before giving it up. She had to do something.

Glancing both ways down the hall to be sure a third man wasn't lying in wait somewhere, Nicole left the stairs and padded toward her parents. Flattening herself against the wall, she darted a quick glance inside the room before yanking her head back out of view.

One of the men had a gun on her father in the back left corner. The other man stood near her mother. A lamp had fallen from the bedside table and the curtains were half pulled down, as if her father had put up a struggle. Unfortunately, in his weakened condition, he'd been no match for the much younger men.

Nicole gritted her teeth. A year ago, no one would have dared accost Anton Renard in his own home. Even six months ago her father would have bested them. The thieves had waited for his illness to do their work for them. Cowards.

Nicole scanned the hall for anything she could use as a weapon. She reached for a decorative porcelain vase perched on the small Chippendale pedestal table between her parents' bedroom and the parlor. Seizing it against her chest, she drew in several fortifying breaths before inching back to the doorway.

"So, Renard," the man taunted, "what's it gonna be? The dagger or your wife's hand?"

"Let her go!" Papa demanded at the same time her mother's soft grunting announced her struggle to free herself.

Visions of her *maman*'s elegant fingers mangled and crooked spurred Nicole into action. Lifting the heavy vase above her head, she ran into the room and slammed it down on her mother's captor's skull.

Porcelain shattered. The man groaned, then crumpled to the floor. His companion shouted.

"He has a pistol in the waistband of his trousers." Her mother pointed as she scrambled from beneath the fallen man.

Nicole dropped to her knees and grabbed the weapon just as the second man lunged forward, his gun targeting Nicole.

"You killed him!"

Nicole extended her arm, pointing her newly acquired pistol directly at Will Jenkins's chest. His brother, Fletcher, must be the man on the floor. Which was a good thing. He'd always been the meaner of the two. The smarter one, as well. If she had to pick a Jenkins to face, she'd choose Will every time. "He's still breathing," she snapped. All those days of playing pirate with Tommy Ackerman were finally paying off. She'd managed to inject just the right amount of disdain into that statement, and her hand wasn't even shaking. "Now, collect your brother and leave our house."

His gaze moved from her face to the gun, then back to her face, an annoyingly smug expression creeping across his features. "I don't think so. You ain't got the first notion how to shoot that thing. Can't even find the trigger, can you." He took a menacing step toward her.

Nicole raised her left brow. "You mean *this* trigger?" She cocked the hammer of the Colt Paterson revolver and released the folding trigger mechanism. Will stopped. "You forget, Will Jenkins — I'm a Renard. Daughter of Anton Renard and granddaughter to Henri Renard, privateer and compatriot of Jean Lafitte himself. I know a thing or two about weapons."

Will swallowed hard, his Adam's apple bobbing in his throat as his attention locked on the gun once again. His own pistol wavered.

Nicole stepped closer to her mother, clearing a path for Will to get to Fletcher and the door without having to go through her. Now if he'd just take the hint. . . .

Fletcher moaned. Will glanced down at his brother. At the same time Nicole's father, all but forgotten in the background, slid his hand around a cane that stood propped against the back wall and leapt forward. He brought the cane down on Will's arm.

Will cried out. His pistol clattered to the floor. Papa kicked it under the bed.

"My daughter told you to leave. I suggest you do so. Now!" He roared the last. Will jumped to obey.

Latching on to his brother's wrist, Will drew Fletcher's arm over his shoulders while shoring him up on the other side with an arm about the waist. The still-reeling Fletcher offered little in the way of assistance. Nevertheless, Will managed to get him up and out the front door. Nicole followed them, the Colt aimed at their backs until they mounted and rode away.

Lowering the weapon, Nicole rubbed her

40

upper arm, suddenly aware of the vicious ache in her muscles. It was amazing how heavy such a small revolver became when one found it necessary to hold it aloft for several minutes at a time. Being in Boston for most of the last two years hadn't done her any favors in that regard. Not much opportunity for target practice in a fancy girls' school. She'd gone soft.

But not so soft that she couldn't run off Will and Fletcher Jenkins. Nicole's mouth curved in a self-satisfied grin as she strolled back into the house and latched the door. All in all, not a bad night's work.

Nicole paused to arrange her dressing gown in a less haphazard manner and to properly tie her sash before reentering her parents' room.

"Do you think they'll be back?" Her mother's voice drifted out to the hall.

"Of course they'll be back. Now that they've seen for themselves how pitifully weak this cursed illness has left me, they'll not stop until they have the dagger."

"But Nicole is here now, surely they wouldn't —"

"Nicole caught them by surprise. It was sheer luck that saved us this night. No matter how well-versed in weaponry she is, no slip of a girl will keep Carson Jenkins at bay.

He has two strapping boys who've just proven they'll do anything to help him secure their family's future. What do I have? A daughter."

The disdain-filled word crashed through Nicole's chest and bludgeoned her heart like a carelessly flung carpenter's mallet.

"Anton! That's not fair."

A heavy sigh echoed through the bedroom. "You're right. Forgive me. I just wish . . . Never mind. It doesn't matter."

But it does matter, Nicole thought. It always had. All her life she'd striven to please her father. To earn his praise, his respect. Yet the one thing he wanted above all else, she couldn't be — a son.

"Nicole is the joy of my life — you know that," her father said. "She's twice as clever as either of Carson Jenkins's boys and has more courage in that tiny body of hers than any man I've ever known. But that doesn't change the fact that she's female. She poses no serious threat to Jenkins or his plans. If anything, her being here simply gives Jenkins one more weapon to use against me."

"Then perhaps I should return to Boston." Nicole stepped through the doorway and tossed the Colt onto the end of the bed, a few inches to the right of where her father sat.

"Nicki!" The color his anger had stirred in his cheeks drained away the instant his gaze met hers.

She gained no satisfaction from his distress. Despite everything, she loved her Papa and knew he loved her, too. He might have always wished he'd had a son, but he'd never once made her believe he regretted having her as a daughter.

"It's all right, Papa." Well, not completely. The words still hurt. But he didn't need to know that. There were bigger issues to deal with than a little girl's hurt feelings. Time to grow up and be the woman her parents raised her to be. "What we need to do now," she said, lowering herself onto the padded divan just inside the doorway, "is formulate a plan to keep Jenkins from creating any more mischief."

Her mother passed by the divan and patted Nicole's shoulder, favoring her with one of those "speaking" smiles of hers. Pride. Approval. Compassion. Then she moved to her husband's side, took his hand, and settled onto the edge of the bed next to him.

"Should we report this to Sheriff Sparks? I know he's got ties to the Jenkins family, but surely when he hears of the threats the boys made —"

Papa shook his head. "Sparks made it

clear when he took office that he would not become entangled in our *feud,* as he calls it."

Nicole bit back a groan. A feud? That was stating it mildly. Jenkins had been her father's fiercest rival for years and blamed him for every financial setback he'd ever incurred. Said it was all because the dagger was stolen from his family. Which was ridiculous. Lafitte had bestowed the dagger on Nicole's grandfather after Henri Renard saved the pirate's life.

"When that scuffle broke out between our two crews last year, the sheriff wouldn't even break it up. Remember?" Her father shot her mother a telling look. "All he did was send for the captains and have them sort things out. He staunchly refuses to hear petty charges from either side."

Maman stiffened. "I'd hardly call what happened tonight *petty.*"

"No one was hurt, nothing was stolen. For a man like Sparks, who spends his nights keeping the lawless element from killing and maiming each other down at the docks, that's the definition of petty."

"We could hire guards," her mother suggested.

"Guards?" Papa reared back as if his wife had slapped him across the face. "And

44

admit to the world that Anton Renard cannot protect his own family? Bah!"

"There's no shame in accepting help from people you know and trust, Anton. I'm sure there are men from your crews who would appreciate earning a little extra money for their families when they're in port by taking on additional responsibilities."

His shoulders curled inward as he expelled a sigh, his chest — once robust and barreled — caving in on itself. "I suppose we must." His gaze lowered to the floor, his pride stripped away. "I won't risk any harm coming to either of you."

"What if the dagger wasn't here?" Nicole quietly inserted into the conversation. "What if I took it back to Boston? That would ensure there'd be no more attacks on Renard House." Her main concern. "Therefore, there'd be no need for guards." Which would save her father's pride and reputation among his men.

Her mother shot to her feet. "Absolutely not! Why, anything could happen to you between here and there. Jenkins wouldn't hesitate to send his boys after you. You'd be defenseless." She spun toward her husband, hands on hips. "Tell her, Anton."

"Your mother's right, scamp. It's too dangerous."

Nicole lunged forward. "It's not too dangerous, Papa. I know how to take care of myself. Haven't I proven that to you, tonight?"

His head snapped up at the challenge in her voice, his eyes hardening. "You got lucky tonight. Taking a man by surprise is an entirely different matter than inviting him to a fight. That's exactly what you'd be doing by taking that dagger."

Did he really have so little faith in her? Nicole folded her arms over her chest. "I can do this, Papa. Just give me a ch—"

"No!" The word stung as if it had been his hand slapping her face. "That's my final word."

Nicole lifted her chin. "If I were a man, you'd let me go." She met his stare, daring him to contradict her.

"But you're not a man, are you, Nicki? You're a girl. And until you have a husband to protect you . . ." His words died away, and with them died her hope of ever being enough.

So wrapped up in her outrage over the injustice of being judged by her gender instead of her merit, Nicole almost missed the odd glimmer in her father's eyes, a glimmer that burned steadily brighter until he finally exploded.

"That's it!"

"Anton," her mother gasped. "You startled me."

"Sorry, my love." Papa patted her hand as she returned to sit beside him on the edge of the bed. "But I've just had the most astounding idea."

"What is it?" The question rang simultaneously from both Nicole and her mother.

Her papa smiled. A scheming, devilish, piratical smile that one would expect to see right before a blade ran him through. Nicole flopped onto the divan.

"Nicki's going to take a little trip to New Orleans."

"But why?" Maman asked. "She just got home."

Papa rubbed his palms against his thighs in anticipation. "Don't you see? It will solve everything. It will keep Nicki away from Jenkins and secure the future of Renard Shipping at the same time."

"How?" Nicole ventured, somehow certain she'd not like the answer.

Her papa's grin confirmed it. "By giving me the next best thing to a son."

"And that is . . . ?" her mother prompted.

"A son-in-law."

CHAPTER 3

Nicole blinked once. Then again.

A son-in-law?

Just who did he expect her to marry? One of his cronies from New Orleans? They were all old enough to be . . . well, her father. Besides that, he'd always sworn to let her choose her own husband, promising never to force her into a union simply because it would aid his shipping interests.

She'd thought herself so lucky when talk at Miss Rochester's school had turned to marriage. Half the girls there were already promised to men who would provide an advantageous match to their families. Two of the young ladies hadn't even met their intendeds. Nicole had bragged of how she'd be free to choose her own man, how her papa was so open-minded, caring more for his daughter's happiness than his business. Yet here he sat, ready to shackle her to someone she'd never met, all to secure the future of Renard Shipping.

How could he do that?

"Papa, you promised . . ." Nicole's voice shook slightly. She cleared her throat and started again, tamping down the emotion that floated too near the surface. "You promised I could choose. Are you breaking your word?"

"No, darlin'." Papa stood on shaky legs and crossed the floor to sit beside her on the divan. "I vowed to give you your choice when the time came, and I will hold to that promise. What I'm asking is that you take an active role in the choosing process. Search for a husband yourself, instead of waiting for him to find you.

"I have contacts in New Orleans. Men of good families. Men who would value a wife with your knowledge and talents."

Men who would value my ties to Renard Shipping, Nicole thought bitterly.

Papa took her hand and squeezed it with what little strength he could muster. "I'm trusting you with the Renard family legacy, Nicki. The Lafitte Dagger will be your dowry. The man you choose will lead Renard Shipping into the next generation."

Nicole finally met her father's gaze. He trusted her to bestow the dagger on the right man. That was something, wasn't it?

Her heart rebelled at the idea of having to marry so expediently, but her papa *was* giving her the freedom to choose. And trusting her with the family legacy. The entire family's future, to be precise — a notion that had her insides rapidly knotting into icy lumps.

Yet, if he had a son, he'd expect his heir to ensure the family's future, too. What he was asking of her was no different. Not really. Nicole sat up a little straighter, a plan of her own formulating. She'd go on her father's husband-hunting expedition. She'd even choose one if she found one to her tastes. But she'd take steps to ensure the safety of those she loved first.

"I'll do it."

Less than a week later, Nicole's trunks were repacked for another voyage. A large trunk held the majority of her clothes and enough funds to keep her in good stead for at least two months, while a smaller one contained the overflow and the necessities required to keep a lady presentable while she traveled. Her mother had insisted they pack nearly every item Nicole owned, neither of them sure how long she would be gone. But one item remained to be packed, an item Nicole intended to fetch on her own.

After slipping from her bed in the predawn darkness, Nicole lit a candle and made her way downstairs, taking care to keep her tread light as the rest of the house slept. She held her breath as she passed her parents' door and finally released it when she reached the privacy of the study.

Nicole crossed the room, purpose driving her steps as her eyes locked on the painting of the clipper ship on the wall behind her father's desk. Sails billowed, masts jutting tall and proud into the gray sky, wooden hull forging ahead through storm-swept seas. Confident. Fearless. Strong. Everything her father admired. Everything she would prove to be.

Setting the candleholder on the corner of the desk as she strode by, she marched forward, refusing to hesitate. Doubt was for the weak. She grabbed the bottom right edge of the painting and lifted it away from the wall just enough for her to ease her fingers into the small slit in the paper backing and retrieve the key hidden inside the frame. Then she turned to the desk, opened the large bottom drawer, and pulled out the ordinary-looking stationery box buried beneath a pile of ledgers. As quietly as she could, Nicole placed the oak writing box atop the desk and inserted the key into the lock at the front. A satisfying *click* echoed loudly in the dark room. Nicole shot a quick glance around to be sure she was still alone, then opened the lid.

Reaching inside, she lifted out the tray of stationery that hid a false bottom. Then, using the edge of a penknife, she pried the wooden cover up to reveal the red velvet bag inside the hidden compartment. A shiver ran through her and raised gooseflesh on her arms as her hand closed around the bag.

The Lafitte Dagger. The talisman every sailor on Galveston Island believed protected the one who possessed it and ensured his success. One had only to look at the success of Renard Shipping over the last twenty-five years, they would say, to prove its value. Renard Shipping was one of the few lines that had survived the political turmoil resulting from Texas moving from Mexican rule to revolution, to an independent republic, and finally to statehood. While other companies floundered, Renard Shipping had flourished.

Of course, Nicole believed her family's success had more to do with her father and grandfather's work ethic, honorable business practices, and extensive business relationships than with any pirate dagger. But it didn't matter what she believed. It mattered what men like Carson Jenkins believed. He would stop at nothing to possess the dagger because he thought it would ensure his success. And taking the dagger was the only way to protect her father and *maman* from further violence.

Just before her ship embarked, she'd slip a coin to one of the kids who ran errands around the docks and have him deliver a letter to Jenkins so he'd know that any further housebreaking at her parents' home would be fruitless. It would take him time to discover which ship she had boarded and therefore her destination. By the time he discovered her whereabouts, she'd have the protection of her father's business associates surrounding her. And if he sent Fletcher and Will after her anyway? Well, she'd have her knife, her wits, and if she knew Tommy Ackerman, an armed escort.

Tommy had moved with his family to New Orleans about the same time she'd first left for school in Boston two falls ago. Mr. Ackerman now ran the Renard Shipping offices in New Orleans, and her father trusted him implicitly. And she trusted Tommy. How could she not, when they'd fought off armadas of imaginary invaders together on the Galveston beaches? He'd made a great first mate when they were kids, and she knew he would have her back as adults, as well.

A creak sounded behind her. Nicole crushed the velvet bag to her chest and spun around.

"Who's there?" she demanded, as her heart nearly pounded out of her chest.

Her gaze darted from the window to the cabinet to the door that led to the dining room, the flicker of her candle making it impossible to discern true movement from dancing shadows. After several heartbeats of silence, the faint clang of pots in the kitchen two rooms away sent a surge of relief through her. Margie. The cook must have risen early to see to breakfast preparations, knowing Nicole would be leaving this morning. All perfectly innocent.

Nevertheless, the scare ignited Nicole into action. She hurriedly replaced the stationery box and key, shoved the dagger, bag and all, into the garter sheath she wore beneath her nightdress, then scampered up to her room.

Her breath puffed out of her in short pants as she leaned her back against the closed door. Could she really take the dagger? It was her dowry, after all — the bait to lure a suitor into matrimony and buy her father an heir. But it was also an act of disobedience, although one that wouldn't be necessary if she wore trousers instead of skirts.

Nicole glared at the traveling costume laid out upon the larger of the two trunks as she pulled the dagger from beneath her nightdress and took it from its velvet bag. She fingered the jewels on the hilt and bit her lip. Her father would be furious if he found out, and her mother disappointed. But what choice did she have? Jenkins wouldn't give up. Fletcher and Will had nearly succeeded in forcing Papa's hand when they broke in. They'd only get bolder in the next attempt. She needed to draw their fire, and this was the best way to accomplish that.

Having made her decision, Nicole proceeded to dress and finish packing. Her usual blade went into her satchel, leaving her garter sheath free for more important cargo. The protection of the Renard family legacy now rested on her shoulders. She'd guard it well.

Nicole paused in the doorway of Renard House later that morning and eyed the waiting coach with a hint of trepidation. Oh, it wasn't the Jenkins brothers who gave her pause. She could handle those two. No, it was the rest of the plan that had her mouth going dry.

A husband.

It had all seemed so straightforward in the beginning. Find a good man, one with integrity and knowledge of the shipping industry. Offer him management of her father's company. But how was she to discern a man's worthiness? With her papa's illness ticking like a clock winding down in her mind, she didn't have the luxury of taking her time. She had to choose wisely, quickly. Yet what if the right man for Renard Shipping was the wrong man for her?

Nicole tightened her grip on the satchel she carried. *I need help, Lord,* her spirit pled. *You led Abraham's servant to Rebekah when he searched for a wife for Isaac, and I ask that you do the same for me. Lead me to the right man, and help me to recognize him when I find him.*

"Having second thoughts?" Her mother came up behind her and gently nudged her out onto the porch. Their full skirts swished together as Nicole turned to reassure her.

"No. Just seeking some direction before heading out."

Maman smiled. "Always a wise choice." She took Nicole's free hand in her own and gave it a heartening squeeze. "I have been praying, too, and I will pray for you every

56

day that you are gone. You have the Ackermans' address?"

"Yes. In my satchel. Though I've read over it so many times, I think I have it memorized."

"Good." She linked her arm through Nicole's, and together they strolled down the steps toward the carriage. "You know, Thomas Ackerman might be a good candidate for you."

Tommy? Nicole's step stuttered. Marry Tommy Ackerman? That would be like marrying her brother. "He's a bit young to be running a shipping company, don't you think? He's only a year older than I am."

Maman squeezed Nicole's arm into her waist and grinned. "He's been raised in the business, just like you have. He'd find his way. Besides . . ." She tilted her head, her eyes warming as she met her daughter's gaze. "There are more important things in life than business. Marriage is one of them. Choose the man who will make you the best husband, not the one who will make the best heir for your father. Agreed?"

How was it that her mother always knew the perfect thing to say? A grin tugged at Nicole's mouth as she nodded. "Agreed."

They reached the end of the walk. Her father stood leaning against the stone pillar that supported the iron gate.

"Well, Nicki," he said, a gleam of pride in his eyes. "Are you ready for a grand adventure?"

She favored him with a saucy wink. "I'm a Renard. I was born for adventure."

Papa laughed. "What did I tell you, Pauline? Nothing to worry about. Not with this one."

He leaned forward and took Nicole's shoulders in his hands, his gaze growing serious. "Take care, daughter."

"I will, Papa."

For a moment it looked as if he would say more. She waited, hoped, but he cleared his throat and stepped back. Nicole squelched her disappointment. Papa never was one to linger over sentimentality.

Squaring her shoulders, Nicole conjured up a cheery grin for her parents' benefit. "I guess it's time to go, then."

After kissing her father's cheek and embracing her *maman* for a final time, Nicole allowed John to hand her into the carriage. She waved her farewells as the team pulled away, then settled back into the seat cushion.

She'd not fail. No matter what it took, she'd smuggle the Lafitte Dagger out of Galveston and find an heir for her father.

Nicole eyed each building they passed, each alleyway. She'd not relax until she was on board ship and locked in her stateroom.

The carriage turned down an unexpected street, two blocks short of where the docks began. Frowning, Nicole tapped on the door between her and the driver. "What's going on, John?"

"Not sure, miss, but I spotted one of your father's men on the street, and he signaled for me to turn. Thought I better see what was up."

"Was it someone you trust?" Alarm bells rang in Nicole's head. What if this was some sort of trap? What if Jenkins had paid off some of her father's men to learn the details of her trip in order to kidnap her and hold her for ransom?

"It was Albert Mathis."

Nicole released a breath and sat back. Albert Mathis had worked for her father for nearly twenty years. He'd not betray them.

John brought the team to a halt at the same time Mr. Mathis dodged around the edge of the nearest building. Just to be cautious, Nicole pulled her knife from the side pouch of her satchel. Trust was all well and good, but she wasn't taking any chances.

CHAPTER 4

Mathis looked up and down the street and then jogged over to the carriage. Nicole lowered the window glass.

"We've got a problem." He didn't really look at her. He continued to search the street as if afraid someone would discover them at any moment.

Nicole's stomach clenched. "Is it Jenkins?"

"Yep." Mathis spoke through gritted teeth. "Those boys of his planted themselves on the dock in front of the *Midnight Lady*. They're just standing there, waiting. My guess is, for you."

"But how did they know?" Nicole laid her knife on the seat cushion, grabbed hold of the window ledge, and thrust her face fully into the opening. She wanted to see his face as he made his explanation. "Papa didn't even put my name on the manifest. None of the crew outside of the *Midnight Lady*'s captain knew to expect me on board."

Mathis met her gaze without blinking. "I busied myself on the docks nearby hoping to overhear something, but the only thing they did was argue over whether or not it was the right ship. Then Fletcher said something about it having to be because it was the only Renard ship scheduled to leave between nine and noon, and that she had specifically said you'd be leaving after breakfast."

"*She* said?" Nicole latched on to the descriptor. "A woman told them?"

"Apparently." A scowl furrowed his brow.

"That doesn't make sense." Nicole plopped her chin on the back of one of her hands still braced on the window ledge. "The only women aware of my travel plans are myself and my mother."

From up in the box, John muttered a curse. "You're forgettin' Margie."

"Our cook?" The very idea was ludicrous. Or was it? Margie had access to the entire house. She could listen at any door she wanted, and they'd never know.

The thought jarred Nicole back onto the cushioned seat. The sound she'd heard that morning in Papa's study. What if Margie had been spying on her? She might have figured out that Nicole had the Lafitte Dagger — information she could sell to Carson

61

Jenkins for a handsome price. And she had likely overheard the details of Nicole's itinerary. The family had discussed it during dinner last evening, never giving a second thought to the woman who came in to remove dishes and serve dessert.

"She's been actin' kind of skittish lately," John said. "Nothing I could put my finger on. But ever since the break-in, I've wondered why she didn't come fetch me from the coach house. Her room is right off the kitchen, easy access to the back porch. If she heard the intruders — and she should have — she could have come running for help. She didn't."

Nicole closed her eyes as her suspicion deepened. "I assumed she'd simply been too frightened to leave her room."

"Maybe." John didn't sound too convinced. "But then there's the trouble with the door. I examined the lock from every possible angle, Miss Nicki. There was no evidence that it had been busted or tampered with. If I had to guess, I'd say someone had simply left it unlocked the night the Jenkins boys paid their call." He pounded his leg with a fist. "I should have talked to your father about my suspicions, but I hesitated to accuse Margie."

Nicole slouched farther into the seat. "It's

not your fault, John. You couldn't know how it would turn out." Why would Margie do such a thing? Her chest ached to think someone she'd trusted could have betrayed them in such a way. But at that moment, the *why*s weren't as important as the *how*s. The chief one being: How was she going to circumvent the Jenkins brothers?

"Maybe you ought to just turn around and take the girl back home, John," Mathis suggested.

Nicole jerked forward. "No!" If she went home now, she would have failed before she'd begun. Unacceptable. There was a way around this. She just needed to think. Turn the circumstances to their advantage.

"Mr. Mathis?" she asked, the germ of an idea taking shape in her mind. "Have any other of my father's ships left port today?"

The older man pulled off his hat and scratched his graying head. "*Morning Glory* sailed with the early tide. Cargo only. No passengers on the manifest."

"Perfect." Nicole smiled as she fleshed out the bones of her rapidly forming plan. It'd be brazen, and there were a few holes she'd have to work out later, but it could work.

"All right, gentlemen. Here's what we're going to do." She fastened her attention on the man in the street. "Mr. Mathis is going to escort me through the alleyways to the west end of the docks, where I will purchase a ticket on one of the riverboats."

"But the riverboats don't go to New Orleans, Miss Nicki," John pointed out, his tone growing rather alarmed. "They go to Houston. And that rowdy town ain't no place for a young lady on her own. Your father would skin my hide if I let you go there."

"Houston's not the only destination," Mathis said thoughtfully. "She could travel up the Trinity to Liberty. It's smaller, more settled. Sam Houston himself prefers it and even keeps a law office there. It'd be safe enough."

"Not to mention closer to New Orleans," Nicole added. "I won't need to stay there long. Just long enough to throw Jenkins off the scent. Then I can come back down the Trinity to Galveston Bay and board one of Papa's steamers to New Orleans as originally planned.

"John, I want you to continue on to the *Midnight Lady,* just as if I'm still in the coach. I'll draw the curtains over the windows and leave one of my trunks tied to the back to keep Will and Fletcher's attention. My guess is they'll pounce on the carriage the moment you leave to see about the luggage. And that's exactly what we want."

"It is?"

Nicole grinned. "Yes. Because when they make their move, you will return to confront them. You'll act as if the information they learned from Margie was nothing more than a clever ruse. We wanted them to believe I was sailing on the *Midnight Lady,* you'll explain, because then they wouldn't be around to witness the sailing of *Morning Glory.*" She smiled. "And it wouldn't hurt for you to gloat a little."

Mathis caught the spirit of her scheme and started nodding. "They'll assume they've missed you and won't search the docks for another possible departure."

"Exactly. We'll discredit Margie's information so the Jenkinses won't trust whatever else she might be tempted to disclose, and we'll clear the path for me to make my run to Liberty. John can leave a message with the *Midnight Lady*'s captain that I will not be sailing as planned, and he can forward it on to the Ackermans."

"I'll also have to explain the situation to your father," John said, dread lacing his voice. "He won't be pleased with this development."

"True," Nicole agreed, "but I suspect he'll appreciate my improvisation. I'm still ac-

65

complishing his plan, just taking a slightly different route to get there. Tell him not to expect to hear from me anytime soon and not to try to contact me. Jenkins will probably be watching the mail, so writing would just give away my position. In fact, no one but the three of us and my parents should even be aware of my detour. Everyone else should be left to assume I traveled to New Orleans as originally arranged."

"I don't like it," John groused.

Nicole sighed. "Well, it's not my first choice, either, but it will work. I feel it."

"Can't argue with the Renard gut," Mathis said with a smile, winking at her through the window. "Believe me, I've tried."

John grumbled something incoherent from the driver's box. Nicole opted to interpret it as agreement. They didn't have any more time to argue. They were perilously close to giving themselves away by being late to the launch. Will and Fletcher weren't exactly the patient sort. If her carriage didn't show up soon, one of them was bound to get antsy and leave his post to come looking for her. She couldn't afford that.

"All right, then," she announced with a slap of her palm against her thigh. "Let's get going." In a flash, she had the window latched and the curtains drawn. She slipped her knife back into the satchel, opened the door, and allowed Mathis to help her alight.

"You need anything from your big trunk, Miss Nicki?" John swiveled in the driver's box to face her, his face as bland as always. She couldn't help smiling at him.

"Just the extra funds Maman packed for me." She circled to the rear of the carriage, where Mr. Mathis was collecting her smaller trunk, but before she could unfasten a single strap, an ominous clacking of hooves against paving stones rent the air.

"Someone's coming," John hissed.

Nicole froze. She couldn't be seen. If word got back to Fletcher Jenkins, their ruse would never work.

"Go, John!" she ordered. The Renard carriage traveling on a side road would stir enough suspicion without it being stopped. There was no help for it. If he didn't hold up appearances for her, they'd be sunk.

"But the money."

"We don't have time. I have enough in my satchel. I'll be fine. Go!" Without giving him a chance to argue, she grabbed her satchel and ran for the far side of the alley, praying Mr. Mathis would follow with the small trunk. He did.

The two ducked into the nearest alleyway

67

and pressed their backs against the wall, Nicole doing her best not to think about how few coins actually resided in the pocket of her satchel lining. It *was* enough to purchase a ticket upriver, but it wouldn't afford her much to live off of afterward. She'd deal with that side of things later, though. Right now, her concern was getting the dagger out of Galveston.

Once the second carriage passed, Mathis stole around the corner and signaled to her. Nicole kept her head down and shadowed his steps, not wanting to draw any attention. Her ears pricked at every sound. Her heart thumped with each footstep. When she and Mathis finally emerged into the bustle of merchants and passengers swarming the west end of the Galveston docks, the crowd offered her anonymity, but she still couldn't relax. Not until she had the dagger safely away. She jolted at every brush against her arm, flinched at every shout. Her muscles had gone so stiff, it was a miracle she could bend when Mathis pushed her into a chair inside one of the river shipping offices and went to inquire about the next boat upriver.

When he returned, Mathis said, "They have a boat leaving in twenty minutes. There are no private chambers available, but there is a ladies' saloon where you can pass the time in the company of other females."

Nicole opened her satchel and extracted her money purse. "That should do nicely. Will you see to my trunk while I purchase my passage?"

Mathis bowed to her. "Of course, miss."

Thankful that he had the wherewithal not to use her name, Nicole smiled her appreciation and made her way up to the ticket counter. She'd been away from home for most of two years and had rarely ventured down to this end of the docks even when home, so most of the men milling about were strangers to her. Hopefully she was a stranger to them, as well. It would make things so much easier should Jenkins decide to ask around about her. It was too late to alter her physical appearance, but at least she could assume a false name. Surely there were enough young brunettes boarding various vessels around the docks to provide adequate cover.

"I'd like to book passage to Liberty, please."

The clerk smiled kindly, if a bit condescendingly. "Name?"

"Juliet Greyson." Jules was one of her dearest friends from school. She was always scheming and looking for ways to circum-

69

vent the rigid rules Miss Rochester insisted they follow. Nicole doubted she'd mind lending her the use of her name for a few hours. The girl would probably think it all a great lark.

"All right, Miss Greyson. Do you wish to purchase a return ticket, as well?"

"No, thank you. I'm not yet sure when I will be returning." Or when she'd have enough funds for another ticket. She counted out the necessary coins and pushed them toward the clerk, trying not to think about the paltry sum left in her purse.

"Very well." The clerk collected the money, made a note in his ledger, then handed her a paper ticket. An illustration of a paddle-wheeler decorated the top along with the name of the boat, followed by her name, destination, and date, all completed in the clerk's tidy script. "Boarding is already underway. You'll need to hurry if you hope to find a chair in the saloon. They fill quickly."

"I'm sure I'll be fine. Thank you." She replaced her purse in her satchel and turned to find Mr. Mathis waiting to escort her.

"I paid for a man to unload your trunk when you arrive at the landing in Liberty. It will be waiting for you when you disembark." He offered her his arm and led her

70

down the dock to the loading ramp.

"Thank you. You've been such a help to me, Mr. Mathis. I'm not sure what I would have done had you not flagged us down with your warning."

He patted her arm and grinned down at her in a very fatherly sort of way. "You would have managed." Steadying her as she climbed the wooden ramp, he remained by her side until the porter examined her ticket and extended a hand to assist her aboard.

"Tell my father not to worry," she whispered fiercely before releasing her escort's arm. "Everything will be fine."

"I'll tell him," he assured her.

As Nicole made her way to the ladies' saloon and found an unobtrusive corner to disappear into, she prayed her parting words proved more accurate than the name on her ticket.

CHAPTER 5

The riverboat cruise up the Trinity to Liberty proved uneventful, and Nicole managed to secure a modestly priced room at a boardinghouse run by a doctor and his wife, a house recommended to her by one of the ladies she'd met in the boat's saloon. The fee included dinner and breakfast the following morning, so when she left the boardinghouse to search for employment, her spirits and energy were high. By mid-afternoon, however, both had sunk to rather dismal depths.

No one was hiring. Or at least no one was hiring an unknown young woman who'd arrived in town the previous evening unescorted and under mysterious circumstances. It didn't help that she was only looking for temporary employment. By the time she figured out that bit of honesty was hurting her prospects, she'd already visited half the businesses in town.

She hated lying. Every time she entered a shop and offered Juliet's name as her own, her conscience cringed. Then she compounded matters by starting to withhold her intention of leaving in a few weeks. No doubt the merchants she'd approached could sense her perfidy. That had to be why each and every one of them sent her away.

But what was she to do? She couldn't draw Jenkins a map by dropping her name like bread crumbs. If he or his sons found her before she made it to New Orleans, the dagger was as good as gone.

Of course, if she couldn't find work, her money was as good as gone. Another bleak prospect.

Nicole groaned and dropped onto a bench outside a tiny frame building painted with large white letters proclaiming it to be Liberty's post office. Her feet hurt, her stomach gurgled from having missed lunch, and the dagger bulging from her too-small sheath had nearly rubbed her inner thigh raw.

She had not wanted to leave it in her room, even buried in her satchel. The doctor and his wife seemed like kind, honorable people, but who knew what the other guests might be like. What if someone started snooping through her things, look-

73

ing for valuables to pilfer? So she'd opted to keep it in her garter sheath in lieu of her usual — much thinner, much more comfortable — blade. The jewels alone would tempt a thief to take it even if he were unaware of the legend surrounding it. So she'd make do keeping it with her. Perhaps the doctor would have some salve she could borrow tonight.

She might need a headache powder, too. Nicole winced and raised her gloved fingers to rub the throbbing place at her temple. The pain had been growing in proportion to the number of merchants who denied her employment during the course of the last four hours.

What would she do if she couldn't find work? She had enough funds for another night or two at the boardinghouse, but then her purse would be empty.

Nicole twisted her head to look through the window behind her. She could write to her father. But that would mean giving up her plan — because her father would surely demand she return home. Worse, it would announce her location to Jenkins. The man's second cousin ran the Galveston post office and could easily be convinced to hold on to a letter addressed to Anton Renard long enough to give Jenkins a head start in tracking her down.

No. It was too soon to give up. She could still make this work. All she needed was a job to . . .

Help Wanted. Nicole squinted at the lettering barely visible on the back wall by the postmaster's counter. Sucking in a breath, she shamelessly pressed her face to the window glass. A notice hung beneath the narrow sign. Several notices. Tacked to the wall. Small scraps of paper curling at the edges. Some fresh and new, others faded and tattered.

They were the most beautiful wall decorations she'd ever seen.

Her hunger forgotten, she sprang from the bench on reenergized legs and dashed to the door. At the last minute she remembered to brush out her skirt and straighten her undersleeves before entering.

"Afternoon." The man behind the counter set aside the papers he was sorting and smiled at her.

"Hello." Nicole dipped her chin. "Would you mind if I peruse the employment listings on your wall?"

"Help yourself, though I don't think any of those will suit you." He straightened his spectacles and turned back to his papers, dismissing her.

75

Nicole swept past him and approached the back wall. Suitability was in the eye of the beholder. And her eye was desperate.

Her gaze brushed the first advertisement. Sawmill operator. Not exactly a position amenable to full skirts and bell-shaped sleeves. Farmhand. Probably not. Several workers were needed at the beef-packing plant at Liberty Landing. The gristmill needed repair. Nicole's heart thumped painfully in her chest. Surely there was something here that required brains over brawn.

Cow puncher. Stage driver. Ferry operator.

Angry tears pooled in Nicole's eyes. *No. No. No!* There had to be something here she could do. There had to be.

Her search came to rest on the last item, tacked high and nearly out of reach over the counter.

Wanted: Secretary.

Secretary? Nicole snatched the notice from the wall, tearing it straight off the nail. Clutching it to her breast, she sent a prayer of thanks heavenward, then held it up and scanned it for pertinent information. It specified the employer was looking for male applicants, but the advertisement was yellowed from age. Obviously none of the local males were interested in or qualified for the position. That could work in her favor.

She marched up to the counter. "Excuse me? Can you give me directions to —" she glanced back at the paper — "Oakhaven?"

The postmaster looked up from his papers, an expression of true alarm on his face. "Oakhaven? You don't want to go there, miss. Trust me."

"Oh, but I do." Nicole gave him her best lady-of-the-manor stare. "However, if you don't feel comfortable directing me, I'm sure someone else will supply the information I need."

"It's not that. I can tell you how to get there." He tugged his spectacles off his nose and began shining the lenses on the tail of his vest. "It's just that I can't recommend the position to you. Not with a clear conscience." He leaned forward over the counter, as if pleading. "He's mad, miss. If you go out there, you'd be taking your life in your hands."

She brushed aside his concerns. "What would a madman want with a secretary? Surely you exaggerate."

"No, ma'am." He shook his head violently. "The fellow moved onto that vacant plantation over a year ago, but he's never farmed a single acre. As far as I can tell, he's never done anything to earn an honest living. All

77

he does is blow things up. None of the merchants will deliver inside the gates after Connor nearly got his leg severed by flying timber last fall. A lady like you would be eaten alive."

It did sound rather daunting, but she couldn't afford to be choosy. This could very well be her only option for gainful employment. No time to be squeamish.

"I'm willing to take my chances," she assured him, lifting her chin in challenge. "Now, if you'd be so kind as to write down the directions for me?" Nicole laid the advertisement in front of him and smiled in such a way that made it clear he'd best not argue.

The man stared at her for a long minute, then shrugged and pulled a pencil from behind his ear. "Your choice," he said as he scribbled a few notes at the bottom of the ad. "Just don't say I didn't warn you."

"I won't." Nicole smiled sweetly as she accepted the paper from him. Then, tucking the paper into her money purse as if it were a fifty-dollar gold piece, she waved her thanks and headed back to the boarding-house.

She'd managed to wring an address out of the postmaster, now all she needed to do was convince a madman to hire a female secretary before he blew her to bits.

Darius Thornton laid down the journal he'd been reading and rubbed his eyes. He'd been up all night again. Reading. Studying. Taking notes. It was always this way when the latest publication from the Franklin Institute arrived in the post. He'd been particularly intrigued by the article on boiler plates. The author proposed a correlation between the thickness of the boiler plates and the likelihood of explosion. It was a fascinating concept, and one he'd not yet considered. It might make for a worthy experiment.

He glanced across his desk and noted the other piece of mail that had arrived yesterday. A letter from his mother. He pushed it farther away, angling it behind a stack of boiler diagrams he'd been working on. If he couldn't see it, he wouldn't fall prey to the guilt it inspired.

Mother didn't understand. No one in his family did. Not really. His father and brother had put a good face on things and told him to take all the time he needed, that King Star Shipping would be there for him when he was ready to resume his duties. But Darius could read between the lines. They all thought him . . . emotionally damaged.

79

They didn't understand his mission. His calling. His need to redeem his greatest failure. The little girl's cry still haunted his dreams. Whenever he closed his eyes, he relived the torture of not reaching her in time. So he rarely closed his eyes anymore. He slept only when exhaustion rendered him unconscious — and dedicated every waking moment to finding ways to make steam engines safer. Read everything he could get his hands on. Studied schematics. Examined old boilers and engines. Conducted experiments.

Steamboat boiler explosions took hundreds . . . no, thousands of lives every year. Innocent lives. Lives that didn't deserve to be cut short. Lives more worthy than his own. Yet God hadn't spared those lives. He'd spared his. The only way Darius could rationalize such an injustice was to assume that God expected him to do something with the time he'd been given. So he poured himself into his work and refused to be distracted from his course. Not by society. Not by business. Not even by well-meaning family members who loved him and wanted him home.

Scratching at an itchy spot on his jaw through his half-grown beard, Darius scowled. Enough of that melancholic nonsense. He yanked open his desk drawer, pulled out his logbook, and began jotting down ideas for an experiment involving boiler plates. He referred back to the article from the Franklin Institute and tried to decipher the notes he'd scribbled in the margins.

Blast. He couldn't even read his own writing — words he'd penned only hours ago. Darius ran a hand over his face. He must have been more tired than he'd thought last night. He flipped through the previous pages of his logbook and examined the contents. His frown deepened. His penmanship wasn't much better there. Too many scratched-out words and sideways notations in the margins. How was he ever going to submit his findings on boiler safety to the Franklin Institute when his notes were in such a sorry state?

Darius shoved his notebook aside and blew out a heavy breath. He didn't have time for this. He'd advertised for a secretary weeks ago. Why had no one applied? It was beyond frustrating.

He pushed up from his chair and paced across the carpet. Passing the untouched breakfast tray his housekeeper had brought hours ago, he snatched up a scone that had gone stale. He shoved it in his mouth, grimaced as he chewed, and washed it down with a swallow of the tea that had cooled too far to even be called tepid.

He had to eat something if he wanted to avoid Mrs. Wellborn's scolding. He was certain the woman kept an accounting of each morsel served him just so she could tell if he ate anything or not. The tyrant. A corner of Darius's mouth twitched upward slightly as he contemplated his housekeeper. At least she'd ceased pestering him about eating his meals while they were hot. She was an intelligent woman, after all, and could recognize a lost cause when she saw one. His work took precedence. Over everything.

Now, if he could just convince one of the mewling cowards from Liberty to hire on as his secretary, he'd really be able to make some progress. It wasn't *his* fault Miles Connor hadn't had the sense God gave a goose. The fellow made the unwise decision to snoop around the pond instead of remaining at the house during one of Darius's experiments. Had he known the grocer was about, he would have warned him of the danger. But no, the man just strolled up to the pond, bold as you please, without a word to anyone. By the time Darius realized he was there, the steam had built up too high in the boiler for the safety valve to release, and the two men had to run for cover. The explosion had been a mild one — fully under Darius's control, of course — but Connor took exception to being showered with a few splintered timbers and iron shards.

Oakhaven had seen few visitors since that ill-fated day.

Darius reached for a boiled egg from the breakfast tray, thinking it would taste better cold than another scone. At the same moment, a knock sounded on his study door.

"Come in," he called as he sprinkled a pinch of salt over the egg.

The door opened, and Wellborn, his butler, stepped inside. "You have a caller, sir."

"A caller?" Darius bit off half the egg, suddenly ravenous now that his stomach had recognized the arrival of food. He chewed quickly and sent the egg the way of the scone before glancing up. "Who is it? I don't have time for idle chitchat with the neighbors, you know."

"Of course, sir." Wellborn's dour expression never altered. Nor did he comment on the fact that no neighbor had come to *chat* in several months. A fact they were both well aware of.

Darius salted the second half of his egg

and popped it into his mouth.

Wellborn didn't so much as raise an eyebrow. "Your caller is an applicant. For the position you posted in Liberty a few weeks back, I believe."

Darius choked the egg down and lunged across the carpet toward his butler. "Why didn't you say so, man? That's the best news I've had in days. Send him in at once."

Wellborn's disapproving gaze raked Darius from his rumpled hair, to his unshaven jaw, to his rolled shirt sleeves. "Perhaps you'd like to freshen your appearance first, Mr. Thornton?"

Darius shook his head. "Time is of the essence, Wellborn. Please show the man in."

Wellborn opened his mouth, held it for a moment, and closed it. "Very good, sir." He bowed his head slightly, then left to collect the applicant.

Darius watched the flawlessly attired butler stride out the study door. The world was far too concerned with superficial trappings to Darius's way of thinking. What difference did a few whiskers or wrinkles make when people were dying? Nevertheless, he took a few seconds to shove his shirttails into his trousers.

"Your applicant, Mr. Thornton," Wellborn's ponderous voice echoed through the

84

chamber. "Miss Nicole Greyson."

Miss? Darius spun around to find a young woman stepping forward as his butler backed out of the room. Her wine-red dress was the height of fashion, sloping over her slender shoulders in a deep *V* and nipping in at her tiny waist before belling out to the floor. The straw bonnet she wore framed her face in a perfect oval, showing off rich brown curls and a smile that projected confidence mixed with confusion as her golden brown eyes scanned his appearance.

She was quite the loveliest creature he'd ever seen. And the worst possible applicant he could have imagined.

CHAPTER 6

Nicole needed a moment to recover from the shock of seeing her future employer in a state of *dishabille*. Shirt sleeves rolled up over muscular forearms, collar open at his throat, eyes red rimmed, dark whiskers lining his square jaw, blond hair tousled as if he'd lost his only comb.

Maybe he really *was* a madman. Thank goodness she'd continued with the false surname. She'd decided to drop Juliet's name in favor of her own since Oakhaven was rather remote, and if the postmaster was to be believed, townsfolk avoided it as much as possible. Yet caution demanded she maintain a measure of anonymity. Was lying about *half* a name less of a sin than lying about the whole thing?

"Miss Greyson." The man offered her a courtly bow, one that would have been right at home in any Boston drawing room.

Perhaps he was just slovenly, not actually

mad. She could deal with slovenly. Especially since he appeared to be familiar with bath water. No stench wafted toward her as he made his bow.

"Mr. Thornton." Nicole dipped her head and offered him a smile. "I understand you're in need of a secretary. I'm here to offer my services."

"Well, I'm afraid your services aren't exactly what I had in mind." He eyed her clothing as if it told him all he needed to know about her. "I'm sorry you came all this way, but I am not looking for someone to help me pen fancy invitations and polite correspondence. You'll be of no use to me." He waved her toward the door. "I'll have my man compensate you for your time."

His out-of-hand dismissal raised Nicole's hackles. How dare he assume he knew her capabilities simply because she'd worn a stylish dress? Was it a crime to want to look her best for this interview?

"Perhaps if I'd arrived donned in a pair of trousers, with my hair in a tangled mess — a style you apparently prefer — you'd have shown me the courtesy of granting an interview before sending me away."

His gaze shot to hers at her scathing tone. His brows arched in surprise, then turned downward in displeasure. "Time is my most precious commodity, Miss Greyson. I refuse to waste it." He stepped closer, and Nicole fought the urge to back away. "I know your type. Well-educated in literature, art, and . . . embroidery. You have lovely penmanship and a high opinion of yourself but no real skill in the things that matter to me. Science, mathematics, mechanics. Besides, you are far too young and much too pretty to work for a man in close company."

This last statement threw a chunk of ice into her rapidly boiling temper. He thought her pretty. Then she remembered he also thought her worthless in all areas that mattered to him. The simmer heated again.

Nicole lifted her chin and stepped so close to him, her skirts brushed his shoes. "I'll have you know, Mr. Thornton, that I am well versed in mathematics, including algebra and Euclidian geometry. My father never had a son, to his great regret, so he passed his business acumen on to me. Instead of reading novels as a girl, I read shipping manifests and accounting ledgers. I will admit to only a rudimentary knowledge of science and mechanics, but I'm a quick study and have a logical mind that can grasp scientific principles with ease."

His brows were arching again, and he opened his mouth as if to say something, but she wouldn't give him the chance.

"Audition me, Mr. Thornton. I dare you."

His head quirked to the side. "I beg your pardon?"

"Give me the chance to prove my value." Nicole raised a brow of her own. "If I fail to meet your expectations, you may send me on my way, and I'll leave without a word of complaint. But if I demonstrate myself capable of the tasks you demand, well . . . then we both end up with what we want. You'll have your secretary, and I'll have employment. Surely that's worth wagering a few moments of your oh-so-precious time."

His gaze sharpened — with curiosity, thank heavens, not anger. Despite her brave words, her knees trembled beneath her skirts. Thoughts of madmen and unpredictable rages had flitted through her head. Yet now that she studied him at close range, she noticed the deep slate-blue of his eyes and a glint of intelligence. Mr. Thornton might be eccentric and rather unkempt, but she doubted he was actually mad.

The man regarded her closely for several seconds, then crossed his arms over his broad chest. "All right. I'll accept your wager." He stalked over to the desk that dominated the center of the room and picked up a small leather-bound book. With a flick of his wrist, he tossed it at her.

It sailed in a shallow arc, spinning like a well-wound top. No doubt he expected her to squeal and lunge out of the way. Instead, she snatched it out of the air with one hand, just as she used to do with the wood-carved guns and cutlasses Tommy Ackerman used to toss her when they were under attack from invisible pirate lords.

Mr. Thornton nodded in appreciation, and Nicole couldn't quite keep her lips from curving in a small smile of triumph.

"What I am looking for," he intoned, "is someone who can interpret my admittedly horrid handwriting, duplicate my diagrams and schematics, and reproduce my computations in an organized and thoroughly legible manner, so that I might submit my findings to the Franklin Institute, the foremost authority on advances in mechanical and physical science." He stepped around the desk and balanced a hip against the flat edge, nodding toward the book he'd just tossed her. "Reconstruct the first five pages in suitable fashion, and we can discuss terms."

Nicole examined the book, flipped it around when she realized it was upside down, then bent back the flexible cover and scanned the first couple pages.

Heavens. He certainly hadn't exaggerated his poor penmanship. If she hadn't spent so many months deciphering her father's scratchings while overseeing his business correspondence prior to heading off to Miss Rochester's Academy for Young Ladies, she would have truly despaired.

As it was, it would be challenge enough. But she hadn't come all this way to give up at the first obstacle laid in her path.

Squaring her shoulders, she smiled at the man who lounged so smugly before her. "Would you mind if I used your desk?" She nodded toward the cherrywood furnishing that surely would have been quite lovely if it hadn't been strewn with untidy papers, journals, and . . . was that a miniature engine?

"Of course." Mr. Thornton stood and gestured for her to come around and avail herself of the chair. "You'll find paper in the top left drawer, and here is pen and ink." He lifted a stack of publications to reveal an ebony inkstand. "I'll just be over here, reading."

Taking the top journal off the stack, he dropped the rest onto the floor and moved toward an upholstered chair situated between a pair of towering bookcases. In less than a minute, he was fully absorbed in his reading, leaving Nicole free to inhale a large breath unobserved.

Collecting the papers scattered over the desktop, she arranged them into a single stack and set them aside. Now that she had room to work, she pulled out a sheet of paper, creased open the logbook, and put pen to ink.

However long it took, she'd not let this task best her.

Darius flipped a page and inhaled a harsh breath. He'd avoided reading this particular article earlier, but putting it off any longer would only prove him a coward. So, steeling his spine, he forced his eyes to scan the words detailing the report of another New Orleans steamboat explosion.

Unlike the *Louisiana,* the *Anglo-Norman*'s boiler hadn't burst as the boat pulled away from the landing, making this case somewhat unusual. In his study of boiler explosions, Darius had learned that around sixty percent occurred either as a vessel pulled away from a landing or while docked. However, according to the journal's accounting, the *Anglo-Norman* had successfully traveled upriver a good distance, had navigated a turn, and was on her way back to the Port of New Orleans when her boiler exploded eight miles from the city. The differences made the report a little easier to stomach, and it wasn't long before his intellect suppressed his emotional response. Images of dead and dying passengers faded beneath the factual description of the type of boiler the boat had carried.

The author of the article supplied wonderful details about the size and layout of the wagon-form design, the diameter of the eight cylindrical flues, the exposure of the water legs, etc. Darius reached for the pencil he always kept on the library table beside his chair and began sketching the steam engine in dark strokes on top of the text of a neighboring article contrasting vertical and radial paddle wheels.

So intent was he on his diagram, he failed to notice the woman standing before him until she delicately cleared her throat. He jerked up from his drawing to see a plethora of red brocade skirts draped just beyond his knees. *Drat.* He'd completely forgotten she was there. Dread sunk deeper into his gut as his gaze lifted to meet her slightly amused eyes.

Drat. Drat. Drat. He'd also completely forgotten her name.

"I'm finished, Mr. Thornton," she said, holding a thin stack of papers out to him.

"The pages are ready for your inspection."

It was *Miss* Something-or-Other. He remembered that much. She wasn't married. Though why that fact should register in his brain when her name failed to stick was beyond his understanding.

"I'm sorry it took so long," she was saying, "but I discovered an error in your computations on page three and had to recopy that entire page after calculating the correct figures."

"What?" No longer caring about her name, Darius snatched the papers from her hand and immediately turned to page three. How dare she presume to correct his calculations?

He held out an empty palm to her, demanding his original logbook as his eyes scanned the page. She must have understood the silent demand, for his notebook slapped against his palm without delay. He took it from her, opened to the page in question, and set about comparing the two equations, eager to point out her mistake.

The little upstart. Just because she fancied herself something of a mathematician did not give her the right to tamper with . . .

His eyes narrowed as he took in her calculations. She'd adjusted the cargo weight. He'd only factored in the difference of engine weight between the double-tier flue boiler and the newer tubular boiler. The amount of cargo would naturally be different on the two types of vessels since the tubular boiler not only weighed less but took up less space, leaving room for more cargo. Therefore, her numbers actually were more accurate when it came to predicting water displacement or draft on a seagoing vessel.

Although, she *had* been kind enough to include his original calculations under a separate heading denoting the even greater difference in draft if the cargo remained unchanged. Of course, no sea captain worth his salt would load less cargo than his ship could carry if it were available. Why would he, when more cargo meant more profit? And she'd known this.

Hadn't she said something about reading manifests instead of novels as a girl? Her father must be involved somehow in the shipping industry. Maybe a female secretary wasn't such a bad prospect after all. If it was *this* female.

Darius glanced up from the papers, peered at her thoughtfully, then frowned. She was still far too pretty.

"You must not distract me from my work." He growled the command at her, but all she did was smile.

She smiled with such untarnished joy that he felt like a man stepping out of a dungeon to behold the vision of a sunrise cresting the horizon. Glorious. Yet so bright, he wanted to scuttle back into the hole from whence he'd come.

"Thank you, Mr. Thornton." She nearly clapped her hands together in her excitement. Hands without gloves, he noted. Hands that consisted of dainty fingers stained with ink at the tips. Capable hands. Delicate hands. The fact that they were *both* intrigued him, even as she stole them from his view by pulling them behind her back as she made an effort to compose herself.

"The advertisement mentioned accommodations."

She was dictating to him again. Odd that he didn't seem to mind. But then, he'd always appreciated people who spoke their minds instead of dallying with polite niceties. He just wasn't accustomed to finding that trait in a woman. Especially one who looked like she belonged on a shopping excursion with his mother and sister, or sipping tea with them in the parlor.

Darius rose from his seat. Time to do some dictating of his own. "There is a small chamber near the kitchen that should suffice. My butler and his wife, my house-keeper, room down that hall, as well, so you'll not be alone. You will work in here" — he gestured around him at the controlled chaos that was his study — "and occasionally with me at the workshop, if I need your assistance. However . . ." He paused to glare down his nose at her, emphasizing the importance of his next point. "You are *never* to interrupt me when I am in the midst of an experiment. Do I make myself clear?"

She nodded, though the stubborn tilt of her chin did nothing to reassure him that she comprehended the absolute necessity of obedience.

"I will leave strict instructions regarding where you may and may not venture on this property, and I expect those instructions to be followed to the letter. Should you fail to comply, you will forfeit your position."

The young lady schooled her features into a properly sober demeanor. "I understand, sir, and will, of course, abide by your wishes."

He swore he could hear the qualifier — *As long as I deem it appropriate* — wafting in the air about her. This was not a woman one contained with threats. No, she'd follow his commands only as long as it suited her purposes. Not that he sensed anything nefarious about her. On the contrary, she was quite the most genuine person he'd met in years. Yet there was something untamed about her. Something below the surface. Like a wild mare that had been broken to saddle even while her spirit stood ready to race the wind the moment the reins were loosened.

Darius turned his face away from her, pretending to peer at something outside his window. The woman was interfering with his focus, drawing him into her puzzle with her bright smile and hidden depths. He couldn't afford to be distracted from his work, from his purpose. Yet neither could he afford to continue on without a secretary, and she was his only applicant. A far more qualified one than he had hoped to find, even amongst the local male population. That outweighed his personal . . . discomfort.

He was master of his own mind, after all. He'd simply refuse to give her the power to distract him. She'd work in the study, and he in the workshop. They would rarely need to cross each other's path. Besides, once she'd been around a few days, he'd grow accustomed to her, much like one grew accustomed to a new piece of furniture in a room. She'd eventually stop standing out

and would be absorbed into the surround-
ings, like everything else about the place.

Yes, he could handle her.

He spun around again to face her, though
he focused slightly to the side to avoid full
contact with her eyes. "Meals will be included, and a stipend will be delivered at
the end of each month."

"Week."

His gaze arrowed back to hers. "Pardon?"

This time she was the first to look away.
"If it wouldn't be too much trouble, I'd
prefer to be paid at the end of each week.
My father is ill, and I'm trying to do all I
can to help him." She looked directly at him
again, and while he didn't detect any un-
truth in her, he did sense there was more to
her story than she was letting on.

Curious.

"A compromise, then." He watched her
closely. "Payment twice a month. Would that
be agreeable?"

A slight tightening about her lips was the
only hint of her disappointment. She nodded. "Yes."

"Good. Then I'll have Wellborn assist you
in collecting your things from town." Right
after he had his man remind him of his new
secretary's name.

CHAPTER 7

Nicole unpacked the last of her belongings in the small chamber that was to be her home for the next two weeks. Most likely the room had been intended for a maid or other servant. No paper decorated the walls, a small rag rug on one side of the bed was all that broke up the monotony of the oak floor, and the only furnishings the room boasted were a washstand, a thin wardrobe, and a tiny bureau that contained two drawers. However, it was spotlessly clean, and Mrs. Wellborn had plucked a handful of buttercups and placed them in a stoneware crock atop the bureau. The yellow blooms cheered the room considerably.

She'd only had space to hang three of her five dresses in the wardrobe. The rest of the space contained table linens and the like. But she didn't mind. With her trunk cleared out, the remaining dresses could be stored there without fear of excessive wrinkles.

A light tap echoed as her door pushed open. "I found another rug and a length of calico that we can use over the window to brighten the place up. What do you think?" The housekeeper bustled into the room, her smile doing more to brighten the place than the pink fabric she carried.

"It's lovely," Nicole enthused, coming forward to take the calico. White flowers dotted the pink cotton in a feminine pattern.

Nicole crossed to the stark bar hanging above the narrow window and began experimenting with the cloth. Perhaps a twist here, then a swag, and another twist . . . She stepped back to eye her handiwork, made a few adjustments so the fabric hung symmetrically, then turned to the housekeeper with a grin. "It really warms the room up. Don't you agree?"

"That it does, dearie. That it does." The plump woman dropped the rug into place in front of the bureau, gave it a tug or two, then straightened, wiping her hands on her apron. "Though I must say, it's having you here that truly warms this old place. I can't tell you how delighted I am to have another female about. Mrs. Graham, our cook, comes in every day to prepare the midday and evening meals, but she never actually dines with us. Says it's not her place.

"I suppose it's natural for a former slave to feel that way, but no matter how many times I explain that Arthur and I are servants on equal footing with her, she refuses to come to the table at lunch, preferring to take a plate out on the back porch and eat on the stairs. In the evenings, she leaves as soon as the food is prepared so that she can get back to her family."

Nicole smiled as the woman took a knitted throw from its storage at the top of the wardrobe and unfurled it across the narrow bed. Mrs. Wellborn seemed always to be in motion. Both with her hands and her voice. Nicole had liked her immediately upon their first meeting, and that impression had only grown stronger over the last hour.

"Yes, indeed. It will be wonderful to have another woman around to talk to. Don't get very many visitors at Oakhaven. Not like we did back in New York. 'Course there were plenty of maids and other household staff to talk to there. Not like it is here with just Arthur and me. But I'm not complaining," she assured Nicole as she wiped a smudge from the tiny mirror above the washstand with a corner of her apron. "Mrs. Thornton was right to send us out here to care for the young master when he decided not to come home after the accident. The man barely eats as it is. If left completely to his own devices, he'd probably wither away to nothing in less than a month's time."

Nicole's ears perked. What accident? Why wouldn't he go home? What was keeping Darius Thornton at Oakhaven? She clamped her lips against the questions, though, fearful that if she drew attention to the details Mrs. Wellborn was inadvertently revealing about her employer, the housekeeper would cease her informational prattle. So instead, Nicole fiddled with the placement of her brush and hairpin box atop the bureau.

But it seemed Mrs. Wellborn was done imparting jeweled tidbits anyway, for she turned around, straightened her apron, and reached for the door handle. "I'll leave you to finish settling in. Come to the kitchen in about thirty minutes, and I'll have supper on the table. Mr. Thornton always dines in his workshop, so you need not worry about dressing for dinner. You may eat in the dining room if you wish or join Arthur and me in the kitchen. Whichever you prefer."

The woman kept her voice carefully neutral, but after the way she'd gone on about having company, Nicole would've had to be dreadfully thickheaded not to guess the correct response. "I'd be delighted to join you and your husband in the kitchen, Mrs. Wellborn. If you'll have me. I can't imagine anything more unappetizing than eating alone in the dining room."

"Splendid!" The housekeeper beamed. "I'll set another place." She bustled out of the room with the same energetic spirit she'd entered with earlier, leaving Nicole smiling in her wake as the door clicked closed.

Should the eccentric Mr. Thornton ever decide to sup in the dining room, her family's status as well as her professional position in the Oakhaven household would demand that she dine in his company, but until then, she'd gladly take her meals with the amiable Mrs. Wellborn and her taciturn husband.

First, however, she had to find a secure place to hide her dagger. Propping her foot against the bedpost, Nicole reached beneath her burgundy skirts and unstrapped the sheath. A sigh of pleasure passed her lips at the removal of the bulky weight. Her finger-tips ran over the reddened skin where the hilt had rubbed against her thigh. She winced a bit at the sting. Obviously, she wouldn't be able to wear her own blade for a few days if she wanted the area to heal. But since transcribing logbooks was a fairly innocuous occupation, she didn't expect to need it.

The Jenkins threat still hung over her head, but John and Mathis would have ensured that the brothers hadn't followed her from Galveston. Fletcher and Will might eventually track her down, but for now she was safe.

Glancing around her room, Nicole tapped the flat of the dagger blade against her hip. The wardrobe was out. With the table linens stored there, Mrs. Wellborn would have cause to dig around inside on a regular basis. The bureau? She could wrap the dagger in a spare petticoat and stuff it in the bottom of a drawer. Nicole frowned. Better not. Should the Jenkins brothers find her, they would immediately search her belongings, and she doubted the presence of frilly unmentionables would deter them.

The bed? Nicole knelt down to peer under the mattress. A rope frame. Nowhere to conceal a dagger there. The washstand wasn't any better. Should she bury it outside? Nicole peered out the narrow window and examined the grounds visible from her vantage point. Beneath that oak tree or behind the shed? She glanced back at the dagger, a sick feeling turning her stomach. No. She couldn't trust it that far out of her sight. There was no telling what could happen out there. A rainstorm could erode away the dirt from where she buried her treasure, or a dog could dig it up.

She paced the floor, her grip on the dagger tightening. She had to find —

A squeak from a loose floorboard severed her train of thought. Dropping her gaze to the floor, she kicked aside the new rug Mrs. Wellborn had brought in and took a few calculated steps, listening for the telltale squeak.

She heard it again, closer to the bureau. Nicole pointed her toe, extending her foot under the bureau, and experimentally pressed on the board she suspected was the culprit. Not only did it squeak, the far edge of the floorboard rose up nearly an inch when she exerted more force on the end closest to her.

Nicole's lips curved in satisfaction. Perfect.

Darius sat cross-legged on the floor of his workshop surrounded by boiler plates. They were each carefully labeled so he would know which exploded boiler they had come from. He had six and a half boilers in his collection. The half being one that had blown so violently, the scrap dealer could only identify a fraction of the parts.

Of course, none of the plates matched. If he'd learned nothing else over the last year, he'd learned to expect inconsistencies. Still, after reading that article, he'd hoped to find *some* common ground. He should have known better. Some of his samples were corroded, others had fractures, and one displayed virtually no wear at all. Some were made of substandard iron, while others were of high quality and appropriate thickness. No pattern. Yet all of these boilers had exploded.

There were simply too many variables. If all explosions were due to boiler plate quality, legislation could be passed to regulate it. But the culprit could be a faulty rivet, a damaged flue, a lack of proper water maintenance, an overtaxed release valve, a clogged pipe, even the accumulation of too much mud from the pump. There were probably a dozen causes that hadn't even been discovered yet. That's what made this work such a nightmare. One malfunction in any of these areas could be the catalyst for an explosion. Though more often than not, a combination of factors set the deadly cogs in motion.

What the industry needed was a regulating body that forced manufacturers and engineers to have their machines held to certain standards and inspected on a regular basis. The 1838 Act had tried to do that by holding captain and crew liable for negligence, but it did nothing to address machinery standards. The number of explosions had actually increased since that act was passed.

They needed a new law and improved safety equipment. An accurate steam-pressure gauge could change everything. If one were found, a crewman could make adjustments to maintain an optimal level of steam without dangerous pressure buildups. It wouldn't be perfect, explosions could still occur with faulty equipment, but it would be a step in the right direction.

Darius sighed. The solution was no simpler than the cause. A multi-tiered problem required a multi-tiered solution. Which led him back to the boiler plates. One tier at a time.

A quiet rap sounded a moment before his door creaked open. Darius didn't look up. "Just set it in the usual place." He waved vaguely, his attention focused on a scorch spot on one of the boilers. Had there been a fire before the actual explosion? Or had the boiler plate simply been overheated in more than one location, and for some reason, this section had held together while another section of the boiler blew? He flipped it over to examine the other side. Similar discoloration, but not to the same extent. It —

"Where, exactly, is the usual place?"

That voice. Darius's head jerked up. The woman holding his dinner tray was definitely *not* Mrs. Wellborn. Far too young. Far too pretty. And far too distracting.

"On the stool by the hearth," he groused, hoping she'd take the hint and scurry away. Alas, Nicole Greyson — he'd made a point to jot her name down in his notebook; he always remembered things once he'd written them down — was not a scurrier. She was a swisher.

Ignoring his impatient barking, she brushed past him, her skirts swishing in a gentle motion as she moved. Swishing in a manner that was far too intriguing. Darius gritted his teeth and forced his attention back to his scorched boiler plate. Although, from his vantage point on the floor, her skirts were impossible to ignore, being at eye level as they were. Maybe if he squinted a bit more as he stared at the boiler plate, his area of peripheral vision would shrink and reduce the pull of —

"You've quite a collection, here."

Drat. Squinting hadn't helped. He could

still see her skirts, and the blasted things had stopped swishing altogether. She couldn't be leaving if her skirts weren't swishing. And what was really annoying was that they'd changed. Oh, it wasn't annoying that she'd replaced her fancy red dress with a navy blue calico one sporting a white ruffled apron. No, that was actually quite sensible. What was annoying was that he'd noticed, and that his noticing had stolen his attention from his boiler plates.

"Did you explode these all yourself?" For once, someone asked that question with curiosity instead of condemnation. But it didn't matter. He needed her gone.

"No, Miss Greyson," he said in his most scathing tone. "*My* explosions are done with models on a much smaller scale. These boilers are from actual steamboats, ones I've collected for my research. And I'll thank you to not touch anything." He raised his voice on this last instruction when his peripheral vision picked up the motion of her hand reaching for one of the internal flue tubes that stood balanced against the wall. "Everything is precisely as I wish it to be in here, and you are not to disturb it. Or me. Now get on with you. I'll see you in the study promptly at eight tomorrow morning. We'll discuss your duties then. Good night."

The skirts swished a step or two, then stopped. "Well, you *did* mention that I would occasionally be assisting you here. That's why I offered to bring out your dinner tray — to familiarize myself with the building and its setup. I'll be sure not to disturb anything until I learn your organizational system."

Darius forced his attention to remain on the boiler plate draped across his lap, even though all his instincts were screaming at him to look her in the face. That would be even worse than watching her skirts. He remembered those golden brown eyes, the way they sparked one minute and went all soft the next, only to be filled with triumph when she bested him a few moments later. No, her eyes were far too dangerous.

"Your presence here is disturbing enough in and of itself."

Had he actually just said that? Darius stifled a groan, praying she'd heed his grouchy demeanor more than the attraction behind it. "Be gone." He waved dismissively in the air above his head, still keeping his gaze turned away from her. "I have more important things to do than converse with a secretary who seems determined to overstep her bounds."

She said nothing for a long moment, and

Darius had to dig the edge of the boiler plate into his shin in order to keep from stealing a peek at her face. Was she angry? Hurt? He had been rather harsh. Or did her expression register a completely different emotion? Puzzlement, perhaps, or . . . intrigue? That last thought made his stomach tighten.

Probably just hunger.

He was never to know what flittered across her face, if anything, however, for her skirts finally started swishing toward the door.

"Mrs. Wellborn asked me to remind you that the biscuits and beef are best eaten warm," she said as the door hinges creaked, announcing her departure. "As are the greens, though they were a tad bitter to my taste. Of course, *you* would probably find them most palatable."

With that, the door clicked closed.

Darius's head came up at the sound, and he peered at the door as if he could see through it to the woman marching back to the house with fire in every step. A reluctant grin tugged the corners of his mouth upward. The woman possessed admirable wit. Having her around might be distracting, but it was rather invigorating, as well. Darius's smile turned downward. All the more reason to keep his distance from her. A man could come to crave . . . invigorating.

Chapter 8

He'd left her a *note*? Nicole stared at the slip of paper carelessly tossed atop the log-book in the center of Darius Thornton's desk the following morning. She'd arrived precisely at eight o'clock, ready to receive her instructions for the day, but apparently her new employer couldn't be bothered with conversing with her in person. No. He'd left her a note.

Miss G —
Transcribe the remainder of this note-book.

— D

So terse. So cold. So . . . begrudging. Did he respect her so little, then? Even after she'd proven herself capable yesterday? Nicole scrunched the slip of paper inside her rapidly closing fist. Why did men have to be such pompous idiots when interacting with female colleagues? Dictating orders instead of sharing ideas, running roughshod over common courtesy.

At least Mr. Thornton's note wasn't dripping with condescension. He seemed to expect her to be able to accomplish the task he'd set before her without supervision. She supposed that indicated some level of trust in her competency. Nicole opened her hand and smoothed out the crumpled paper against the flat surface of the desk, then took her seat in the chair. Perhaps she shouldn't jump to conclusions about the man's character when he wasn't there to defend himself. It was entirely possible he simply treated his correspondence with the same negligence he treated his personal habits. No need to take it personally. She should just be thankful she had employment.

Pulling out fresh paper and ink, Nicole set to work. She was halfway through the first page when a percussive roar rattled the desk lamp and shook the floor beneath her feet. She screeched and dropped her pen, ink splatting all over the page as she grabbed for the solid wood of the desk to brace herself.

What on earth . . . ?

A man's shout echoed outside. Nicole

launched out of her chair and ran for the window. Nothing.

Had Mr. Thornton fallen victim to one of his explosions? Nicole spun away from the window and dashed out into the hall. Wellborn, the butler, stood at the base of the stairs, polishing the banister.

"Wellborn!" she called. "What's happened?"

The man continued polishing, as if deaf.

"Wellborn!" she barked again, coming up beside him.

He finally glanced up. "Oh. Sorry, miss. I didn't hear you." He left the polishing rag draped over the balustrade and reached both hands up to his ears. He removed a wad of cotton from each and then smiled at her.

"Was there something you wanted?"

Was there something she wanted? Had he not felt the very earth quake beneath his feet a moment ago? This entire household was mad.

"Your master might be injured. I heard him shout after that horrendous roar." She grabbed his arm and started tugging him toward the front door. "We must hurry —"

"Easy, miss. There's no cause for concern." He gently extricated his sleeve from her grasp, smoothed the fabric, and dragged

116

to a halt. "I take it Mr. Thornton failed to inform you of his schedule?" He shook his head as if answering his own question. "He can be a bit absentminded about things like that. I apologize. I'll take it upon myself to warn you of future experiments before they occur. You shouldn't be caught off guard again."

As if that were the issue.

Wellborn sketched a quick bow, then turned back to his work, completely unconcerned that his master could at that very moment be lying somewhere outside in a mutilated heap, breathing his last. All right, so he probably wasn't *too* mutilated if he'd been able to shout, but still . . . someone should check on the man. And apparently she was the only resident of sound enough mind to volunteer for the task.

Fine.

With a huff, Nicole gave up on the butler and marched out the front door. She'd start with the workshop and move on from there. Crossing the yard, she swept her gaze from the barn to the workshop, searching for any sign of Mr. Thornton, mutilated or otherwise. Nothing. At least if the man had indeed blown himself up, he'd had the courtesy to do so out of sight of the house. Mrs. Wellborn and Mrs. Graham would no doubt be thankful for that favor.

She stomped toward the workshop, arms swinging, spine stiff. He better not be dead. She needed this position. Needed the wages. How else was she supposed to get to New Orleans and scare up an heir for Renard Shipping? Was his endeavoring to stay alive too much to ask? She'd known the man was a tad eccentric and enjoyed exploding things, but couldn't he hold off on his destructive hobby long enough to let her collect a round of wages?

A few paces away from the workshop entrance, Nicole paused to examine the structure before storming the castle. As far as she could tell, the roof hadn't caved in. All four walls were standing. No smoke poured from the windows. The structure appeared to be sound. Bracing herself for what she might find, she strode to the door, flung it open, and stepped inside.

"Mr. Thornton?"

She blinked against the dim interior, her attention drawn to the sunlight streaming around the back door that hung ajar. Tentatively, she started across the room. "Mr. Thornton?"

A grunt echoed from the other side of the door. A low rumble that grew into a lion-esque roar.

Good heavens. Was the man dying? "Mr. Thornton!" Nicole surged across the remaining distance and pushed the door open with such force it crashed back against the opposite wall as she stepped outside.

"Blast it all, woman! You made me drop it. I could have lost my foot."

Darius Thornton, perfectly hale and hearty, straightened his posture and stepped away from a thick free-standing log wall that looked as if it had been cut from the side of some poor family's cabin.

"The thing's as heavy as a steamer trunk full of lead." He glared at her. "What are you doing here, anyway? You're supposed to be in the study transcribing my notes."

"I heard the explosion and your shout. I thought you might have been injured."

Her employer shook his head at her a moment before he rolled his eyes. "God save me from interfering females," he muttered before turning back to his log wall . . . thing.

"I was perfectly fine," he called out as he bent to grab the handholds that had been worked into the wood a few feet off the ground, "until you showed up." He grunted as he strained to lift the heavy piece and began dragging it, the tendons in his neck bulging as he threw his full weight behind the motion.

A set of grooves in the hard-packed dirt beside the workshop indicated where man and wall were heading, and the snake-like trail stretching for several yards behind them demonstrated how far they'd already come. Gracious, the man must be part ox. Unable to stand still and watch another person slave away when she was in a position to lend aid, Nicole darted around to the far side of the logs. She bent her shoulder to the end piece, dug her feet into the dirt, and pushed. The logs picked up speed as they slid over the dirt.

Once the structure was settled where it belonged, she stood back and dusted tiny bits of bark from her sleeve.

"Thanks for helping move the barricade," her employer groused, little actual gratitude detectable in his voice.

"Barricade?" For the first time, Nicole recognized what she'd helped him move. She gasped and staggered back a step.

The barricade looked like a remnant from the Alamo. Scarred logs. Bark blasted away in more places than not. Deep gouges. But what truly haunted her were the hundreds of metal scraps embedded so deeply into the logs that no one would have been able to pry them out. The thing looked like a giant pincushion.

Merciful heavens! If an explosion could shoot iron fragments that deeply into a solid log wall, what would it do to the flesh of a man?

"Are you insane?" she blurted. "Why in the world would you do this? It's a miracle there aren't bits and pieces of you blasted all over the yard."

All he did was raise an eyebrow and nod toward the log shield they'd just moved. "That's what the barricade is for, Miss Greyson."

She stomped toward him, hands clenched at her sides. "And what if an explosion occurs before you get behind the barricade? What then? Have you no care for your family, your parents? And what of your staff? People depend upon you. You have no right to be so careless. Scientific advancement isn't worth your life. And that's exactly what you are risking every time you —"

"I know exactly what I'm risking!" He lunged away from the wall, his face halting mere inches from hers. "And I know exactly what it is worth compared to the thousands of innocent lives that have been sacrificed already to steamboat explosions. Women. *Children.* All dead because the demand to transport more things faster has superseded our understanding of the mechanics we use to accomplish it.

"The more we can learn about what causes these explosions, the better chance we have to create safety measures that will prevent them. That's why I do this, Miss Greyson. Not to get my name in some scholarly journal. Not for the thrill of brushing close to death. I do it because too many innocents have died for me to stand by and do nothing."

His vehemence speared her. She couldn't move, could barely blink. She'd been around shipyards and boats her entire life, and never had she given more than a passing thought to the lives that were taken when accidents occurred on board. She'd read newspaper accounts of riverboat explosions that had injured or killed dozens of passengers and crew, but those people seemed so far removed from her, she'd felt little more than a brief stirring of pity — a stirring that dissipated as soon as she moved on to the next article.

Darius Thornton, on the other hand, read those same accounts and decided to make a difference, to risk his life in the pursuit of knowledge that would change an industry.

It shamed her.

Her employer pivoted away and slapped the heel of his hand against the workshop wall. Nicole followed and laid a hand on his arm. "What can I do to help?"

His chin came around slowly, his gaze resting on her hand a moment before lifting to her face. Passion still blazed in his eyes, but it had faded just enough for her to catch the tortured gleam behind it. He'd been touched by this. Personally. Hadn't Mrs. Wellborn mentioned an accident? Had Darius Thornton lost a loved one in a steamboat explosion? A family member? A friend? A . . . wife?

He stepped aside, pulling away from her touch. "Just do what I hired you to do. Tidy my notes, check my figures, catch my errors."

"And assist with your experiments." She lifted her chin in challenge. If he was going to risk his life in such a noble quest, the least she could do was watch his back in the process. Somebody had to.

Mr. Thornton's gaze sharpened and once again found her face. "Assist?" He raised a supercilious brow.

Nicole sniffed and crossed her arms. "Honestly, Mr. Thornton. You can't convert me to your cause, then ban me from participation. It just isn't done."

A spark she'd never seen before lit his slate-blue eyes as he said, "And we all know

how I hate to flout society's conventions."
Somehow he managed to say that bit of
balderdash with a straight face. He carried
it off so well, Nicole couldn't help but
laugh, which finally brought that smile of
his out in full force.

Oh dear. There might be more risk involved in this endeavor than she'd first
thought.

CHAPTER 9

Three days later, Nicole arrived in the study for her morning transcription instructions, not surprised to see the room void of her employer's presence. He seemed to have forfeited not only the study for her use, but the entire house. She never saw him — not at meals, nor at the end of the day. As far as she could tell, the man never relaxed, rarely ate, and if he slept, she couldn't imagine where.

His bed was perfectly made every morning even before Mrs. Wellborn made her rounds — she'd sneaked peeks the past couple mornings before reporting to the study. A man who couldn't be bothered to straighten his clothing surely wouldn't take the time to make his own bed. The only logical conclusion, therefore, was that he didn't sleep in it. Perhaps he'd stashed a cot somewhere in his workshop. Though judging by the clutter she recalled being scattered about the place, there wouldn't be room to set one up.

Shaking her head at the eccentricities of her absent employer, she grinned a little as she made her way to the desk, where a stack of papers laid waiting for her. Darius Thornton's untidy scrawl peered up at her from the note tossed haphazardly atop the pile.

Miss G —

Continue transcribing logbook #1. Should you finish, begin logbook #2.

Confirm calculations and tidy up the diagrams on the schematics to your left.

Report to the workshop at three o'clock.

— D

Nicole blinked. Report to the workshop? The man was actually inviting her into the hallowed sanctum. Remarkable.

A frisson of anticipation buzzed through her. There hadn't been an explosion in the last three days. Could it be that this invitation to his workshop was actually in response to her offer to help him with his experiments? His silence over the last days had led her to assume he'd decided she'd not be of much use, but perhaps she'd been wrong. Perhaps Darius Thornton did see more than her skirts when he looked at her. He'd hired her, after all, even though he'd advertised for a man. And he hadn't fussed at her when she'd helped him move that barricade of his.

The man might be odd, but no one could doubt his practical nature. Perhaps he'd seen enough promise in the work she'd produced to accept her assistance in other areas. Nicole battled a smile and lost. She always had been unable to resist an adventure.

Of course, she still intended to watch Mr. Thornton's back. Though his intelligence couldn't be discounted — his research was thorough, his experiments logical, and conclusions sound — the man was too reckless by half.

She supposed the fact he remained alive and in possession of all his limbs after more than a year of experiments should relieve her concerns. Yet oddly enough, she felt more compelled than ever to keep an eye on things. If ever a man needed looking after, it was Darius Thornton.

In the meantime, however, she had schematics to copy.

The morning plodded on at an excruciatingly slow pace. Nicole managed to get the boiler diagrams copied to scale, but she had to constantly wrestle her mind away from thoughts of what might transpire that afternoon. Losing her train of thought for the third time on one of Mr. Thornton's computations, Nicole tossed her pen down in disgust. At the same moment, the study door creaked open and Mrs. Wellborn toddled in, a basket of cleaning supplies dangling from the crook of her arm.

"Good morning, Miss Greyson," the housekeeper sang out as she crossed the room to the bookcases. She set her basket on the small table near the armchair. "I hope you don't mind if I invade your privacy for a little cleaning. I always polish the furniture on Saturdays, and there's so much wood in this room, I fear I won't be able to finish it while you're having lunch."

Nicole fiddled with the papers on her desk and reclaimed her pen, suddenly feeling guilty over her lack of attention to the task at hand. "Of course I don't mind." She dragged a logbook in front of her and dutifully opened it to the last page she'd transcribed. "You won't bother me."

At least not any more than she was already bothered.

Several minutes passed in silence, the soft sounds of a skirt rustling and the smells of linseed oil and lemon the only evidence of

Mrs. Wellborn's presence. Then a quiet hum developed, followed by an occasional flourish of the dust rag, which caught Nicole's eye. The housekeeper's white cap bounced up and down in Nicole's periphery as the cheery woman fairly danced through her chore. It was so infectious, Nicole itched to twirl about the room herself. Instead, she smiled and bent her head over the logbook, trying to concentrate on deciphering another line of her employer's cryptic handwriting.

"I understand you've been taking your lunches down by the pond," Mrs. Wellborn ventured as her dust rag glided over the bookcase shelves nearest the desk. "It truly is a lovely spot. Arthur and I sometimes take a stroll along the banks in the cool of the evening."

Her rag paused midstroke, and her gaze fogged over as a sigh escaped her. In a blink, clarity returned and the housekeeper shot Nicole a flirty smile. "He's been known to steal a kiss under the branches of that big oak, too. You'd never know it to look at him, but my Arthur can be quite the man of passion."

Nicole giggled, charmed by the idea of the staid butler sharing a passionate embrace with his wife in such a setting. "I can't imagine a better place for a tryst. It's a shame I don't have a beau to share it with."

The housekeeper's expression sharpened an instant before the dust rag resumed its fluttering — a fluttering that seemed rather more frantic than necessary. "So you have no young man paying court to you? Hard to believe, as pretty as you are."

Nicole blushed and became suddenly fascinated with the logbook in front of her. "Not yet," she said, fingering the pages, "but my father has a few prospects in mind." Prospects she was supposed to be considering at that moment in New Orleans.

"I'm so glad to hear that your father is involved." The fluttering converged upon the desk. Nicole circled a protective arm around the schematics. "So many young people these days fail to see the wisdom in arranged marriages."

"Oh, it won't be arranged," Nicole corrected as she carefully stacked the papers into a tidy pile and dragged them a safe distance from the overeager duster. "Papa promised to give me a choice. He just has a few . . . suggestions about where I should start looking."

"Sounds like a fair compromise." The dusting flurry ceased as quickly as it had begun. Mrs. Wellborn smiled her cheery smile before turning her attention to a lamp with a smoky chimney. "I wonder if you found someone acceptable on your own if he would approve."

"If the man were truly acceptable, I don't see . . ." Nicole's brow furrowed. Somehow this conversation seemed much less hypothetical than it had a moment ago. "Goodness. Is it really almost noon?" It was actually only 11:35, but the housekeeper couldn't see the clock face from her position by the lamp, and Nicole decided a liberal definition of *almost* was acceptable in this circumstance.

She pushed to her feet and backed away from the desk. "All this talk about the pond has me itching for a visit. I think I'll head to the kitchen and see if Mrs. Graham has any leftovers I can pilfer for luncheon." And escape any further probing questions. The less the people at Oakhaven knew about her, the better it would be for everyone.

"Oh, all right, dear." The housekeeper waved her rag as if she were a fancy lady waving farewell with a lace handkerchief, but the confusion in her eyes pricked Nicole's conscience. "Have a nice time."

She didn't want to hurt Mrs. Wellborn's feelings, but neither did she wish to encourage any matchmaking impulses the woman might be prone to. Especially if those efforts involved a man handsome and noble enough to tempt her heart while being completely unsuitable for taking the helm at Renard Shipping. An obsessed, eccentric, social misfit would be a disaster for her father's company, no matter how intelligent and driven the man might be. No, she needed to do her job, earn her wages, and get on to New Orleans. Memories of her father's weakened condition spurred her determination. He was counting on her to find him an heir. She'd not disappoint him.

After collecting her bonnet from her room and thrusting it upon her head with a careless abandon that would no doubt make her disheveled employer proud, Nicole strode into the kitchen, where Mrs. Graham was pulling a pair of Dutch ovens from the coals in the hearth. The cook thumped them onto the worktable and pulled off the lids, releasing the heavenly aroma of fresh-baked bread.

Nicole's stomach gurgled.

"Bread's gotta cool." Mrs. Graham lifted her eyes just enough to let Nicole know she was speaking to her. "If you're wanting somethin' to eat, there's part of yesterday's loaf in the cupboard. You can take some ham from the skillet, too. I ain't got around to warmin' it yet." Defensiveness edged the cook's voice, as if she expected a reprimand for not anticipating Nicole's early lunch plans.

"Cold ham and day-old bread sounds perfectly acceptable, Mrs. Graham. Thank you." She crossed to the cupboard, found the bread, and began exploring the other occupants resting within its recesses. Lifting the corner of a flour-sack towel, Nicole smiled at the treat she'd uncovered. "Would you mind if I cut off a few slices of this cheese, as well?"

Mrs. Graham shrugged. "Suit yourself."

Nicole gathered her luncheon items, tied them up in a towel, and headed for the back door. Sunshine warmed her face the moment she stepped outdoors, and in that moment her concerns shrunk to a manageable size. She closed her eyes and breathed deeply of the clean, sweet air. God was good. He'd blessed her with a beautiful spring day and, with it, the reminder that he was in charge. She didn't have to carry her troubles alone. He would watch over her father's health, take care of her, and if it fit his plans, lead her to the man who would fulfill both her and Papa's needs.

Nicole hiked around to the far side of the pond and settled herself on the large exposed root she'd discovered on her first visit. It had just enough curve in it to be comfortable, especially when she leaned back against the oak's trunk. The natural bench offered a delightful view of the pond. She tore off a piece of her bread and tossed it toward the pair of ducks gliding along the surface. Both birds dove beak first for it, their feathered bottoms popping up at the same moment, stirring a laugh from Nicole.

After whispering a quick word of thanks for her meal and a heartfelt plea for her father's healing, she relaxed against the tree trunk and ate. The ducks hovered on the edge of the pond, silently pleading for her to share. She obliged, tossing her last two scraps into the water.

"That's all there is, I'm afraid." She held up empty hands, then shook out her napkin, scattering the crumbs upon the dirt. A line of ants came to investigate, and she watched the procession carry away the evidence of her lunch. Industrious little bunch. Wonder how far away their home —

A quiet splash broke off her thought.

Nicole jerked her gaze back to the pond but saw nothing — nothing but ripples spreading out beneath the landing. Someone was in the water.

In a flash, she grabbed her knife from its

sheath and jumped to her feet. Dashing behind the tree, she gathered her full skirts tightly against her legs and tucked the excess material between her knees.

Had the Jenkins brothers found her?

She should have known better than to let her guard down. How stupid could she be? Nicole pounded the oak with her fist. She'd grown lax. Let herself feel safe just because Oakhaven sat ten miles from town and rarely entertained visitors. Fool! If Will and Fletcher walked up to the front door and asked for a woman named Nicole, Wellborn would no doubt direct them to the study. Or the pond. Or wherever she happened to be at the time. He had no reason not to.

Peeking around the tree, Nicole frowned. A line of bubbles drew a path across the pond, but no one surfaced. Had it been an animal instead of a man that dove into the pond? It seemed too long for a man to hold his breath. An alligator, maybe? While a gator *would* be preferable to a Jenkins, she'd rather not confront either one.

She stood behind the tree, debating the merits of hiding versus making a run for the house, when all at once the surface of the water shattered and a man shot up from the depths, his chest breaking the plane of the water as he gasped for breath.

He lingered only a moment in the shallows, lifting his face to the sun, eyes closed, dark blond hair slicked back over his head. Water poured off him in rivulets, plastering the white cotton of his shirt against his torso. A smile touched his mouth, serene and unfettered for a blissful heartbeat before his features tightened again in concentration, and he plunged back into the water.

That was no Jenkins.

Nicole braced her weight against the oak's support, all ability to breathe having fled her body.

He swam on the surface this time, his powerful strokes driving him across the pond as if he had been fitted with one of the new screw propellers her father found so fascinating.

He reached the landing faster than she could have had she run along the path, and once there, he thrust himself out of the water in a long, graceful push onto the platform before stretching out flat on his back to absorb the heat of the sun-soaked wood after what must have been a frigid swim. It was only April, after all.

Nicole withdrew behind the tree, confident now that hiding was her best option. Only she couldn't hide from the images bombarding her consciousness. *Good heavens,* she thought as she pressed her sagging spine into the tree at her back. Who would have guessed that an overly eccentric, obsessive, mechanical scientist could be such a riveting physical specimen?

And that smile. A sigh eased out of Nicole's lungs. For an instant, a single moment, Darius Thornton had released his fierce drive to conquer the world's boiler problems and allowed peace to rest upon his soul. Yes, it had been only a moment.

But in that moment, he'd been glorious.

CHAPTER 10

Darius's chest heaved as he sprawled on the landing, eyes closed while he tried to borrow heat from the sun. A spring breeze brushed over him, sending shivers across his body, but it was a small price to pay. He'd needed that swim to clear his head. Water relaxed him. Nourished him. It reset his internal compass, helped him focus on what was important. Like his next experiment.

Boiler plates. He'd fashioned two miniature boilers with the boiler plates he'd taken from his collection. Both in relatively good condition. No noticeable corrosion or fractures. Yet the first stood at one-quarter-inch thickness while the second expanded to three-eighths. He'd constructed the experimental boilers with the same number of rivets, the same soldering. Plate thickness should be the only variable. Should be. Yet since yesterday, doubt had itched beneath his skin until he couldn't stand it any longer. He was missing something.

That's why he'd summoned *her*. She'd caught his error with the cargo weight during her interview, and she'd proved adept with the schematics, drawing them to scale as if she understood how each piece fit with the others. He hoped her keen mind would decipher what was missing from his current equation. Unfortunately, knowing she'd be in his company again had played havoc with his concentration all morning. Hence the swim.

He lay there several minutes, emptying his mind of swishing skirts, copper-brown eyes, and . . . feminine penmanship. Darius's brow wrinkled as he squeezed his eyes more tightly closed against the sun — the sun and the vision of his words in Miss Greyson's tidy script.

Bah! He flung an arm over his eyes, but even that failed to banish the loops and flourishes he'd come to associate with his new secretary.

It was no wonder he saw pages upon pages of her script in his mind. It was the last thing he looked at each night before collapsing for a couple hours of sleep, usually on the sofa in his study. And somehow in those lonely hours before dawn, the evidence that someone understood his words, scratched and ugly as they were, made it easier to pretend that someone understood *him.*

Growing uncomfortably cool in his wet trousers and shirt, Darius rolled to the side, intending to push himself to his feet, but a quiet yelp stilled his motion. His eyes flew open. The catalyst for all his concentration complications stood not five yards away, her eyes round and wide, like those of a flushed rabbit an instant before it bounded away from the hunter.

Neither of them said a word.

Afraid she'd bolt if he moved, Darius remained on his side. But when her gaze flickered ever so briefly from his face to his chest, he recalled the inappropriate nature of his wet attire. His neck heated. Followed by his temper.

"You shouldn't be here, Miss Greyson." Darius shoved to his feet and glared at her, anger a much easier emotion to wear than discomfiture. "My summons was for three o'clock. You should be working in the study, not out wandering the grounds."

Her eyes narrowed and her chin lifted, all resemblance to the scared rabbit of a moment ago gone. "So I'm not to be allowed a break for luncheon, then?" She released her grip on her skirt and stiffened her posture.

Luncheon? Was it noon already? Darius squinted up into the blue sky and noted the sun's rather obvious placement overhead. *Drat.* He never was one to keep tabs on the time. And now his lack of temporal awareness left him looking like some kind of fiendish overlord.

"Of course you're allowed a break for luncheon. Don't be ridiculous," he blustered, trying to somehow salvage the situation. "But it would be best for you to do so at the house. I run my experiments at the pond, you know. At times, it can be quite dangerous down here."

"There were no boilers or machinery of any kind when I arrived," she protested, her blasted logic blowing holes in his weak-kneed argument. "And I've grown quite fond of taking my midday meal here. Surely you wouldn't deny me such a simple pleasure."

Her cheeks reddened at the word *pleasure.* Darius cocked his head, his blood growing warm beneath his wind-chilled skin. Had she witnessed his swim? He didn't see how she could have missed it if she'd indeed been lunching by the water. The more intriguing question was, had she liked what she'd seen? Ever the scientist, Darius couldn't let the hypothesis go unchallenged. Ignoring his boots where they lay in the grass at the edge of the landing, he strode barefoot toward his quarry.

"So I'm to understand that you lunch by the pond every day, Miss Greyson?" he asked as he stalked her through the shin-high grass. Her chin wobbled just a bit, and she took a nearly imperceptible step back. He'd probably not have noticed it if he hadn't been observing her so closely. But what kind of scientist would he be if he didn't attend to the tiniest of details?

"Every day," she confirmed, her voice impressively free of tremors. The lady knew how to put up a strong front. "After working indoors for several hours, it's nice to have the benefits of fresh air and a change of scenery. The pond offers both."

He halted his advance about a foot away from her. "I imagine the scenery changed a little more than you were expecting today." His lighthearted tone surprised him nearly as much as it did her. Her brow puckered as if he were an equation she couldn't quite decipher. Well, that was only fair, since he didn't have a clue about what he was trying to do, either. Surely not flirt with the woman. He didn't have time for such vain endeavors. He needed to extricate himself from this situation. At once.

Not knowing what else to do, Darius sketched a short bow and begged her pardon as if he were a gentleman in his mother's drawing room instead of a soggy scientist dripping all over the vegetation. "I apologize for intruding on your solitude, Miss Greyson, and I hope I have not offended you with my . . . ah . . ." He glanced helplessly down at his wet clothing.

"Dampness?" The amusement in his secretary's voice brought his head up. "My father used to be a seaman, Mr. Thornton, and I grew up swimming in the Gulf. You aren't the first man I've seen take a swim." Though the way her gaze dipped again to his chest and the slow swallowing motion of her throat that followed seemed to indicate that she hadn't been as unmoved by the sight as she would have him believe. That thought pleased him far more than it should have.

"Be that as it may, I'll take special care not to avail myself of the pond during the midday hours in the future."

He expected her to murmur some polite form of thanks for his consideration, but she didn't. No, she stared at him instead. Long enough that he had to fight the urge to squirm under her perusal.

"You know, Mr. Thornton," she said with a cock of her head that gave him the distinct impression she was testing her own hypothesis. "I believe your . . . dampness has restored your ability to converse with genteel manners." Her lips curved in a saucy grin that had his pulse leaping in response. "Perhaps you should swim more often."

She left him to stew in his own muddy juices, and he watched her go, strangely captivated by the way the wind wrapped her bonnet ribbon around the delicate curve of her neck.

Darius wrenched his attention away. Taking another cold swim suddenly seemed like a *very* good idea.

Later that afternoon, Nicole stood biting her lip outside the storage shed that housed Mr. Thornton's workshop. She could do this. Just because memories of her employer's wet, well-honed form had proven incredibly difficult to banish and had kept her from accomplishing anything of note in the last three hours did not mean she couldn't converse with him in an intelligent manner during this appointment. She was a professional. A woman of education. A Renard. And Renards faced their challenges head on.

Renard though she may be, her hand still trembled as she raised it to knock on the door.

"Enter," came the impatient call from within. Nicole smiled. Apparently their encounter hadn't altered her employer's demeanor. Good. She was starting to think she liked him better without his manners. At least she knew what to expect.

Nicole let herself into the workshop and picked her way past piles of steel and iron scrap until she reached her employer's side. She waited for him to turn or somehow acknowledge her presence, but all he did was mumble to himself and pace between two machines that bore an uncanny resemblance to steam engine boilers.

Curious, Nicole stepped closer and craned her neck to see around Darius Thornton's broad shoulders. The boilers were nowhere near the size of the actual mechanisms used to power riverboats, but the two of them together took up an entire wall of the workshop.

"Did you build those yourself?" she asked, impressed. The craftsmanship was really quite good. Apparently his construction skills were more finely tuned than his drafting ones. These models looked nothing like the disproportioned schematics in his log-books.

"What? Oh, ah . . . yes." He shot a quick glance at her, frowned, then continued his pacing. "But there's something missing. I can't conduct my experiment until I diagnose my error." He ran a hand through his short-cropped hair, his jaw clenching as he looked from the first boiler to the second.

At least he'd thrown on dry clothes, even if his shirttail was half-untucked at the back. She dropped her gaze to his feet. And shoes — thank heaven. There was something far too intimate about being in a closed room with a barefoot man.

"Well, don't just stand there, Miss Greyson." Darius Thornton reached out, clasped her wrist, and tugged her forward. Heat from his hand penetrated her sleeve, and tiny sparks shot up her arm. He positioned her in front of himself and started rambling off facts about the two boilers, his body hovering near hers as he pointed out the various details.

"Same quantity of new rivets, same soldering, same flue design in each," he was saying.

Nicole ordered her mind to concentrate on the task at hand, *not* on the man standing close enough to brush against her shoulder every time he gestured to one of the scaled-down boilers. The brief contact between them obviously meant nothing to him, as focused as he was on his experiment.

What would it be like to be the object of such focused attention?

The stray thought so staggered her, Nicole had to lock her knees to remain upright. Where in the world had *that* come from? Mr. Thornton was the oddest, most socially defiant gentleman of her acquaintance. Still . . . there was something about him that intrigued her. Something deep inside that drove his obsession. Something she wanted to excavate and examine for herself.

Simple curiosity, of course. That's all it was. Nicole eased forward, putting an inch more distance between her and Mr. Thornton. It was natural to be curious about one's employer. Who wouldn't be?

Yet if he were ever to look at her with the same intensity he reserved for his boilers, she'd probably combust on the spot. The woman who gained his attention would have to be made of sturdy stuff. And while Nicole had always considered herself of that breed, she was also savvy enough not to get tangled in a mess that didn't concern her. She was at Oakhaven to earn passage to

New Orleans, not to unravel Darius Thornton's mysteries. Best she leave him to his boilers.

Determined that their proximity would mean as little to her as it did to him, Nicole reined in her thoughts with a strong hand and turned her attention back to the situation at hand.

"Thickness of the boiler plate should be the only variable," her employer was saying, "but I can't escape the feeling that I'm missing something." He paced a few steps away from her. "I need you to tell me what it is."

Her heart gave a panicked flutter. "Me?" What made him think she would know anything about boilers?

"You're an intelligent woman with a logical mind. You found my error with the cargo weight. You can find any errors here, as well." He finally looked her full in the face, and she was struck by the desperation in his features. It was as if he feared failure at a level that far exceeded what this simple experiment warranted.

And *she* was the one he was turning to for help. Because he respected her intellect and considered her capable.

"Please," he said. "I can't afford the waste of time and precious equipment for an experiment that the Franklin Institute will throw out as useless because I overlooked a control element."

One had only to see the angst etched across his brow to know this had nothing to do with personal prestige. He was a crusader, and even though she didn't fully understand his cause, Nicole felt herself being drawn into it.

"I'll do what I can."

Some of the tension drained from his jaw and forehead. He dipped his chin in an abbreviated bow. "Thank you."

Nicole nodded back, then took a step closer to the boilers. "Have you made any notes?" The words were barely out of her mouth before a logbook was shoved into her hand.

It was difficult to concentrate with her employer pacing the room behind her, but Nicole did her best to examine his work and search for any discrepancies that might interfere with the experiment's outcome.

"Both have safety valves in the same position," she murmured. "Dampers, fireboxes, water pumps. They seem to be identical in every way. As long as you are careful to use comparable water levels and heat them at the same rate, everything should be fine. Although . . ." She made a few mental calculations.

"What?" Mr. Thornton demanded, coming beside her. "What are you thinking?"

Nicole hesitated. "It's just that . . . Well, I don't know how much difference the thickness of the boiler plate will make in the heating rate of the water. You might have to use more fuel, or greater heat, to induce the same amount of steam in the second engine due to the barrier between the fire and the water being thicker. Once a steady temperature is achieved, the differences should even out, but if you are testing to see which thickness can stand up to increased steam pressure the longest, you might need to factor in the initial difference in heating the water through a thicker plate."

Nicole finally glanced up from the logbook to gauge Darius Thornton's reaction. The poor man looked rather frozen, his face expressionless, his body eerily still. Nicole returned her attention to the notes, unsure what such a response meant.

"Of course, I have very little practical experience with the workings of such machines," she hurried to remind him. "It's very possible that the difference an eighth of an inch of plating would make on the heating rate is negligible. I've never actually witnessed a side-by-side comparison." She knew she was rambling but couldn't seem to stop. His continued silence had stretched her nerves nearly to the snapping point.

"Miss Greyson?" His deep voice cut through her babble, sparing her from further maligning her own intelligence.

"Yes?" She forced her chin up. The lines that had grooved his face mere moments ago were now barely visible. It was as if ten years of hard living had just fallen away. Her own heart lightened in response.

A grin broke out across Darius Thornton's face. "I think I might just have to kiss you."

CHAPTER 11

And then, unbelievably, he did.

His warning gave Nicole no time to react, for as soon as the words left his mouth, Darius Thornton gripped her upper arms and planted a fast yet fierce kiss on her lips. Oh, it was perfectly chaste — a celebratory kiss, not anything with romantic intent — but it rattled her just the same.

He laughed, called her a genius, and immediately snatched his logbook from her fingers and began jotting notes in the margin as he returned his attention to the boilers.

Nicole followed his lead, adding her laughter to the mix while hoping he was too absorbed in his boilers to recognize how forced the sound was.

Darius Thornton had just kissed her. That fact roared so loudly in her mind that all thoughts of boilers, heating rates, and explosions dimmed in comparison. Her first kiss from a gentleman, and he hadn't even meant anything by it. Not that her pulse could tell the difference. She hadn't felt this light-headed since the time she bet Tommy Ackerman that she could hold her breath longer than him and nearly passed out from the effort.

Nicole backed a few steps away, needing some distance. *Get ahold of yourself, Nicki. The man's eccentric. That's all.* He probably would have kissed Mrs. Wellborn had she been the one to mention heating rates. No need to blow anything out of proportion. *Just be thankful you were able to help.*

Yet that was half the trouble. She'd helped him puzzle through a problem, and at the moment the solution clicked in his mind, his demeanor became as unburdened as it had been when he burst out of the water after swimming the length of the pond. *She'd* done that. She'd given him that bit of peace. Her heart swelled with the knowledge even as an alarm sounded in her mind. For deep inside, a need was growing within her — a need to ease this man's burdens, to restore whatever it was he had lost. But it was a need she couldn't afford to indulge. Not while her own family's burden lay heavy on her shoulders.

"So, want to help me set up the barricade?"

Nicole's head jerked up. Darius — No, *Mr. Thornton.* She had to keep a professional distance with the man. Unfortunately it was hard to think of her employer as *Mr. Thornton* when he was grinning at her like a young boy with a new toy. Numbly, she nodded and followed him outside.

"Grab hold," he said, gesturing to the barricade handle nearest her, "and help me cart this old girl toward the pond. You'll see a well-worn groove in the ground about fifteen yards from the landing. That's where we'll set her down."

The scarred logs — an all-too visual reminder of the very real threat these experiments posed — still sent an unwelcome shiver through her. Nevertheless, she hurried forward and wrapped both hands around the cylindrical peg that jutted out on the right side. Most men would assume she was too weak to help with such a task or would consider it improper for a woman to take part in an endeavor so obviously fitted to a man. Others would prefer to show off their manly prowess by hefting the thing themselves while the lady looked on in awe. Not Darius. He respected her desire to be included as well as her strength and capability and therefore asked her to help. Simple.

Straightforward. No murky social considerations to confuse things.

Nicole hid a grin as she bent her knees and lifted her end of the barricade. That nonconformist quality of his was starting to grow on her.

The barricade was heavy, and her end dragged much closer to the ground than the side Darius — Mr. Thornton — carried. By the time they reached the groove indicating where the thing was to sit, her arms burned.

A tiny grunt escaped her as she dropped her end. A masculine version echoed beside her at the same time, making her feel better. Apparently, she wasn't the only one who'd struggled under the weight of the barricade.

"Thanks for the help," her employer remarked as she turned to face him. "It usually takes me twice as long to move it on my own."

"Glad to lend a hand." Nicole glanced back toward the workshop. "Will you need assistance with the boilers, as well?"

"I can manage those on my own, but we'll need two wheelbarrow loads of wood to fuel the fireboxes. There's a barrow out by the woodshed. If you would start loading it while I move the boilers down to the pond, that would save considerable time."

"Aye, aye, Captain." Nicole clicked her heels together and snapped a salute.

Her employer seemed a bit nonplussed by her actions until she winked at him and allowed the smile she'd been fighting to bloom across her face. He laughed then and gave her a playful push in the direction of the shed. "Hop to, sailor, before I make you walk the plank for insubordination."

Nicole scurried away, giving her best imitation of a cowed crew member, bowing and scraping as she trotted over the packed dirt of the yard. Darius's deep chuckles followed her, the rich sound warming a place inside her that she hadn't even realized had been cold.

An hour later, everything stood ready. The boilers floated on small rafts tethered to either side of the pond's landing. The firewood lay piled in the middle. Her employer did his final checks, made a note or two in his logbook, then trudged up the slight incline that led to the barricade where Nicole waited.

"Remember, you are not to remove yourself from behind this barricade for any reason." His eyes met hers in an unyielding stare. Nicole immediately nodded her agreement.

He'd wanted her to wait in the workshop or even the house, but she'd been determined to see the experiment up close. Partly to appease her curiosity, and partly to appease the worried voice inside her head that demanded she watch over the man who cared more about saving future lives than protecting his own.

After she vowed to obey his instructions to the letter, he finally relented and granted her permission to watch the experiment from this protected spot. The log wall was only about five feet tall, so if she stood on the crate she'd purloined from the shed, she would have an unobstructed view of all that led up to the explosions.

"I promise to take every precaution." Her stomach fluttered in anticipation, a strange mix of nerves and excitement. "And as soon as you wave at me to get down, I'll duck fully behind the wall and cover my head."

The grim line of his mouth eased just a bit as she recited his instructions back to him. "Right."

He reached for the long caped greatcoat that he'd hung from the edge of the barricade and slid his arms inside. He dug a pair of leather gloves from one of the coat pockets and quickly donned them, as well.

His armor, Nicole realized. A little shiver ran down her back as she imagined scalding steam spewing from an exploded boiler and iron shrapnel flying like bullets from a gun. And all Darius had for protection were a wool greatcoat and a pair of gloves. *Inadequate* didn't begin to describe it.

He gave her a final stern glance, then marched down to the pond. Nicole leaned her back against the barricade and wrapped her arms about her middle. Her eyes slid closed.

Watch over him, Lord. Keep him safe.

Climbing onto her crate to peer over the barricade, she comforted herself with the knowledge that Darius Thornton had conducted several of these experiments in the past and had survived each one. He knew what he was about. Still, her gaze never left him as he worked the water pumps and fed the fireboxes.

She had no idea how much time had passed when the release valves finally began to whistle. Her legs felt slightly numb from standing in one position for so long, but she dared not move from her perch. Steam had obviously built up pressure in the boilers, yet Mr. Thornton continued stoking the fires of each one. Just as a riverboat pilot

158

would do to gain speed or to fight a current.

The hiss of the steam grew louder. The whistle's pitch higher. Mr. Thornton hovered near the boiler with the thinner plate, no doubt listening for the groans of the metal that would signal an escalation of pressure. Then he added more wood.

Nicole wanted to shout at him to stop feeding the devils, but she held her tongue. Her fingers grasped the top of the log wall with such force, splinters jabbed her skin. She leaned forward, pressing up onto her tiptoes.

The bodies of both boilers bulged as the steam pressure continued to rise. Nicole gritted her teeth against the whimper rising in her throat. Darius pulled out his logbook and made a note. So calm. So controlled. The crazy man should get out of there. Surely the fires were hot enough to continue building sufficient steam without him. He should observe from behind the barricade. Make his notes from there.

However, boilers needed a continual source of water and heat, and like any good steamboat engineer, he kept to his post, feeding both.

He edged closer to the boiler on the right, the one with the thinner plate, and tipped his head as if listening to the sound of the metal itself. But as he focused his attention on the right side boiler, it was the one on the left that continued swelling. As Nicole watched in horror, its sides bulged to a size she'd never dreamed possible.

Cupping her hands around her mouth, and praying her warning would be heard above the fevered hiss of the steam, Nicole screamed with every bit of breath in her body.

"Darius!"

The instant his head came up, she pointed to the other boiler. He turned. His eyes widened in alarm, and he began to run, waving and shouting for her to get down.

She obeyed, jumping off the crate and hunkering behind the barricade, making herself as small as possible so there'd be plenty of room for Darius to take cover.

A blast like cannon fire rent the air. The ground shook from the force. Nicole's arms instinctively shielded her head. The logs vibrated as shards pelted the barricade — a barricade sheltering only one person. Her.

CHAPTER 12

The instant the boiler blew, Darius yanked
the collar of his greatcoat over his head,
tucked his knees beneath him, and hit the
ground.

Blast. He hadn't mistimed an explosion
this poorly in months. But it was supposed
to have been the thinner boiler plate that
blew first, not the thicker one.

Water slapped his back. The heat of the
boiling liquid scalded his flesh through his
coat. He gritted his teeth and forced himself
to remain still while instinct screamed at
him to throw off the coat burning him.

Something slammed into his hip with the
force of a mule kick. He flinched and bit
back a groan. No stabbing pain followed.
That meant a blunt end. *Thank God.*
Smaller pieces pelted him like hail. He'd be
black and blue for the next week, but at
least he didn't have to worry about finding
someone to stitch him up.

When the pounding of debris slowed, Darius crawled toward the barricade. His back burned like the dickens. Too risky to throw off the coat yet, though. The second boiler could blow any moment.

He thought he heard Miss Greyson shout his name again, but the coat muffled the sound. That, and his ears still rang from the explosion, so he couldn't be sure of anything.

Then all at once a pair of arms wrapped themselves about his shoulders and tugged him upward. "Hurry, Darius. Hurry!"

His heart iced over in an instant. She was out from behind the barricade!

With a roar, he shot to his feet, grabbed her off hers, and ran for the safety of the wall. As he rounded the corner, the second explosion hit. Throwing himself on top of her, he smothered her with his body and prayed nothing would get past him.

She didn't make a sound. For a moment he feared he'd knocked her unconscious with his rough handling, but once the rapid thunking of iron careening into logs ceased, he could feel her uncurling beneath him. Immediately, he rolled off, then sucked in a sharp breath when his scalded back connected with the ground.

"Where are you hurt, Darius?" She

crouched beside him, her gaze scouring his torso, arms, and legs for injury. Slowly, her attention traveled to his face, the concern in her golden brown eyes a balm to his scarred heart. He wanted to bask under that look for hours. Days. To listen to her say his name — was she even aware she'd called him by his first name? To watch her lips form it, shape it — lips he suddenly recalled kissing. Lips he wanted to kiss again, only this time he'd take his time to savor their sweetness.

"Darius? Focus." She grabbed his shoulders and gave him a little shake. Then she stroked the hair off his forehead and brought her face closer to his. "Where are you hurt?" Deep furrows creased her brow as she ran her fingers through his hair, lifting his head, massaging his scalp. All thought of bruises and burns faded under her ministrations. He hadn't felt this good in ages.

"I don't feel any lumps," she said. "Did anything hit your head?"

An examination. Of course. That's all it was. Not any particular offer of comfort. She'd simply been trying to ascertain his injuries while he lay around like a sluggard, too drained from his panic over her being in harm's way to form a coherent response to her questions. He'd best get off his back and show some life before she started examining anything else.

"I'm fine, Miss Greyson," he grunted, pushing her hand away from where it had just settled against the plane of his chest, a touch he would no doubt enjoy far too much if he allowed himself the luxury. "Just some scrapes and bruises. Nothing to be concerned about." He rolled to his side, then onto his feet, trying not to wince as his shirt stretched across the tender flesh of his back.

He must not have hidden his reaction as well as he'd hoped, though, for she was at his side in an instant, grabbing for his coat. "You're wet," she accused. "Why didn't you tell me you'd been scalded?" She reached for his lapels and pushed the heavy wool fabric off his shoulders.

"The coat took the brunt of it." He arched his back to avoid the slide of the garment as it fell toward the ground, then slowly peeled off his gloves as if his butler were waiting to accept them. "It's not the first time I've been hit by the spray. I'll have to sleep on my belly for a few days, but it'll heal."

"It'll heal faster if you quit being so stoic about it and treat it." The woman actually had the audacity to glare at him. "I'm going up to the house to fetch some salve and a fresh shirt for you. In the meantime, I suggest you take one of your swims."

Darius raised a brow at her authoritative tone. "I believe, *Miss Greyson,* it's customary for the employer to give the orders, not the employee."

She crossed her arms over her chest, her brown eyes shooting sparks at him. "When one's employer nearly blows himself up, he forfeits the right to give orders. At least for the rest of the day."

Darius fought a smile. She was certainly a bossy little thing when she was riled. But when she unfolded her arms to jab a finger at him, the trembling in her fingers firmed up his frown. The woman might exhibit a brave front, but the explosion had left her shaken. She needed someone to tend to her, not the other way around.

"The cold water will soothe your burns," she was saying, still harping at him about that swim. "They'll heal faster if —"

"Enough." He spoke gently, but with a firmness she couldn't run roughshod over. "I'll make you a deal. I'll follow your orders if you follow mine."

She eyed him skeptically. "What orders?"

"I'll soak in the pond and let Wellborn slather me up with salve if you'll go up to the house and have a cup of tea. You've been through an ordeal, and my mother swears that nothing fortifies a body like a good cup of tea."

Her shoulders visibly slumped at the mention of tea, as if the prospect of a warm cup of Darjeeling overrode her desire to continue lecturing him. That tiny motion revealed her vulnerability and made him want to pick her up in his arms again, carry her to the house, and ply her with the tea himself.

"Your man knows how to tend injuries properly?" she asked, straightening her posture.

"Wellborn's put me back together more than once over the last year. He'll manage."

"All right, then," she finally conceded. "I'll send him down straight away."

She turned to go, but he stopped her with a hand to her arm. "I have one more order for you, Miss Greyson."

She glanced back, and he met her gaze, holding it for a long moment before he spoke. "Never, under any circumstances, put yourself in danger for me again. Is that understood?" He released her arm and stepped back. "I'm not worth your life."

Her eyes bored into his. Then she sighed and gave her head a little shake. "Another calculation error. Really, Mr. Thornton. You need to brush up on your computational skills."

She hadn't agreed to his terms, Darius realized as he watched the stubborn woman return to the house. He should be angry, or at the very least, plotting ways to extract a vow of obedience from her. Yet, the sudden burst of warmth inside his chest made it impossible to do anything but smile.

Fifteen minutes later, Wellborn in his starched collar and impeccably pressed trousers handed a towel to Darius as he climbed out of the pond.

"I have clean clothes and the salve you requested in the workshop, sir," the butler intoned. "Miss Greyson insisted I tend to your back. Threatened to do the task herself if I refused."

"Did she?" Darius grinned as he toweled his hair dry. The thought of Nicole's fingers delicately applying salve to his scalded skin was a rather tantalizing prospect. Too bad it was also highly improper.

Darius ran the towel down his bare chest, leaving his back and arms to dry in the breeze so he wouldn't have to touch them with the rough fabric. The cold pond water had helped soothe the burn, but the skin still pulled and ached like the dickens.

"What are your impressions of the lady, Wellborn?" Darius asked as he handed his man the towel and walked to the edge of the landing to collect his boots. "You've had more occasion to be in her company than I have the last few days."

"It's not my place to have opinions, sir." Wellborn followed, carefully sidestepping the iron fragments and exploded boiler parts littering the landing. As he watched Darius pull on his boots, a slight tightening at the corner of his mouth was the only indication he might disapprove of his master's chosen pastime.

"Come now, Wellborn," Darius teased as he strolled up the incline to the workshop. "This isn't New York. This is Texas, where a man is judged by his character and his actions, not by his social station." He reached the door and turned to face his butler. "You've been with my family for years and have served us with impeccable integrity. I respect you, Wellborn. Not your position in my household, but *you,* the *man.*" Darius clapped him on the shoulder. "Surely, under all that straight-laced formality is an intelligent being with observations and opinions like any other. That's who I'm asking."

Wellborn's eyes widened, as if he believed Darius had completely taken leave of his senses, talking to him in such a familiar manner. Perhaps he had. But Wellborn was the only masculine opinion around, and as a married man he was bound to have a better understanding of women than Darius did. Besides, Wellborn was the epitome of stoic sensibility. His opinion was sure to be unbiased, a trait Darius could no longer claim when it came to Nicole Greyson. The woman had him tangled up in knots.

"Why don't you change your trousers, sir, while I see to the salve."

Darius sighed. He guessed he couldn't expect a man to set aside a persona he had carefully constructed and cultivated all of his adult life in the blink of an eye. The fellow probably thought him a lunatic for asking.

Neither spoke a word after that. Darius changed into dry trousers and a pair of wool stockings, then bent over one of the worktables so Wellborn could smear the greasy, medicinal concoction onto his back.

Wellborn had applied the stuff to his shoulders and neck, and was halfway down Darius's back, when he finally broke the silence. "She's diligent with her work. Miss Greyson. Always prompt to her post in the study each morning."

Darius went very still. He made no effort

169

to turn around, afraid that if he did so, Wellborn would cease his recitation.

"She comports herself well," the butler continued, still hesitant but apparently warming to the topic. "By the quality of her clothing, I'd say she comes from money, but she doesn't put on airs."

Darius hadn't thought much about her clothing beyond the fact that it looked well on her, yet Wellborn's observations reminded him that upon first meeting, he'd considered her a woman of his sister's ilk. Wealthy, educated, refined. Which begged the question, why would a woman like that be seeking employment? And from a man with no connections to her family. Imagining his sister doing such a thing sent a shudder through him when he thought of how easy it would be for an unscrupulous employer to take advantage of the situation.

Wellborn dipped out another dollop of salve and rubbed it across Darius's lower back. "She dines with the missus and me in the kitchen. Flora's taken quite a shine to her. The two have become quite . . . friendly."

Wellborn reached for the towel and wiped his fingers clean. "All finished, sir."

Darius straightened and allowed his man to help him don a shirt. The cotton fabric stuck to the salve, but it would keep the dirt out and keep him decently clad.

"She saved my life today." Darius spoke softly, slowly meeting Wellborn's gaze.

His butler didn't lower his eyes, as was his custom. No, he met Darius's look straight on — one man to another. Darius's respect for him swelled.

"She called out a warning that gave me time to outrun the blast." He never would have survived the explosion standing as close to it as he had been. The steam would have melted skin from bone. "I find myself in her debt."

Wellborn nodded but didn't say anything for a long moment. Then, when Darius thought he would collect his supplies and return to the house, he cleared his throat instead. "I might know a way we could repay that debt."

Everything inside Darius sharpened at that comment, just like it did when he stumbled across an idea for a new experiment. "Oh?" he asked, trying to keep his voice casual.

"The young lady drew me aside after she returned from her luncheon today. She made an odd request."

Darius recalled their earlier run-in at the pond. *Odd* didn't begin to describe it —

him stalking her through the grass in his sodden clothes and bare feet. She'd handled herself with plenty of spirit, though, and he'd thought they'd left on good terms.

"I did have words with her this morning," he admitted, though it seemed like forever ago now, with all that had happened since.

"Her request did not pertain to you, sir. At least, not directly."

Darius arched a brow. "What *did* it pertain to?"

Wellborn was always serious, but something in the man's expression made the back of Darius's neck prickle. "Miss Greyson requested, if anyone came to Oakhaven asking after a young woman matching her description, that I not reveal her presence here. Also, that I make her aware of the situation at once."

Darius fell back against the worktable. He grabbed the edge to steady himself. "She's in some kind of trouble."

Wellborn dipped his chin in agreement. "It seems a logical conclusion. I'd thought to discuss the matter with you later this evening."

"Thank you for bringing it to my attention," Darius said, ironically slipping into the same formality he had chided Wellborn for earlier. However, when a man lost his equilibrium, he tended to resort to old habits to regain his footing.

"I found her phrasing of the request a bit odd." A contemplative look came over the butler's face.

Darius mentally reviewed Wellborn's account, analyzing each section as he would one of his journal articles until a hypothesis formed. "She's more concerned over someone recognizing her appearance than her name."

Wellborn nodded. "That is the impression I gained."

Interesting. It seemed his new secretary might have accepted the position under false pretenses. Well, a false name, at least. Not that it mattered. The woman had proved herself more than capable. Her name didn't matter.

"Let's adhere to her wishes for now. With one deviation." Darius pushed up from the table and braced his legs apart, as if preparing for battle. "If anyone comes looking for her, inform me first. She deserves our protection, Wellborn. I intend to see that she gets it."

A light glowed in Wellborn's eyes, and Darius knew he had an ally. The man would bring his wife in on the plan, as well, he was sure. Which left Darius to deal with his

173

enigmatic secretary.
What secrets was Nicole Greyson hiding?

Chapter 13

Nicole lingered about the kitchen, assisting Mrs. Wellborn in laying out the evening meal. Thankfully, the housekeeper kept up a steady stream of idle chatter that required little more than an occasional *hmm* from Nicole to maintain its momentum. She wasn't exactly fit for intelligent conversation at the moment. Not when all of her mental processes were devoted to worrying over the state of her employer's health.

Was Wellborn tending to his injuries properly? Had any of the exploded iron bits dug themselves into Darius Thornton's flesh? She hadn't noticed any blood during her inspection, and the man hadn't mentioned any painful gashes or impaled objects about his person. Of course, if he were anything like her father, he wouldn't admit to an injury in her presence. Men tended to be muleheaded when it came to their frailties. Never admitting weakness around women. Even those in their own family. Heavens, her father could barely get out of bed, and Mama still had to tiptoe around his pride.

Perhaps Darius had sent for Wellborn for that very reason. Nicole stilled, the bread she'd been slicing only half cut, her hand going lax on the knife handle midsaw. Perhaps he had hidden a serious wound from her, preferring to reveal it only to another male so she wouldn't think him weak. As if she ever would. Nicole tightened her grip on the knife and sawed through the rest of the slice with far more vigor than was necessary.

Fool man. She'd never think him weak. How could she when she could still feel his arms about her as he caught her up to his chest and carried her effortlessly back to the barricade? His weight had rested atop her as he shielded her from whatever projectiles were hurling at them, not giving any thought to his own peril, only her protection. *Weak* was not a word she would ever associate with Darius Thornton.

As she cut the final slice, Nicole took advantage of a rare lull in Mrs. Wellborn's cheerful prattle. "I'll fill a tray for Mr. Thornton," she offered, eager for any excuse to check up on the man and judge the sever-

176

ity of his injuries for herself, "and take it to the workshop."

"That won't be necessary, Miss Greyson, but thank you."

Nicole spun toward the doorway. "Dar— Mr. Thornton!"

She raked her gaze over his tall form. He moved a bit gingerly as he entered the kitchen, but that was to be expected after the abuse his body had taken that afternoon. No bandages in evidence, at least none that she could see. She supposed it was possible he had a wound concealed beneath his dark trousers, but she gauged his movements as he ambled to the table and didn't detect a limp or any hitch in his stride.

"Do I pass inspection?" The amusement in his voice brought a rush of heat to her cheeks.

"That depends," she brazened, lifting her chin. "Are there any hidden injuries I should be concerned about?"

He made his way around the table, running his fingers along the back of each chair. "Such a personal question, Miss Greyson." A teasing gleam lit his eyes as he steadily approached. Nicole dropped the bread knife and turned to face him fully, reaching behind herself to grip the cabinet top for support. "But you can put your mind at ease." He didn't stop when he rounded the table. He kept coming.

Nicole's pulse fluttered, and her grip on the cabinet doubled.

"Except for a pile of bruises and some overheated skin, I'm fine." He ceased his advance. Finally. She had to tilt her head back to hold his gaze, though, so close had he come.

"I'm glad to hear it. Sir." She added the last to try to force some distance between them. With him standing so close, all she could think about was that unexpected kiss they'd shared. Not the healthiest train of thought for a young woman who planned to leave as soon as monetarily possible. He was her employer. That was all. Yet her attention drifted down toward his mouth anyway. Realizing what she was doing and suddenly recalling the housekeeper, Nicole yanked her attention away from Darius's face and scanned the room. But the kitchen stood empty.

"She's setting places for us in the dining room," Darius said, apparently reading her mind. "I thought we might discuss possible explanations for why the boilers burst in the wrong order, among . . . other things." He paused, and Nicole found her eyes drawn to his once again. A strange gleam lit them, as if it were *her* and not the boilers he was puzzling over. A completely ridiculous notion, of course. Nothing fascinated Darius Thornton more than boilers.

"All right." Nicole turned away from his probing eyes and busied herself with arranging the bread slices in a basket and covering them with a cloth. "I'll join you in a moment." She finished with the bread and sidled past him toward the stove, where she began ladling chicken stew into the tureen Mrs. Wellborn had set out. From the corner of her eye, she saw him exit, and a relieved breath whooshed from her lungs.

Steady, Nicki. Just because the man suddenly wanted to dine with her instead of taking his meal on a tray didn't signify that anything had changed between them. It was simply expedient. This way he wouldn't have to wait for her to eat before discussing the results of the afternoon's experiment. After all, Darius did value his time. They might have shared a harrowing experience and a celebratory kiss, but they were still employer and employee. Nothing more.

Nicole frowned as she hefted the heavy tureen into her arms. Darius Thornton was on a mission to save steamboat passengers. She was on a mission to save her father's shipping enterprise. They traveled divergent paths — paths that had met and intertwined for a brief time, yes, but paths that would necessarily split once again. She'd do herself no favors by letting her heart get tangled up with his in the interim. It would only make the leaving that much harder.

"Goodness, Miss Greyson," Mrs. Wellborn fussed as she came through the door and caught sight of Nicole lugging the tureen toward the dining room. "There's no need for you to be carting around heavy serving pieces. Arthur will get that."

"Please, miss," Wellborn intoned, indicating with a wave of his hand that she should set the tureen down on the table. "Go join the master. We'll tend to the meal."

Not wanting to intrude on anyone's territory, Nicole complied. "I left half the stew in the pot on the stove, and the bread is cut and in the basket." She knew she was rambling, but somehow the idea of being alone with Darius suddenly made her jittery.

"Now, don't you worry about us, dearie." The housekeeper clutched Nicole's hands, then scooted behind her to work on her apron strings. With a practiced twist and flip, Mrs. Wellborn had Nicole's apron off her shoulders and over her head before she quite knew what had happened. "That's better." The woman circled Nicole, approval warming her eyes. "You look lovely, dear. The green of that gown sets off your complexion perfectly."

Nicole swallowed a groan. The last thing she needed after the day she'd had was to dodge a barrage of well-meaning but ill-aimed Cupid arrows. Her feelings were in turmoil enough as it was. "Thank you, Mrs. Wellborn, but I'm sure my appearance is of no consequence. Mr. Thornton requested I dine with him so we can discuss business. Nothing else."

"Of course." The housekeeper waved her hands about as if erasing Nicole's argument. "It's just that it's been such a long time since we've actually served a meal in the dining room. The excitement has me all aflutter. Humor an old lady, will you?" she asked as she aimed Nicole toward the door and gave her a little push. "Let me pretend the master has finally set aside those horrible exploding machines for good and is ready to resume life as a normal Thornton."

Pretending is dangerous, Nicole thought as she stepped into the dining room. But when Darius crossed the floor to greet her, the smile on his face warm and inviting, Nicole found herself all too eager to pretend. To pretend this was her house, her dining room, her *man.* No, it was far safer to stay rooted in reality.

"Let me get your chair for you, Miss Greyson."

Was it her imagination, or was there a strange inflection in the way he said her name? Well, her assumed name. She squirmed inwardly as Darius led her to a spot near the end of the table. The more time she spent at Oakhaven, the guiltier she felt about her deception. It was as much for the protection of the people here as it was for herself, but it still felt disloyal.

Darius pulled out her chair and seated her with all the grace of a well-trained gentleman. He still wore no coat or cravat, as most gentlemen would when dressing for dinner, but his shirt sleeves were rolled down to his wrists, which for him was quite a concession. Of course, even that was probably due more to the salve plastering the cotton to his skin than any nod toward formality, but Nicole was finding she rather liked his flouting of convention. One knew what one was getting with Darius. No insincere flattery or pretentious nonsense designed to turn a woman's head. He simply said what he meant and did what he said. She'd take integrity over pretty manners any day.

He took his place at the head of the table

to her left and signaled Wellborn. The butler carried over the tureen while his wife served. They left the basket of bread, a crock of butter, and a plate of jam tarts on the table, then disappeared into the kitchen.

"How is your back faring?" Nicole asked after Darius offered grace. She dipped her spoon into the thick broth and captured a dumpling.

Darius shrugged. "Sore, but manageable. Soaking in the pond helped take some of the sting out." He drew a piece of bread from the basket, buttered it, and handed it to her.

When her fingers closed around the crusty edge, she expected him to let go. He didn't. She glanced up into penetrating blue-gray eyes.

"You saved my life today, Miss Greyson. I owe you my thanks."

Nicole lowered her lashes, the intensity of his regard giving her pulse a ragged rhythm. "I'm just glad I was there to call a warning."

Darius grinned, then released his hold on the bread. "Me too." He took a second piece and turned his attention to buttering it. "So what do you think caused the boiler with the thicker plate to explode first?"

"I have no idea," she said, glad to be back

on familiar footing. Talking to Mr. Thornton, the obsessed scientist, was clinical. Safe. Exchanging singular glances and grazing fingertips over bread with Darius, the *man,* was anything but. "Did we overcompensate for the difference in heating rate?"

"I considered that," Darius said between bites. "I suppose it could have played a role. However, it occurred to me that the thicker plating might have created greater rigidity in the iron."

Nicole paused with her spoon halfway to her mouth and tilted her head as she considered the implications. "If it was less pliable, it wouldn't expand as easily, possibly making it more brittle under pressure." She nodded, her enthusiasm building. "It's a sound theory."

"Of course, the explosion could have been caused by a faulty rivet or a weakness in the soldering. I do my best to ensure quality craftsmanship," he said with a shrug, "but I'm not perfect."

Nicole offered to help him collect the scrap from the explosion in order to examine it for evidence of contributing factors, and the two animatedly discussed the possibilities of what that evidence might entail. Ideas and postulations flew back and forth as their dinner disappeared.

Nicole had always enjoyed scholarly discussion and had often debated with her schoolmistresses back in Boston. But there was something incredibly stimulating about sharing such discourse with a man she respected. The girls at Miss Rochester's Academy were constantly being cautioned about not revealing too much intelligence around the young men they encountered at social events. Gentlemen preferred ladies who were accomplished hostesses and charming conversationalists, not bluestocking termagants who were too free with their opinions, especially if those opinions differed from those of the males in their company.

But Darius was different, she noted with a smile as he punctuated the air with his spoon while ranting about the need for an accurate instrument to measure steam pressure. He treated her as an equal. Respected her knowledge, even sought her opinions. There was no place for personal pride in his work. It was all about advancing mechanical understanding and saving lives. If a young woman with a penchant for mathematics could help achieve that goal, he didn't hesitate to include her.

Too bad her father and his men couldn't see her in such a light. Her skirts seemed to blind them. Yet, to be fair, even if they did support her as the heir to Renard Shipping, it was unlikely the account holders would. They'd no doubt transfer their business to Jenkins the minute she took the helm. Nicole let out a tiny sigh as she used the last piece of bread to sop up the dregs of broth in her bowl.

"Ready for dessert?" Darius held the plate of tarts out to her.

Nicole quickly swallowed the bread she'd just popped into her mouth and dabbed her lips with her napkin. "Yes. Thank you."

She reached for a strawberry one from the pastry plate, smiling shyly. He smiled back, and Nicole savored the ease that had built between them.

"Wonderful," he said, selecting a blackberry tart for himself. "Then perhaps you are also ready to tell me about the trouble you're running away from."

Nicole's gaze flew to his, the peace of the moment obliterated as effectively as a hunter's shot blasting through a morning meadow.

What did he know?

CHAPTER 14

Darius watched the play of emotions on his secretary's face move from shock to panic to caution all in the space of few heartbeats.

"Trouble?" she asked, obviously reluctant to volunteer any information.

Darius sighed. His gut had told him she'd not want to open up about it, but he hadn't been able to stop himself from hoping his instincts were wrong. It would be so much easier if she just laid her cards out on the table for him to diagram and dissect. Probing around in private matters required a delicacy he'd never mastered. His conversational tools had all the delicacy of a sledgehammer.

"Wellborn told me about your request." If he was going to bludgeon, he might as well smash straight to the point and minimize the damage. "Regarding Oakhaven visitors."

A slight tightening around her mouth was the only indication of her distress. Keeping her attention firmly locked on her tart, she collected her dessert fork and used the side to break off a piece of the pastry. "I'd rather hoped you'd be too busy with your work to care about any comings and goings that didn't concern you. Wellborn shouldn't have bothered you with such a trifling matter." She brought the bite to her mouth and chewed slowly, as if savoring the sweet. But he knew better. She was stalling. Using the tart as an excuse to occupy her mouth so she couldn't answer his questions.

Darius tugged her plate out of reach before she could stab a second bite.

"Nicole."

His use of her given name had the desired effect. Her chin jerked up and her eyes widened as she scanned his face.

"Your safety is not a trifling matter." The urge to cover her hand with his speared through him, but he resisted, not knowing how she'd interpret such a gesture. Unsure, as well, how he'd *want* her to interpret it. "While you are at Oakhaven, you are under my protection. Whatever you are running away from —"

"I'm not running away." Her eyes sparked, and she visibly bristled as if he'd offended her. "I'm simply taking care of an . . . an errand for my father. It requires a bit of secrecy, is all, and there are competitors who wish to . . . interfere."

She chose her words with care. Too much care.

What father would send his daughter on a secret errand knowing others would attempt to *interfere*? Had he no concern for her well-being? Surely her errand had not originally entailed gaining employment as a secretary, which meant something had already gone wrong and she'd been forced to improvise. He thanked God her improvising had brought her to him and not to some brigand who would toss her to the sharks at the first hint of trouble.

Why hadn't she returned home? Who was after her? What was this mysterious errand that she risked so much for? And how much was she truly risking? Her father's favor? Her reputation? He stilled. Her life?

He wanted nothing more than to demand answers from her, but the mulish set of her jaw warned he'd only hit a wall of silence should he choose that route. So he bit his tongue and made a few mental calculations.

If he'd learned nothing else from his experiments with boilers, he'd learned that if one didn't get the answers he sought with the first attempt, one must approach the problem from a new angle. So he slid her dessert back in front of her and casually took a bite of his own.

"Why has this . . . errand fallen to you? Most fathers would see to business matters themselves, especially if there are competitors who might . . . interfere." He chanced a look at her as he raised his fork to his mouth for a second bite, careful to keep his tone mild and his expression only slightly interested.

She poked at the jam in her tart with the tines of her fork, her gaze downcast. "I'm afraid his health is failing," she finally admitted. "His competitors are eager to take advantage of his deteriorating condition with unscrupulous schemes. As his only child, the duty of safeguarding the family and securing our business fell to me." Nicole glanced up then, her eyes blazing with a determined fire. "I'm not the type to sit idly by and wait for solutions to fall from the sky when trouble arises. I find much more is accomplished when one analyzes a problem and takes the necessary action to overcome it."

Darius lifted another bite of dessert to his mouth, mentally cataloguing all the details he could sift out of her conversation while he chewed. Ill father. Only child. A family business. "Very practical of you," he conceded. "I employ similar methods myself when designing my experiments."

"Precisely." A smile broke across her face with such radiant beauty that for a moment Darius could only stare.

Forcing himself to look away, he struggled to recoup the strategy that had exploded into tiny, unorganized bits the moment her smile hit. Something about trouble. Competitors. Plans. *Ah, yes.* "So what part of your plan led you to Oakhaven?"

Her smile dimmed even as her chin came up in that defiant way of hers that was as annoying as it was admirable. "I was on my way to New Orleans to seek aid among my father's business associates when an unfortunate incident forced me into a detour that depleted my funds."

"I see. So you intended your employment here at Oakhaven to be a temporary arrangement." Stunning how much that prospect distressed him.

"I'm sorry, Darius. I know I should have told you from the beginning." She dropped her fork and laid a gentle hand on his forearm, her touch playing havoc with his thought processes. "I was just so afraid you wouldn't hire me if you knew I planned to leave after a few weeks."

"It *will* be rather tiresome to train a

replacement," he grumbled. As if a comparable substitute even existed. The woman was perfect for him. . . . *As my secretary,* he quickly amended, grabbing his nearly empty glass and swigging down the last mouthful of water.

How had their conversation gotten so far off track? He thumped the glass back onto the table and rubbed absently at the pulse throbbing in his temple. The length of Nicole's stay wasn't important. Keeping her safe for the duration was.

"So, these competitors . . . What do they hope to gain by *interfering* with your journey?" The instant the question left his mouth, he knew it was too direct.

Nicole dropped her gaze and removed her hand from his arm. "With all due respect, Mr. Thornton . . ."

Drat. They were back to *Mr. Thornton* again.

". . . the details of the business I'm conducting for my father are not your concern."

"They are if they put you in danger. And what of the rest of my staff?" Darius snatched the napkin from his lap and threw it onto the table before lurching to his feet and pacing behind his chair. "I have a right to know if having you here is putting them at risk."

"No greater risk than they face from your exploding boilers!" Nicole shot from her seat, color running high in her cheeks.

The audacity of the chit. "I take every precaution —"

"As do I." She glared at him. "The Wellborns are in no peril, especially if they keep my presence here a secret. It's doubtful that Jenkins's sons will find me, anyway. Heaven knows they aren't the sharpest knives in the drawer."

"As master of this house, it's my duty to know the business of those under my roof." He didn't know what nonsense he was spouting now. He didn't care. Nicole had let a vital piece of information slip in her anger, and he wasn't about to let the argument cool long enough for her to notice her lapse.

"Well, perhaps it's time I collect the pay I've earned and leave you and your roof to your own devices."

Not on her life. The woman would be unprotected. Vulnerable. Easy prey for that Jenkins scum. But he couldn't let her know his refusal was out of concern for her. She'd simply assure him she'd be fine and walk out the door.

Darius crossed his arms over his chest and looked down his nose at her. "You agreed to accept payment after a term of two weeks. I'll not pay a cent before then. You owe me ten more days, Miss Greyson. Or do you plan to renege on our agreement?"

Her hands fisted at her sides. "I never go back on my word."

"Good. Then be dressed and ready to journey with me to Grand Cane first thing in the morning. Church services start at ten o'clock, and everyone at Oakhaven is expected to attend." And on that ridiculous bit of imperious blather, he turned and strode out of the room.

The moment Darius left, Nicole plopped onto her chair in an undignified heap. Suddenly cold, she hugged herself and rubbed her arms with trembling hands.

She'd nearly ruined everything. And for what? Her pride? If Darius had taken her up on her offer to vacate his home, she'd be back to where she'd been five days ago — short on funds, with no likely employment prospects on the horizon.

He would have been well within his rights to send her packing, probably should have, truth to tell. Despite her posturing, her being at Oakhaven *did* present a risk to Darius and his household. So why did he insist she stay? Was he that desperate for someone to organize his notes and assist with his experiments, or was there another motive at play?

A creak from the door leading to the kitchen kept her from further analyzing that thought. Mrs. Wellborn slipped into the room and began clearing the table.

"Saw the master pass the kitchen on his way to the study," she said in explanation of her presence. "I swear, sometimes I think that man wouldn't stop working even for the second coming. Barely touched his tart." The housekeeper tsked and shook her head as she collected Darius's dishes. "Oh well. At least he ate in the dining room tonight. That's progress, I suppose."

She brushed past Nicole and laid a hand on her shoulder. "Don't let his rush dictate your pace, dearie. I have some tea steeping in the kitchen. I'll bring you a cup so that you can relax while you finish your dessert. You deserve at least that much after the day you've had."

Nicole craned her neck to meet the older woman's eyes. Sympathy shone there, a sympathy that seemed too fresh to be related to the afternoon's explosion. No, most likely it stemmed from a combination of thin walls and raised voices. The woman was simply too well trained to acknowledge that she'd overheard their . . . discussion.

"Would it be all right if I brought my tart into the kitchen?" Nicole asked. "I'd enjoy some company along with that tea, if you can spare the time to sit and chat for a bit."

The housekeeper beamed. "I'd like nothing better." She patted Nicole's arm, and some of the chill seemed to leave the room.

Nicole answered with a smile of her own, then rose and collected her dishes before following Mrs. Wellborn into the kitchen.

It didn't take long for the housekeeper to have two steaming teacups on the table. Nicole lightly curved her fingers around the china cup, savoring the warmth and bending close to inhale the fragrant steam.

"You're an angel, Mrs. Wellborn. This is exactly what I needed." Nicole stirred in a teaspoon of sugar and set the spoon on her saucer with a delicate *clink*.

The lady smiled as she lowered herself into the chair across from Nicole. "If there's one thing I've learned over the course of my fifty-five years, it's that warm tea and warm company can shrink any problem down to a manageable size." Leaving her tea to cool, Mrs. Wellborn fiddled with her lace cap for a moment, then met Nicole's gaze. "Arthur told me of your request. That we not reveal your presence to any visitors who might show up looking for you."

Nicole's chest tightened. The stress that had begun to dissipate under the influence of sweetened tea and Mrs. Wellborn's kind smiles came back with a vengeance. "I'm sorry," she mumbled, dropping her gaze to her cup. "I know such a request puts you in an awkward position. I wouldn't have asked if it wasn't important. But please don't ask me to explain my reasons. It's a private matter that I will deal with alone, should the need arise."

"Slow down, dearie. No one's asking you to explain anything." The housekeeper reached across the table and clasped Nicole's hand. "I only brought it up because I wanted to assure you that Arthur and I will do everything we can to help."

Nicole raised her chin in time to catch the twinkle in the older lady's eye as the dear woman continued. "This won't be the first time Arthur and I had to deploy discretion for the good of the family."

"But I'm not family." Strange how bitter those words tasted on her tongue.

"That's where you're wrong." Mrs. Wellborn's grip tightened on Nicole's hand. "You're family to us. You have been since the day you entered this house with that sweet, sassy spirit of yours, willing to work hard and help with tasks far beneath a woman of your station."

"Oh, but I'm not —"

"Goodness, child." The housekeeper tittered. "I knew you had breeding the moment you swept through the front door. You might have fallen on hard times, but I know a lady of quality when I see one." She patted Nicole's hand, the simple gesture strangely effective in inspiring reassurance, when from another it would have felt patronizing. "Whatever trouble you're facing, miss, I'm fully confident it's not of your making."

A stinging sensation radiated around the back of Nicole's eyes. She'd done nothing to earn this woman's faith, yet she gave it without reservation. It was humbling. Somehow Nicole managed to push a thank-you past the knot in her throat.

Mrs. Wellborn lifted her teacup to her mouth and sipped, then regarded Nicole thoughtfully over the brim. "You've been good for him, you know. For all of us, really, but especially for the master."

Nicole's pulse sped at the thought even as her mind discounted the comment as illogical. "I don't see how you could think that. I've been here less than a week, and before today he avoided my company as much as possible."

A knowing grin curved the housekeeper's lips. "You're young, dearie. You don't have the experience to see what I can. Believe me, I've noticed a change in him since your arrival. That burden he's been carrying for the last year and a half has been grinding him down with its weight month after month, draining his life like an insatiable leech. Then you came, and it was as if the load lightened." As Nicole opened her mouth to respond, Mrs. Wellborn hurried to add, "And not just because you're helping him transcribe all those notebooks of his."

She winked at Nicole over her teacup, and Nicole immediately raised her own cup to her lips, desperate for an excuse to drop her gaze. "You give him something to think about besides those horrible boilers. Something much more uplifting, if you ask me."

The housekeeper's words pleased Nicole far too much. Pleased her, and plagued her with guilt. As much as she wanted to be the one to help shoulder Darius's burden, she had a weight of her own to carry. Her father was depending on her to find him an heir, and family had to come first.

So why did she find herself hoping the

wages she'd receive in ten days' time would be so paltry they would require her to extend her stay?

Chapter 15

Nicole took special care with her appearance the following morning, opting for her light green silk. It was the nicest of the dresses she'd brought with her, the lace lining the bodice a bit extravagant, but the relatively plain skirt making it perfectly acceptable for a country church service. The rag curls she'd slept in framed her face to advantage, and her gloves added just the right touch of formality. But even knowing she looked her best, her stomach still churned uneasily as she left her room and headed to the parlor. She had much to make up for after last night's squabble, and Darius was not the type of man to forgive a woman's transgressions just because she cleaned up well.

After sharing tea with Mrs. Wellborn last night, Nicole had closed herself up in her room and, instead of simply checking on the dagger to make sure it remained safely tucked away, she'd taken it out of its hiding place, unwrapped it, and stared at it until her eyes began to cross. She'd done it to remind herself of her mission, but instead of clarifying her purpose, it only left her more torn.

Did Darius have a right to know what trouble he courted by letting her stay at Oakhaven? Surely Will and Fletcher Jenkins wouldn't do anything to harm him or the Wellborns, even if they found her here. They wouldn't want to risk bringing the law down on their heads. Then again, she never would have dreamed they'd attack her parents in their own home, either. If anyone at Oakhaven was harmed because of her, she'd regret her silence for the rest of her days. Yet, if she lost the Lafitte Dagger because she confided in the wrong person, her family's legacy would be forfeit. Such a loss would kill her father for sure.

I don't want anyone hurt because I made a wrong choice, God. I need all the wisdom and guidance you can spare.

Before Nicole reached the parlor, Mrs. Wellborn met her in the hall and shooed her toward the front door. "Come along, dearie. The master doesn't like to be late."

Nicole immediately lengthened her stride. "I'm sorry. I didn't realize . . . I don't have a timepiece. . . ." Her excuses dissipated into the air. The *why*s didn't matter. She knew how much Darius valued time, yet she'd let herself get distracted by vanity and worry — two of the most worthless pursuits known to womankind. Not exactly the best start in repairing her relationship with her employer.

They exited to the porch, and while the housekeeper paused to latch the door, Nicole hurried down to the wagon that stood hitched and ready to go. It was more of a buckboard, really, with a second bench seat bolted into the bed to allow for more passengers. Wellborn and Darius stood at the horses' heads, conversing quietly. Nicole approached, an apology on her lips.

"I . . ." Whatever she'd been about to say vanished from her mind the moment Darius turned to face her.

Goodness and mercy. The unkempt scientist with wrinkled trousers, rolled sleeves, and mussed hair had been replaced by a debonair gentleman handsome enough to make even the sturdiest female swoon. Clean-shaven jaw, hair dampened and combed, a pressed suit including a tailored jacket, vest complete with watch chain and fob, starched collar, and tie. The effect left her quite speechless.

"Ah, Miss Greyson. Good of you to join us." Darius stepped around the butler and moved to her side. Inwardly, she winced at his subtle barb, yet outwardly, as he took her arm, she presented the composed facade Miss Rochester had insisted they all perfect at the Academy. He led her past the horses to the side of the wagon where a stepstool had been placed in line with the second bench seat. "Allow me to assist you."

The man looked far too smug. Too polished. Too . . . tame. Suddenly she wanted the obsessive scientist back, the man who praised her intellect and rescued her from exploding boilers, not this . . . this . . . bland fellow.

So she prodded him.

"I take it you enjoyed your morning swim?" she asked as he handed her onto the stool.

His head reared back slightly. "How did you know I . . . ?"

That's more like it. A smile curved her lips as she gathered her skirts to ascend the rest of the way. "Easily enough. I recalled how much your manners improved after your last dip in the pond." Clasping his hand to steady herself, she boldly met his gaze. "I hope you swam long enough to ensure your manners last all the way through church. I know how much of a strain it will be for you to be imprisoned in that suit for the next few hours."

His only reaction was a single raised brow, but as she turned away, she could have sworn she'd seen his mouth twitch as if he were struggling to contain amusement. At least she *hoped* it was amusement. Anger wouldn't serve her purposes nearly so well.

Darius bit his tongue to keep from grinning as Nicole hoisted herself into the wagon. He managed to keep the smile contained until he stepped aside to allow Wellborn to assist his wife. The moment he turned his back on the little minx, however, he let it loose.

She was making it awfully hard to keep up the disgruntled employer pretense that he'd started last night. He usually had no trouble being disgruntled around people, especially when he was trussed up in a jacket with ridiculously tight sleeves and a collar that made his neck itch. His bad temper was legendary in the Thornton household. 'Twas why his mother finally stopped forcing him to attend parties and why his father put him in charge of King Star's accounting records.

Yet a few teasing comments from Nicole

had him mighty close to whistling, for pity's sake. He actually liked the chit. Outside of his sister and mother, he couldn't remember ever actually *liking* a woman before. Oh, he'd been attracted to several and even admired a few, but he'd always felt pressured to put on an act for them, to cover up his flaws so they wouldn't see his true self. When the act became too tedious, he simply forfeited the chase. Without much regret.

Nicole, however, had already seen his flaws. He'd paraded them before her since the moment she arrived for her interview. Yet instead of turning up her nose, she'd come to accept them as part of him, even teased him about them. It left him with no tedious act to maintain, only a growing hunger to learn more about her, to prove that he could accept her flaws, as well. Starting with that bullheaded stubbornness that kept her from asking for help.

As he climbed into the driver's seat and took up the reins, he leaned close to Wellborn on the seat beside him. "Tomorrow I want you to go to the landing in Liberty and see what you can learn about a family named Jenkins," he murmured in a voice too low for Nicole to hear over his housekeeper's chatter and the jangle of the harness as the horses set the wagon in motion.

"It seems they're the ones making trouble for our houseguest. Competitors of some sort for her father's business. I recall her mentioning something about reading shipping manifests from a young age, so her father might be involved in freight or import/export endeavors." Their conversation by the pond came back to him, as well, the part where she'd tried to convince him that she was unruffled by his soggy condition. "She grew up near the Gulf, so you might start by questioning the crews coming up from Galveston."

Wellborn dipped his chin. "I'll see to it first thing in the morning, sir."

Darius straightened. "Thank you."

In the meantime, he planned to keep a close eye on his new secretary. Perhaps make a few discreet inquiries of his own. And if the prospect of spending more time with her happened to speed his pulse every time he thought of it, who was he to complain? With the sadly insufficient amount of sleep he acquired each night, a rush of fast-pumping blood every now and again would help keep him alert.

And the distraction she presented? Well, he'd find a way to deal with it.

After a thirty-minute wagon ride, a two-hour church service, and another thirty minutes in the wagon on the way home, Darius was seriously reconsidering his ability to deal with the distraction his secretary presented. On the ride to Grand Cane, he'd run countless scenarios through his head about how he could best protect her from the unknown Jenkins brothers. During church when the preacher extolled the congregation to look not only to their own interests, but to the interests of others, his first thought was of her. Even now as he steered the horses onto the drive that led to Oakhaven, he found his senses straining to eavesdrop on the ladies' conversation behind him instead of concentrating on his driving.

"I can't believe I just attended the church that Sam Houston's wife established. Maman won't believe it." Nicole's giddy enthusiasm reminded him for the first time of the difference in their ages. She carried herself with such maturity, self-possession, and intelligence that he'd never given much thought to her age. Yet by physical appearance, he'd guess her to be of similar age to his sister who'd just turned twenty this past year.

And the way she called her mother *Maman*. French ancestry. Another clue to have

208

Wellborn follow up on.

"Oh, yes," Mrs. Wellborn cooed. "She and her sister-in-law, Nancy Lea — she was the lady in the yellow bonnet — were the ones to suggest building a church near the Houston home. Did you meet Nancy?"

"I'm sure I did." Nicole laughed, the light sound carrying an edge of self-consciousness. "However, all the names and faces are rather a blur right now."

"Don't worry about that. A few more visits, and you'll have everyone straightened out."

"Of course." Nicole responded politely, but Darius heard the change in her voice, as if someone had snuffed the light from it. And he knew she was thinking the same thing he was — she wouldn't be here long enough to learn the names.

Darius frowned and turned his attention back to the horses, guiding them between the barn and the house and pulling them to a halt near the front porch. He had just reached for the brake lever when Mrs. Wellborn screeched.

"Thief!"

Darius whipped his head around. There. The parlor window. A boy. Halfway in, halfway out. Though in a blink he was all the way out. Out and running like blue

209

blazes across the open field on the far side of the house.

Passing the reins to Wellborn, Darius prepared to give chase when a tiny growl echoed behind him.

"Oh, no, you don't." Heedless of her finery, Nicole leapt over the side of the wagon as if it were three inches off the ground instead of three feet and ran after the boy at a speed he'd never witnessed in a woman.

Darius vaulted after her, immediately lamenting his Sunday garb. Running down a fleet-footed lad and a gazelle of a woman would be so much easier sans necktie and jacket. Eventually, his longer legs prevailed, catching him up to Nicole.

"I'll get him," he huffed as he passed her, assuming she would pull up and catch her breath. But the crazy woman never slowed, even when he passed her. Her feet continued slapping against the earth behind him.

Did she doubt his ability to apprehend the lad? The thought pricked his pride and added an extra surge of energy to his stride. "Ho, boy!" he called. "Hold up there."

The young thief glanced over his shoulder at the shout, then tripped over something and fell sprawled on the ground. He started to scramble to his feet, but when he got on all fours, he froze.

Darius sprinted faster. Was the lad hurt? Whatever he had stolen, it wasn't worth the child coming to harm. But as he rushed up behind the boy, his heart dropped to his stomach and he careened to a halt.

A coiled rattler lay not two feet in front of the boy. The deadly *shhhh* of the snake's tail had the hair standing up on the back of Darius's neck. The creature's head lifted another inch, its forked tongue darting out as if measuring the distance of the strike.

"Easy, lad," Darius murmured in a soft voice. "Keep still. I'll not let him bite you." Though how he was going to keep that rash promise, he hadn't quite figured out. He had no pistol. No knife. There wasn't even a decent-sized rock within arm's reach. All he could think to do was grab the boy and fling him behind himself, praying the rattler would either miss or strike him instead of the boy.

Darius inhaled a steadying breath and braced his feet. He'd have only one shot at this. *God, you closed the mouths of the lions for Daniel. Please do the same with this snake.*

He leaned forward, his eyes glued to the boy's middle. His fingers spread slightly in readiness. *One. Two. Thr—*

Thwack!

A small blade pierced the snake's head and pinned it to the ground. A precision shot.

Together, Darius and the lad turned in the direction from which the throw had come.

His intrepid secretary stood glaring at the rattler, her face flushed, her breathing heavy, and her outstretched right hand in perfect post-throwing position.

CHAPTER 16

Nicole gulped air into her lungs, doing all she could not to bend over and brace her hands on her knees. Even with the loose lacing she'd always preferred, she swore she could feel her corset compressing her lungs. But she dared not show any weakness. With the snake out of the way now, the boy might try to take off again.

When Mrs. Wellborn had cried *thief*, Nicole's heart plummeted to her stomach. Had Will and Fletcher paid the boy to ransack the house while they'd all been away at church? It wouldn't be hard for the boy to pick her room out from the others. How much time had he spent inside before they'd come home? Enough time to search the few drawers and under the mattress and realize that the Lafitte Dagger must be hidden elsewhere? Had he been clever enough to notice the uneven floorboard? He was a small lad, his eyes closer to the floor than a man's.

Most likely the boy was simply looking for a few baubles to pawn, but she couldn't be too careful. Her family's future rested on that dagger. If even the slimmest chance existed that this boy had it, she'd chase him all the way to the Gulf. She needed to see his cache.

She turned to address the lad and found two pairs of eyes staring at her as if she'd just sprouted a horn in the middle of her forehead.

"Gadzooks, lady! Where'd you learn to throw like that?" The awe in the boy's tone brought heat to her cheeks.

"A pirate taught me," she snapped, stomping forward to reclaim her blade. For heaven's sake. Did *all* males assume women to be helpless creatures incapable of fending for themselves? Pressing her shoe against the snake's neck, she held the lifeless rattler down and yanked the knife free. There wasn't much blood, but still, she couldn't exactly lift her skirts and slip it back into the sheath strapped to her thigh with Darius and a child looking on in rapt attention.

"A pirate, Miss Greyson?" Darius regarded her with a raised brow, obviously not as awestruck as the gaping boy at his side.

She sighed. "All right, so my father was an ordinary seaman, not a pirate. But I used to imagine him a pirate while we had our lessons." She tossed a wink at the boy. "Made it so much more fun, you know. My father ensured I was proficient with pistols, too, but I preferred the blades. So much more elegant and lighter weight. Much better suited to a lady, wouldn't you say? Pistols are dirty things, what with all that black powder and the flash from the flintlock every time one pulls the trigger." She gave a little shudder, and the boy cracked a smile.

Now was as good a time as any, she supposed.

Gesturing toward the odd-shaped lump bulging around the boy's middle with a tilt of her head, Nicole kept her tone light, nonthreatening. "Care to show me what you've got hidden beneath your shirt?"

The boy's arms wrapped tentatively around his belly, and his gaze dropped to the ground. His shoulders slumped. "I guess it's only fair I give it back. Since you saved me from that rattler and all." He tugged his shirttails free from his trousers and cupped his hands beneath to catch the loot.

Loot that amounted to a round loaf of bread, a jar of jam, and a small wedge of cheese.

He extended the offerings to her, the thinness of his wrists evident as they stretched past the ends of his too-short sleeves. Nicole's heart twisted into a painful knot as she stepped forward to accept the stolen items from him. Moisture collected at the back of her eyes. *She* felt like the thief, taking food from a boy so obviously in need of nourishment.

"Where are your parents?" Darius asked in a voice carefully devoid of recrimination as he stepped closer and placed a hand on the lad's shoulder.

The child flinched, but whether from Darius's touch or his question, Nicole couldn't decipher.

"Dead, sir."

"And your guardian?"

The boy's face blared mutiny, his lips a thin line, his eyes narrowed. "I ain't tellin' 'cause I ain't goin' back. Not ever."

Nicole met Darius's gaze over the youngster's head. What atrocities had the boy suffered that made scrounging around on his own preferable to living with his guardian? Her heart broke for the little warrior, his arms crossed over his bony chest, his determination not quite hiding the fear in his eyes.

They couldn't turn him over to the law.

He'd be forced to return to his guardian or sent to a workhouse. What kind of life was that for a young lad? He'd only taken food, nothing of monetary worth.

As if Darius had read her thoughts, he hunkered down in front of the boy. "My name's Darius Thornton, and I own the house back there." He tipped his head in the direction of Oakhaven. "I'm a very busy man with important work to see to, and chasing you out into this field has inconvenienced me greatly."

The boy hung his head, his spirit draining out of him. Nicole gritted her teeth and surged forward to intervene, but Darius stopped her with a look.

"There might be a way you could make it up to me, however." He paused, not saying more until the boy met his eye.

"You see, it occurs to me that I might be able to get even more of my important work done if I had additional help around the place." He leaned close and lowered his voice as if imparting a secret. "Wellborn, the other fellow back there? Well, he's a bit of a dandy, always dressed to the nines. Hates to get dirty. So half the time, I'm the one mucking the stalls in the barn when what I should be doing is researching steam pressure and boiler plates. You ever muck a stall, boy?"

The lad eyed him speculatively. "Yes, sir."

"Know how to saddle a horse or harness a team?"

"I done it a time or two."

Darius thumped him lightly on the shoulder, then pushed up to his feet. "Excellent! I thought you had the look of a lad who knew his way around a barn. I bet you can even milk a cow."

"Shoot, mister. I been milkin' cows since I was big enough to carry the pail without spillin'." A light of understanding suddenly lit the boy's eyes. His arms uncrossed in a flash, and he bobbed around in front of Darius like a dog waiting for his master to throw him a ball. "I can feed chickens, too," he said, "and collect eggs. And I know the difference 'tween a weed and a carrot top. I used to help my ma out in the garden back home. I bet I could save you all kinds of time, Mr. Thornton."

He glanced guiltily at the food in Nicole's hand.

"I don't eat much. Honest. That would have lasted me several days. And I could bunk in the barn. I'm used to sleepin' outside. I wouldn't even need a blanket or nothin'."

Darius sharpened his gaze on the lad.

"Now see here, young man. If you come to work for me, I expect you to eat every morsel placed in front of you. You're scrawny enough as it is. I don't care to have walking skeletons on my payroll. They're too fragile."

The boy stood tall. "I'm strong, mister. I swear. I won't be lettin' you down. No, sir. I'll clean my plate every night, just like my mama taught me. You'll see."

Nicole suppressed a smile. "You better promise the same for breakfast and noon, as well. Mr. Thornton can't abide waste."

The boy's jaw slackened, as if he couldn't quite imagine such bounty as three meals in the same day. Then he closed his mouth with a snap and nodded like a soldier accepting orders. "Breakfast and noon, too."

"And when I set up your cot in the tack room," Darius continued, his tone serious, "I expect you to make it up every morning, no matter how many blankets there are. Understand?"

"Y-yes, sir."

"And when I pay your wages at the end of the month, no running off to town to fritter them away on candy if there's still work to be done."

"W-wages?" The poor boy looked completely overwhelmed.

Darius did, too, though he did a better job of hiding it. There was a definite shimmer of compassion in his eyes, and his voice had gone rather thick. In fact, he had to clear his throat before he continued.

"You heard me," he said gruffly. "Wages. I'm from the north, boy. I don't believe in slavery. What I do believe in is respect, hard work, and integrity. Give me that, and we'll get along just fine. So what do you say? Will you come work for me?"

The boy nodded, his eyes still a bit glazed. "Yes, sir."

Nicole's chest felt near to bursting, not only for the child so in need of a home, but for the tender heart of the man offering one for the lad's use. Not exactly what she expected from an obsessive scientist, even one with a noble purpose. For despite his arguments to the contrary, she expected having the boy underfoot would hinder more than help, at least at first, as the boy learned his way around. But Darius was willing to take him on anyway. Even after the lad had stolen from him. She couldn't imagine many of the men she'd met in Galveston or Boston taking such charitable action.

Before the dreamy sigh rising up in her throat could escape, however, Nicole clamped her lips shut and forced her attention away from her employer. Going soft for the man would do neither of them any favors. She was on her way to New Orleans to find a husband, an heir for her father. And no matter how good a man Darius Thornton was, or how his smiles made her heart skitter, she couldn't lose sight of her mission. He might know the inner workings of a steam engine, but that wasn't enough. Her father needed a man who knew the shipping business in its entirety: from hiring crew, to managing inventory, to selecting trade routes, to generating new business contacts. Losing her heart to a man who could never be her father's heir would be a disaster.

She needed to leave. Sooner rather than later.

"What's your name, son?" Darius asked, gesturing for the boy to walk beside him back toward the house. Nicole made no move to follow the twosome. Distance was what she needed now.

"Jacob."

The pair moved past her, and despite her pledge to keep herself distant, Nicole couldn't suppress a grin as Jacob mimicked Darius's stride, matching right arm to right arm and left to left as they walked. She remembered doing much the same thing when her father would take her sailing — imitating his wide stance on deck, the angle of his jaw as he shouted orders, even ducking her head as he did when they entered his cabin despite the fact that there was about as much chance of her hitting her head on the crossbeam as there was of the Gulf running dry.

Hanging back to get her reaction under control, she wiped her knife on the edge of her petticoat, then angled her body away so she could raise her skirts enough to slip the knife into its sheath, taking care not to drop the pilfered food cradled in her other arm. When she straightened, she expected Darius and Jacob to be well ahead but instead found her companions only a few yards away, their far-too-curious eyes riveted on her.

"So that's where you keep it." Darius's attention dropped to a spot halfway down her skirt. "I had wondered."

Nicole lifted her chin. "Yes, well, I tried carrying it around in one of those lacy little reticules, but it kept getting tangled in the ribbons. Not very practical." Keeping her eyes averted from Darius's face, she marched past the gawkers and headed for the house. She'd make her own distance.

■ ■ ■ ■

Darius watched her sweep past, her head high as a queen. The woman was full of surprises. Who would have guessed such a beauty not only had the mind of a scholar but the skills of a pirate?

"Your missus is somethin' else, Mr. Thornton. You think she'd teach me to throw a knife like that if'n I asked her?"

My missus? Darius balked, yet not as much as he would have expected at such a notion. "Miss Greyson is my secretary," he quickly corrected, "not my wife. She's my employee, just as Wellborn and Mrs. Wellborn are, and as you soon will be."

"So you don't have any family, neither?"

Darius resumed walking, the boy's words pricking at his conscience like a stinging nettle. "My family is in New York."

Jacob, who had been dogging his steps, jerked to a halt. "You just left 'em there?"

The stinging nettles morphed into cactus spines.

"I'm not married, Jacob," he justified, though the boy looked far from mollified. "I didn't abandon a wife or children. It is my parents and siblings who are in New York. I'll return to them when I've accomplished

223

the work I came here to do."

"Your work must be awful important, then." Jacob started walking again.

"It is," Darius assured him.

"Still," Jacob said, a thoughtful expression on his face, "if my folks were alive somewhere, I think I'd find a way to do my work closer to home. Pa always used to say work was easier when you had a family to come home to."

"Your pa sounds like a very wise man."

Jacob nodded and fell silent. But the quiet did nothing to dilute the guilt roiling in Darius's gut. Was that letter from his mother still buried on the desk in his study? Surely he could spare a few minutes to read it this afternoon. Maybe he'd even jot a note in reply. He hadn't written them in . . . How long *had* it been? He couldn't recall.

Needing something to distract him from the shame of that realization, Darius turned his attention back to the boy at his side. "How old are you, Jake?"

"Eleven."

Darius raised a brow but didn't question him. The boy looked more like eight or nine. Then again, a kid on his own, eating only what he could steal, wouldn't exactly have a diet conducive to steady growth. Mrs. Wellborn would have her hands full fattening this one up. Yet he had no doubt his housekeeper would be up to the task. As much as that woman harassed him about eating, Jacob didn't stand a chance.

He wished Nicole's problems were as easily solved. He watched the light green skirts ahead of him sway as she extended her lead. Why did he get the feeling she was putting more than physical distance between them? He couldn't allow that. Not if he planned to protect her. Nicole might try to run, but he'd not let her hide. Not from him.

CHAPTER 17

For a man who had gone out of his way to
avoid her during the first few days of her
employment, Darius Thornton had become
annoyingly attentive of late. He'd dined with
her each of the last three nights, to Mrs.
Wellborn's delight and Nicole's dismay. He
insisted she attend him in the workshop
every afternoon, either to talk through his
latest investigative hypothesis or to assist
with his efforts at salvaging what parts he
could from the exploded boilers. And tonight, he'd called her into the study hours
after the sun had set to go over the article
chronicling the results of the boiler plate
experiment she'd been working on for
submission to the Franklin Institute's journal.

How in the world was she supposed to
maintain a healthy emotional distance from
the man if he insisted on constantly thrusting his physical self into her presence day

and night? It was like trying to climb out of a bog when the mud sucked your legs farther down every time you took a step. But she'd slogged her way through quagmires before — one of the benefits of growing up on Galveston Island. She'd get through this, as well. It simply required determination and mental strength, two qualities she possessed in abundance.

Or she had, before she'd started fighting a battle that a growing part of her really didn't want to win.

Be strong, Nicki. Your future depends on it.

Nicole halted outside the study door and breathed deeply, steadying her nerves.

Marrying a man to provide her father with an heir was bad enough, but doing so without a heart to invest in the offer would make her miserable. No matter how many times Darius Thornton with his endearingly crusty manners and gallant offers of protection tugged on her to stay, she would not succumb.

Fortified, she squared her shoulders and rapped briskly on the oak door. A deep voice bid her enter.

Darius sat behind the desk, the one she usually worked at in the mornings, his head bowed over a thin stack of papers. He'd reverted back to his usual attire — smudged and wrinkled shirt gaping at the throat, sleeves rolled up over tanned forearms, unshaven jaw, and hair hanging carelessly over his brow. Yet when he glanced up to wave her in, the haggard look on his face arrested her.

How had she missed that? She'd seen him at dinner not two hours ago and could not recall him looking so weary. Of course, she'd been doing her best to avoid his attention, spending more time staring at her plate than at her companion. But surely if he'd looked this worn she would have noticed. She seemed to notice everything about the man, whether she wanted to or not.

"Darius" — the name slipped off her tongue before she could catch it — "what's wrong? You look . . ."

"Ghastly, I know." He smiled then, a self-deprecating twist of his lips that made her want to wrap her arms around him, run her fingers through his hair, and promise him that everything would be all right. "I'm just tired. Nothing to fret over. I'll force some sleep upon myself tonight."

Nicole frowned over the odd phrasing as she slid into the seat in front of the desk. She knew his dedication to his work drove him to burn the candle at both ends more often than not, but surely sleep wasn't so elusive as to require force? The man looked ready to drop.

"Did you have more edits for the article?" She restrained a sigh. She'd already rewritten the thing twice.

"No. Everything looks in order. I only added one note to the front page and thought you should see it." He turned the sheaf of papers so she could read the change he'd penned in at the top.

There, beneath the dry, mechanical title of *Experiment in Boiler Durability When Plating Thickness Is Varied,* Darius's bold, yet completely legible script listed a second contributor to the article. Miss Nicole Greyson.

She felt tears pooling.

"You deserve as much of the credit as I do," Darius said in a gruff voice. "You helped me refine the procedure and bore witness to the results. Did you think I wouldn't notice where you added your own observations to the report?"

"I just thought to clarify a few details and —"

"And you did so with an expert hand." Darius leaned back in his chair, braced his elbows on the chair arms, and pressed his fingertips together into a peak. "I couldn't be more pleased with your work, Nicole. I wish you had been working with me from the beginning."

Warmth flooded her at his words. Warmth. Satisfaction. Belonging. Dangerous belonging. Only . . . she had no true claim to that belonging. How could she? The name he'd written with such beautiful regard wasn't even hers.

She scooted the papers back toward Darius. "That's very kind of you, Mr. Thornton, but not necessary. Surely the article will have a better chance at publication without a female listed as a contributor. And really, all I did was tidy your notes and observe from a distance. I contributed very little."

"On that point," Darius said, leaning forward in his chair, his blue gaze boring into hers with an intensity that left her a mite breathless, "I'm afraid I'll have to disagree. But it is neither here nor there. The change is made, and the article will be placed in tomorrow's post."

"I don't need the recognition," Nicole insisted. "Please reconsider. I'd hate to be the cause of your article not appearing in the journal." Would publishing under a false name be considered fraud? Her stomach clenched. She couldn't allow him to do anything that could possibly tarnish his reputation. First thing in the morning, she'd need to rewrite the front page, removing the falsified name. She could switch out the pages and rewrap the packaging so no one would know.

Darius waved his hand, then tapped the stack of papers with a stiff finger. "Publication was never the goal. Congress funds the Franklin Institute, having tasked them to investigate steamboat explosions with the purpose of discovering safety protocols that can be mandated to prevent future disasters. My goal is to add to their knowledge so they can convince the government to pass new, more stringent legislation. I couldn't care less about seeing my name in print."

"You're a noble man, Darius Thornton." She meant the words as an expression of admiration, for admire him she did, despite the danger that presented — because, really, she couldn't help it, not when his motives were so selfless and pure.

But Darius reared back as if she'd struck him across his stubbled cheek. "I'm not noble. Far from it." He shoved to his feet with such a jerk, the chair tumbled backward onto the rug. Paying it no heed, Darius stalked to the window and lifted the curtain to stare out at the black night.

Nicole sat frozen in her seat, the violence of his reaction leaving her stunned. She watched him across the room, her heart aching at the pain radiating from him, even as her mind struggled to puzzle out what had caused it.

"I don't deserve your regard, Nicole." He spoke quietly, but the low timbre of his voice slammed into her like a battering ram, laying waste the walls she'd erected to protect herself. What good were walls if they kept her from offering comfort? This wasn't about sparing herself pain. It was about sparing him. Something was haunting him, some poison from his past that he couldn't quite work out of his system.

Slowly, she rose from her chair and padded across the floor until she stood within arm's reach of him. "Why, Darius? Why don't you deserve it?"

His knuckles whitened as he crushed the curtain fabric in his fist. "I'm a selfish man. And a failure. Not strong enough to save . . ."

She waited, but the rest of the sentence never came. "Who?" she prompted. "Who couldn't you save?"

His face turned toward her then. Harsh lines traversed his forehead above blue eyes so tortured it pained her to meet his gaze.

Yet she refused to look away. She'd not let him fight this battle alone. He stared at her long and hard before finally twisting away, his attention once again focused on the darkness beyond the window. Or perhaps the darkness within his spirit.

"It doesn't matter," he said, a heavy sigh accenting his words.

"I'd say it matters a great deal. To you." Dared she touch him? The fingers on the hand nearest him trembled and even stretched toward him a little. Yet before she could lift her arm, Darius flung the curtain away from himself and strode back to his desk. He righted the fallen chair, then braced his palms upon the polished cherry-wood tabletop.

"Forgive me, Miss Greyson. I grow melancholy when I'm overtired. Pay me no mind."

As if that were possible — he filled her mind to overflowing. Nicole traced his steps back to the desk, not ready to let the matter drop. He had no family nearby to confide in, only servants. Somehow she couldn't imagine Darius baring his most personal hurts to his butler. But perhaps he would confide in her. One friend to another. They were friends, weren't they?

"Darius, I —"

"Here." He picked up a stack of journals

and thrust them at her belly, effectively cutting off her attempt to converse as she juggled to gain hold of the volumes. "I marked several articles I'd like you to read in preparation for our next experiment. We need to narrow down our options, and I'd like you to be informed as to what has already been reported. You can take a break from transcribing my notebooks and spend your morning researching instead."

"All right." She stared intently at his downcast eyes, silently pleading for him to look up. But he never did. He just kept shuffling papers around, pretending to be busy, dismissing her.

Perhaps it was for the best. Sharing secrets bred intimacy. She was willing to risk closeness if it would ease his burden, but if he refused to let her in, there was nothing she could do. At least this way, she could refortify her defenses.

"Will that be all, Mr. Thornton?" She settled the journals against her waist, crooking her right arm around the stack.

The man still didn't look up. "Yes. Thank you. Good night."

Nicole hesitated, debated with herself, then reached her left hand across the desk to cover his. He stilled, tension vibrating through the muscles of his hand and wrist, but he stayed focused on the papers.

"Sleep well, Mr. Thornton." She gave his hand a brief squeeze, then turned and headed for the door.

His voice rumbled softly behind her, so softly she almost didn't hear him.

"I never sleep well."

Nicole didn't sleep well, either, that night. Her mind spun in fretful circles as she lay in bed, worrying over Darius, praying for him. Something from his past held him captive, something he was too ashamed to discuss. She wanted to help him, but what could she do? She'd be leaving in a few days.

When sleep finally claimed her, it was the fitful variety that produced very little rest. She awoke to pitch blackness, her legs tangled in the bed sheets, her sleeping gown twisted so tightly about her knees, she could barely move. Yanking the cotton fabric out from beneath her, she sat up and swung her legs over the side of the bed. She ran her hand over her face, then flung her braid off her shoulder to slap against her back.

What time was it? It had to be after midnight, yet it seemed nowhere near dawn. Darkness lay too thick in the room. Restless energy coursed through her even as weariness made her limbs heavy. She sighed, all too familiar with the symptoms. Lying down now would just result in hours of fruitless staring at the ceiling. She'd have to get up. Pushing against the edge of the mattress, she gained her feet.

Whenever she would get this way at the Academy, usually the night before a comprehensive exam, she'd sneak down to the kitchen and heat some milk. The warm reminder of childhood tended to relax her and make her drowsy enough to drift off again. She hadn't needed the remedy in a while, but she knew of nothing else that would work. Sliding her feet into a pair of felt slippers, she shook her bunched-up gown down over her legs, collected her wrapper from the end of the bed, and threaded her arms through the loose sleeves. After tying the belt, she opened her door and quietly stole down the hall.

She had just reached the entrance to the kitchen when a dim light escaping from beneath a door farther down the hall drew her attention. The study. Darius wasn't still awake, was he?

Unable to resist the pull, Nicole approached the study. She didn't want to disturb him if he was working, and heaven knew she wasn't dressed to be in mixed company, but something unexplainable urged her forward.

As she neared the door she heard a muffled sound, deep and resonant. She pressed her ear to the crack in the door. It came again — a moan. Darius was moaning. Was he hurt? Injured somehow?

She clasped the knob and turned it gently, striving for as much quiet as she could manage. Nudging the door open an inch, she peered through the tiny opening, searching the room for Darius. The dim light from the lamp on the small table near the bookshelf banished enough shadows for her to make out his figure stretched out across the length of the sofa.

His face contorted in anguish. His head tossed back and forth. Cords protruded from his neck as he strained for something, his hand outstretched at his side. He moaned again, the sound flaying Nicole's heart like a lash.

"No," he muttered. "No!" His legs thrashed. Even the toes on his bare feet curled down upon themselves as the nightmare claimed him.

Nicole rushed forward, not sure what to do but needing to be beside him. She wanted to hold him, to soothe away his torment, but he thrashed too much for her to get close. He was still clad in the same wrinkled shirt and trousers he'd been wearing earlier in the day, but a fine sheen of sweat had plastered them to his skin. His hair lay damp across his forehead, and his mouth twisted in a painful grimace.

Kneeling on the rug just out of his reach, Nicole wrapped her arms about her waist and rocked in a gentle motion, exuding comfort the only way she knew how. "Shh, Darius. It's all right," she crooned. "I'm here."

She hadn't thought it possible for his body to stiffen any further, but it did. "Where?" he demanded in a surprisingly clear voice. "Where are you?"

"Here, Darius. I'm here." She reached out to touch his arm, but he jerked away before her fingers could make contact.

"Where?" he demanded again, his voice breaking. "I'll save you, I swear. I won't let you die this time. I'll find you. I promised. Remember? I promised."

Tears rolled down Nicole's cheeks. "Darius," she called in a louder voice. "Darius, wake up."

"I won't stop. I won't." He waved his arm in front of him like a blind man searching for an object.

Not knowing what else to do, Nicole clasped his probing hand. "You found me,

Darius. I'm here."

His fingers closed around her wrist in an iron vise. "Thank God," he sighed.

Then he yanked her. Hard. The force of his movement jerked her from the floor and in a flash had her sprawled across his muscular chest.

He clutched her to himself so tightly she could barely breathe, let alone move. Then, after a final kick of his legs, his flailing ceased.

CHAPTER 18

Darius swam through the nightmare waters, searching. The girl was in the water. Sinking. Drowning. Dying. He had to find her faster this time, had to save her. In the twisted way of dreams, he saw her face through the murky river depths. Pale. Frightened. Accusing. He kicked harder. Reached for her. She floated out of reach. Always out of reach.

He groaned in anguish, slashing his arms through the dark currents that taunted him with his failure, his guilt. His heart hammered in his chest. He couldn't fail again. Not again.

A voice called his name from far away, but he couldn't afford to listen. He had to reach the girl. Then all at once, the vision changed. The nameless girl with the accusing gaze became a young woman, a woman with sable brown hair and copper eyes. Her hair floated around her face in waves as her lips formed his name. *Darius.*

Nicole.

No! Not Nicole. It couldn't be her in the water, sinking to her death. But it was. She called out to him again and again, gouging his heart with her cries.

"Where are you?" he shouted into the depths. He stroked harder, deeper. But the water thickened, became like molasses, holding him back, holding her captive. He fought against the resistance, his muscles straining to the point of pain. He reached for her, but the vision faded. "I won't stop," he vowed. "I won't." He couldn't lose her. Not Nicole.

He swept his hand wide, pleading with God to let him find her in time.

That's when the miracle occurred.

A hand clasped his. *Her* hand. Firm. Substantial. Not the mist he usually encountered. He held it fast. Nothing would tear her hand from his. Not this time. "Thank God." He pulled her against his body, reveling in the solid feel of her, gripping her with all his might so there'd be no chance of her slipping away. Then he kicked for the surface, leaving his nightmare world behind.

"Darius?" The soft voice that had called to him before, called to him again. Urging him to wake. But he didn't want to wake.

Not this time. He'd finally succeeded. He'd saved Nicole from the river. He clutched her closer to his chest, strapping both arms around her, afraid she'd turn again to mist and leave him. She couldn't leave him. Not now. Not when he'd finally found peace.

Yet it was her voice calling him. Begging. Pleading.

"Darius, please. You're hurting me."

He opened his eyes at once. "Nicole?"

She lay draped across his chest, her face angled up to his, her dark braid curling beneath her chin. A ragged breath escaped him. She was the most beautiful sight he'd ever beheld.

Until she winced, and he realized he was holding her tight enough to crack her ribs. He released her immediately.

She wiggled against him as she struggled to sit up, finally bracing a hand upon his chest to lever herself upward. His pulse reacted to her touch, and he had to close his eyes to keep from clutching her to himself again. The haze of sleep was clearing, but his control hadn't yet been fully restored. A small groan vibrated in his throat.

Cool fingers stroked his brow, his face, his hair. "Darius, it's all right. It was just a dream. I'm here, now. Safe. We're both safe."

He opened his eyes and turned his face

toward her voice. She had slid from atop him but knelt by the side of the sofa near his head. His gaze roamed her face, her shoulders, the area around her ribs. "Did I hurt you?"

She shook her head, and he expelled a heavy breath in relief. Forcing himself to sit up, he lifted away from her soothing touch, dropped his feet to the floor, and braced his elbows on his thighs. He rubbed his trembling hands through his hair, then drew them down over his face as he battled to pull himself together. He didn't have the luxury of privacy to let the panic subside on its own.

What had she seen? Heard? How had she ended up draped across his chest? Well, he supposed he knew how that had happened. She'd simply gotten too close while he'd been in the throes of his nightmare. It had been so vivid this time. And different. Nicole had been the one in the water, not the girl from the *Louisiana.* Her presence had heightened his fear. *And my relief,* Darius thought, remembering the peace that had settled over him when he'd successfully captured her in his embrace. Surely, if she hadn't awakened him, he would have slept soundly the rest of the night with her pressed to his chest. It would have been the first decent night's rest he'd had since the accident. Yet as much as he hated to let her leave, he couldn't in good conscience stay alone in her presence.

"Do you want to talk about it?"

He dropped his hands from his face at her soft question, finally trusting himself to meet her gaze without revealing the extent of his neediness.

She was kneeling, hands folded in her lap, wearing some kind of robe, the neckline and sleeve edges embroidered with tiny yellow flowers and green leaves. The robe gaped a bit at the knees, exposing the white cotton of what had to be her nightgown. Swallowing hard, Darius turned his head and pretended to contemplate the shelves of books to his left.

"I'm a good listener," she cajoled. "It might help."

Darius clenched his jaw. He'd never told anyone the details of that day. Not even his father when he'd come to visit him in New Orleans after the accident. Saul Thornton must have sensed some of his torment, for he'd probed Darius for an explanation of why he refused to return home with him, but the pain had been too raw for Darius to put into words. Too fresh. So he'd begged his father to let him deal with the accident in his own way, to give him some time alone to come to grips with what had happened. And his father, being the insightful, loving man he was, had agreed.

That had been a year and a half ago. Time had certainly not healed his wounds, but they'd scarred over pretty well. The rawness had eased, only emerging at night in his dreams. Was it time to speak of that day, of his failure? Would it drain some of the poison from his soul? Recalling the utter contentment that had flooded him when he felt Nicole pressed safely to his chest, he thought perhaps it would.

"I'll make it easy on you," she said, a hint of a smile touching her lips, a smile free of judgment or censure. "I'll tell you what bits I've already pieced together. That way you'll only have to fill in the gaps instead of telling the entire tale." Her eyes warmed as he watched, aglow with compassion, and in that moment he wanted nothing more than to unburden himself and tell her all.

Nicole rose from the floor in a graceful motion, then pivoted in order to join him on the sofa. As soon as he recognized her intent, Darius slid over to make more room for her, yet not so far that there would be a gulf between them. He craved her closeness.

"Mrs. Wellborn mentioned something

about an accident that occurred some time ago," Nicole began, arranging her wrapper over her knees to completely conceal her nightclothes. "I assume that this accident happened on board a steamboat, prompting your passionate devotion to boiler safety." That subtle, almost teasing smile appeared again only to retreat beneath the swelling sympathy in her eyes. "You are driven, Darius. I've recognized that from the first time we met, and I couldn't help wondering at the source of your obsession. What would drive a man of wealth and breeding to leave his family and hide away on a small plantation in Texas to conduct explosive scientific experiments?"

She laid her hand across his forearm, the coolness of her fingers seeping into his overheated skin. His muscle twitched, and something more than comfort traveled up his arm and into his chest.

"You lost someone, didn't you?" she queried, the softness in her eyes taking some of the sting from the words. "Someone you tried to save? Was it your brother? Sister? Is that why you isolate yourself from your family and work day and night to try to fix what went wrong?"

He glanced away, choosing the safety of staring at the floor instead of her lovely face as he shook his head.

"She was a child," he murmured, somewhat amazed he could actually give voice to the awful truth. "About a year or two older than Jacob, I'd guess. I didn't even know her name."

Nicole's thumb stroked the sensitive underside of his forearm. How could she continue to offer him comfort when he'd just admitted to letting a child die? He didn't deserve her kindness, her support. Yet he didn't have the willpower to pull away. Her ready acceptance felt too good.

Silence stretched between them. However, silence wouldn't protect him from the tale. He lived with it every day. He had nothing to lose by giving it voice. Except Nicole's good opinion. A shudder passed through him at the thought, but her touch on his arm lulled him. It promised understanding — an understanding he couldn't resist trying to attain.

"Did you ever hear accounts of the *Louisiana*'s sinking in New Orleans?" His heart thudded so hard in his chest, he almost couldn't hear his own voice. Inhaling and exhaling slowly through his nose, he attempted to calm his raging pulse. "Her boilers blew while pulling away from the levee in the fall of 1849."

Nicole shook her head. "I was away at school. And to be honest, I didn't pay much attention to the newspapers. Too wrapped up in my studies." Her thumb stopped its stroking then, but her hand remained in place on his arm. "Did many lose their lives?"

"Over one hundred fifty."

Nicole sucked in an audible breath. "Dear God in heaven. So many."

"Countless more were wounded. Some bodies were never recovered." Suddenly no longer able to stomach her comforting hold, Darius shoved up from the sofa and paced a few steps away. He couldn't look at her, couldn't accept her sympathy. He needed to insert space between them, between the ugliness of what he remembered and the innocence that radiated from her. He wanted to shield her from the truth, to protect her.

But when he peered over his shoulder, the determination lining her face stopped him from sending her away. It was the same determination that likely had sent her off alone through the wilds of Texas to help her ailing father. The same determination that took out a rattler with one throw of her knife. Nicole might be young and innocent, but she was strong, too.

"Tell me, Darius," she insisted, a thread

of steel in her tone. That steel cut through the last of his resistance.

"I didn't want to be there that day," he admitted, crossing to the bookshelves and idly fingering the cloth and leather spines. "I remember grumbling about how my brother should have been the one meeting with my father's investors. He was the diplomat of the company, after all, and was used to such affairs. My job entailed balancing the ledgers and keeping the company solvent, not parties and business meetings where I would be expected to hobnob with men who cared more about the cut of their waistcoat than dirtying their hands with actual work. But David's wife was pregnant with their first child, and she wanted him close at hand."

Darius rested his right arm along the edge of a shelf and tapped his fisted hand against the wood. "I was so selfish, Nicole, so wrapped up in my own petty disappointments that I couldn't see past the end of my nose. Did I celebrate with David over his impending fatherhood? No. I crabbed at him about letting his wife dictate his actions and tried to make him feel guilty enough to change his mind about the trip."

His hand trembled as he opened his fingers, and the sting of tears pricked at the back of his eyes. "I thank God every day that David didn't give in to my demands." His voice broke. "If he had died, and his child had been born fatherless . . ." Darius couldn't continue, the thought too horrible to contemplate.

Suddenly she was there, behind him. He hadn't heard her move, but he felt her lean against his back, press her cheek into the divot between his shoulder blades, and wrap her arms about his waist. He shuddered at the contact and nearly wept at the comfort and acceptance she offered.

The words came easier then. He told her of the horrific explosions that concussed with such force that large hunks of shrapnel flew hundreds of yards, crushing anything that stood in their path. Surrounding ships, trees, horses, carriages . . . people. All fell beneath the onslaught. He recounted how the hull shattered and water rushed over his shoes. How people were trapped in the inner cabins. How they screamed.

He spared her the grisliest details. The mutilated bodies. The smell of scalded flesh. The cries of the wounded, who'd not been blessed with a quick death. She already gripped his middle like an iron band, and warm tears soaked the back of his shirt. She didn't need the details for her to picture the destruction of that day.

"The ship was going down," he said, covering her arms with his. "I knew I could swim to shore, but I couldn't abandon the women and children. I tried to reach the upper deck, but debris blocked the stairway. I ran back outside and started to climb the railing when a woman from above saw me and dangled her child over the edge, pleading with me to save him. He couldn't swim.

"I grabbed the boy and handed him off to another man who was helping with the evacuation. A second child followed the first. Then another. And another. The chain seemed never to end. But then it did. Only one girl remained, older than the rest. No parent in sight. She clung to the upper railing, too far away for me to reach."

Darius closed his eyes, the vision that had haunted his dreams for the last year and a half rising in his mind. Her thrashing legs. Her panicked eyes. Her slipping hands.

"I climbed up to get her," he recounted, "promising her I wouldn't let her fall. She was scared out of her mind, but when her gaze met mine, she gave a little nod. She trusted me, Nicole. She trusted me, and I let her fall."

Darius hung his head, grabbing on to Nicole's arms with both hands, like a drowning man grabbing a life preserver. "The boat had taken on too much water. It pitched sideways, and the jerking motion shook the girl off. I tried to catch her but only brushed her skirt with my arm before she splashed into the river. I dove in after her. The water was too murky to see anything, but I submerged again and again until my lungs nearly burst, searching with my arms, my feet, begging God to let me find her.

"When I did, it was too late. I finally caught hold of her and pulled her to the surface, then onto shore. I tried to pump the water out of her lungs. I begged her to breathe. But she never did." A broken sob erupted from his throat before he could catch it back.

The tears fueled his rage. He lashed out, slamming his fist so hard against the shelf nearest him, it cracked. "Why, Nicole?" he demanded. "Why would God spare a self-absorbed, embittered man like me and take the life of an innocent? It's not right! *I* should have died that day. Not her." His throat closed up then, and his knees grew weak. He curled in on himself and slowly sank to the floor. "Never her."

CHAPTER 19

Nicole followed Darius to the floor, curving her body farther over his back as she glided her arms upward to wrap about his shoulders. His agony shredded her heart.

"The girl's death was not your fault," she whispered near his ear. "The accident was to blame. You did everything you could. More than most people would have done."

"It wasn't enough."

And that was the issue, wasn't it? Darius blamed himself for not rescuing a girl who was most likely dead moments after hitting the water. He held so tightly to his guilt that his wounds were torn open day after day, never getting the chance to heal. Why wouldn't he forgive himself? Or was it God he couldn't forgive?

"I should have died. Not her."

Nicole stiffened against him. There it was again, that woeful statement belittling his value, his worth. When he'd first uttered the words, she'd heard only his grief over the girl's death. Yet this time she detected hints of bitterness and suppressed anger — corrosive elements that had no place in healing. She would gladly comfort Darius in his pain, but she would do him no favors by fueling his self-pity.

"So, you think God made a mistake." She leaned away from him, her voice hardening just enough to get his attention.

He twisted to face her. "Why should an innocent die while a reprobate lives?"

"I see," she said. "Only sinful people should have died in that accident if God were indeed just. Of course, all have sinned, so I suppose only the tiniest of babes should have survived according to your reasoning."

Darius turned fully toward her, his features tightening in anger. "You're being deliberately obtuse."

"Am I? Well, you're being deliberately arrogant, thinking you know better than God."

"I am not! I —"

"Yes. You are." Nicole crossed her arms beneath her breasts and glared at him. "What happened was an accident. A horrible, tragic accident. But accidents happen in this fallen world we live in. Innocence is no guarantee of protection. Rain falls on both the just and the unjust."

He scowled at her, and Nicole nearly lost her nerve to continue. But a still, small voice inside her urged her on.

"God sees things in a scope so broad our narrow-focused minds can't even comprehend. If you had died that day instead of that young girl, what would have become of me? Have you asked yourself that, Darius? I was out of money and out of options when you took me in and offered me a job. And what of Jacob? He'd still be running about on his own, sneaking into people's houses to pilfer food. Without you to offer him work, food, and a place to sleep, the boy might have been shot by an irate home-owner by now. I thank God he spared you that day."

Nicole steeled herself as Darius's piercing blue gaze bored into her. Some of the anger seemed to have left him, but the intensity of his scrutiny made her squirm. She'd not back down, though. If she could say something to help him heal, somehow give him the strength to let go of his guilt, perhaps leaving him later wouldn't be so hard.

Darius finally turned away from her and braced his back against the edge of the bookshelf. Propping his knees up, he rested his forearms across them and stared blankly into the empty space in front of him.

"After the accident," he said, "I wrestled with that idea — that God had saved me for some divine purpose. That's why I started collecting boilers and conducting experiments. It was the only thing that made sense. If I could discover a way to prevent future explosions, maybe then I could redeem my greatest failure."

"Oh, Darius." Nicole scooted next to him and took hold of his hand. "Don't you know? You *can't* redeem your failures. None of us can. Only the Redeemer has that power, and he's already wielding it on your behalf. He's bringing good out of that tragedy, good that we are only beginning to see."

He yanked his hand from hers as if she'd scalded him with the steam from one of his boilers. He shoved his fingers through his hair and closed them into a fist that had to be painful pulling against his scalp.

"You don't understand, Nicole." The anguish etched across his features brought new dampness to her eyes. "I have to fix it. I have to atone for my mistakes."

" 'There is therefore now no condemnation for them which are in Christ Jesus,' " Nicole softly quoted. "The work you are doing is important, and I believe God led you to it. It is one of the ways he is working his good in your life. But when you continue clinging to your feelings of guilt, this God-given mission becomes nothing more than self-imposed penance.

"Forgive yourself for the child you were unable to save, Darius, and praise God for the many who are alive today because of your actions."

Deciding she'd lectured him enough for one night, she rose up on her knees, checked her balance with a hand to his shoulder, then leaned close and pressed a gentle kiss into the side of his forehead. "You're a good man, Darius Thornton. I'm proud to know you."

Surround him with your comfort and your mercy so he won't feel alone as I leave, Nicole prayed as she pushed to her feet and crossed the room. Casting one last look over her shoulder when she reached the door, Nicole couldn't help wishing she had the right to stay by his side the rest of the night, to hold him and guard against the nightmares that had haunted him for far too long. But she had no such right and never would — not with the promise she made to her father hanging over her head.

Biting back a sigh of regret, she slid quietly from the room.

■ ■ ■ ■

Darius watched her leave from the corner
of his eye, careful to keep his face angled
toward the darkened window so she
wouldn't realize where his gaze rested. He
could still feel the touch of her lips above
his temple. A kiss that soothed the sore
places her words had scraped raw moments
earlier.

"I'm proud to know you."

Darius closed his eyes and leaned his head
against the bookcase behind him. After all
he'd told her — his failures, his selfishness
— and she making no bones about her
opinions regarding his drive to atone for
past mistakes and defeats, she still managed
to say the one thing his heart most needed
to hear.

"I'm proud to know you."

If he were to be honest with himself —
and tonight certainly seemed the time for
such brutal observations — he'd have to
admit that she'd touched on the real reason
he'd yet to go home. Fear that he'd never
hear such a sentiment from his father or
brother. Fear that if they learned the full
truth of his failure, he'd lose their respect
and become the son and brother they

simply tolerated, not the one they embraced without reservation. Such a turnabout would erode his insides and leave him as hollow and useless as an old steamship scavenged for parts.

There were ponds and vacant acreage in New York as well as Texas. He didn't have to hide away so far from home in order to conduct his experiments. Yet he'd *wanted* to keep himself distant, to give himself time to fix things before facing his family.

Darius snorted and shook his head at himself. What was he — a young lad determined to glue together his mother's favorite vase before she came home so her disappointment would be tempered by the evidence of his efforts to repair the damage? Did he truly believe she wouldn't notice the cracks and jagged edges? Would his remorse after the fact erase the sin of his disobedience?

"There is therefore now no condemnation to them which are in Christ Jesus."

Could that really be true? Could Christ make the vase new again with no cracks or imperfections? Perhaps Nicole was right. Perhaps he was keeping Christ from making all things new by letting guilt run rampant in his soul. But how was he supposed to let go of it? It haunted his dreams, drove his work, and even motivated his kindness. Heaven help him, it defined the man he had become. Who would he be without it?

The image of the broken vase lingered in his mind. He couldn't fix it. No matter how hard he tried, it would never be the same. *He* would never be the same. Not in his own eyes. Not in the eyes of his family. It was impossible.

"The things which are impossible with men are possible with God."

The verse from Luke resonated in Darius's mind as if it been spoken aloud. He jerked his head up and straightened away from the bookshelf.

I am the potter; thou art the clay.

The potter. Of course.

New energy pumped through Darius as he stood and crossed to his desk. He opened the top right drawer and grabbed hold of the small leather volume he kept there, a volume he'd been neglecting of late in favor of his work. He turned up the wick on the desk lamp, opened the cover on his Bible, and began flipping pages until he found the passage he sought in Jeremiah 18.

" 'Arise, and go down to the potter's house,' " Darius murmured beneath his breath, " 'and there I will cause thee to hear my words. Then I went down to the potter's house, and, behold, he wrought a work on the wheels. And the vessel that he made of clay was marred in the hand of the potter.' "

Marred. Cracked. Broken. Yet for the first time Darius realized that what truly mattered was not that the pot was marred, but that it remained *in the hand of the potter.*

He continued reading. " 'So he made it again another vessel, as seemed good to the potter to make it. Then the word of the Lord came to me, saying, O house of Israel, cannot I do with you as this potter? saith the Lord. Behold, as the clay is in the potter's hand, so are ye in mine hand, O house of Israel.' "

Darius stared at the page until his vision blurred.

I've taken myself out of your hand over these last eighteen months, haven't I, Lord? So sure I could fix things myself if I could just accomplish enough good to fill the cracks. But you don't want me to fill the cracks, do you? You want me to put myself in your hands and allow you to create a completely new vessel.

Forgive my arrogance. My stubbornness. Help me to yield to you, to submit, to surrender. To release the guilt that steals my peace and turns your calling on my life into burdensome penance. Create in me a clean heart, O God; and renew a right spirit within me.

He sat motionless at his desk for several minutes, the words of his prayer rolling over in his mind and seeping into his heart. His eyelids closed and his head bowed until it rested against the open pages of the Bible. Deep breaths moved in and out of his lungs as he remained still before the Lord.

Then slowly, almost without him recognizing it, the germ of an idea planted itself in his consciousness. The longer he sat at his desk, the deeper the roots penetrated. Soon leaves were sprouting and branches stretching until it consumed him so fully, he knew he had to act on it at once.

Straightening, Darius pulled open the left drawer of his desk and rummaged around for paper, pen, and ink. He had to tell them. Had to tell them everything. To trust in their love for him. To rely on God's grace no matter their reaction. To steal the devil's power by facing what *will* happen instead of cowering away from what *might* happen.

Darius steeled himself as he dipped his pen in the well and slowly stroked his parents' names across the top of the first page. If he could tell Nicole the truth, he could tell his family. He owed them that much. Blast. He owed them a lot more than that.

The words flowed from his pen. Pages of them. By the time he finished the task, a rosy glow glimmered outside the study window. Dawn had come. A new day full of promise and hope.

Darius sat back in his chair, stretched his back, and flexed the fingers of his right hand to work the cramps out. His eyelids drooped with weariness, his energy completely spent. Pushing up out of his chair, he braced his legs beneath him and turned off the lamp. Then he stumbled to the sofa, collapsed upon its cushions, and for the first time in months, fell asleep without dreading what was to come.

CHAPTER 20

Nicole woke late the following morning and rushed through her ablutions before dashing off to the kitchen to grab something portable for breakfast.

"Yer late," Mrs. Graham groused in her usual terse style. "I already tossed the leftover mush in the slop bucket." She nodded toward the pail kept by the back door.

Not particularly fond of cornmeal mush anyway, Nicole suffered little regret as she eyed a half loaf of bread wrapped in a cloth on the cabinet near the hearth. "I overslept, I'm afraid. But don't worry, I'll just cut myself a thick piece of that bread you baked yesterday and be off. Mr. Thornton expects me to be in the study promptly at eight each morning, and it's nearly that now."

After leaving things so unsettled between them, the last thing she wanted to do was show up late for work. Besides, she needed to change that article page before he could mail it off with her pseudonym scrawled across the top.

"At least throw some butter on it." The cook's gravelly voice broke into her thoughts a moment before the woman slapped a small crock onto the counter beside Nicole. "I won't have the master accusin' me of not feedin' you. Skinny thing like you is bound to blow away in the first strong breeze of the day if we don't anchor you proper-like."

Nicole smiled as she set down the journals Darius had given her to read and picked up the bread knife. "Well then, I'd better spread it on thick, for everyone knows your bread is too light and airy to anchor anything."

"Oh, get on with ya," Mrs. Graham protested, swatting her with a damp dish towel before she turned her attention back to drying the freshly scrubbed mush pot. Nicole decided to act as if she hadn't noticed the white-toothed grin that flashed momentarily across the dark-skinned woman's face. Mrs. Graham took great pride in her surly demeanor, after all.

Once she had her bread sliced and buttered, Nicole retrieved the journals and hurried down the hall. Her skirt swept side to side, like a ringing bell, driven by her accelerated pace, until she whisked around the corner into the study and careened to a halt.

Papers littered the top of the desk — papers, a small book, an inkstand, pens. Nicole frowned. She never left Darius's desk in such disarray. Neither did Darius. He'd always left her a short note outlining her duties for the day, perhaps a stack of schematics to copy, but nothing this . . . chaotic.

Had his temper gotten the better of him after she left last night? Somehow she couldn't quite imagine him flinging pages about in a fit of frustration, at least not any pages that pertained to his work. It was too important to him. Even as the thought crossed her mind, she noted the stack of papers on the corner. The Franklin Institute article. Still there, carefully stacked, tied together with a piece of twine.

Slowly, she edged around the desk. If the papers scattered hither and yon weren't from the article, what were they from?

Darius's familiar script covered the ivory sheets from top to bottom, although he seemed to have taken pains to keep his handwriting more legible than he did when scribbling in his notebooks. One page, however, lay atop the others. It had writing only in the center, the words large and jumping off the page. An address.

Mr. and Mrs. Saul Thornton
Castlewood Manor
New York City, N.Y.

His parents. Nicole's heart fluttered faster than a hummingbird's wings. He must have written all of this after she left, pouring his soul out on paper as he had done in person with her. She blinked to clear the sheen rapidly glazing her eyes. *Oh, Darius. You're learning to trust again. To let go.*

Curiosity burned a hole in her midsection, teasing her with snippets of the letter exposed to her view. How she longed to read what he'd written, to bear witness to his reconciliation with his family. But the correspondence was private, and she'd not betray his trust in such a manner. Averting her eyes, she turned her head from the desk and nearly choked on the startled cry that rose in her throat.

Darius lay sprawled upon the sofa not five feet away.

Nicole clamped her lips closed and managed to muffle most of her surprised squawk, but a tiny squeak escaped before she could swallow it. Darius's brow crinkled a bit, and he rolled onto his side to face her more fully, yet his eyes remained closed.

How had she missed him? The man was

so large the sofa could barely contain him. Legs dangled off the side. Wide shoulders dwarfed the curved lines of the upholstered back. Even the yellow cushions beneath him jutted at odd angles as if trying to rearrange themselves to better accommodate his stature.

A smile danced across her face. Her mighty scientist looked like a young boy now, gangly limbs draped every which way, a relaxed, peaceful expression upon his face. So different from the tortured man she'd encountered a few hours ago, tension screaming through his muscles, anguish etched into his features. He had thrashed and moaned when she'd found him, but now his chest rose and fell in a deep, steady rhythm. It was beautiful to see.

He was beautiful. Nicole inched closer. With him asleep, she didn't have to worry about keeping her guard up. She could paint a mental portrait of him to carry with her when she left. Just for a friendly remembrance, of course, not because her heart bled at the thought of never seeing him again.

Lowering herself to the rug, she let her gaze roam slowly over Darius. She started with his tousled honey-gold hair, then lingered over his face: his strong jaw, dark with whiskers; the brush of his lashes against tanned cheeks; the smooth, supple line of his lips. Ah, his lips. They'd once kissed her in playful celebration. What would it be like to have them meet hers with more personal intent?

Heaven. She was pretty sure it would feel like heaven.

Which was exactly why she shouldn't be staring at them, she admonished before forcing her attention away from his face. Of course, his throat wasn't much better, leading as it did to the top of his chest and exposing a hint of masculine hair to her view through the open collar of his shirt.

Nicole bit her lower lip. Perhaps this mental-portrait notion wasn't such a good idea. Her pulse was leaping all over the place. And what if he somehow sensed she was ogling him and woke up? She'd be mortified.

The thought threw her into action. Lurching to her feet, she backed away from the sleeping man, then turned and scurried for the door. At the last minute, she remembered the article. Going back, she set her breakfast down, grabbed the article and a clean sheet of paper from the drawer, then tossed everything on top of the journals and pivoted back toward the door. She had pen and ink in her room.

Her eyes swept over Darius a final time, her attention snagging on the bare feet dangling off the end of the couch. What was it about this man and his bare feet? Whenever she saw them, they inspired the most ridiculous thoughts in her head. Thoughts of closeness and shared secrets.

Botheration. They were just feet, for pity's sake. Darius's were nothing special. Built for standing, walking, running. Same as any man's.

Yet feet were intimate things. She couldn't recall ever seeing a man's bare foot except for her father's, and that only when the family went sea bathing during the summer. She'd seen Tommy Ackerman's feet of course, helped bury them in the sand more times than she could count, but that hardly signified. They'd both been children.

A man, in contrast, kept his feet covered at all times. He might doff his hat, remove his gloves, roll up his shirt sleeves or even remove his shirt if involved in physical labor. But he never removed his shoes unless he was getting ready for bed.

Bed? Nicole jerked her attention away from Darius's feet and practically ran the rest of the way to the door.

Nicole Camilla Renard, she scolded with

the best mental imitation of her mother she could manage. *You get your head out of that man's bedroom and back on your shoulders where it belongs. Darius doesn't need you mooning over him like some lovesick debutante. He needs you to help with his experiments and transcribe his documents. And you need his wages so you can get on to New Orleans and find a man to marry and save Renard Shipping.*

So what if she couldn't imagine anyone else having feet as perfectly formed as Darius Thornton's with his thick soles, long toes, and strong arches? What difference did feet make at all? None — that's what. Her future husband could have hairy feet or unclipped nails or even webbed toes as long as he fulfilled her other requirements. What mattered was his character, his skill in running a business, his knowledge of the shipping industry, and . . . hopefully . . . his affection for her. That's what she needed to focus on. Not feet.

So why did she feel like crying at the thought of seeing some other man's feet in her future bedroom?

Pathetic creature. Time to grow a spine. Nicole firmed her jaw and quietly clicked the study door closed.

"Miss Greyson?"

Nicole whirled around, nearly spilling her stack of journals.

"Mrs. Wellborn," she said in a voice too soft to carry into the study. "You startled me." She steadied the article with the back of her left hand, taking care not to get any butter from her breakfast on the pages.

The housekeeper raised a brow as she approached from the direction of the kitchen. "I'm sorry, dear. But I thought there might be some kind of problem for you to be leaving the study so early. Are you out of ink again?"

"No, no. Nothing like that." Nicole led Mrs. Wellborn back down the hall, away from the door. "I just won't be working in the study this morning."

"You won't?" The older woman's brow puckered. "But you always spend your mornings in the study."

Nicole drew to a halt a few steps from the kitchen door. "Mr. Thornton will be making use of it today."

"That man," Mrs. Wellborn grumbled. She heaved a sigh, then straightened and brushed out her apron. "Well, I suppose I ought to fetch his breakfast tray from the workshop then, hadn't I. The master really should learn to inform me of his plans. How else am I supposed to know when he gets the urge to switch rooms on me?"

"I wouldn't bother with the tray, Mrs. Wellborn." Nicole grinned as the furrows in the housekeeper's brow deepened.

"And why not? Getting that man to eat is almost as difficult as getting him to stop working long enough to sleep. If he doesn't get his tray, there's no telling when he'll actually . . . Why are you smiling like that?"

"He's sleeping now." Nicole couldn't have contained her smile if Darius himself had ordered it. And the way Mrs. Wellborn's arching eyebrows nearly disappeared into the lacy edges of her cap only added to Nicole's delight. "I think he was up most of the night working on some correspondence, but he's sleeping now. Peacefully. On the sofa. I didn't want to chance disturbing him. He needs his rest."

"Oh, miss. You don't know the half of it." The housekeeper lifted the corner of her apron to wipe at her eye. "That bed upstairs is never used. Never. He prowls through his workshop all hours of the night, then heads to the study for more of the same. Every now and again, he'll collapse on that sofa for a few hours, mussing the cushions just enough for me to know he had laid there. But never enough to get any true rest. It's like the man's afraid to fall too deeply asleep

— crowding himself onto that narrow sofa instead of using the perfectly good bed he has upstairs."

Nicole blinked. Of course. If memories of the *Louisiana* attacked Darius in his dreams, it was no wonder he avoided sleep. What amazed her was that the man was still functioning at an intelligent level after more than a year of such torment.

"If he's slumbering now, with the sun streaming through the curtains and the sounds of everyday activity humming around him," Mrs. Wellborn continued, "the man's either half dead with exhaustion, or he's finally found a bit of peace."

Nicole clutched her stack of papers more tightly against her chest. "Let's pray it's the latter."

Mrs. Wellborn's chin bobbed in agreement. "I'll see that he's not disturbed, miss, and will do my best to keep the house quiet."

"Excellent. I have a few details to see to in my room, but after that, I'll find Jacob and do *my* best to keep the boy outside. We'll stay close in case Mr. Thornton awakes and has work for me to do."

"We won't have to worry about Arthur," the housekeeper added as she reached the kitchen door. "He took the rig to town to run an errand for Mr. Thornton. He'll be gone several hours."

Odd, Nicole thought. Wellborn had run errands Monday, as well. Three days ago. One would think a single trip would be sufficient. Had something urgent come up to warrant a return trip?

Nicole brushed off the thought as she continued down the hall toward her bedroom. She didn't have time for puzzles. She had an article page to edit, journals to study, an energetic young boy to distract, and a slumbering scientist to insulate. Wellborn and his mysterious errands would have to wait.

CHAPTER 21

Darius woke with a crick in his neck. A crick. Imagine that. He couldn't remember the last time he'd slept long enough to get a crick in anything. He grinned and reached behind his head to rub the sore spot at the base of his skull while rising to a sitting position.

What time was it? He glanced around the study, noting the light flooding the room. The tick of the desk clock lured him from his seat on the disheveled sofa, promising answers, but when he got to his desk, it was the letter he'd written to his parents that drew his attention.

Gathering the pages one after the other, he arranged them in order and carefully folded the address sheet around them. After cutting off a wafer seal from the sheet he kept in his desk, Darius affixed it to where the four folded corners met on the back, then set the packet atop the article he'd

bundled yesterday evening. A bundle someone had wrapped in brown paper and addressed for him. A grin tugged at the corners
of his mouth. *Nicole.*

Still taking care of him, even while he
slept.

Darius grabbed up the desk clock and
stared it in the face. *A quarter after eleven?
Truly?* If he'd fallen asleep around dawn,
that would mean he'd slept for at least four
hours, possibly closer to five. And not once
had he dreamed of the accident. Remarkable. He'd never gone more than two hours
without falling into one of those hellish
nightmares.

He needed to find Nicole. Tell her. Thank
her.

He scooped his leather gaiters from the
floor with a single swipe of his arm and
hastened upstairs to change into a fresh
shirt and trousers.

As he yanked clean clothes from his
bureau, he recalled the feel of her arms
wrapped about him, the way her cheek had
rested against the planes of his back. She'd
coaxed him out of his torment even before
he'd awakened, then drew the poison of his
guilt from him — first with her patient acceptance of his story, then with a fiery challenge that dared him to get out of the way

and let God redeem his failures. Darius grinned as he recalled her fearless prodding. Not much of a gentleman at the best of times, he must have been a bear last night. Yet his little pirate never once backed down. She said what needed to be said then left him with a kiss and words of hope.

The woman might think God spared his life in part so he could be here when she found herself in desperate need of employment, but he knew the truth. God had not brought Nicole to Oakhaven for a job. He'd brought her here to pull the thorn out of a stubborn bear of a man's paw so that he could finally start to heal.

And something told him if he allowed her to leave him, an even larger thorn would take its place. One from which he might never recover.

Darius haphazardly shoved the tails of his linen shirt into his trousers and ran a comb through his overlong hair. *Bear* was right, he decided, gazing critically at his reflection in the mirror above his washstand. He looked half-wild. But he had no time to worry over his appearance. He had to find Nicole.

He found her by the pond with Jacob, behind the big oak tree. Darius slowed his step. She stood behind the boy, her arm in line with his as she helped him perfect his throwing motion.

"That's right," she encouraged. "Keep your arm relaxed. Your last throw was close, so just release a little earlier. Feel that wrist movement?"

"Yes'm." Jacob nodded, his face a study in concentration.

"Good. Now, aim for the dirt between those two tree roots. Remember, keep your throw strong, but controlled. Wrist and arm work together in one smooth motion." She let go of the boy's arm and backed up a few paces. "Cock, release, follow through. Go!"

Jacob drew the knife back, stepped toward the tree, and flung the blade. It landed with a satisfying *thwack,* tip buried in the sand, off-center but within the designated area.

"I did it!" Jacob cried, his face beaming as he spun toward his mentor, who was already squealing and clapping in delight. Nicole ran forward and embraced the kid with such abandon it made Darius's chest ache. She spun Jacob in a circle, both of them laughing as they celebrated. Then they slowed, and as she lowered the boy to the ground, her gaze lifted to collide with his.

"Darius." She straightened immediately, like a child caught doing something wrong. "I-I mean, Mr. Thornton. I was . . . um . . .

just giving Jacob a few lessons on knife throwing." She backed away from him, and Darius frowned. Why was she acting so skittish? Where was his fearless pirate?

She tugged the blade from the earth and wiped it clean on the hem of her skirt. "I'm sure you're wanting me back up at the house, though, aren't you? Now that the study is . . . ah . . . available. I'll head there straightaway."

"Hold, Miss Greyson," he said, not about to let her go hying off without him. "There's no rush."

She stopped abruptly and finally looked him in the eye. "There's not?"

More than one question shone in her golden-brown gaze. He wanted to spend time answering them all. As well as asking a few of his own. But they weren't alone.

"You're not mad, are you, Mr. Thornton?" Jacob asked, worry creasing his brow. "Miss Nicole made sure I finished all my chores before we started the lessons. She even helped me with some of 'em."

"Did she now?" Darius arched a brow but couldn't keep the stern expression in place for more than a second. Grinning, he ruffled the boy's hair. "I'd say you two had a perfectly productive morning, then. I've got a clean barn and a stable hand who is well on his way to becoming rather skilled with a blade. That was an impressive throw, Jake."

The boy glowed with pride at the praise. "Thank you, sir. Miss Nicole says I'll have to practice every day if I want to get as good as her."

"I suppose you'll need a blade of your own to be able to accomplish that feat." Darius stroked his chin in what he hoped was a thoughtful manner. "I guess it's a good thing I'll be riding into town to post some mail today. You can ride along with me and pick out a knife from the ones at the mercantile. I've decided I can't have my employees running around out here without some kind of protection. Snakes, you know."

"Do you mean it, Mr. Thornton? My own knife?" Jacob hopped around Darius's legs like a popping kernel in hot oil.

Darius chuckled and ruffled the boy's hair again. "Yep. Go on up to the house and see what jobs Mrs. Wellborn has for you. Now that the house is no longer under quarantine due to a sleeping dragon, we can get on with our work. Then, when the chores are done and we've had some lunch, we can be on our way."

"Yes, sir!" Jacob didn't hesitate. He sprinted up the hill to the house, his short legs pumping as fast as they could go.

"A sleeping dragon?" Nicole raised a brow, her tone wry. "The creature looked more like a drowsing puppy the last time I saw him."

"Thanks to you." Darius stepped close and brushed a lock of hair that the wind had blown free behind her ear. His finger lingered, savoring the feel of soft skin along the hairline of her neck. Her teasing grin faded, and her breath hitched.

"Darius?" Her gaze raked his face as if searching for answers to questions she couldn't find the words to ask.

He was more than ready to answer her questions, spoken or otherwise, but there were a few things he needed to say first. So he stepped back. But not without purpose. No, he had another hypothesis to test, and he aimed to establish conditions conducive to achieving the desired results. Hence, when he stepped back, he made sure to move in a direction that would take him closer to the tree — the large oak that would afford them a measure of privacy if Nicole would be accommodating enough to follow him.

Darius crunched through the dead leaves that had fallen around the base of the tree to make room for new spring growth, holding his breath until he heard her steps behind him. Excellent.

"Darius? What is it? You're not acting like yourself. Are you angry that I didn't wake you this morning? I know how much you hate to waste time, but I really thought you needed the extra —"

His laugh cut her off. "I'm not angry with you, Nicole." How could he be angry? She'd given him back his life last night. His family. Shone much needed light into the dark places of his soul. He owed her a debt, one he intended to repay with a first installment that would free her from whatever snag she found herself in with that Jenkins person, and the rest to be paid back slowly, over many years, with incredibly exorbitant interest.

"If you're not angry, then what is wrong?" Nicole demanded. Well, maybe not demanded. She was biting her lip, after all. A sure indication that she wasn't nearly so composed as she would have him believe. But then, his little pirate hated to show weakness. She preferred to go on the attack . . . or just go — handling things on her own.

That last thought cinched around his heart like a too-tight belt, but he willed the desperation away. He had to be strong to win the respect of his pirate princess, strong and bold.

"Really, Darius. First you sleep nearly to noon, then you promise Jacob a trip to town for a knife he doesn't really need, at least not immediately, and now you're out here being all quiet and mysterious when you're supposed to be barking orders or handing me a page of instructions so I can get back to work."

"Mysterious, am I? Hmm. I rather like that." He edged closer to the tree, angling his body in such a way that she would have to step in between him and the oak in order to look him in the eye. Which she did. Darius fought to keep the smile from his face. *Like a tug pilot guiding a barge up the Hudson,* he thought smugly. *Not that she is anything like a barge,* he quickly amended. *Blast.* He'd have to do better than that when it came time for courting, or he'd lose her for sure.

"You never go to town," she insisted, an attractive shade of pink rising in her cheeks. "You always send Wellborn, and you've already sent him this week. Twice. Including today. Why aren't you running off to your workshop or burying your nose in a mechanics journal or . . . Stop staring at me like that."

"All right." Darius complied by advancing

toward her, cupping her delicate jaw in his hand, then closing his eyes . . . while he pressed his mouth to hers.

She stiffened in surprise. At least he hoped it was surprise, for she still held a weapon in her hand. A detail he'd failed to recall until just that moment. But then a *thud* vibrated the earth near his foot, and Nicole's palms came to rest against his chest. Blissfully empty, knifeless palms. Palms that sent delicious shivers dancing through him as he closed the distance between them, leaning her back against the tree.

His hypothesis had been correct. She tasted sweet — sweeter than honey fresh from the comb. And she kissed him back with an intoxicating mixture of shyness and fiery abandon so essentially Nicole that blood surged through his veins in recognition. She was his match.

Raising a second hand to cup the other side of her face, Darius drew her mouth even closer and deepened the kiss. His fingers caressed the hair at her nape; his thumbs stroked her cheeks. The clean scent of her filled his senses, building a craving for more. More that wasn't yet his to claim.

Slowly he gentled his hold and eased the pressure of his lips against hers. Unable to let her go all at once, he weaned himself with short, sweet kisses to her lips, her cheeks, her forehead. Then he tucked her head beneath his chin and concentrated on steadying his breathing.

He'd intended to talk to her first, to explain how much her being there for him last night had meant. But once he'd had her positioned safely behind the tree, the need to kiss her had erupted over him with such force that all thought of conversation fled.

A gentleman would apologize for such indelicate behavior, he supposed. Darius grinned. Good thing Nicole had never mistaken him for a gentleman, for he couldn't seem to dredge up one iota of remorse.

CHAPTER 22

Nicole closed her eyes as Darius folded her into his chest, her breathing ragged, her body trembling. He'd kissed her. Well and truly kissed her. On purpose. And merciful heavens, how the earth had shifted.

She remembered wondering once what it would be like to be the object of Darius's focused attention. Now she knew. *Glorious. Absolutely glorious.* The intensity of his gaze, the passion of his kiss, the tenderness of his touch. Even now his hands stroked her back as he held her. She'd give up anything to be able to stay with him like this forever. Anything except her family's future. That she couldn't sacrifice.

Gathering the remnants of her shattered resolve, Nicole pushed against Darius's chest and stepped away from his embrace. "We shouldn't have done —"

"Shhh," he interrupted, placing a finger over her lips. The touch shot a new wave of

warmth through her that Nicole was helpless to stop. "No regrets."

She turned her head aside, away from his
touch, his scrutiny. "You don't understand.
I —"

"I understand that you were there for me
last night." His soft voice rippled over her
like the gentle lapping of a lake upon the
sand, slowly eroding her resistance. "You
were there for me in the darkness of my
nightmare, Nicole, a nightmare that has
tormented me every time I closed my eyes
over the last eighteen months. Yet you
banished it with the touch of your hand."

He captured her fingers and lifted them
to his mouth. His breath stirred against the
skin on the back of her hand a moment
before his lips descended. The kiss lingered
with a sweetness that made her heart leap
even as despair sliced it in two.

"Please don't," she whispered. "I have to
leave soon, and this will only —"

"I wrote to my parents." He squeezed her
hand and trapped it against his chest, refusing to let her finish her explanation. "I told
them everything. The *Louisiana.* The girl
who drowned. My compulsion to study
boiler explosions."

Nicole nodded. When she'd seen the
pages, she'd known he'd held nothing back

from them. "I'm glad, Darius. That gulf needed to be crossed. I'm certain they'll understand. They'll support you. Love you."
Like I do.

Oh, heavens. It's too late. Nicole bit back a cry and tugged free from his grasp. She spun from him, her only thought to escape. But he was too fast. He caught her wrist and turned her back to face him.

"I also wrote them about you." His blue gaze bored into her with paralyzing force. She couldn't move. Couldn't flee. Could only stare at the social travesty of his un-groomed features — the scruffy half beard shadowing his jaw, the too-long hair falling over his forehead — and feel her heart beat with love for this unconventional man.

Darius's grip softened on her wrist until his fingers were tracing tiny circles over the sensitive skin. "I told them that I had met a woman who wasn't afraid to stand toe-to-toe with me. A woman who had seen my flaws and learned my darkest secrets, yet didn't immediately run for the hills."

His self-deprecating chuckle coaxed a reluctant smile from her, the sound sooth-ing the sharp edges of her turmoil.

"I told them how this woman seemed instinctively to know when to comfort and when to confront, and how I was better with her in my life than I'd ever been on my own." His voice deepened as he spoke, the huskiness brushing over her like an angora shawl on a cold winter night. *Better with me than on your own?* Oh, how his words caressed her, thrilled her. She wanted to snuggle up in him and block everything else out.

But that was impossible.

Blinking back tears, Nicole touched a hand to his face, praying he would feel her regret even though she dared not speak it aloud. "Did you tell them I am your employee?" she said instead, trying not to flinch as the warmth in his eyes suddenly cooled. "Did you tell them I would be gone by the time your letter reached them? That a promise made to my dying father would keep me from ever returning?"

"What?" His voice sharp, Darius's fingers bit into her wrist, and he jerked her toward him. "Why can't you return to Oakhaven once your errand is complete?" He searched her face, but she offered no explanation. The truth hurt too much. He released her and rubbed his hand over his face. "You know, it occurred to me this morning that perhaps it would be a good idea to get away from the boilers for a while. Take a break. Start again with a fresh perspective. I could

take you to New Orleans myself, show you
—"

"No!"

Hurt flashed in his eyes at her shouted denial, and she hated herself for putting it there. But what choice did she have? Darius in New Orleans? A violent tremor shook her core. She'd never survive. The warring halves of her heart would tear her in two.

As she watched, the hurt faded from his eyes, replaced by scientific curiosity. He straightened, crossed his arms over his chest, and regarded her in much the same way he did his boilers. Examining. Calculating. Determining weaknesses.

Merciful heavens. Her greatest weakness was Darius himself. How could she defend against that?

"Why?" he asked calmly, his tone detached, as if it were a scientific inquiry he posed. "Why don't you want me to accompany you to New Orleans? I might be a bit rusty on my etiquette, but I believe it is much preferred for a young woman to travel with an escort than alone."

He was right, of course, which only made the question that much more difficult to answer.

"Why, Nicole?" he pressed.

"It would make things harder on me," she

hedged. "It's better if I go on my own."

He didn't even blink, just stared at her as he would a puzzle that needed solving. "Why?"

"It's not your concern!" Nicole stomped her foot, her toe kicking the hilt of her fallen knife. She bent to retrieve it, the weight of the blade a reminder of who she was and what she needed to be about. "I'll handle my father's business the way I see fit, and I'll thank you to stop interfering." Her heart pounded more from fear than anger, but she held her ground, needing to prove to herself that she was strong enough to do what had to be done.

"Why?"

Nicole fought to restrain the scream rising in her throat. "Leave it alone, Darius. *Please.*" Her voice broke on the last word, and a tear slipped past her lashes.

"Why?" Compassion crept into his tone this time, and that touch of feeling was her undoing.

"You want to know why, Darius?" she shouted up at him. "Fine! I don't want you with me because I'm going to New Orleans to get married!"

He reeled backward, as if she'd shot him, and Nicole couldn't bear it. A sob wrenched straight from her heart and flew past her lips as she turned and ran for the house.

Married? Darius staggered, his shock dulling his response for critical seconds, allowing Nicole to stretch out a sizeable lead. Shaking off his stupor with a jerk of his head, he sprinted after her. She couldn't fire a shot like that over his bow and expect no return fire.

"Wait!" He yelled after her, not surprised when she ignored his call and ran even faster. But he wasn't about to let her outdistance him. He had no fancy clothes to hinder his movement today.

Muscles straining, stride lengthening, he closed in on her. Whimpers echoed in the air around him as he drew abreast of her, but he hardened himself against the sound, against the sight of tears rolling down her cheeks. He refused to let her run away from him without an explanation.

"Nicole! Stop!"

She paid him no heed. Again.

Fine. If she wouldn't stop on her own, he'd see to the task for her. With a surge of speed, Darius passed her and veered sharply into her path, turning toward her as he did so. He tightened his abdomen an instant before she crashed into him. A grunt squeezed from his lungs at the contact, but he locked his arms around her. She fought to escape his hold but was no match for his greater strength.

All at once she gave up and wilted against him. Turning, she wrapped her arms around his waist and buried her face in his shirt. Her hot tears scalded his chest more painfully than any boiler steam ever could. Yet even as his hold softened, the angry questions welling inside him demanded release.

"Are you betrothed, Nicole?" he asked through clenched teeth, bracing himself for her answer. Heaven help him. If she was, she never should have responded to his kiss with such sweet abandon. That kiss had touched places within him he'd forgotten existed. She *couldn't* belong to another. She belonged to him.

No response. Why didn't she answer?

"Blast it all, woman." He grabbed her by the shoulders and pried her away from him so he could see her face. "It's a simple enough question. Are you betrothed? Yes or no?"

She shook her head, and Darius had to lock his knees to keep his legs from collapsing in relief beneath him.

"No," her voice scratched, "but I might as well be. I must choose a husband from among my father's business associates, those he trusts to take over his company upon his death. I am to procure him an heir."

An heir? Darius released his hold on Nicole, so many dark emotions raging inside him, he was afraid he'd hurt her. His hands fisted at his sides, longing to slam into her father's face. He didn't care how sick the old man was, he had no right to use his daughter's love and affection against her in such a way. "He's selling you off to the highest bidder," Darius growled. "He deserves to lose his company."

"It's not like that!" Nicole scrubbed the tears from her cheeks with an impatient swat of her hand, then grabbed him by the shirtfront. "None of the men in New Orleans know why I am coming. I will be the one in control.

"Don't you see? My father could have ordered me to marry a man of his choosing, but he didn't. He trusted me to make the choice, gave me the freedom to choose a man I could come to love. He wanted that for me, he just needed to speed the timetable up a bit. It was supposed to be simple. I sail to New Orleans, have an old family friend introduce me to eligible young men of good character and knowledgeable backgrounds. I determine for myself which man would make a suitable husband for me and heir for my father, then present him with the . . . gift my father set aside for my dowry, and we would marry."

Darius noted her stumble over the word *gift*. She was holding something back.

"I wasn't supposed to meet *you*, Darius." The pain in her words cut through him, driving all other concerns from his mind. Her balled hand loosened to lie flat against his chest. "I wasn't supposed to come to Liberty at all. I was supposed to arrive in New Orleans with my heart fully intact and free to give to the man I deemed worthy."

Was she saying her heart was no longer free? Darius's pulse gave a little leap as his resolve steeled. If there was a way around this promise she'd made to her father, he'd find it. He just needed a little time. Time and a conversation with Wellborn. He had to get to town.

Darius reached up and covered Nicole's hand with his. She peered up at him, her lips begging to be kissed. Yet her anguished brown eyes held his desire in check. Leaning forward, he touched his forehead to hers, his eyes closing as he breathed in her scent.

"I won't ask you to break your promise to your father, Nicole, but I will ask you to give me time to find a way around it. I'm

296

certain there's a way to provide your father with his heir without you pledging your life" — *to a man other than me* — "to a stranger."

She shook her head slightly, the movement vibrating through him from where their heads met. "Time is something I don't have, Darius. My father is too ill, possibly dying. I can't delay. I will stay here until the end of our agreed time, but then I will leave for New Orleans. Alone."

She pulled her head away from his, and Darius fell forward at the loss. Then her lips brushed against his brow, and everything inside him stilled.

She'd given him six days — six days to untangle the web her father's promise had trapped her in, six days to unravel her mysteries, six days to convince her that she belonged with him and no other.

When she pulled away from him, he made no move to stop her. Time was of the essence, and the instant Nicole entered the house and closed the door behind her, he sprang into action. Sprinting to the barn, he called out to Jacob, who was carrying wood from the shed up to the house.

"Time to go to town, Jake. Go tell Mrs. Wellborn we'll grab a bite to eat in Liberty, and then meet me at the corral."

The boy gave a whoop of glee and scampered off. Darius saddled his mount before striding to the house to collect his letter, article, and sufficient funds to cover whatever necessities might arise — lunch, posting fees, bribes to entice certain parties at the levee to share information that Wellborn might not have been able to pry free.

He had six days to solve Nicole's mysteries and claim her heart. He'd not waste a single minute.

CHAPTER 23

Two hours later, Darius sat at a corner table in the only café Liberty boasted, jabbing a piece of fried ham with a questionably clean fork as Wellborn looked on. He'd crossed paths with his man on the outskirts of town and convinced him to circle back so they could discuss what information he'd been able to ferret out of the river pilot he'd come to town to meet.

Once entering town he'd had to post his parcels, and then he'd dug through every blasted blade the mercantile had to offer before Jacob managed to select one. Once they finally reached the café, he'd ordered their food — which apparently had to be butchered and cured after their order, considering how long it had taken to arrive — and all the while his tight-lipped butler had sat with that infuriatingly neutral expression on his face, hiding any clues Darius might have been able to glean.

"Spill it, Wellborn," Darius growled impatiently. The wait was killing him.

"You're not concerned the boy will overhear?" Wellborn tipped his head toward a table a short distance behind him, where Jacob was gulping down a glass of milk and working to devour a slab of ham of his own.

Darius shook his head. "The boy's focused on his food. And when that's gone, he'll no doubt drool some more over his new knife. Besides, I explained we needed to discuss a few matters. He won't bother us."

Wellborn raised a brow. "He might not bother us, but there's a good chance he'll hear. This place is as empty as a beggar's purse."

Darius glanced around the room as he shoved a forkful of mashed potatoes into his mouth. At nearly two in the afternoon, the three of them were the only patrons in the place. Even the staff had disappeared into the kitchen.

"Just keep your voice down," Darius rumbled in a quiet tone of his own. "The boy will be fine."

"All right, but part of what I have to say concerns him." Wellborn leaned across the table and spoke so low Darius had to stop chewing in order to hear him clearly. "I visited with the sheriff again."

Darius nodded. He'd asked Wellborn to check in with the lawman two days ago, after he'd offered Jacob a place at Oakhaven. The boy had refused to reveal his surname or provide any details about what had driven him from his guardian, but there was no doubt in Darius's mind that it had been a grave offense. This boy was no idle runaway. Yet his conscience demanded he at least notify the law as to the boy's presence. He couldn't knowingly harbor a fugitive, no matter how justified.

"Has someone reported him missing?" Darius swallowed the lump of half-chewed food in his mouth, no longer tasting it. If Jake's guardian showed up, he wasn't sure what he would do. Press charges against the man for abuse when the boy sported no scars?

Thankfully, Wellborn shook his head. "No. But Sheriff Davenport asked around a bit and heard of a man with a small spread north of here, near Cold Spring. The fellow took in his brother's kids last year, after their parents died of influenza."

"Kids?" Darius set his fork down and leaned over his half-full plate, his forearms pressing into the table.

"A boy and a girl." Wellborn fell silent for a moment, cast a surreptitious glance over

301

his shoulder, then whispered, "The girl died a couple months back."

"How?"

"The sheriff didn't have any details. But he did say the man who took the kids in is a known drunk."

Darius's throat constricted. His eyes immediately found Jacob at the next table stuffing a whole biscuit into his mouth in one overlarge bite.

If Jacob had had a sister, Darius could easily imagine her death being the catalyst for his leaving. Especially if his uncle contributed to it in some way.

"The sheriff is in no hurry to volunteer information about Jacob's whereabouts. Seems to think the boy's better off away from that drunk of an uncle, even if he is blood kin, so he won't pursue the matter unless the man comes looking for the boy."

"Good." Darius took a swig of his coffee. "And the other matter?" He picked up his fork and pressed the side of it into his ham to disguise his level of interest, though inside he churned with impatience.

Wellborn took his time answering. As if he knew this was the information Darius cared most about.

"Well?" he growled.

Did the edges of Wellborn's eyes crinkle

just a touch? The man was probably laughing his head off behind that proper mask of his. Impertinent fellow.

"Did you find Captain Stewart?" Darius pierced Wellborn with his most imperious, lord-of-the-manor glare. Not that it had any noticeable effect. The man was obviously immune. However, the directness of the question finally succeeded in loosening the man's tongue.

"I did." Wellborn dipped his head slightly. "He was good enough to spare me a few minutes of his time after he landed this morning."

"Did he know of this Jenkins person and what business the man is in?" When Wellborn had asked around at the landing on Monday, he'd learned that Stewart was the man most familiar with the Galveston routes. Stewart had been farther up the Trinity delivering cargo, but the dock workers expected him back today, hence the second trip to town that week.

"Yes, he knew of a *Carson* Jenkins. The fellow apparently runs a coastal shipping company, his two main routes encompassing Cuba and New Orleans. The man's not very well respected, it seems. Rumor has it that Jenkins isn't above making an unscrupulous deal if it means enlarging his profits

303

— though Stewart insisted he had no first-hand knowledge of such maneuvers."

"Of course the man's unscrupulous! His sons are hunting an innocent young woman."

Wellborn gave a slight shake of his head and drew his eyes upward meaningfully. Darius clenched his jaw, realizing he'd spoken louder than he'd intended. He glanced past his butler to where Jake sat, his meal finished. Thankfully the boy was too busy admiring his new knife to give the adult conversation any heed. Nevertheless, Darius grasped his temper with both hands and modulated his voice to a low rumble.

"What I need to ascertain is how far this Jenkins fellow will go in his pursuit of Nicole. Would he allow his sons to inflict bodily harm, or heaven help us, even kill her to get what he wants?"

Wellborn's eyebrows shot to his carefully pomaded hairline. "Surely you don't think he'd . . . ?"

"I don't know what to think — that's the problem. There are still too many missing pieces." Darius dug the fingers of his left hand into the flesh above his knee with such force, pain ratcheted up his leg. "What of a competitor for Jenkins? Could Stewart shed any light on that?"

Wellborn eyed him intently, his mouth curving ever so slightly. "He did have a few observations of interest."

Darius scowled at his butler. "Quit toying with me, man, and spit it out," he growled. "You've tortured me enough for one afternoon."

All hints of a smile vanished from Wellborn's face as he nodded. "Very well, sir. It might interest you to know that Jenkins's fiercest rival is a man by the name of Anton Renard. He has an outstanding reputation among pilots and businessmen alike. Efficient. Honest. Maintains quality machinery and knows how to make the customer happy."

Darius seized upon the name. "And he's French."

"So it would seem," Wellborn concurred. "Stewart said there was bad blood between the two that goes back many years, but he didn't know the details. He spoke highly of Renard Shipping, though. Said it was a shame Anton Renard had no son to carry on the family business. Only a daughter, he believed."

Wellborn casually lifted his cup to his mouth to sip his coffee as if he hadn't just dropped an informational gem worth more than a king's ransom on the table between them.

Darius shook his head, a laugh of disbelief escaping him as he thrust his fingers through his hair. "Her father's in shipping. Shipping!"

All this angst about finding an heir for her father's business and here he sat, already an heir to one of the most successful shipping companies in the country. Renard would be hard-pressed to find a man with more knowledge of the industry to take over the helm of his company. Yet Renard had specifically charged his daughter with choosing a man from among his New Orleans contacts, someone who knew the local routes and could immediately step into the business. Darius lacked those associations. Not to mention the fact that he'd abandoned King Star Shipping for more than a year. Two strikes against him. Three, if she considered his rough social edges.

Darius sobered. Maybe convincing her of his suitability wouldn't be as easy as he'd first thought. Nicole's blind devotion to her father could still take her away from him. And even if he convinced her he was the best man to take over her father's business, that only solved one of their problems. There was still Jenkins to deal with.

"I need to learn more about this bad blood between Renard and Jenkins. My gut tells me the answer to this entire mess lies somewhere in that dispute."

But he only had six days. How was he supposed to find the answers he sought in such a short time when any overt action on his part could raise the suspicions of the very men Nicole was hiding from? Even the discreet questioning Wellborn had done for him increased the chance someone would suspect the reason for his interest. Yet he couldn't just sit back and wait for trouble to find them. If something should happen to Nicole . . .

Darius slumped forward. "I can't lose her, Wellborn."

The man held his gaze, strong and steady. Then his lips slowly curved. "Flora always said that when you fell, it'd be hard and fast. Guess she was right."

Darius didn't welcome the change in conversation, but he couldn't deny the truth of Wellborn's observation, so he held his tongue.

"We knew David would have a slow, polite courtship. That boy always does what's expected. But you? Well, your mama despaired of any woman getting past that abrupt manner of yours to see what you have to offer. It's a good thing they grow a hardier breed of females down here in Texas."

"It's not Texas, Wellborn. It's Nicole." Darius swiveled his head and glanced out the window, embarrassed to reveal his softer feelings, yet at the same time determined to give Nicole her due. "She's young, but she has this wisdom about her that cuts through foolishness and lays bare the heart of a matter. She's intelligent, unafraid to speak her mind, and loyal to a fault."

That fault being blindly obeying her father's request for an heir at the expense of her own happiness. But even then, he only faulted her steadfastness because of his own selfish desires. He didn't want her giving herself to some rich New Orleans dandy with fancy manners and social charisma. *He* wanted her loyalty, her devotion, her love.

"Miss Nicole is quality, through and through," Wellborn agreed. "A true woman of character. You've chosen well, Mr. Thornton."

"Unfortunately, mine's not the only choice that matters." Darius turned from the window and regarded his butler — no, his friend — with a serious air, allowing him to see a hint of the desperation clawing for purchase inside him. "She plans to leave me, Wellborn."

"What?"

This time Darius was the one shooting meaningful glances to remind his companion to keep *his* voice down.

"You must be mistaken, sir." The man looked genuinely rattled. Darius had never seen Wellborn rattled. Not even the first time he exploded a boiler on Oakhaven's pond. "She mentioned no such plans to me, nor to Flora. I'm sure of it." He fidgeted with the cuff of his perfectly pressed coat, and for a moment Darius thought he might actually *crease* the thing. But then he seemed to gain control of himself and smoothed the wool back into place.

"Perhaps you misunderstood. I've seen the way she looks at you, Mr. Thornton. If I might be so bold, I'm quite certain she holds you in some esteem."

Darius shoved his plate aside, his appetite irrevocably gone. No use staring at the stuff any longer.

"There's no misunderstanding. She made her position quite clear to me just this morning. In six days, if I cannot convince her to stay, she will leave Oakhaven and never return."

"But . . . why?" The plaintive tone in Wellborn's voice nearly made Darius smile.

The man was as besotted with the idea of Nicole joining the Thornton family as he was.

"I don't feel comfortable sharing details of what she has told me in confidence, but I can tell you her reasons have nothing to do with any feelings she might have toward me or anyone at Oakhaven. She has made a promise to her father, and honor demands she fulfill it."

The older man's face crumpled, but only for a moment. As Darius watched, his butler stiffened his posture, threw back his shoulders, and jutted his chin. "So what are we going to do about this development?"

Darius did smile then. Such a show of loyalty was heartening. "We're going to find a way to help her keep her promise to her father without leaving us behind, and we're going to make sure Jenkins and his men don't harm a hair on her head in the process."

An expression that was downright crafty slid over Wellborn's features. "Would it help if I told you that a Mr. Edmund Whistler, formerly employed by one Carson Jenkins, is due in town this afternoon? He used to be a member of Captain Stewart's crew, but he now works on board the *Polly Anne.* I checked the shipping schedules, and the

Polly Anne is scheduled to dock at three o'clock."

"Then I suggest you be there to meet him, Wellborn." He'd prefer to meet the boat himself, but a manservant would draw less notice than Oakhaven's crazy, boiler-exploding landowner.

The butler gave a brisk nod. "My thoughts exactly, sir."

Darius dipped his chin, an unspoken vow humming through the air between the two men. Rising to his feet, he pulled a few coins from his pocket and tossed them onto the table to cover the price of the meals.

Talking to Whistler at all was a risk. If the man still had ties to Jenkins, Nicole could be exposed. But if they didn't talk to him, Jenkins might find her anyway, and Darius would be caught off guard. Better to fight an enemy you understood and could prepare for than one you knew nothing about.

At least that's what he told himself as he called to Jake and strode out of the café.

CHAPTER 24

When Darius reached the yard at Oakhaven, he lowered Jacob down from the horse, knowing how anxious the boy was to show off his new blade. "Don't forget to send Miss Greyson out to meet me in the workshop after the two of you are through," Darius called as Jake dashed toward the house.

"I will," came the answer, though Jake never turned.

Darius grinned at the boy's eagerness, yet very little of the weight pressing into his chest lightened. Exhaling a ragged breath, he dismounted and led his horse into the barn. His mind churned while he rubbed the horse down and put up the tack.

There had to be an answer, an answer that didn't involve Nicole breaking her vow to her father *or* marrying someone besides him.

Darius leaned against the barn wall and

forked his fingers into his hair, clutching an overlong hank in his fist. The roots tugged painfully at his scalp, but he tightened his grip.

You opened the Red Sea for the Israelites, God. You made the sun stand still for Joshua. Surely you can provide a solution for us, as well. I love her. I don't want to lose her. Please, please work this out for our good.

Darius surged to his feet, crossed to the barn opening, and slammed the heel of his hand against the doorframe. He hated feeling helpless, powerless. He wished he could hem Nicole in like one of the variables in his experiments, controlling everything around her to ensure the outcome he wanted. But she had a mind of her own. A stubborn mind. A clever mind. And hemming her in would only alienate her further. The only trump card he held was his connection to King Star Shipping. However, playing it too early could lead to losing the hand. No. Better to hedge his bets and wait to see what Wellborn learned at the docks this afternoon. So much depended on what Whistler might reveal.

No, he corrected himself, letting his palm trail down the wooden beam until his arm hung loosely at his side. *Everything depends on God. That's where my trust belongs.*

313

Yet even as that truth settled over him, he couldn't completely banish the slithering fear that wound itself around his heart and squeezed with increasing strength.

What if God said no?

By late afternoon, anxiety had worn Darius's mind down to mush. He hissed out a pain-filled breath as the hammer he'd been using to pound out a dent in a section of boiler plate collided with his thumb. For the third time. He lifted the digit to his mouth, then shook his hand out in an effort to ease the throbbing.

"Are you all right?" Nicole glanced up from the inventory list she was compiling, her brows arched with concern.

So much for hoping she hadn't noticed.

Nicole stepped toward him as if to offer aid, but Darius quickly waved her off. "I'm fine. Just a bit distracted. So many possibilities running through my head, you know."

She frowned but thankfully remained on her side of the workshop. "All right, but you might consider setting the hammer aside while working through experimentation ideas next time."

"Perhaps you're right." Darius smiled, and made no effort to correct her misconception. Boilers were the last thing on his mind.

He hadn't given a single thought to his next experiment. How could he when every piece of his brain had been consumed with thoughts of what was happening in Liberty?

He tossed his hammer onto the worktable. Iron plating, rivets, and soldering gear jangled in protest, as loudly as if Mrs. Wellborn had just upturned the box of good silver onto the floor.

"Darius? Are you sure you're all right?"

Back turned to Nicole, he closed his eyes. Of course he wasn't all right. The woman he loved was bound and determined to leave him in six days, and he had no feasible plan to stop her. His hands balled into fists.

How had he thought working alongside her would make the waiting more bearable? It was killing him. One minute he wanted to storm across the workshop, confront her with what he knew, and demand answers. The next he wanted to pull her into his arms and make her promise never to leave him. With a grunt, Darius yanked the protective apron he wore over his head and strode for the door.

"I'm going to get some air," he announced without meeting her eyes. "Continue your work. I'll be back shortly."

Closing the door behind him, Darius made for the pond. If ever he needed a swim, it was today. The enforced quiet under the water. The strain of muscles. The soothing rhythm of the strokes.

He reached the landing and barely paused long enough to pull the boots from his feet and the shirt from his back before launching his body into the water in a shallow dive.

The frigid temperature shocked his system, and for a blessed moment, freed his mind. Scissoring his legs and thrusting his arms, he propelled himself deeper and faster, as if the key to winning Nicole's hand lay on the opposite side. He didn't surface when the water began to grow shallow, as he usually did. He let his lungs burn until his hands collided with the muddy bank. Then, finally, he planted his feet and shot up.

Gulping in a deep breath, he turned to continue back to the landing, his muscles aching but ready for more. That's when he heard a voice. High pitched. Excited. Sharpening his focus, Darius scanned the yard. *There.* Jacob, his legs flying, waved wildly as he ran toward the landing.

"Wellborn's back!" he shouted. "Wellborn's back!"

Darius surged off the bank. His arms cranked through the water as his legs powered him forward.

He reached the landing in record time, hoisted himself out, and made a grab for his shirt as he leapt from the dock to the grass. Not taking the time to replace his shoes, Darius rubbed his head and face with the dry cotton of his shirt while he picked his way, barefoot, up the hill that led to the house. He gave his chest a cursory swipe before cramming the wet shirt over his head. His arms got stuck in the sleeves, but he muscled his way into them, ignoring the small seam-popping sounds that accompanied his efforts.

Jacob came alongside, trotting to keep up with Darius's long, hurried strides. "Do you think he's got news from that whistling fella?"

Darius jerked to a halt and spun to face Jacob. "You know about Whistler?"

The boy shrugged. "Only what I heard Wellborn tell you at the restaurant. But don't worry. I didn't say nothin' to Miss Nicole." He paused, his little throat working up and down as he swallowed. "I don't want her to leave, neither. She saved my life. I figure I owe her."

He planted his hands on his hips and gave Darius a man-to-man look. "I don't want nobody hurtin' her. She might be good with a knife an' all, but she's still a girl. And girls

317

tend to get hurt when they get in the way of angry men."

A sheen shimmered across the boy's eyes for a moment, a sheen that proclaimed Jacob's firsthand experience in the matter. But before Darius could comment, the kid blinked it away and resumed his march to the house.

"Come on, Mr. T." He gestured for Darius to follow. "Time's a wastin'."

No one had to tell him twice. Darius overtook Jacob in three strides, threw him a wink, and set off at a run. Jacob hollered and gave chase, moving ahead when a rough-edged stone hiding in the grass stabbed Darius's arch. He pulled up like a lame horse, hobbling the last few yards to where Wellborn was climbing down from the wagon seat.

"Well, I suppose we won't be having our discussion in the study, will we?" Wellborn commented dryly, his brow lifting as he took in Darius's soggy trousers, muddy feet, and torn shirt. "Flora would have my head if I let you set foot on her carpets in that condition. You're like a wet dog in need of a good shake. An *outdoor* shake."

Darius gave his head a quick wag, causing Jacob to sputter with laughter as he moved to unhitch the horses. As soon as the boy was busy, Darius sobered. "The barn will do."

"What of Jacob?" Wellborn murmured. "If he's seeing to the horses, we can't be assured of privacy."

"He already knows." Darius made for the barn door, ignoring the sore spot on his foot.

Wellborn kept pace, glancing over his shoulder at the boy as he went. "He overheard at the café?"

"Apparently. But he's got sense enough to hold his tongue." Darius crossed into the barn's dim interior and immediately headed for a back stall, his eyes adjusting as he went. "Nicole knows nothing." He dropped his voice. The subject of their conversation remained safely ensconced in his workshop fifty yards away, yet he'd take no chances. Too much depended on the proper timing of his challenge. If she discovered what he was up to before he had his arguments in order, he'd be sunk.

"Jake sees himself as her protector," Darius continued, sliding into the last stall and bracing his back against the end wall. "He'll keep quiet and do what he can to aid us."

Wellborn grimaced at the pile of droppings left behind by the previous occupant and gave it a wide berth, taking care not to brush up against any of the walls as he followed Darius inside.

"So what did you learn? Did you find Whistler?"

The butler cleared some old hay from the floor with a brush of his shoe, as if checking for hidden muck before settling into a spot. Darius bit his tongue to keep from snapping at the man. Who cared if a little manure ended up on his shoe? Darius would plant his bare foot in the stuff if it meant getting to the answers he sought more quickly.

After an agonizing minute that seemed to stretch into eternity, Wellborn finally ceased playing with the straw and turned his attention back to Darius.

"When the *Polly Anne* docked, her captain pointed Whistler out to me. After I promised to buy him a bottle of his favorite beverage at the local saloon, he became rather friendly. Chatted with me for over an hour at one of the back tables."

Tension radiated through Darius. He leaned forward. "And . . . ?"

"And I believe I may have ascertained the source of contention between Jenkins and Renard, though it seems a bit of superstitious nonsense, if you ask me. I can hardly countenance our sensible Miss Nicole crediting such a tale."

Impatience rumbled in Darius's throat. "I don't care if it involves purple monkeys riding orange dolphins. I need to know what I'm up against so I can plot a course around it."

"Yes. Well. Thankfully, there are no monkeys or dolphins of any variety involved, at least not to my knowledge."

"Wellborn." The man's name vibrated between Darius's clenched teeth in a clear warning.

"It does involve a pirate, though," the butler announced. "A fellow by the name of Lafitte."

Jean Lafitte? The man was a legend. Pirate. Privateer. Spy. What young boy growing up along the coast hadn't pretended to be one of Lafitte's men, living in the pirate colony of Campeche? Darius had taken on the role of Lafitte himself more than once, strutting around with David and the other boys as they each took their turn as the mighty leader. "If I recall correctly," Darius said thoughtfully, "Jean Lafitte established a pirate colony on Galveston Island."

"That's correct. And according to Mr. Whistler, before the Navy forced the pirate to evacuate the island in '21, he bequeathed a jeweled dagger to one of his trusted men who opted to remain behind. Legend holds that whoever possesses the dagger will rule the Galveston shipping trade. Both Jenkins and Renard claim the dagger belongs to them, yet the dagger has been in a Renard's possession for the last two generations. Jenkins believes Renard's success is due to his retention of the dagger and is determined to gain control of the talisman for himself."

A frisson of anticipation reverberated along Darius's nerves as doors previously locked to him began to open. Snippets of memory flashed as his mind assimilated what Wellborn was telling him.

Nicole's insistence on seeing the goods Jacob had stolen from the house.

Her father's desperation for an heir.

Her fear that Jenkins's sons would catch up with her.

Her odd hesitation when she mentioned the gift she was supposed to present to the man she chose to marry.

"God save us, Wellborn," Darius erupted. "Nicole's got the blasted pirate dagger with her!"

Chapter 25

Nicole forced herself to finish the inventory of arched flues, cylindrical flues, grate bars, steam drums, water gauges, and blow cocks after Darius left, determined she'd not become one of those weepy damsels who moped just because life handed her a disappointment or two. Things could be much worse, after all. Poor Jacob was a perfect example. All alone in the world. No family. Stealing food to survive until Darius took him in. She'd be self-centered indeed to think her momentary troubles could even compare.

Closing the logbook, she meandered toward the small window along the back wall, not really paying attention to the scenery before her. She tapped the side of her pencil against the window ledge. There were bound to be kind gentlemen in New Orleans — gentlemen she could respect, perhaps even come to care for in time.

She'd make her choice and live a good life. A life that would make her father proud. And eventually, if God blessed her, she'd have children to spend her love upon, children who would be free to follow their hearts when the time came for them to choose a mate. She'd see to that.

Nicole tried to convince herself she could be content with such a scenario, but her heart rebelled.

Perhaps her father would be satisfied with an heir who excelled at building steamboat machinery. The pencil slipped from her grasp as the idea wormed its way into her mind. Darius might not have business connections or intimate knowledge of the shipping industry, but the man was certainly intelligent enough to learn. He'd gone from some kind of bookkeeper in his father's company in New York to a mechanical engineer in a matter of months, conducting scientific experiments that she was sure would lead to safer steam engines in the near future. He might not be the most congenial of men, but she could aid him in that area, smooth out his rough edges when necessity demanded they make social appearances. Surely that would satisfy her father, wouldn't it?

Yet in her mind's eye she pictured Anton

Renard as he'd looked the day she left on this crazy journey. Weak. Pale. Barely able to stand. He needed someone who could step in immediately and run the company, not simply a man with a penchant for learning.

Her father had entrusted her with the Renard family legacy. Hope and pride had radiated from him the morning she'd set out, and oh, how she longed to be the daughter who saved the day. Nicole's teeth pinched the inside of her cheek. She couldn't disappoint him, not even for the sake of her own happiness.

Bending down, she retrieved the fallen pencil and, with it, her practicality. Wishing for things one couldn't have only led to bitterness and melancholy. She'd do better to count her blessings and turn her mind to making the best of her situation. After all, God could bring good out of any hardship. Hadn't she said as much to Darius? She'd not prove herself a hypocrite by denying that truth now.

As she turned away from the window, she caught a glimpse of a familiar wagon standing abandoned outside the barn. So Wellborn had finally returned. The man had become a regular visitor to town of late, but this trip had lasted nearly all day.

Had something happened? It had been nearly an hour since Darius left, and he wasn't exactly the type to let frivolous distractions keep him from his work. A sudden thought cut through her calm. The Jenkins brothers. Wellborn had promised to report to her at once if he spotted any strange men around Oakhaven. But if Darius got to him first . . .

Her stomach lurched. She needed to get back to the house. Check on the dagger. Question Wellborn.

Nicole clutched the logbook to her breast and hurried out of the workshop. Intent on her destination, she failed to notice Darius until he strode out of the barn directly into her path.

"Mr. Thornton!" Somehow she managed to reverse her momentum before ramming into him. "I . . . ah . . . didn't see you there." A movement to her left drew her gaze. Dread nestled in her stomach. "And . . . Wellborn. What have the two of you been up to?" She forced a laugh from her throat, trying to emulate a teasing tone, but she doubted the strangled sound fooled anyone.

The butler, who was busy extracting a piece of straw from where it had caught near his cuff as he exited the barn, jerked his head up at her comment. The trace of guilt that flashed in his eyes set fire to her belly.

They'd been discussing her. For certain.

Nicole bristled. They had no right to scheme behind her back. Who knew what inadvertent damage they could have caused, no matter how well intentioned their investigation? At once, the mystery behind Wellborn's repeated town visits cleared like a freshly washed windowpane. He'd been asking around about her. On Darius's order.

Heaven help her. Her anonymity was as good as gone.

"What have you done?" She whispered the accusation, the sound barely audible as she pierced Darius with her stare.

He reached for her, but she stepped away, sure if he touched her she'd fall apart. "Nicole, I . . ." His words died when she shook her head at him.

"You can't always fix everything, Darius. Sometimes tinkering just breaks a machine further, leaving it beyond repair."

"But it's only through tinkering that improvements can be made, that new solutions can be found that would have remained undiscovered otherwise." Darius closed the distance between them, his eyes imploring. Her heart thudded in her chest, wanting to believe him, wanting to clasp the hope he offered. "I can help you, Nicole," he said. "Please, let me."

It would be so easy to shift her responsibilities onto his broad, capable shoulders. To let him take charge for a while. Yet, even if he could protect her from the Jenkins brothers, that didn't change the fact that she'd still have to search out a husband in New Orleans — a man other than Darius — to fulfill her pledge to her father.

She couldn't let him risk his life, the lives of his staff, the life of young Jacob, to help her when the ultimate outcome would not change. If anyone suffered on her behalf, it would haunt her the rest of her days, knowing she could have prevented it if only she hadn't weakened and accepted his offer.

"You're a good man, Darius Thornton," she said, lifting her hand to his cheek. His eyes closed a moment as he leaned into her touch. When they opened, they glowed with an intensity that wrenched her heart. Emotion clogged her throat, but she forced the rest of what had to be said past her lips. "I believe in you. In your work with the boilers. In your scientific mind. You will accomplish great things. I know it in my heart. Never forfeit your passion, Darius."

It was good-bye, and they both knew it. His slate-blue eyes blazed denial, but she turned from him before he could give it voice. Not caring that she would appear the coward, she grabbed up her skirts and ran to the house.

Darius lunged after the fleeing Nicole, but a firm hand grabbed his arm from behind.

"Let her go, Mr. Thornton," Wellborn cautioned.

"No." He'd never let her go. He couldn't.

"Not forever. Just for now."

Darius flung an impatient glare over his shoulder. "*Now* may be all I have." She'd had a look of finality about her as she'd spoken that terrified him. She was leaving Oakhaven. Leaving *him.*

"It's too late in the day for her to go anywhere," Wellborn stated in an annoyingly logical tone as he released Darius's arm. "You have time to convince her. Time to woo her over to your way of thinking. And that will be easier to accomplish once you've both calmed and you no longer have an audience looking on."

Darius pressed his lips together to keep the growl building inside his chest from erupting. Wellborn was right — if Nicole felt backed into a corner, she'd run. Shoot, she was already running. Stubborn, infuriating woman.

If he pursued her now, his attempts at

persuasion might become a tad too adamant for her taste. She'd likely accuse him of bullying her, and his chances of talking sense into her thick head would go right out the window.

"Why do women have to be so complicated, Wellborn?" he grumbled.

The butler shook his head, a hint of a smile lighting his eyes. "I suppose God wanted to ensure we never grew bored, sir."

Darius exhaled a long breath and concentrated on relaxing his muscles. He'd give her time to compose herself, but he wasn't so generous as to leave her to her own devices for long. She might not believe the two of them had a chance to find their way out of this crazy maze together, but until she wore another man's ring on her finger, he planned to do everything in his power to change her mind. Nicole Renard was a woman worth fighting for, even if he had to fight the woman herself.

"Have Mrs. Wellborn set the dining room for two tonight," he ordered the butler, "and see that we're not disturbed."

His man bowed. "As you wish."

"Oh, and . . . make sure she shows up, will you?" Darius glanced sideways at Wellborn, embarrassed by the request. "I have a feeling she won't be particularly eager for my company this evening."

"I'll set Flora to the task. That woman can talk a cat into a bath before the poor creature even grasps what has happened. She'll get your young lady to the dining room. Have no fear."

Darius nodded, a portion of the weight lifting from his shoulders. He scrubbed a hand over his whiskered chin. Perhaps a shave was in order. Hard to properly woo a woman when he looked like a disreputable brigand.

"Do you suppose you'd have time to press a pair of trousers for me, Wellborn?"

The staid fellow's face split into a grin as wide as the Mississippi. "I'll see to it at once, sir. A shirt, as well. Your suit coat should be in adequate condition. I brushed it out after services last Sunday. Would you like your shoes polished?"

"Whoa." Darius held up a hand, a sudden urge to laugh welling up inside him. "Let's not get carried away, man. We wouldn't want the woman fainting dead away from shock, now would we? I need her conscious. Hard to have a productive conversation otherwise."

And that's what scared him. He was lousy with words on a good day, and today was far from a good day. Not when the woman he loved was almost certainly packing up her trunk this very moment, determined to leave him. If a few social trappings could give aid to his cause, he'd swaddle himself gladly.

The most critical conversation of his life awaited him in the dining room tonight. He needed every possible weapon at his disposal.

CHAPTER 26

"So it's true, then."

Startled, Nicole glanced up from where she knelt at the foot of the bed clutching a folded petticoat and spied Mrs. Wellborn standing in the doorway. Twisting her face away from the housekeeper's view, she quickly brushed away the still-moist tear tracks from her cheeks and gave a little sniff to clear her nose before speaking.

"Mrs. Wellborn. I-I didn't hear you knock." How long had the woman been standing there? And how long had Nicole been holding her petticoat while staring blankly into her trunk?

Nicole tossed the undergarment into the open trunk and snatched up the rolls of stockings piled on the floor near her hip. "Did you need something?"

Mrs. Wellborn strolled into the room, seated herself on the end of Nicole's bed, and flipped the trunk lid closed. "What I need is for you to come to your senses, dearie. You can't just leave us. You're part of the family."

"I can't stay." She grabbed the latch and started to reopen the trunk, but Mrs. Wellborn slid right off the mattress and landed her plump derrière squarely atop the lid. The woman had the balance and aim of an acrobat.

"Why not?" The housekeeper clasped her hands to her knees and stared Nicole straight in the eye. "Has the master done something to scare you off? I thought you'd learned to see past his brusque ways. He might be a bit rough around the edges, but his heart is as golden as they come. You know it's true."

Nicole scrambled to her feet and pivoted away from Mrs. Wellborn's scrutiny. Must *everyone* stick their nose into her business? She made a grand show of opening and closing bureau drawers as if double-checking to make sure she hadn't left anything behind, but she knew the drawers were empty, and somehow staring into their vacant depths only made her heart ache worse.

"Mr. Thornton has done nothing wrong. It's just time for me to leave. That's all. It can't be helped." She quietly clicked the last hollow drawer closed. "I enjoyed my time here very much," she said, finally turning to face the housekeeper, "and I will miss you all dreadfully." A tiny sob caught in her throat, and in an instant, Mrs. Wellborn was on her feet, tugging Nicole into a warm embrace.

"Forgive an old woman her nattering." The housekeeper's voice trembled with tears of her own as she squeezed Nicole tight. "Here I was thinking only of my own grief without giving a care for yours." She stepped back and stroked the curls framing Nicole's face, just like Nicole's own mother did whenever her daughter needed soothing. "Deep down, I knew you didn't want to leave us, but when Arthur told me the news, all I could think about was finding a way to make you change your mind."

"You have no idea how badly I want to change my mind." The words burst through the widening fissure of her heart, no longer able to be contained. "I want to stay more than you can imagine. And that wanting is tearing me apart." Nicole lifted her chin and forced a deep breath into her lungs. "Unfortunately, I have obligations — responsibilities that can't be ignored. My family is depending on me. I can't let them down."

"Of course not," Mrs. Wellborn clucked

as she rubbed Nicole's arms. "If you've given your word, there's no question but that you must keep it."

The defensive starch Nicole had been using to keep herself upright crumbled, and she collapsed back into the housekeeper's arms. "Thank you for understanding," she said, hugging the woman close for a moment before stepping back. "I wish the men could be as accepting. It would make everything so much easier."

Mrs. Wellborn pulled a handkerchief from her apron pocket and dabbed at her own eyes. "It's not in their nature. They don't see this situation as a certainty that must be accepted. No, in their minds, it is a challenge thrown down like a gauntlet. Accepting equals defeat, so they won't hear of it. Instead, they'll do everything in their power to find a solution. Men are fixers, dear. Just one more thing we women have to . . . accept." The housekeeper winked, and Nicole felt her mouth twitch into something that felt amazingly like a smile.

"I suppose it's not fair of me to admire that quality in Mr. Thornton when he's busy solving boiler safety issues only to berate him for it when he employs the same strategies on me."

Mrs. Wellborn smiled and patted Nicole's

shoulder. "Love would be boring if it were simple, dearie."

"Oh, but I —"

The housekeeper took hold of her arm before she could find the right words to protest. "What you need after all that packing is a nice hot meal to fill those empty spaces inside you." Mrs. Wellborn tugged her gently toward the door. "Everything looks so much brighter with a full belly. I have a place already set for you in the dining room."

"No, I — !" Nicole jerked to a halt. "I mean, no, thank you. It's sweet of you to go to all that trouble, but I'd rather spend my last night at Oakhaven with you and Jacob in the kitchen."

The only reason Mrs. Wellborn would try to direct her to the dining room was if Darius was there. Waiting for her.

"Arthur took Jacob down to the pond to sail the raft the two of them made this afternoon. You should have seen them huddled over the table, tying all those sticks and twigs together with bits of twine." The housekeeper chattered gaily, as if nothing were amiss, all while gently maneuvering Nicole down the hall. "You would have thought Arthur was as much a boy as young Jacob. They gobbled their supper and disappeared out the back door faster than a pair of lightning bugs."

She shook her head, laughter bubbling forth as she nudged an elbow into Nicole's ribs. "I haven't seen Arthur move that fast in ages. I think I'll just grab a couple biscuits and meet them down by the water. See what kind of fun they get up to."

Unable to escape the frothy yet forceful current that was Mrs. Wellborn without being rude, Nicole floated helplessly along beside the housekeeper, the dining room door drawing ever nearer. Her stomach clenched with an odd mixture of dread and anticipation. No matter how painful it would be to spend time alone with Darius, she couldn't deny that deep down she wanted to do exactly that.

One last meal together. What harm could it do?

Mrs. Wellborn drew to a halt, clasped Nicole's hand, and patted the back of it with motherly affection.

"Let him say his piece, dearie. That's all he asks. Then, if you still want to leave, my Arthur will drive you to town in the morning. The master has already given instructions regarding your wages, so you need not worry on that score. You won't be leaving us penniless. Of course, we hope you won't be leaving us at all, but be assured that we'll support your decision, whatever it may be."

"Thank you." Nicole blinked back the moisture gathering in her eyes. This wasn't the time for tears. She'd handle this final meeting with dignity and decorum, just as her mother had taught her. No hysterics. No angry demands. Just patience and kindness. She'd been absorbed in her own disappointment long enough. Time to focus on someone else for a change.

Darius. This entire situation was even more unfair to him than to her. At least she'd known about her promise to her father from the beginning. Darius hadn't. He'd simply given a needy woman employment, involved her in his mission, and given her the respect she'd always craved. Whatever he planned to say, she would listen. She owed him that much. No matter how much it hurt, she'd listen to his arguments, his strategies, his pleas.

And if he didn't plead? Nicole swallowed hard, the possibility scalding her as it went down. Well, if he didn't plead, she'd listen to that, too. She'd accept his good-bye with graciousness and be thankful for his good sense. It would be cruel for her to expect him to grow old pining for her, unable to move on even after she married another.

Much better for him to put her behind him like one of his unsuccessful boiler experiments and move forward. Just because her own heart would always belong to him didn't mean she wanted him to suffer the same misery.

Only . . . a small, wretched part of her wished exactly that, God forgive her.

After giving Nicole's hand a final pat, Mrs. Wellborn released her grip and smiled that cheery smile of hers that never failed to brighten Nicole's spirits. "Food's on the sideboard. Venison stew. One of Mrs. Graham's specialties." She winked. "Go on, now. Don't keep the master waiting."

Nicole's lips curved. Trust Mrs. Wellborn to sum it all up in such beautiful simplicity. This was dinner, not the guillotine. With a nod of her head, Nicole took hold of the door handle and let herself into the room.

Movement drew her gaze at once to where Darius paced along the wall to her right. At her entrance, however, he spun to face her.

"Nicole." Her name floated from his tongue like a leaf drifting to earth from an autumn tree. He crossed to her in four strides and took up her hand. "Thank you for coming."

His fingers trembled slightly, as if he were nervous. Darius — the no-nonsense man who faced down exploding boilers without batting an eye — was nervous. For some odd reason the notion served to calm her own rioting emotions.

A smile tugged at the corner of her mouth. "I heard venison stew was one of Mrs. Graham's specialties. I couldn't turn down the opportunity to taste it."

"Then taste it you shall." Darius grinned as he placed her hand onto his arm and led her to the sideboard.

Nicole breathed in the scent of his shaving soap as he uncovered the tureen and ladled a serving of stew into a fine china bowl. He'd shaved. For her. Blinking, she took in the rest of his attire. Pressed trousers, suit coat. He even wore a starched cravat at his throat. He hated cravats. But he'd worn one. For her.

And what was she wearing? The same rumpled gown she'd worn among the machinery in the workshop and crawled about her room in while packing. She hadn't even taken the time to check her hair or wash her face. *Good heavens.* Were her eyes still red and puffy from her crying?

Darius placed her food on the table by one of the filled water goblets, then held out her chair.

Nicole thanked him with a nod of her

head. "I'm sorry I didn't dress for dinner," she said as she slid into her seat. "I was busy pa—" She broke off, not wanting to mar the peace with talk of leaving. "Time got away from me," she said instead.

Darius's thumb drew a line between her shoulder blades as he stepped from behind her chair, sending tiny shivers down her back. "You look lovely."

Bless the man. The warmth in his blue eyes actually had her believing him. Then he smiled — a private, intimate sort of smile that set her heart to pounding against her ribs.

She glanced away and seized her napkin, taking refuge in the ordinariness of shaking out the linen square and placing it in her lap.

Really. Where did an obsessive scientist learn to smile like that? It was grossly unfair. Had he been a practiced rake, she'd know how to rebuff him. But how did one defend against a man who actually meant all that was implied in such a look? Tenderness. Affection. Love?

Thankfully, Darius moved back to the sideboard to dish up his own meal, affording Nicole a moment to recover.

When he returned, he claimed his seat at the head of the table, directly to her left. He bowed his head and offered a brief prayer of thanks, then picked up his spoon and began eating. Nicole followed his example, cultivating the careful truce between them. She commented on the rich flavor of the stew. Darius told her about an article he'd read on the possible benefits of employing larger or more numerous safety valves on boilers.

The familiar pattern set her at ease to the point that she found herself suggesting ideas for experimentation, which soon had Darius shoving aside empty dishes in order to work out scenarios upon the table linen using knives and forks and a leftover biscuit or two as off-scale representations. Nicole watched him work, amazed as always at the quickness of his mind and his ability to work through several possibilities at once.

She reached into her hair and tugged a pin free from behind her ear. "What if we added a second valve" — she laid the pin across the tines of one of the forks — "here?"

Darius looked over at her, the gleam of appreciation in his eyes making her a tad light-headed.

Before she could retreat, Darius captured the hand she'd used to place the hairpin and brought it to his lips. With his other arm, he latched on to the seat of her chair and dragged her to his side.

"You know, it used to take me days to make the kind of progress on my own that the two of us just completed in an hour."

His husky voice made her quiver as his soft breath fanned over her cheek. His face was so close to hers, she could nearly feel his lips move against her skin as he spoke. "You make me better, Nicole. Not just a better scientist, but a better man. You challenge me, encourage me, and help me dream of the future instead of the past."

His lips did brush against her temple then, and Nicole's breath caught. Her eyes slid closed. She didn't want to think about the future *or* the past. All she wanted was now.

"Do you remember what you told me this afternoon?" Darius's deep tones rolled through her like a sip of hot tea on a cold day, warmth permeating her insides in a long, slow wave.

Remember? No, she didn't remember. She could barely think at all.

"You told me never to forfeit my passion."

Yes, his passion. His boilers. He could achieve so much good with his work. Save so many lives. She was proud to have played even a small role in that work. She thought to tell him so, but as her eyelids lifted, his gaze locked on to hers with such force everything else evaporated from her mind.

"I make you a solemn oath here and now never to forfeit my passion." He cupped her face with both hands. Nicole scanned his features, trying desperately to puzzle out what he was saying, even while her heart thundered the answer. "*You* are my passion, Nicole. And I refuse to forfeit you."

His mouth claimed hers, sealing his pledge. Nicole whimpered slightly but thrust her fingers into his hair and held on for all she was worth. His kiss was hard, possessive, and carried the taste of desperation. A taste she recognized well. She answered in kind, giving him her love, her wishes, her dreams. For this moment there was no future, no past, only now. Beautiful, glorious *now.*

All too soon, however, Darius gentled his kiss. The desperation eased and sanity returned. He dropped tiny kisses along her jaw, then her forehead, then a final touch to her mouth.

"Two minds are better than one," he murmured in her ear. "In scientific inquiries . . . and in more personal matters."

Nicole stiffened slightly. He must have felt it, for he reached for her hands and held them as if afraid she would bolt.

"It's time to let me in, sweetheart. Let me help. We can solve this dilemma together. I know we can."

But she'd already solved it. Just not in the way Darius approved. Truth be told, she didn't approve of it, either, but there was no other option. Was there? Could there possibly be something she'd overlooked?

She twisted toward him, wanting so badly to hope — to believe they *could* find a way. "I-I don't know where to begin."

Darius smiled and stroked the back of her hands with his thumbs. "Why don't you start with the Lafitte Dagger?"

CHAPTER 27

Darius studied the woman at his side, attuned to her every movement, her every breath. How could he not be after that kiss? The way she'd buried her fingers in his hair and clung to him had left him shaking. Yet it wasn't her reaction to his kiss, delightful as it had been, that had him focusing on her now. No, it was her reaction to his words.

"You know about the dagger?" Her voice wobbled slightly. Nicole looked down and shifted in her seat, but she didn't tug her hands free of his grasp. A good sign. He hoped.

"And Renard Shipping." Darius caressed her fingers as he spoke, trying to ease the tension that radiated down her arms and into her hands. "You are the daughter of Anton Renard, aren't you?"

He'd been careful to keep his tone void of accusation, but still her head jerked up like a frightened hare, her eyes darting about as if looking for a way to flee. Darius gripped her hand tighter, unwilling to allow her escape.

"Your name doesn't matter, sweetheart. I know the truth of who you are. You are kind and loyal and more intelligent than most of the men of my acquaintance. You are the woman I love."

"Darius, I . . ." Moisture shimmered in her eyes, giving them a luster that only made them more beautiful. "I never wanted to deceive you. But it was as much for your protection as mine. I couldn't risk someone discovering my identity and bringing trouble to your door. You don't understand what these men are capable of."

"Carson Jenkins and his sons, you mean?"

She reared back. "You know about the Jenkins family?"

Darius eased his grip on her fingers and resumed stroking the soft skin along the back of her hand in what he hoped were soothing motions. "Only that they are your father's main competitors for the Galveston shipping routes and that there is some bad blood between them and the Renards. Something having to do with the Lafitte Dagger."

He paused, his gaze meeting hers. "You

have it with you, don't you, Nicole? It's the gift you mentioned as part of your dowry, the one intended for your . . . the heir." Darius couldn't bring himself to say *husband.* Not when referring to a man other than himself. "That's why Jenkins sent men after you. He wants the dagger."

She nodded shakily. "He's been after it for years. Claims the dagger belongs to his family, not the Renards." Her chin jutted out, and a spark of fire ignited in her golden-brown eyes.

"Jenkins insists that the dagger was bequeathed to his uncle back in '21 when Lafitte left Galveston. He says my grandfather stole it. Complete nonsense, of course. His uncle never even served with Lafitte. He was simply one of the many smugglers who took advantage of the loose slaving regulations to make his fortune. My grandfather, on the other hand, worked for Lafitte at the Maison Rouge headquarters and saved the pirate's life when he took a bullet meant for him. It was for that act of courage that the dagger was bestowed."

In her agitation, Nicole pulled her hands free from his grasp and fisted them. "Unfortunately, there is no documented evidence beyond a note in a doctor's log regarding Henri Renard's injury to dispute Jenkins's claim. But it's more proof than Jenkins has ever produced to substantiate *his* story. Which is probably why the sheriff in Galveston never chose to get involved. He figured that since the dagger was in the Renard family's possession and no one could offer proof that it didn't belong there, he had no cause to interfere. Made Jenkins furious, especially since the man is related to him by marriage. Through a cousin, I think."

Darius digested the information as she rattled it off, his jaw growing increasingly tight. Feuds rarely fostered an atmosphere conducive to reason. High emotion, adamant demands, the rationalizing of unjustifiable actions as acceptable if they produced the desired results. It was fanaticism. And Nicole was stuck right in the middle of it.

"He envies my father's success," she continued, frown lines creasing her brow as she spoke of Jenkins. "He's convinced that success would be his if *he* possessed the dagger. The fool. Hard work, integrity, and intelligent investing earned my family their success, not some mystical dagger."

"If that's how your family feels, why not just give the thing to Jenkins and be done with it?"

Nicole fidgeted in her chair, her dark

lashes shuttering her eyes as her attention fell once again to her lap. "Because not everyone in my family feels that way."

Her chest heaved as she sighed, her breath so heavy he could feel the movement of air across the backs of his hands where they rested on his knees. Darius held his tongue, some instinct warning him from probing further until she was ready.

Finally her eyes met his. "I know it sounds crazy, but my father treasures the Lafitte Dagger above all other possessions. It's more than a family heirloom — it's the Renard family legacy. Irreplaceable. Meant to be handed down from father to son for generations. Giving it up to Jenkins would be tantamount to . . . to forfeiting every penny of the inheritance my father has built up for his heir — giving it to his enemy."

She bit her lip and turned her face away. He reached for her hand, gently pried open the fisted fingers, and slid his palm next to hers. Intertwining their fingers, he lifted her knuckles to his mouth and kissed them. *You're not alone,* he tried to communicate each time his lips touched her skin. *Let me share your burden.*

Her face swiveled back, her gaze fixed on their interlocked hands still raised to his mouth.

"I-I don't know if Papa truly believes his business will suffer if the dagger is lost to him or if it's just a matter of family pride, but I can't disappoint him, Darius. I can't. It's bad enough that I'm not the son he would have preferred. If I cost him the dagger, too —"

"Hush." Darius cupped his free hand around her cheek, forcing her to look at him. "No one's going to cost him anything. I promise. All right?"

She hesitated, then gave a tiny nod.

"Good." Darius had to make a conscious effort to keep his touch gentle, a challenge when he wanted nothing more than to pound his fists into the table in front of him. How could a man be blessed with a daughter like Nicole and not find her sufficient? Fiercely loyal, keenly intelligent, poised, beautiful, and brave enough to face down exploding boilers. In his estimation, the woman was worth more than any pirate dagger, no matter who had owned it.

Slowly, he dropped his hand from her face and leaned back in his chair. He maintained his hold on her hand, however, as he delicately pressed for more information. "So, what transpired to escalate things?" Her fingers twitched against his. "I assume something must have frightened your father quite severely or he never would have conceived this scheme to secure an heir." What sane man would put his only child, his daughter, in danger if he wasn't desperate?

"Will and Fletcher Jenkins broke into our home, held my parents at gunpoint, and threatened my mother."

The stark simplicity of the statement slammed into him like an unmanned sailing boom swinging into his midsection without warning. He felt as if all the air had suddenly pushed from his lungs.

"And these are the men who are looking for you?" No wonder she carried a knife strapped to her thigh. But what good would one little knife do against two grown men armed with pistols? He prayed God would never let them find out.

"They threatened to break my mother's fingers if Papa didn't tell them where the dagger was."

Break her mother's . . . Darius clenched his jaw. He wasn't letting those fiends anywhere near Nicole. He'd ship her off to New York if he had to. His parents would take her in, protect her. But she'd never leave her father, and her father would never leave his company. Which left Nicole in harm's way.

"That's why I took the dagger," Nicole explained, only making Darius's jaw clench tighter. "I had to lure Jenkins away from my family. They weren't safe even in their own home. Papa argued it was too dangerous —"

"And he was right!" Had the woman no care for her personal safety? "Blast it all, Nicole. You shouldn't take such risks."

She stiffened, her brow arching. "Because I'm a woman? Incapable of looking after myself?"

Darius arched his own brow and glared. "No, you wretched girl. Because you're worth more than a thousand blasted pirate daggers, and no one in their right mind would wager a fifty-dollar gold piece for the chance to win back a nickel."

Her eyes widened as if the idea had never even occurred to her, which only served to aggravate him further. Darius shoved to his feet and paced the length of the table.

Maybe he could buy Jenkins off, bribe him to move his business to another port. But what guarantee would he have that the man wouldn't simply take his money and then resume his hunt for the dagger?

A lawman. Darius seized upon the idea. The sheriff in Galveston might not have been willing to get involved in the feud, but that didn't mean they couldn't approach another. Especially if an innocent woman's life was at stake. Sheriff Davenport in Liberty seemed an honorable man. He'd handled the situation with Jacob in a reasonable manner and didn't seem the type to shy away from a fight.

"We should notify the sheriff in Liberty." Darius squared his shoulders, readying himself for her protests.

"Is he trustworthy?"

It wasn't a protest, Darius supposed, but judging by her frown and the way she was shrinking back against her chair, it didn't qualify as agreement, either. "I haven't had much interaction with him — outside of the situation with Jacob — but the man is well respected. I heard Sam Houston himself recommended him for office."

Her brows peaked. "Well, that's certainly a ringing endorsement. It's just . . ." She sighed. "The more people who know about my connection to the dagger, the greater the chance that information will slip out and lead Will and Fletcher to Oakhaven. I don't want to risk anyone here getting caught in the middle. If the Wellborns or Jacob were hurt because of me . . ."

Her words fell away, and she suddenly surged to her feet before him, her right palm pressing against the wall of his chest. "Darius, if something happened to *you,* I'd never forgive myself."

His heart rate tripled. He looked into her face, memorizing every curve and line, each facet eminently precious. "How do you think I'd feel if something happened to you?" he rasped out. "Nicole, I love you, and I swear that I will do everything in my power to keep you safe."

"Oh, Darius." The whispered words skimmed over his skin in a feather-soft touch, raising his senses into keen awareness. Her eyes glowed with a sad, inner light even as her lips curved upward. "I love you, too. I tried so hard not to, knowing I had to move on to New Orleans in order to fulfill my vow to my father. But it was no use. My heart ignored all logic and dove right into your hands."

"And I'll never let it go," he declared fiercely as he grabbed her shoulders and pulled her into his arms. "Never."

He kissed her then the way he'd wanted to earlier. Fully. Branding her as his. Leaving no room for her to consider any other man as her husband. He'd restrained himself before, not wanting to frighten her, not sure of her feelings, wanting only to convince her of his. Yet now, with her declaration of love still vibrating in his ears, he released the reins and kissed her with all the passion raging in his heart.

His hands moved over her back, searching out the small arch above her waist, then using it to pull her closer to him. Her palms came up between them, burrowing beneath his suit coat. The feel of her fingers splayed against his chest sent tremors through him. His lips left her mouth to trail tiny kisses along her neck, and when her head fell back to give him better access, a tiny growl of satisfaction rumbled in his throat.

She was his. Nicole belonged to him and he to her. God had brought them together, and he'd see to it that no man put them asunder. No New Orleans dandy, no Jenkins brigand, not even her father.

He worked his way back up her throat to her jaw, her ear, then reclaimed her mouth. Her lips met his with equal fervor. Her hands climbed from his chest to his shoulders and then to his nape. Her fingers tangled in his hair, sending a wave of delightful shivers coursing through him. She rose up on tiptoes, and her hands came around to frame his face, holding him to her as she returned his kiss.

As if he would pull away, he mentally scoffed.

But then he did, for he felt her withdraw, felt her mouth ease back, her body shift as her feet returned fully to the floor. Thankfully she didn't try to step out of his arms. He doubted he would have been physically capable of releasing her at that particular moment. Instead, she rested the side of her face against his chest. The top of her head brushed the edge of his jaw, and the perfection of the fit made him smile. He closed his eyes, his ragged breaths loud in his ears as he stroked her arm.

"Oh, Darius," she said, despair lacing her passion-thickened voice. "What are we going to do?"

His arms tightened around her. "We're going to find our way through this. Together." He leaned his cheek against her hair. "Tomorrow I'll visit with Sheriff Davenport. I'll not mention the dagger, only that two men are hunting for you. If you'll write out their names and descriptions, I'll pass that information along so he can be on the lookout for them. He won't be able to arrest them based on suspicion, but he can send word to us if they are spotted. Maybe even send a deputy or two to help defend against them."

"But what about my father? We can't just hide out here forever. He's not long for this world, Darius. He needs an heir."

"I'll be his blasted heir." Darius winced. That hadn't come out the way he'd intended. "What I meant to say is that I can escort you home, present myself to your father, and officially ask for your hand. I may not have the extensive connections in New Orleans that your father might wish, but I know shipping. I can be an asset."

Nicole lifted her head from his chest and glared up at him. "Don't you think I haven't already thought of that? But he needs someone who can take the helm right away, not a businessman used to keeping books, no matter how quick a study you are. Just because you understand the mechanics of steam engines and can take apart boilers with your eyes closed, that doesn't mean you know shipping."

"Maybe *that* doesn't," Darius snapped, irritated that she'd so easily discounted him as heir material, "but the fact that I've spent the last six years overseeing the business interests of one of the largest steamship lines in the country certainly does. Ever heard of King Star Shipping?"

CHAPTER 28

"King Star Shipping?" Nicole staggered backward, out of his arms. *Good heavens.* They practically owned the Atlantic, with regular lines to Liverpool and Plymouth in England, Havana in the Caribbean, as well as hitting all the major American coastal ports like Boston, Baltimore, Charleston, and New Orleans. "I-I think I traveled home from school on a King Star vessel. The *Starlight.*"

"That would be Captain Sanders's ship," Darius replied, the name rolling off his tongue with such ease it made Nicole dizzy. She grasped the back of her chair to steady herself. "Fine little coastal steamer," he continued. "If I remember correctly, we fitted her out with a new screw propeller system before I . . . took a sabbatical."

"That's right," she murmured more to herself than him. Her body seemed to have gone numb, even the words falling from her lips echoed in the room as if someone else were speaking them. "I remember questioning Captain Sanders about it so I could inform Papa of the innovation when I returned home. He'd been fascinated by it."

Darius crossed his arms over his chest and jutted his jaw a bit. "I researched that project myself and made the recommendation to my father. We plan to install the new propellers on a rotating schedule until the entire fleet is rigged out. Increases engine efficiency and speed output."

Nicole dragged her gaze up from the floor, desperate to make this new information fit with what she'd assumed she knew about Darius, needing to witness the truth in his eyes. "I thought you were just a man of business, tallying numbers in ledgers, overseeing investments for your father. You said as much," she accused.

"And it was true," he said, his voice irritatingly calm while she felt as if one of his boilers had just exploded here in the dining room. "It just so happens that my father owns a shipping company, and when I'm not balancing the accounts, I'm perusing the latest mechanical journals and deciding which improvements are worth incorporating into our vessels. Why did you think I made that fateful trip to New Orleans in the first place?"

"You said you were meeting with investors. I just assumed it had something to do with expanding into the growing western markets."

"Well, you were half right. We *were* considering expansion — from ocean steamers to riverboats. The river transport industry is quite lucrative, you know." His mouth turned up at the corners then, and the shock that had immobilized her began to thaw.

"I do know," she said, unable to resist returning his smile with a small one of her own. "My father has amassed a considerable fortune shipping immigrants and supplies in and cotton out."

Darius uncrossed his arms and closed the short distance separating them. The heat in his eyes scalded away the last vestiges of her numbness. "Something tells me you'd be a great asset to a man who suddenly found himself inheriting such a company."

Nicole's mouth went dry. Could it really be so simple? Could Darius truly be her father's heir and her husband? *Please, Lord. Let it be so.* "Would you really consider taking on such an inheritance?" she asked, her heart pounding in her chest as his hands alit on her shoulders and traced feather-soft lines down to her wrists. "You'd be away from your family — permanently. And your experiments." She swallowed. Hard. "Darius, there'd be no time for them any longer. You'd have to . . . to give them up." The words seemed to slice her open as they left her tongue.

The two things he valued most, his family and his work. . . . How could she ask him to sacrifice both? No. It wasn't fair. He shouldn't have to —

"We'll figure it out, Nicole." His caress traveled down to her fingers. He gently pried them from the chair back, then lifted them to his mouth and pressed a kiss upon the sensitive skin just below her knuckles. "I'll have twice as many steamships at my disposal as I do now and can easily run the two of us up to New York several times a year to visit my family. And they, no doubt, will visit us, as well. It will work out, sweetheart."

He kissed her hand again, and she actually started to believe him. Yet one barrier blocked her full acceptance. "What of your boilers, Darius?" She forced the question past the thickness in her throat. "They are your life's work."

He shrugged. "I seem to remember you calling them a self-imposed penance."

She shook her head, intending to argue, but he shushed her with his words.

"I know. It wasn't the work so much as my obsession with it. It's past time to regain some balance." He stroked the line of her jaw with the back of one finger, such tenderness and love imbued in the touch, Nicole could barely breathe. Her eyes locked on his as tiny tremors danced along her skin. "I'll find a new way to contribute to the effort," he vowed. "Perhaps one that doesn't even require explosions." A smile crinkled his eyes.

How could he look at her like that, with so much love and not one speck of regret? She searched for the tiniest glimmer of resentment or bitterness but found nothing. Nothing! The last of her stone-heavy doubt dissipated, leaving her as buoyant as a cork bobbing light and free atop the waves.

"I love you, Darius Thornton." Nicole wrapped both arms about his neck. Her gaze captured his and held it fast. "I choose you. As my husband *and* as my father's heir. If you'll have me."

He leaned close, his lips a mere breath away from hers. "Darling, I'd thought you'd never ask."

Nicole spent the following morning *un*packing everything she'd stored away in her trunk the previous afternoon. When the last handkerchief lay neatly in the dresser across from her bed, she closed the empty trunk with a satisfying *thump*. Unable to help herself, she spun in a circle, her skirts belling out around her as laughter bubbled to the surface. She wasn't going anywhere. Not without Darius.

Imagine — a son of King Star Shipping right under her nose this entire time. Nicole shook her head. Only God could have managed such a feat. He'd led her to the one man who could fulfill not only her father's needs but her own heart's desire. And she'd nearly run away from him. The thought sobered her, but only for a moment. No use dwelling on what almost happened when current events were so much more pleasant.

Humming a cheerful little ditty she'd learned to play on the piano at Miss Rochester's Academy, she waltzed out of her room and down the hall. She spied Mrs. Wellborn polishing the banister at the base of the staircase and immediately swept the older lady up into her dance, leading her around the narrow entryway with more enthusiasm than grace.

"What in the world?" the housekeeper exclaimed before dissolving into giggles.

The two of them twirled and sashayed until Nicole finally released her partner near the dining room door.

"Sorry," Nicole managed between heavy breaths, her tone not in the least repentant. "I couldn't resist."

Mrs. Wellborn waved her dust rag as if it were a debutante's fine lace handkerchief, then curtsied. "It was my pleasure." Her eye twinkled with shared mirth. "I'm so happy you're staying, miss. We all are. Why, I haven't seen the master smile this much since he was a boy. It wouldn't surprise me if he were to come home from town today with something more than just a deputy to watch the road. I seem to recall the mercantile in Liberty having a decent selection of . . . Well, let's just say I've happened to notice the jewelry case a time or two when I've been shopping for foodstuffs. It's not as fine as the offerings in New York, of course, but a man who is eager to stake a claim could do worse."

Heat rose to Nicole's cheeks. "Mrs. Wellborn, I have absolutely no expectations along those lines." At least she hadn't until the housekeeper planted the thought in her brain. Now she could scarcely think of anything else. What would it be like to wear his engagement ring? To proclaim to all the world that she belonged to him? Her stomach quivered. Delightful. That's what it would be like. Utterly delightful.

But they had more pressing matters to contend with today, and she refused to be disappointed when he returned without a ring, as he certainly would. Besides, she'd proposed to him, not the other way around.

There was nothing the least bit conventional about their engagement. She wasn't even completely sure they were engaged. Nothing would be official until Darius presented himself to her father and asked for her hand, so imagining what kind of ring he might possibly bring back from Liberty was a pointless exercise.

"I'm sure he won't take the time for something as frivolous as shopping. You know how focused he gets when he sets his mind to a task. He'll deliver my descriptions of the Jenkins brothers to the sheriff, then do his best to enlist the man's aid. Once he's accomplished that, he'll return home."

Mrs. Wellborn shrugged. "You may be correct. The master does tend to be a bit, well, oblivious to things not immediately within the purview of whatever his current undertaking might be. Somehow I think you'll be able to break him of that habit, though."

The housekeeper's eyes sparkled with a teasing gleam. "Or at least drag him back to reality every now and again. He seems conspicuously unable to ignore you, my dear. A rather handy trait for a wife."

Mrs. Wellborn winked, sending another annoying flash of heat down Nicole's neck. "And may I just say that Arthur and I could not be happier. It will be a joy to welcome you to the Thornton family, miss."

Eyes stinging at the kind gesture, Nicole impulsively wrapped the plump woman in a quick hug. "Thank you. I promise to take good care of him."

"I know you will, dearie. I know." The housekeeper patted Nicole's back a moment before stepping away. "Now, get on with you and let an old lady finish up her duties. Luncheon will be here in less than an hour, and I've a table to set and a cook to assist. Mrs. Graham will grow sulky if I'm not there to help lay out the food."

Nicole laughed as the older woman vigorously shooed her toward the front door. "All right," she said. "I'll go find Jacob and see if he would like another lesson."

She should probably work on Darius's logbooks some more, but she doubted she'd be able to concentrate on the sedentary task. Energy thrummed through her, making her feel like a thoroughbred straining at the reins, needing desperately to run. Unpacking her trunk had kept her hands busy for a time, but even that had failed to dispel the restlessness inside her. She needed physical exertion, and Jacob, with his boundless supply of liveliness, was just the one to provide it.

"The lad's stacking firewood in the woodshed," Mrs. Wellborn called after her, "or at least he was the last time I peeked out the upstairs window. Arthur didn't want him underfoot while he started boxing up the master's machinery in the workshop. Mr. Thornton is quite particular about his machinery."

That was stating it mildly. Nicole grinned. She couldn't help it. Everything about Darius seemed to make her grin this morning. The way he'd eaten his eggs at breakfast, tucking into them as if afraid they'd somehow escape his fork. The way he'd spared a moment to kiss her cheek before riding off to meet with Sheriff Davenport. And now even his obsessive scientific nature had her smiling.

Love did rather strange things to a woman.

Leaving the house, Nicole traipsed past the barn to the woodshed. A pile of logs stood in front of the lean-to, the split wood lying about in disarray. "Jacob?"

It wasn't like the boy to leave a job before he was finished. Of course, he might have just run off to the privy for a moment. She might as well take over his chore until he returned. That way they'd be able to continue their knife lessons all the sooner.

Cheered by the thought, she bent to collect a log. Once she had three pieces in her arms, she crossed to the shed and began placing them atop the shortest of the stacks.

"Miss Nicole?" A thready voice called her name from behind the shed. "Help me. I've . . . I've hurt myself."

"Jacob?" Nicole dropped the last piece of wood without a care and rushed around the shed. "Where are you?" Her eyes scanned the landscape, but the trees were thicker here, impeding her view.

"Please. Hurry." Tears sounded in the boy's voice, and Nicole's heart gave a painful twinge.

"I'm coming, Jacob." She picked up her pace, jogging into the trees.

Please, God, let him be all right. Visions of the rattlesnake that had nearly struck him the day they'd met sent desperation surging through her. Had he fallen? Broken a leg? She had to find him!

Turning in the direction his voice had

come from, she rounded a large oak. She caught a glimpse of Jacob lying on the ground in front of a tree to her right.

"Jacob!" She lunged forward, focused solely on reaching him.

That's why she didn't hear the rustle until it was too late. Strong arms captured her from behind, wrapping around her middle like iron bands and lifting her feet from the ground. She tried to scream, but a hand clamped over her mouth, and she soon found herself struggling to draw sufficient breath. She kicked and flailed anyway, then in a moment of blessed clarity remembered the trick her father had taught her.

Letting her body go limp, she dropped her chin forward. The instant she felt her assailant relax, she drove her head backward with all the force she could muster. Her skull slammed into his chin with a satisfying *crack*. The man cursed and shoved her away. Nicole stumbled but managed to keep her feet. She reached for her blade, but the deadly sound of a gun being cocked stilled her hand.

"Quit beating up on my brother, Nicki, or I'll shoot the kid."

CHAPTER 29

Nicole released her skirt hem and slowly straightened, taking care to position her arms nonthreateningly at her sides. Fletcher Jenkins gripped Jacob by the upper arm, his hold so rough and high, the boy's left foot dangled above the ground as he tried to lean away from the pistol barrel pointed at his head.

"Afraid you couldn't take me on your own, Fletcher?" Disdain dripped from her tongue as she glared at the older Jenkins. "Is that why you're using the boy as a shield? Only a coward would hide behind a boy to face a woman."

"Shut up!" Fletcher yanked his gun hand around and leveled the pistol at her chest.

Good. That was exactly where she wanted it. Away from Jacob. She lifted her chin for good measure and even managed a haughty little sniff. The lines around Fletcher's mouth tightened as his eyes narrowed.

"Uppity wench," he spat. "You high-and-mighty Renards think you run the world, but you're no better than us. Soon as we get the dagger, you'll see how worthless you really are. Too bad your daddy won't live long enough to see his company run aground."

The barb hit home. Nicole flinched. It wasn't more than a squeezing of her eyes, but the scum recognized it. His mouth twisted into a gloating sneer. Back in control, he slid his attention to a point beyond her shoulder.

"You done babying that scratch yet, Will?"

"Scratch? She loosened two of my teeth with that steel head of hers. I can't get my lip to stop bleeding."

"You deserve worse for letting a woman best you."

"Yeah? Well, next time *you* sneak up on her while I hold the gun on the kid. See how good you do against the little she cat."

While the brothers bickered, Nicole met Jacob's gaze. She saw the apology in his eyes, yet determination glowed there, as well. The boy was a survivor. He'd be a capable ally. One the Jenkins brothers would underestimate even more thoroughly than they did her.

Be ready, she mouthed. He nodded.

Keeping an eye on Fletcher's gun, Nicole shifted her weight forward. Distracted by his brother's whining, his arm drooped, the pistol's barrel now pointing somewhere below her waist. If he would just drop it a little lower . . .

"Hey!" The gun snapped back into place. *Drat.*

She stared at Fletcher, unwilling to let him think he'd won any sort of victory. But then a calculating gleam flared in his dark eyes, and his gun arm slowly bent until . . .

No, no, no!

Fletcher pushed the pistol's barrel so firmly against Jacob's temple the boy's head angled downward until his ear nearly touched his shoulder. A sick certainty churned in her stomach. He wouldn't be taunted away from Jacob this time. He'd found her weakness, and the scurvy dog knew it.

"Now, *Miss Renard.*" Fletcher sneered as he pronounced her name. "You have five minutes to fetch me the Lafitte Dagger."

"That's barely enough time to get to the house and back," Nicole exclaimed, heart thumping painfully in her breast as her mind raced. How would she leave word for Darius? Even if she ran, she'd not have time to do more than grab the dagger and return.

Could she fetch Wellborn from the workshop on her way in? "I need at least ten. You can't expect me to leave something so valuable just lying around. I buried it. It will take —"

"You have five minutes. No more." Without taking his eyes from hers, Fletcher reached into his vest pocket, extracted a watch, and flipped open the lid with his thumb. "For every minute you're late, I'll have Will break one of the lad's fingers. He's been pouting about not getting to try his hand with your mother, so I'm sure he wouldn't complain about you taking your time. Would you, Will?"

"Nope."

Nicole lunged forward, desperate to protect Jacob somehow, but Will snaked an arm out and caught her around the elbow, yanking her to a halt. She jerked against his hold. "You monster! He's just a child."

Fletcher shrugged. Shrugged! As if Jacob's fate was no more important to him than that of a spider beneath his boot. "If you don't want the boy harmed, I suggest you hurry."

"It's all right, miss." Jacob looked up at her, his young face stoic and brave. "I'll be fine." He straightened his head a bit against the pistol and rolled his shoulders back. Nicole wanted to scoop him up, hug him close, and keep him safe. She'd brought this trouble here, and God help her, she intended to ensure it left no permanent mark.

Straightening her own posture, she ceased struggling against Will's greater strength and nodded to Fletcher. "I'll go. But if you lay a hand on that boy before I get back, I'll deliver Lafitte's dagger directly into your black heart."

"And I'll put a bullet in his brain." Fletcher tilted his head as if weighing the two outcomes. "Last time I checked, bullets still fly faster than knives. Better a busted finger than a hole in the head — don't you think?"

Will chuckled at his brother's obscene comment, and Nicole fought the urge to ram her skull into his mouth a second time. The pig.

"Oh, and plan on Will watching you from the tree line," Fletcher said. "If you happen to call out to the old man clanging things about in the shed, I'll know. And the boy will pay." Fletcher's eyes hardened as if he'd suddenly grown weary of their sparring. "No detours. No tricks. No trouble. Just fetch the dagger and get back. Understand?"

Nicole gritted her teeth and nodded. As long as Fletcher had Jacob, her hands were bound as surely as if manacles encircled her wrists. Yet her loyalty to her father bound her, too. Could she really hand over the Lafitte Dagger to a Jenkins? Or could she save Jacob without it?

"You have five minutes, Nicki."

Dear Lord. Only five minutes. She'd never figure it out in time.

"Go!"

God help me!

Will released her arm, and Nicole shot through the trees. Skirts hiked up to her knees, she ran like a deer fleeing a hunter. A muffled curse echoed behind her followed by plodding footsteps as Will struggled to keep up. Yet once she hit the clearing, all thoughts of Will evaporated. All that mattered was the dagger and Jacob, and how in the world she could possibly save them both.

She pounded up the back porch steps and flew past a bewildered Mrs. Graham. The instant the door slammed behind her, she screamed the housekeeper's name and scrambled down the short hall to her room. Tearing at the floorboard, her bosom heaved as her lungs gasped for air. She had just pulled the red velvet bag containing the Lafitte Dagger from beneath the floor when Mrs. Wellborn burst around the corner, hand to her chest.

"What's happened?" The woman's eyes stretched wide with terror. Nicole didn't have time to soothe.

She yanked open the gathered cord at the top of the velvet bag, dumped the dagger onto her bed, hoisted her skirts, and slid her own blade free of its garter sheath. Once she had her own throwing knife secured in the red velvet bag, she snatched the strip of toweling hanging from the washstand and wound it around the Lafitte Dagger, covering the tooled silver scabbard and jeweled hilt.

"I don't have time to explain," Nicole said, taking hold of Mrs. Wellborn's arm, "so please listen. Give this dagger to Darius the minute he returns." She thrust the towel-wrapped package at the housekeeper who accepted it with trembling hands. "He must keep it safe. It's essential." She waited for Mrs. Wellborn's nod before she released the dagger fully into her keeping. "Tell him to take it to Galveston, to my father. I'll meet him there."

Hearing the imagined tick of Fletcher's watch in her head, Nicole grabbed up the velvet decoy and pushed past the housekeeper. She couldn't spare a single second. She had to get back to the woodshed.

"Wait!" Mrs. Wellborn called after her. "If

you're not traveling with the master to Galveston, where will you be?"

Nicole didn't stop to explain. She couldn't. She had no answers.

Darius would be upset — of that she had no doubt. But what choice did she have? None with Jacob caught in the middle. She had to get the boy away from Fletcher and somehow manage to lead the Jenkins brothers away from Oakhaven. It was the only way to protect the people she loved. At the same time, it would grant Darius the head start he needed to get the true dagger back to Galveston. She'd outwitted the Jenkins brothers before. God willing she'd do so again.

Passing the shed, Nicole ran into the trees. Lungs throbbing, she refused to slow, even when a rustle to her left told her Will was nearby. She didn't stop until she reached the edge of the small clearing where Fletcher held Jacob.

Her gaze scoured the boy. No tears. No mangled fingers or cradled hands. Just a wonderfully mutinous expression that screamed his readiness to teach these scallywags a lesson. *Thank you, God!*

Fletcher's gun remained pointed at Jacob's temple, however, cautioning Nicole that the danger hadn't yet passed.

"I'm impressed," Fletcher drawled, snapping his watch lid closed and sliding the timepiece into his pocket. "Back with time to spare. How fortunate for our young friend here."

She forced her breathing to slow, not wanting to appear winded. Fletcher had always been a bully. If he sensed fear or weakness, he pounced. Her best chance was to brazen through with a strong front. He'd already determined her vulnerability where Jacob was concerned, yet his lust for the dagger made him equally susceptible. They were evenly matched.

Fletcher's attention flickered down to the red bag gripped in her right hand. Hunger lit his eyes. "Bring it to me."

At his barked demand, a horse whickered and stomped somewhere to Nicole's right. A flash of gray winked in her peripheral vision, but she kept her attention on the man before her. "Release Jacob first."

"I don't think so. Will," Fletcher called, "get the dagger from her. Smack her one if you have to."

Nicole glanced swiftly to her left. Will was striding out of the trees, rubbing the jaw she'd knocked, apparently eager to dole out some retribution. He was bigger, stronger. He'd wrest the false dagger from her in short order. Her only chance was to beat him to the punch.

"You want the dagger?" Heart thumping wildly, she took off running — directly toward Fletcher. "Here!"

With all her might, she flung the red velvet bag over Fletcher's head. He gasped, and his gaze followed the arc of the dagger. He released Jacob to make a grab for the bag, but it was too high. The instant Fletcher's hold loosened, Jacob yanked free and ran for Nicole. She waved him away. "Run for the house, Jacob. Don't stop. Not for anything. Go!" She was already veering to the right, praying she could get to the horses before Fletcher realized the knife was a fake.

Jacob disobeyed, following her path for a few steps, matching her frantic pace. "Here!" He reached behind his back and pulled out the blade Darius had bought him. His untucked shirt had kept it hidden. He tossed it. She snatched it from the air and nodded her thanks. His eyes met hers for a split second before he swerved away and sprinted toward the house. His feet flew so fast, she knew neither Jenkins would catch him.

An outraged shout hit the air. Nicole ran faster.

"Get her!" Their footsteps pounded the

earth, growing louder, closer.

Please, God. The horse. I need the horse!
Nicole searched the narrow pines blocking her view. She should have reached the gray by now. Hadn't he been behind that trio of trees? Then a movement to the left registered at the corner of her vision. The horse! She'd overshot.

Correcting her path, Nicole tucked Jacob's blade into the waistband of her skirt. The gray wasn't alone. A second horse stood pawing the ground, a black with white stockings. More high-strung than the gray, the black danced sideways when she approached and shook its head. The gray watched her but didn't shy.

"Easy," Nicole said, taking up the reins that dangled in front of the ground-tied gray. "We're just going to take a little ride." Thrusting her foot into the stirrup, Nicole swung up onto the gray's back, then reached over to slap the black hard on the rump. "Yah!"

The skittish horse reared and took off through the trees. Will burst through at the same time, running straight for her. Nicole kicked out her left foot and caught him square in the jaw. Again. He spun away from her, howling.

"Nicole!"

She turned at Fletcher's scream, her horse rearing slightly. Fletcher staggered around the trees. He was closing in. Nicole grabbed Jacob's knife from her waistband and held it aloft. Fletcher wasn't so close yet that he'd be able to note any details about the blade. "The Lafitte Dagger belongs to the Renards. I'll never hand it over!"

Hatred scorched his features. "Then I'll take it from you!" Fletcher raised his gun.

Nicole spun away and kicked the gray into motion. A shot rang out. Pain slashed across her arm. The gray surged forward, spooked. Nicole leaned low over the horse's neck and held on for dear life as the horse thundered through the trees. The too-long stirrups flapped unused against the animal's sides, urging him to greater speed. The reckless pace would kill them both if the horse stepped in a hole or stumbled over an exposed tree root, but Nicole made no effort to rein him in. Every stride they took away from Oakhaven meant increased protection for those she loved and safety for the dagger her father cherished.

CHAPTER 30

Darius urged his bay to an easy canter as he turned down the road leading to Oakhaven, eager to see Nicole and tell her what he'd accomplished that morning. He'd put the sheriff on alert, hired three locals to serve as guards over the next few days while he made preparations to leave for Galveston, and stopped by the bank to withdraw travel funds. But it was the revealing of his last errand that he most anticipated.

The small gold band pressed against the top of his thigh from inside his pocket as he rode, the edges of the red stone at its center rubbing slightly with each stride of the horse. Their engagement might not be official until he'd had a chance to speak with her father, but Darius intended to have his ring on her finger well before that, not so much as a mark of possession as a symbol of promise.

Nicole had chosen him last night —

chosen him above all the wealthy dandies of New Orleans, the polished gentlemen of Boston, even above her father's original stipulations, and the thrill of that moment still sent shivers over his skin whenever he recalled her declaration. He wanted to gift her with the same pledge, to make it clear that he'd chosen her, as well, above all others.

When he'd seen the delicate gold band in the mercantile's jewelry case, its sides looped into matching hearts that cradled a glimmering garnet at the center, it had spoken to him. The crimson stone reminded him of the red dress she'd worn when they first met, and how, even then, he couldn't get the swish of her skirts out of his mind. The stone lay caught between the hearts of the two men who loved her, her father and her soon-to-be husband. He longed for her to see that each of those hearts supported her, that they would work together to shelter her. She didn't have to choose one over the other.

Oakhaven came into view, and in an instant, all thoughts of the ring in his trouser pocket vanished from Darius's mind. What was Wellborn doing pacing the yard with that ancient rifle of his? A tickle of unease raised the hairs on the back of Darius's neck. He was about to call out his question when the butler spun toward him, shouldered the rifle, and aimed the barrel directly at his chest.

"Whoa, man." Darius slowed his mount and held up his hands. "What's going on?"

The rifle dropped instantly. "Oh, thank heavens you're back, sir!" Wellborn jogged across the short distance separating them.

Darius frowned. Wellborn never ran. Ever.

Dread knotted Darius's gut as he swung down from the saddle. Nicole was all right, he told himself. She had to be. He'd only been gone a couple of hours. Something must have spooked the household — that's all. Wellborn had always been the cautious sort. Perhaps he'd caught a stranger wandering about and decided to stand guard as a precaution. Yet Darius couldn't fully buy in to that idea. Wellborn might be cautious, but he was no alarmist. It would take something of magnitude to shake him to this degree.

And shaking he was, like loose rivets on a boiler at full steam. Despite his quaking hands, the butler grabbed the reins from Darius and shoved him toward the house. "Hurry, lad. Flora and the boy will fill you in on the details. I'll get you a fresh mount."

A fresh mount?

Nicole. All his clever rationalizations died a quick, brutal death. Somehow the Jenkins brothers had gotten their hands on his woman.

Darius sprinted to the porch, took the stairs in a single leap, and barreled through the front door. "Nicole!" He shouted her name as he made for the kitchen, praying she'd answer and prove his instincts wrong. She didn't.

Before he could push open the kitchen door, Mrs. Wellborn bustled out of the study and held the door wide. "In here, Mr. Thornton."

He strode across the hall and entered the study to find Jacob pushing up from a chair to face him. The boy's eyes were red-rimmed and tear tracks stained his cheeks, but he squared his shoulders like a miniature soldier and looked Darius in the eye. Well, almost. His gaze got stuck somewhere around the third button on Darius's shirtfront.

"It's my fault, sir. I wasn't payin' attention. I was stacking firewood at the shed, and they snuck up behind me. They used me to bait the trap."

Darius lowered himself to one knee in front of the boy. "You're not the one to blame here, Jake. They are. Now, tell me

387

what happened." Blood pumped furiously through his veins as his worst fears were confirmed, but he forced a layer of calm into his voice. "What happened to Miss Renard?"

"She came looking for me. They forced me to call out to her, to pretend I was hurt. I didn't want to, but the dark-haired one pointed a gun at my head and said he could shoot me instead, if I wanted, and just grab her when she came to see what happened."

Darius bit back a growl. Must be Fletcher. Nicole had called him the meaner of the two. "You did right. How many men were there? Do you remember?"

Jake nodded. "Just two. Fletcher and Will they called each other. Will tried to grab Miss Nicole from behind when she came looking for me in the trees, but she fought him off. Smashed him good with the back of her head. Clanged into his mouth hard enough to draw blood and send him staggerin' sideways like a bowlegged drunk."

The boy's lips curved into an almost-grin at that, and Darius couldn't deny a certain satisfaction at the knowledge that Nicole had inflicted her fair share of damage. His fists itched to finish the job.

"She stood up to 'em," Jake continued, pride lacing his tone. "Made Fletcher so mad he pointed his gun at her instead of me. I thought about reaching for my knife then, jabbin' it into his leg and making a run for it, but I was afraid he might shoot her. Then, before she left to fetch the dagger, he pointed the gun back at my head, and I was too scared to try for the blade."

And thank God for that, Darius thought. He didn't want to contemplate what could have happened to the youngster if he had tried to stop the Jenkins brothers on his own. "What happened next?"

"He gave her five minutes to fetch the dagger," Jacob recounted, "and warned her not to call Wellborn for help. Said he'd start breaking my fingers if she took longer."

Just like her mother. Darius clenched his jaw so tightly his teeth ached. Blast that Jenkins scum. Nicole must have been beside herself.

"She made it back in four," Jacob boasted. "I knew she would. She's nearly as fast as me."

Yes, she was, but even so, Darius didn't feel good about the two-to-one odds she faced. The fact that she wasn't here now meant something had gone wrong. Had Fletcher and Will taken her hostage? Surely Wellborn would have searched the area when Jacob escaped to ascertain if she'd been shot or wounded. But why would the Jenkins boys take her hostage if she turned over the dagger? They'd have no use for her. Unless they were afraid she'd go to the law. How far would they go to silence her?

Icy chills crawled up Darius's arms and nested in his heart, wrapping freezing tendrils about it until even drawing a breath became a painful endeavor. His head dropped forward and his eyes slid closed. He'd get her back somehow. He had to. She was his life.

"Fletcher told her to give him the dagger," Jacob continued, his voice bringing Darius's head back up. "She told him to let me go first. Then Fletcher told Will to just grab her and take the dagger away. Told him to hit her if he needed to."

Darius forced a shaky breath into his lungs. He had to ask. "Did Will hurt her?"

"Nope." Jacob crossed his arms over his chest as he shook his head. "She was too fast for him. She ran right at Fletcher and threw the little bag high into the air. It sailed over his head. They both went after it like trouts going after a worm."

Thank God.

"So why isn't she here?" Darius glanced about the room, as if she might be hiding behind the sofa or the curtains. "Did they catch her before she could make it back to the house with you?"

"No, sir. She never ran for the house. She ran for the horses."

Darius scowled. "What horses?"

"Must've belonged to Fletcher and Will." Jacob gave a small shrug. "All I know is that she sent me to the house while she ran for the horses. I slipped her my knife before I left, so she's got some protection. You should probably still go after her, though." Jacob's mouth pulled into a disconcerted line. "I heard a gunshot as I ran. Wellborn didn't find anything, so she's probably all right, but Fletcher'll be real mad when he catches up with her."

That was stating it mildly.

Darius placed a hand on the boy's shoulder. "I'll find her, Jake. I just need to grab a few things" — like his hunting rifle, pistol, and sailor's knife — "and then I'll go after her."

"Pardon me, Mr. Thornton," a feminine voice cut in, "but that's not what Miss Renard wishes you to do."

Darius pushed to his feet and turned to frown at his housekeeper. "Of course she'd want me to go after her. Do you think she'd prefer I leave her at the mercy of those villains chasing her?" There wasn't a chance in the world he'd be doing that, even if Nicole *was* crazy enough to wish it of him.

Mrs. Wellborn stepped closer, her hands trembling as she held out what looked like a wadded towel. "She told me I was to give you this as soon as you arrived home." A sick certainty churned in his belly as he stared at the toweling. He could swear it changed shape before his eyes, from an ambiguous wad to something more elongated and defined. The housekeeper pushed the object into his hands. The metallic weight of it dragged on his soul like an anchor.

The muscle in his jaw throbbed as he tore open the wrapping. A fine-tooled silver scabbard slightly tarnished with age lay in his palm, taunting him. The jewels encrusted in the handle winked up at him like a gambler who'd just revealed his winning hand.

Blast it, Nicole! When would the woman get it through that thick skull of hers that safeguarding her life was more important than safeguarding that troublesome dagger? He closed his fist over the Lafitte blade until the metal gouged his hand through the toweling. He wanted to hurl the infernal thing against the wall, then pull it from its sheath and smash it against the stone hearth until the blade snapped off and all the gems turned to dust.

"She said it was essential that you take it to Galveston, to her father. Those were her very words," the housekeeper prodded. "Essential. Said she'd meet you there."

If she survived the Jenkins brothers. Which was doubtful. If they hadn't caught her already, they'd be hot on her trail. Her tricking them out of the dagger would only make them more vengeful and relentless. If they were willing to break fingers before, what would they do once truly provoked?

Darius shuddered.

"I don't care what she said," he bit out. "I'm *not* taking the blasted thing to Galveston. I'm taking it with me and chasing down that headstrong, too-brave-for-her-own-good fiancée of mine before she gets herself killed." He waved the blade under Mrs. Wellborn's nose, her startled expression stoking his ire. "And if I have to forfeit her precious pirate dagger to ransom her back, by all that's holy, that's exactly what I'll do. Nothing you or she can say about it will change my mind. Do I make myself clear?"

Instead of nodding obsequiously and scurrying away like a sensible servant, his housekeeper placed one hand on her ample hip and, with the other, pushed the decorative dagger out of her face and back toward him. "Well, thank heaven one of you has the sense God gave a goose. I agreed to pass on her message, but I gave no promise to endorse it. That child is so concerned with protecting everyone else, she gives no heed to protecting herself."

Mrs. Wellborn clasped Darius's forearm and looked up at him as if fully confident in his ability to rectify the situation. "Bring her back to us, Mr. Thornton. She's family."

Yes, she was, and he wasn't about to let the Jenkins boys take her away from him.

"Jacob." He pivoted around to the boy, who stood watching him with wide eyes. "Meet me at the woodshed in five minutes. I'll need you to show me where to look for tracks."

Mrs. Wellborn scuttled out of his way as he marched toward the study door. "I've got a bag of food and another of medical supplies packed and ready to go," she called to his back. "I'll have Jacob bring those out to you, sir."

He flung a thank-you over his shoulder and kept moving, trying not to think of the need Nicole might have for the medical supplies, or the gunshot Jake reported, or the cruelty of the men pursuing her. To contemplate the possibilities would only drive him mad, so he focused solely on the immediate problem — finding her trail and tracking her down. He'd deal with the rest when it presented itself. For now he would hunt.

And pray.

CHAPTER 31

Nicole glanced behind her for what must have been the hundredth time as she rode into Liberty. Still no sign of the Jenkins brothers. She knew they were out there, could feel them gradually closing the gap. Her best chance was to procure immediate transportation out of Liberty and away from Galveston, clearing the path for Darius.

Had Mrs. Wellborn given him the dagger yet? The sooner he made his way to Galveston the better. She didn't know how long she could hold off Will and Fletcher. Hopefully long enough.

As she passed the buildings at the outskirts of town, Nicole slowed the gray to a trot, not wanting to attract undue attention. A woman riding astride was enough to draw comment on its own should someone happen to note her arrival. A woman galloping recklessly through the streets would turn every head in town.

The gray shook his head and snorted as he adjusted to the new pace, pricking his ears when he realized Nicole was directing him toward the livery. "Almost there," she cooed, reaching down to pat his slightly lathered neck. "You did well, my friend."

A man in worn trousers met her at the livery doors, a straw dangling from between his teeth at the side of his mouth. He raised an eyebrow at her as he came forward to take the reins. "You ain't the feller I rented this horse to. Whatcha doin' with ol' Sam?"

Nicole shifted in the saddle to slide her left foot into the stirrup before swinging down to the ground. There was no use hoping the man hadn't noticed the ill-adjusted tack. His sharp eyes seemed to take in everything about her.

"I borrowed this fine creature from a Mr. Fletcher Jenkins after running into him up near Oakhaven." She flashed her most brilliant smile, gratified when the grizzled man blinked up at her and lost his toothy grip on the straw. "I'm sure Mr. Jenkins will be along shortly to settle his account. Your Sam's a real goer," she said as she brushed past the stableman. "He deserves a good rubdown after our little excursion." Then, with a wave of her hand, she escaped across the street before the man's suspicious nature reasserted itself. The fewer questions she had to answer the better.

Reaching into her skirt pocket, Nicole felt for the small woven bag she'd stashed there earlier. Her fingers brushed against a metal clasp. It had survived the wild ride to town. Her coin purse was woefully thin — she'd never collected her wages from Darius, after all — but she'd grabbed it from her trunk while switching out the daggers, knowing she'd need every resource she could gather if she was to have any chance at escaping the Jenkins brothers. She wouldn't be able to travel far, but if she could find a place to hide, she could send a message to Darius down in Galveston, and he or Wellborn could come after her.

It wasn't much of a plan, she admitted to herself as she ducked into the stage office, but it was all she had at the moment.

"Hello, miss." A jovial young man jumped up from where he'd been sitting behind a desk and hurried to meet her at the counter. She appreciated his ready grin even though it made little headway in soothing her frazzled nerves. "How can I help you to-day?"

"I need to purchase a ticket." She pulled out her purse and dumped the contents onto the counter, cupping her hands around the coins to keep any from rolling onto the floor. She quickly tallied the amount. Four dollars and thirty-two cents. At a dime a mile she'd not have enough to get to Beaumont or Houston, but surely there were smaller communities along the way.

The clerk's smile slipped a bit as he eyed the paltry assortment of silver on the counter. "And where are you . . . ah . . . hoping to travel?"

Nicole met his gaze without flinching. "The *where* isn't important. What matters is the *when*. What time does your next stage leave?"

"Not until morning, miss."

Morning? The tiny piece of calm she'd managed to grasp ripped from her like a bandage from a wound, leaving blood to flow freely. Fletcher would run her to ground for sure. She couldn't allow that, for not only would she be caught, but Darius could be compromised, as well. No, she had to lead the Jenkins brothers away from Liberty. Now.

"You don't understand," she said, trying to sound firm yet hearing a hysterical edge creep into her voice. "I have to leave today. Within the hour at the very latest." She could rent a horse, but the livery would be the first place Fletcher went once he arrived in town. If she ran into him there, it'd be all over. "Do you have horses to let here?"

The clerk's eyes softened in sympathy. "I'm afraid not. They're for company use only. The livery has —"

She cut him off with an impatient shake of her head. There had to be something else. She didn't have enough funds for steamboat passage upriver, but what if . . .

"What about a freight company?" She grabbed the clerk's arm, desperation surging through her. "Do you know of any wagons making afternoon runs today?"

The clerk gently disengaged his arm from her grip and straightened his sleeve. "Holsten usually makes a run up to the logging camp fifteen miles northeast of here on Fridays, but that's no place for a lady to . . ."

Nicole stopped listening and started stuffing coins back into her purse. Right now she wasn't a lady — she was a decoy. And if a logging camp was her only destination option, she'd take it and thank God for his provision.

"Thank you for your help." She shot him a quick smile and hurried away.

"But, miss! I don't think you should —"

Nicole closed the door, cutting off the man's well-meaning warning. No time to second-guess. She had to find the freight office.

Checking over her shoulder toward the edge of town and praising God when she found the road empty of irate Jenkinses, she turned down the street that led to the river. Too much urgency pumped through her veins to keep her steps modulated, so she half walked, half trotted toward the wharf and ignored the curious stares of those milling about the market square. Let them notice. She needed to leave a few bread crumbs for Fletcher to follow anyway. Just as long as he didn't find them before she got good and away.

She recalled seeing a sign for Holsten's Freight Service when she'd first arrived in town, so she headed directly for the rough-hewn log building situated near the ferry landing. A bearded man in a fringed, buckskin jacket was tying down a canvas tarpaulin over a wagon bed. Sharp corners and flat edges creased the canvas where crates had been loaded at the front of the wagon, but the canvas hung relaxed near the back.

Did she dare?

Nicole swept her gaze up and down the street. No one seemed to be paying her any mind. She could make it if she timed it right. But what if the driver caught her?

How could she possibly explain? Biting her lip, she debated, watching as the freighter walked around his wagon for a final inspection. When his back was toward her, she crept closer, moving into position. Then, when he climbed up onto the bench and reached for the reins, she sprinted forward, hoisted herself over the closed tailgate, and ducked beneath the tarpaulin just as the wheels began to roll.

The wagon lurched forward before she had a chance to anchor herself. The motion flattened her and threw her roughly against the side of the wagon bed. She threw out her hands to brace herself, and her elbow collided with one of the crates. Burning pain shot up her right arm. Only then did she remember the sting she'd felt as she rode away from Oakhaven. Curling onto her left side in a protective ball, she reached around and gently probed the sore place on her arm. The fabric of her sleeve felt ragged, torn. Steeling herself, she ran her fingers over the flesh exposed by the hole in her sleeve. When her fingertips made contact, her breath hissed, and her eyes squeezed shut.

Cakes of dried blood flaked away as she explored. Fletcher's bullet must have grazed her. The crease in her upper arm ached like the very devil now that she was aware of it, but it didn't seem too serious, thank the Lord. She eased her hand away and forced a few deep breaths in order to calm her racing heart. She was safe. For now. Hidden beneath the canvas, she'd not have to worry about Fletcher spotting her should they pass him on the road. And once they reached the logging camp, she would gladly pay the freighter for his transport. Surely he wouldn't be too upset as long as none of his goods were damaged. Right?

Pillowing her head with her good arm, Nicole settled into the rocking rhythm of the wagon and prayed that Darius would meet with much less excitement on his journey.

"Why is everyone so all-fired interested in that brown-haired gal? Females is nothin' but trouble, and that one's no different. Mark my words."

Darius trailed after the liveryman as he paced from the barn entrance to the hay wagon that had just arrived. The fellow snatched up a straw from the mound of fresh hay in the wagon bed, jabbed it into his mouth, and took up the hayfork.

"So someone else asked after the young lady?" Darius prodded. He'd been pretty sure two sets of tracks had left Oakhaven land, the second set pressed deeper into the earth, as if the horse was carrying a greater weight. No footprints had been in evidence more than fifty yards outside the ambush site, so Darius concluded the Jenkins brothers had ridden double in their pursuit of Nicole, giving her the advantage. But once the tracks hit the road, there were too many other hoofprints to decipher anything specific. He'd simply had to assume they'd all come to town. Realizing that they'd need to acquire a second horse, he'd made the livery his first stop.

The stable hand pushed past Darius, moved to the back of the hay wagon, and began to unlatch the tailgate. "Look, mister. I got work to do. I can't stand around jawin' all day."

The man's callous attitude ignited Darius's already simmering temper. He marched over to the man in three angry strides, yanked the hayfork out of his hand, and tossed it aside. "That woman you so casually dismissed is my affianced bride," he ground out between clenched teeth, his face thrust so close to the other man's he could see individual whiskers poking from the fellow's chin. "The men following her mean her harm. If you don't tell me everything you know about the situation this very moment, I'm liable to loosen your tongue with my fist. Now start talking."

The man glared up at him in defiance, not intimidated in the slightest. Yet he reached up and slowly pulled the straw from his mouth. "You sure the gal's in trouble?" His mouth turned down in a frown. "She was all smiles when she rode in. Course ol' Sam was lathered like he'd been ridden hard, and the stirrups were dangling far too long for a gal her size. I thought something was off about that."

Darius stepped back, thankful that physical force would not be necessary. "Where did she go after she left the livery?"

"To the stage office. Though I don't know what good that'd do her if she were trying to outrun those other two fellers. Next stage won't leave until tomorrow."

"How much of a lead did she have on them?"

" 'Bout thirty minutes. Them other fellas rented fresh horses and set out after her. Said she was their sister, always playing practical jokes on them like stealing their horse and leaving them to ride double. Seemed odd, but wasn't my place to question, so I just pointed them in her direction and told them to take better care of my stock. Didn't like the idea of them running the poor beasts ragged."

Darius nodded and crossed over to the livery wall to retrieve the hayfork. With a dip of his chin, he handed it back to the man. "Thanks for your help."

The man accepted the fork — and apparently the unspoken apology, as well. "I had me a gal once. If I had chased after her like you're doing instead of letting her run off with my best friend, maybe I'd still have her." He stuck his straw back into his mouth and turned toward the waiting hay wagon. "Hope you find her."

"I won't stop until I do," Darius murmured, then set off for the stage office.

CHAPTER 32

The crack of a gunshot jerked Nicole from her doze. Her heels kicked out in reaction, ramming into the side of the wagon. Pain ricocheted up to her knees. A small moan escaped before she could smother the sound. Not that anyone would hear her over the creaking wagon wheels, harness, and . . . were those pounding hoofbeats approaching from *behind*?

The Jenkins brothers. It had to be. Heart skittering and slamming around in her chest like a bird desperate to escape a glass box, it was all she could do to remain hidden when every instinct demanded she throw back the tarpaulin and see what was going on.

"Hold freighter!" Fletcher's voice. Nicole bit her lip. "Hold, or the next bullet goes into your back."

"Whoa, there," the man called to his team, his voice surprisingly steady as the wagon began to slow. Hoofbeats pounded by on either side, drawing Nicole a vivid picture of the brothers surrounding the unsuspecting freighter.

"Reach for that shotgun, and you'll regret it," Will said.

Nicole clenched her eyes shut, praying the man would obey. Two against one were unlikely odds in any case, but she'd prodded the bear with Fletcher earlier. No doubt he'd nursed his rage over the last hours. It'd take little to push him over the edge.

"I don't take kindly to threats, son." The freighter's gravelly voice resonated with authority and impatience. Nicole could imagine him staring Will down with narrowed eyes until the younger man looked away. "I got no goods worth stealing unless you're craving new saw blades and coffee stores. Why don't you two fellas take your little raidin' party elsewhere."

"We don't want your goods, old man," Fletcher growled. "We want the woman."

"Woman?" The freighter gave a hoot of laughter. "Shoot, boy. I ain't had a female ride a route with me since the time Clarabelle Stanton paid me twenty dollars to let her ride along to Dever's Woods to meet the feller who'd been courtin' her through letters. Poor cowpoke took one look at the six-foot woman and ran screamin' for cover, leaving me to cart the snifflin', sobbin' creature all the way back to Liberty. No twenty dollars is worth that grief, I promise ya. I don't know who set you after me, but you got the wrong freighter."

"You're the only freighter that fits the timeline. I got witnesses who remember seeing her in your vicinity before you left and none who recall seeing her afterward."

"You callin' me a liar, boy?" A chunk of granite would have been softer than that voice.

Nicole winced. Why couldn't Fletcher just take the man at his word and let him pass? If the two powder kegs kept throwing sparks at each other, it wouldn't be long before something exploded.

"Maybe she stowed away."

"Impossible," the freighter insisted. "I tied down the canvas myself and pulled out immediately after. I never left the shipment unsupervised."

"Then you won't mind if we take a look." She could hear the snide smile in his tone, and her pulse rate tripled. She was done for.

Out of options, Nicole crawled to the end of the wagon bed. She peeked from beneath the tarpaulin and released a breath when she saw the thick stand of cypress trees lining the road. She had to go now, before they started searching the wagon. It was her only chance. Pulse throbbing, she counted to three, flung herself over the tailgate, and sprinted for the trees. Fletcher's shout echoed all too soon behind her. Hoofbeats followed.

If she could just get closer to the river, where the woods grew thicker, his mount wouldn't be able to maneuver and she'd have the advantage. She could find cover. Hide herself.

But even as the thought formed in her mind, she recognized the flaw. Fletcher was too close. There'd be no escape this time.

She ran in a zigzag pattern, darting around trees in the hopes of slowing him down, yet still he gained on her. The rush of the river grew louder, urging her not to give up. She ran faster. Harder. Her shoes churned the soft earth.

Hooves echoed directly behind her. Closer. Beside her. Nicole caught a glimpse of Fletcher's looming shape in the edge of her vision. She cried out and dodged sideways, but not far enough. A heavy weight slammed into her back, knocking her to the ground.

"No!" She clawed at the earth, desperate

to free herself. Tight arms locked around her legs, trapping her. Pinning her. She tried to kick him, but his weight wouldn't budge. Then something hard connected with the side of her head, stealing her senses. Her vision blurred and her ears rang. She ceased her struggles, hoping the stillness would help reestablish her equilibrium. Unfortunately, Fletcher took that as a sign of capitulation and roughly hauled her to her feet.

"I'm in no mood for any more of your games, Nicki," Fletcher all but spat at her. "You'll hand over the dagger or I'll . . . What's this?" The arm he'd wrapped around her middle brushed against the knife she'd stashed in her waistband. Grabbing the handle, he yanked it free. "Another fake? Where's the real one? Where's the Lafitte Dagger?"

He shook her so hard she feared she'd lose consciousness. She almost wished she would, just to escape his bellowing.

"Answer me!" He flung Jacob's dagger aside. The boy's treasured blade clattered against a nearby tree trunk before falling into the dirt and pine needles littering the ground.

A moment later the flat of Fletcher's hand slapped her face. Stinging pain ripped through her. Tears seeped from the corners of her eyes.

"Where is the dagger?" he roared.

"I don't have it!" Whipping her head around to face Fletcher, she glared at him defiantly. "Did you think I would be so foolish as to carry it with me when I knew you'd follow?"

"Liar!" His hands roved over her body, searching for the dagger.

Nicole slapped at his hands. "Beast! Stop that!" But he was too strong. Too determined. The only thing that made his hands' moving over her bearable was the fact that he was so intent on discovering a bit of metal, he didn't linger over softer areas. Still she felt soiled by his touch, and when he moved to feel about beneath her skirts, she kicked so wildly he had to call his brother for help.

"You take care of that freighter?" Fletcher grunted the question as he wrapped both arms around Nicole's middle, trapping her arms to her sides, and heaving her backward until her feet left the ground.

Will dismounted and strode forward, accepting the squirming package Fletcher thrust at him. "Yep. Took his shotgun and knocked him cold with my pistol butt. Then set the wagon off with a slap to the lead

412

horse's rump. He won't be interferin'."

Nicole screamed anyway, hoping someone, anyone might hear. But the sound died against the wall of trees closing her off from the road.

Will's arms tightened around her midsection, crushing her chest and making it impossible to draw a full breath. Her screams faded into whimpers, which turned into silent tears of humiliation as Fletcher's rough, filthy hand climbed up her stocking-clad leg. Her gaze curled upward toward heaven as she tried to distance herself from what was happening. Thankfully, Fletcher was efficient, and found the garter sheath quickly.

"Empty," he growled, then yanked up her skirts to verify with his eyes what his fingers had told him. "Where is it?" he demanded as he flung her skirts back down and pushed to his feet. "Where's the dagger?"

Nicole pressed her lips together in answer.

Fletcher stared at her long and hard. She stared back. Then all at once he turned away. Her heart soared for one precious moment of victory before plummeting to her toes when he grabbed her away from Will and started marching deeper into the trees.

"Stand guard," Fletcher ordered. "I got an idea."

"Where're you taking her?"

Nicole wanted to know the same thing.

"To the river."

The river? Nicole struggled to keep pace with Fletcher's longer stride. Every time he jerked her arm forward, she nearly fell on her face.

"I won't tell you." She tossed the words at his back, wishing she had something more substantial to throw. "No matter what you do, I'll never reveal the dagger's hiding place."

The look he flung back at her chilled her blood. "We'll see."

CHAPTER 33

Darius held his mount to a slow canter as he tracked the wagon wheel grooves he'd been following since leaving Liberty. Not knowing how long it would take to catch up to the freighter, he didn't want to risk exhausting his mount. Yet the restraint was taking its toll. A giant clock ticked in his head, the sound growing louder the longer he rode without overtaking the wagon. Had the Jenkins brothers found Nicole? Was she even now suffering at their hands?

His tracking skills were minimal at best — growing up in New York he'd had little use for the skill, after all — so he didn't even try to decipher the myriad hoofprints lining the road. No, he focused on the wheel marks, praying they were indeed from the freight wagon and not some random farm vehicle.

Even if the Jenkins brothers had already made off with Nicole, Holsten would be able to tell him what happened.

If the man was still alive.

A sweat droplet beading on Darius's forehead rolled into the corner of his right eye. He swiped his sleeve impatiently against the sting and squinted back at the wheel tracks. So intent was he on the ground directly in front of his horse that he nearly missed the buckskin-clad man limping unsteadily toward him along the west side of the road. A quick glance north revealed a listing wagon bed protruding from between a stand of pines.

Darius immediately reigned in his mount. "You Holsten?"

The man lifted his head, his stare hostile. A line of blood trickled along his temple from beneath his dust-laden hat. "Who's askin'?"

"Name's Thornton." When no recognition brightened the man's eyes, Darius hastened to add a bit of context to his name. "I bought the Oakhaven plantation outside of Liberty a year or so ago."

Holsten cocked his head. "The crazy easterner who blows things up?"

Darius winced. Perhaps he should have left the context off. "Only in the name of scientific inquiry, I assure you. But my choice of pastime is not at issue here. I'm looking for a woman. Average height, brown hair, red dress. I believe she stowed away in your wagon."

"What you want with her?"

Darius bit back a growl. Must the man respond to everything he said with a question? Getting information out of Holsten was like getting steam out of lukewarm water.

"She is to be my wife," Darius said, leaning over the saddle to better meet the man's eyes, "and she's in danger. I believe you may have had a run-in with the two villains chasing her." He tipped his head in the direction of the abandoned wagon.

The freighter stared up at him as if he couldn't make up his mind as to whether or not Darius could be trusted.

"Please," Darius begged. "If you saw which way they headed or know anything about Nicole's whereabouts, please tell me. They will stop at nothing to get what they seek. I fear for her safety."

"I do, too. It's why I'm hiking down this dad-blamed road with my head poundin' and my eyes crossed from the pistol butt I took to the skull. Didn't even know the gal was there until them yahoos started waving their guns around, demandin' I hand her over. Poor thing lit out like a scared rabbit,

417

hoppin' out of the wagon and dashin' for the trees as if she were lookin' for some kind of hole to hide herself in. Didn't see her for long," the freighter admitted, scratching at his beard, "but I do recall that red dress of hers. She'll have a hard time hidin' anywhere with a flag like that waving around."

"Where?" Darius demanded, jerking straight in the saddle and scanning the trees for clues.

"See that sapling with the broken crown?" Holsten pointed to a spot about ten yards behind Darius, where a young pine's top dangled sideways. "I saw her run that way, headin' toward the river. The first feller lit out after her, cursin' and hollerin'."

Darius didn't wait for more explanation. He kicked his mount into action and raced for the sapling.

"The second one's got my shotgun as well as a pistol," Holsten called out after him. Darius shifted the reins to his left hand and retrieved his percussion pistol with his right.

"Don't let me be too late, Lord," he whispered. "Not this time."

Nicole gasped and sputtered when Fletcher finally yanked her head out of the river. Wet hair slashed across her face, making it even harder to breathe. Coughs wracked her

418

body as she fought to expel the water she'd swallowed. She couldn't see anything, feel anything. Her entire being focused on drawing air into her aching lungs.

How many times had he forced her head under the water? Four? Five? She'd lost count. Waist-deep in the Trinity, she couldn't feel her legs any longer. Her energy flagged. The cruel hand clutching the hair at the top of her head might very well be the only thing keeping her upright. The river's current tugged at her sodden skirts, tempting her to just float away and leave her troubles behind.

But leaving her troubles behind also meant leaving her family behind. Leaving Darius. She didn't want to leave him. She wanted to feel his strong arms about her, to feel his lips press into hers, to hear him whisper words of love in her ear.

"Where . . . is . . . the dagger?" Fletcher's growl brought Nicole's mind back into focus. His heaving breaths told her he was winded, as well, weakening. If she could last just a little longer, maybe he would falter.

Not wanting to waste the energy it would take to choke out the same answer he'd already punished her for multiple times, Nicole kept her mouth shut.

"Come on, Nicki. This feud has gone

on . . . long enough. The Lafitte Dagger . . . belongs to the Jenkins family. Your . . . grandfather stole it from us." He paused and glanced over at the riverbank. Searching for answers? Patience? A rock to finish her off with? "Your father's had his whole life to reap the dagger's rewards. It's our turn."

His grip tightened on her hair, and terror leaked into Nicole's veins. He was going to send her under again.

"Give up the dagger, and I swear I'll not threaten you or anyone in your family again."

The pressure built against her neck. She tried to resist, but she'd lost too much strength. Fletcher's arm slowly bent her head down. The water rose up to meet her.

No! Not again.

Gulping what air she could, she braced herself for the shock of cold and the smothering swirl of water.

She couldn't forfeit . . . had to hold tight . . . stay strong. For her father. For Darius. If Fletcher found him with the dagger, he —

Her face hit the water, then the icy blanket closed over her head. She didn't fight it. Not anymore. It did no good. Yet when her feeble supply of air grew thin and her lungs protested, panic crawled over her like a thousand tiny spiders.

She started to thrash, grabbing at his hand even though she knew it would do her no good. He wouldn't let her up until the black edges of unconsciousness threatened. Yet this time something changed. A garbled rumble reached her through the water, the sound deep and resonant. An instant later, Fletcher yanked her upward, blessed air finding its way back into her lungs.

"Nicole!" The deep rumble she'd heard underwater turned into an anguished roar.

She knew that voice. Nicole clawed at the dripping hair swathing her face, desperate to confirm with her eyes what her ears had already told her.

Darius! Her heart gave such a leap of joy it nearly flew from her chest. But as quickly as it leapt, it plummeted to the ground like a bird shot out of the sky. What was he doing here? He was supposed to be on the way to Galveston with the dagger.

He met her eyes briefly before turning his attention to Will. Only then did she realize that the two men had pistols trained on each other. Will stood on the riverbank slightly upstream from her position, while Darius, still mounted, was situated closer to the trees.

"Let her go, Fletcher," Darius demanded, "or I'll shoot your brother."

"You can try, but he'll get a shot off, as well. Then who will rescue the lady?" Fletcher spun Nicole around in a half circle, forcing her into deeper water. Her footing slipped. She squealed as the current swept her feet out from under her.

"Nicole!"

Fletcher grasped her about the waist and hoisted her upright, just as a gunshot rent the air, his distraction a success. Darius fell from his horse, and in that moment, Nicole didn't care one fig about the blasted Lafitte Dagger. All she cared about was the man she loved and whether or not he was alive.

"No!" She fought Fletcher's hold, desperate to get to Darius, but her enemy's grip was as unshakeable as iron.

"Get his gun, Will," Fletcher shouted, but Darius was already regaining his feet, the pistol still in his hand.

Nicole searched his form for injury but saw nothing. Surely he must have been hit to have been thrown backward off his horse. Keeping his pistol trained on Will, who had traded his pistol for the freighter's shotgun, Darius turned toward her, easing his way closer to the river. That's when she saw it — a line of red blooming against the white cotton of his shirt beneath his coat. How deep had the bullet penetrated? It could be a scratch or a mortal wound; she had no way of knowing. At least he was on his feet. Yet even as she watched, the red line on his shirt widened and spread. He'd not be able to hold them off for long. And what would happen to him then?

"I have what you want, Fletcher." Darius's voice resonated with a forcefulness that heartened Nicole's anxious spirit, until she realized what he was holding.

He was going to forfeit the dagger.

Nicole shook her head in slow denial, even as logic told her it was the only chance to save both their lives.

She never should have taken the dagger. Should have left it at home with her father's guards. But, no. She'd wanted to prove herself. Show her father that she was as good as a son. Sure, she'd also wanted to keep her parents safe, but had that been her true motive or just an excuse?

"Will?" Fletcher's grip tightened painfully about her waist, but Nicole made no protest. She stood against him, limp. It was over. Jenkins had won.

"It looks like the real thing," Will called out. "I can see the jewels from here."

Darius took another step closer to the

river. "Let her go, Fletcher, and it's yours."

A sob caught in Nicole's throat. She hated feeling helpless. Trapped. Responsible.

"Set it down on the bank and step away," Fletcher ordered. "Once you're clear, I'll release the girl."

Darius obeyed, keeping his pistol trained on Will so the other man would not be tempted to make a premature move for the dagger. "The dagger's yours," Darius called. "Now, release Nicole."

Fletcher's grip loosened from around her waist. Nicole staggered for purchase, having lost her anchor. The current eroded the sand from beneath her shoes and her sodden skirts tugged her downstream. Losing her balance, she lifted her arms to steady herself, but just as she found her footing, a boot shoved against her backside, sending her sprawling into the river.

The greedy current snagged its prize and pulled her deeper into its grasp. She tried to swim, but the toll of fighting Fletcher had sapped her strength. Her skirts dragged her under. She fumbled with the fastenings as the river turned and twisted her beneath the surface, frantic to free herself from the leaden fabric. But her fingers were too numb. As the blackness rose to claim her, she battled to the surface a final time, gulped a breath, then let the river take her.

CHAPTER 34

When Nicole's head disappeared beneath the river's surface, Darius's heart stopped beating.

No!

In that instant he forgot about Will Jenkins and his shotgun. He forgot about the wound throbbing in his side. Every ounce of his attention focused solely on the patch of red fabric floating away from him with alarming haste.

Dropping his pistol, he sprinted for the river. His boots tore up the bank as he ran past a dripping Fletcher. The man made a dive for the dagger, yelling at his brother to shoot, but Darius never slowed. Nothing mattered more than getting to Nicole.

Her head broke the surface once, but the current immediately sucked her back down. She wouldn't have the strength to fight the current and the weight of her skirts for long.

Darius slid down the muddy bank and hit

the water. High-stepping through the shallows, he rushed forward on foot until the river reached his thighs. Then, after a final glance to pinpoint Nicole's position, he dove headfirst into the Trinity.

Never had he swum so hard. Agony pierced his injured side each time he stretched his right arm over his head for a full stroke. He steeled his mind against it, defiantly stretching his arm even farther the next stroke. He would not slow. Not for anything. His waterlogged boots dragged at him like twin anchors, but he simply kicked harder. If he couldn't reach her in time, all would be lost, and his well-being would no longer matter.

Feeling the currents swirl and tug, Darius did his best to swim with the river instead of against it, but even so his fatigue grew. He lifted his head, needing to gauge his distance from Nicole, make sure he wasn't off course. For one heart-stopping moment, he saw nothing but dark water. Panic seized him.

Scenes from his last nightmare flashed through his mind — him searching the waters for the drowning girl from the *Louisiana* only to have her identity shift as he watched her face take on Nicole's beloved features.

This couldn't be happening again. He couldn't lose another girl. He couldn't lose Nicole.

Then, as if the Lord had heard his unformed prayer, he glimpsed a bit of red. *Thank God!* She was close. Only a few yards ahead.

He cut through the water toward her, choosing a line that would take him slightly past his target so the current would push her directly into his arms. But he had to fight the current to get there. He kicked and stroked, pulling with all his might. Just as he lifted his head to check his position, something heavy thumped into his side. He grabbed for it, knowing it had to be Nicole, but she eluded his grasp.

He hadn't had time to take a breath, but he didn't care. He had to get a hold of Nicole before the river dragged her away from him again. Working beneath the surface, he opened his eyes and fumbled with the seemingly endless fabric of her dress to find her arm or waist to latch on to. Murky water clouded his vision. He could make out a swirl of red but little else. Then all at once, the mass rubbing against him slid beneath, escaping.

His lungs burned for air, but his heart screamed louder. He would *not* let the river take her. With a forceful kick he lunged downstream and threw his arms wide before closing them like a crab's pincer around something blessedly solid. Darius clasped it to his chest and surged to the surface.

Sunlight hit his skin and air rushed into his lungs, but the woman he held hung limp over his arm. Her back was to him, one arm pinned upward at an awkward angle, her hair full of river soil and debris. He turned her toward him, gaining a better hold around her ribs. Desperate to see her face, he swiped roughly at the hair covering her features. All color had been drained from her skin. Her neck flopped against his arm like that of a lifeless doll. Like the girl from the *Louisiana*.

No! Nicole was a fighter. No woman who could run as well as she and kill snakes with a toss of a knife would let a river take her down. She was his pirate, raised on the isle of Jean Lafitte, king of the pirates. She knew how to swim, how to survive against the odds. He'd not give up on her.

Turning onto his side, careful to keep her face above water, Darius swam one-armed toward the bank. With each pull toward shallower water, the current's grasp on him eased. When his fingertips finally scraped the muddy bottom, Darius's strength was so spent, he struggled to get his feet under him. He wobbled as badly as a newborn foal, but somehow he managed to gather the woman he loved into his arms and stagger onto solid ground.

He fell to his knees when he cleared the bank, Nicole still clasped in his arms. Gently, he laid her upon the grass and bent over her to listen for breath.

Nothing.

She lay too still, her skin too pale. Memories flooded his brain of the last female he'd pulled from a river.

Grabbing her shoulders, he thrust his face into hers. "You will not die," he ordered. "Do you hear me?" He shook her shoulders as if he could somehow rouse her if he just startled her enough. "You will not die!"

Yet her limp form looked too much like death already.

Darius ran a hand over his face. *Think, man!* There must be something he could do. If he could build a boiler with a pump that moved water from the — Of course! He'd pump the water from her.

Kneeling over her supine body, he pushed against her chest, firm and sharp. He repeated the action. Again. And again.

"Come on, Nicole. Breathe, honey. Breathe for me."

Her head lifted slightly with each press of his hands, but she gave no sign of life. A vine of despair slithered through his wall of determination, cracking the mortar. Mentally uprooting it, he flung it from his mind. He refused to consider that she wouldn't recover. He could still save her. He just needed to stay focused, to expel the water that kept her from breathing. But a second vine slid past his barrier, then a third.

Don't take her from me. I beg you. A hot tear rolled down Darius's cheek as he worked, his pace growing frantic. *I need her. I love her. You restored Lazarus to his sisters. Restore Nicole to me. Please.*

Darius put more and more of his weight behind each push until his entire torso acted like a piston, moving up and down. Up and down.

"Don't you dare give up, Nicole," he growled at her. The salt from a second tear rolled over his lips and leaked onto his tongue. "You promised to marry me, blast it all, and I intend to hold you to it. Now, breathe!"

He rocked forward, desperation lending a greater sharpness to his motion. All at once, water spewed from Nicole's mouth. Darius snatched his hands from her chest and immediately turned her head. He rolled her to her side and pounded the flat of his hand against her back as she coughed up more of the river.

"That's it, sweetheart. Get it all out," he crooned, his heart doing such crazy flips his whole body shook.

She drew up her knees as more spasms wracked her, but the tiny gasps she took between the coughs echoed in his ears like the finest concerto ever played.

He mouthed a thank-you toward the heavens, then cradled Nicole in his arms, stroking her hair, pressing kisses to her forehead, murmuring words of love. Her lashes slowly lifted, and brown eyes met his.

"Dar-ius?" she croaked.

"I'm here, love." He smiled down at her and gathered her just a little closer as he rocked her gently. "You're safe now. Everything's going to be all right."

"The d-agger?"

He stilled. She wasn't going to like his answer, but he refused to give her less than the full truth. "Fletcher has it."

She moaned and turned her face away from him. The action stabbed him like a sword to the gut.

"We'll report it to the Rangers. Give them a description of the Jenkins brothers as well as the dagger." He turned her face back toward him, but she closed her eyes, as if she couldn't bear to look upon him. She couldn't have cut him any deeper had she thrown her knife into his chest. "We know where they're headed," he cajoled, his gut clenching as a new panic set in. He couldn't lose her. Not now. Not when he'd just gotten her back. "The Rangers will track them down and retrieve the dagger. You'll see."

Nothing. Not so much as a flutter of lashes.

It was too much. After all they'd endured, he wouldn't let her give up on him. Not without a fight.

"Look at me, Nicole," he demanded in a rough voice he barely recognized as his own. His grip on her chin tightened. "Quit hiding like a coward and face me."

That got a reaction. Her lids flew open and her eyes shot brown fire at him.

Good.

"I didn't drag you out of that river to have you mope around like a dog that lost her favorite bone. And I'll not apologize for exchanging that blasted dagger for your life, either. It's a knife, Nicole. A dull, ancient blade no longer good for anything except causing friction between two feuding families. No matter how valuable it is, it's not worth dying over."

Nicole stiffened and jerked her chin out of his grasp. "Don't you think I know that?" she shouted at him, her voice a hoarse rasp. "I don't blame you for handing over the dagger, Darius. I blame myself for taking it in the first place. I thought myself so clever. So capable. So noble for taking the danger upon myself instead of leaving my parents to face it." Her bitter tone scraped his heart raw. "I disobeyed my father, and thanks to my pride, the Lafitte Dagger — the Renard family legacy — is in the hand of our enemy."

Darius glared down at her. "Do you think having the Lafitte Dagger hanging on the Renard family wall would comfort your father if your lifeless body was delivered to him in an undertaker's wagon?"

She flinched at the callous question, uncertainty clouding her eyes. Darius ruthlessly pressed his advantage.

"That dagger is not the Renard family legacy, Nicole. You are. You are the next generation, your parents' hope for the future. Any man who would choose the welfare of a knife over that of his child is a fool, and from what you've told me, your father's no fool."

"But if I hadn't taken the dagger, none of this would have happened."

"And we never would have met." A tragedy that didn't bear contemplation. Darius crooked a finger beneath Nicole's chin and forced her to meet his eyes. "There is no way to predict what could have happened if you had chosen another path. For all you know, something even more dire could have occurred. Fletcher and Will could have murdered your parents and stolen the dagger while you danced with a bunch of New Orleans dandies."

She hissed in a breath. "Never say such a thing!"

Darius released her chin and ran his hand through his wet hair. "I didn't mean . . . Sorry . . . I just . . . Look. What I'm trying to say is that torturing yourself with *what if*s and *could have been*s serves no purpose. Take it from one who speaks from experience. Repent of your mistakes, learn from them, and move forward. Trust God to bring good out of whatever mess you're in."

She sniffed and ran her hand beneath her nose. "He's already brought good from it," she said in a quiet voice he had to strain to hear. "He brought me you."

Darius's heart thudded against his ribs. "Am I enough, Nicole? Is my love enough?"

Please let her say yes. Please.

She said nothing for six long heartbeats

435

— the throbbing intensifying with each pulse. Then she pulled slightly away from him, and it was all he could do not to seize her by the arms and imprison her against his chest.

"All my life," she said, her gaze resting somewhere in her lap, "I've tried to prove to my father that I was as valuable to him as a son, because deep down I feared that no matter how much he loved me, having a daughter wasn't enough." Slowly her eyes lifted and met his. "I have never felt that way with you, Darius. From the beginning, you've respected me, partnered with me, treated me as an equal. Your love is a blessing I can barely comprehend."

She reached out and touched his face, her fingers stroking over his brow, past his temple, down to his jaw. "No, Darius. You're not enough." Her finger paused atop his lips. "You are *everything.*"

Darius seized her, clasped her to his chest, and melded his mouth to hers. Nicole cupped his jaw in her hand and returned his kiss with a fervor that matched his own. She tasted of hope, of forgiveness, and of love.

Thank you, God, his spirit shouted as he bent over her to deepen the kiss. *Thank you.*

CHAPTER 35

Nicole gave herself fully to Darius's kiss, eager to assure him of her love. He groaned his appreciation, his arms tightening around her and bringing her even closer. This man's love was worth any price. Even the loss of the Lafitte Dagger.

Nicole broke away from the kiss and buried her face in Darius's shoulder. Her labored breaths rasped loudly in her ears, a product not only of the passion they shared but of the realization that had just rammed into her. If Darius had been the one in Fletcher's grasp, his life hanging in the balance, she would have handed over the dagger to save him in a heartbeat. No matter how disappointed her father would be over the dagger's loss, she couldn't regret setting out on this path. Not when it led her to Darius.

Nestling into the crook of his shoulder, she gloried in the feel of his arms around her, of his cheek pressed against her fore-head. This man had saved her. Had nearly given his life for her. Jumping in the river as he did, swimming for who knew how long to reach her and pull her back from the edge of death. All of this after being shot from his horse —

Nicole sat up abruptly and yanked the flaps of Darius's coat wide. The red stain glared up at her, the river having spread it to encompass his entire side.

"You're injured!" she cried. "How could I have forgotten?" She immediately began tugging the shirt from his trousers, intent on assessing the damage, but the rumble of a warm, masculine chuckle stilled her frantic motions.

"I'm fine, Nicole." His hands covered hers, keeping her from her goal. "The bullet took a chunk out of my flesh, but everything vital is still in good working order. The cold from the river helped stem the bleeding. I'll be sore for a few days, but I'll heal."

"Not if infection sets in. That river is filthy. Just look at all the grime sticking to us." She scraped the side of her hand against her skirts and collected a disgusting amount of silt. She must look like a half-drowned mud creature. Lovely.

But her appearance was of little consequence. What mattered now was ensuring Darius's recovery by tending to his injury with all possible haste. Nicole jumped to her feet and grabbed Darius's hand. She yanked on him until he finally rose to his feet. "We've got to get you cleaned up and bandage that wound before it turns septic."

He stumbled a bit and swayed unsteadily as he worked to plant his feet solidly beneath him. Had a fever already set in? Darius was the strongest man she knew. He could swim for days in that pond of his. No little jaunt in the river to pull her out should have depleted him. She rushed forward and wrapped her arm about his waist. Her own limbs felt as limp as an unstarched crinoline, but she'd gladly loan him what strength she had.

"Here. Lean on me. Let's find your mount and get back to the road. It shouldn't be too far."

Darius raised a brow at her. "It's at least half a mile."

"Half a mile?" Nicole straightened and looked around her. Surely he exaggerated. But as she looked around, she saw nothing familiar. The river didn't even look the same. Cypress roots dangled in the water here, where there had been only grassy banks before.

"You were unconscious for most of the ride." Darius teased, chucking her under the chin. "Take it from the man who was awake and swimming every inch of the way — we have a bit of a walk ahead of us."

He held out his hand, and she slipped hers into it. Together they followed the river upstream, staying as close to the banks as they could. The cypress groves lining the water blocked the sun, sending cold shivers through Nicole every time the breeze blew. Her wet skirts dragged on her like iron chains, and it wasn't long before she had to stop to catch her breath.

"I've got to get rid of some of this weight," she grumbled as she braced an arm against the nearest tree trunk.

"I'm going to duck over here for a moment." Darius nodded toward a cypress a few yards ahead of where they'd stopped. "Give you some privacy in case you want to . . . make some adjustments." He waved his hand in a vague manner, then pressed a quick kiss to her cheek before turning his back and hiking to the far side of the tree.

Nicole yanked up her skirt and immediately set to work on her petticoats. She wore three of the wretched things, the top one woven with horsehair for extra stiffness. All it gave her now were extra pounds to carry around. Her cold fingers made slow work of the ties, but eventually all three petticoats fell to the ground in a soggy circle around her feet. She stepped over the ring, feeling worlds lighter, though without the supporting crinolines her skirt hung several inches too long.

She moved toward the tree where Darius waited, bunching up the extra dress fabric in her hands so she wouldn't trip. "Do you have a blade with you?" she asked as she rounded the tree. "My skirt needs a trim."

He pulled a hunting knife from the sheath at his belt and knelt before her like a knight before his lady. With a couple quick slashes, he had the cloth ripping, and soon a long strip several inches wide tore off in his hands.

"Thank you." She sighed in contentment. Now if only they could get dry.

Darius draped the red fabric over a low-hanging limb, and as it flapped in the wind, he offered her his hand. She reached for him, but the sound of approaching footsteps had Darius shoving her behind him before she could make contact.

"You leaving me a trail to follow, Thornton?"

Holsten. Thank heavens. She hadn't even given the freighter a single thought in the midst of all that had happened. A shameful oversight she intended to rectify at once. She immediately offered a silent prayer of thanksgiving for his well-being.

Darius, too, relaxed and stepped aside. The moment he did, Nicole rushed forward. "Mr. Holsten, I'm so sorry for putting you in danger. Please forgive me."

The man held up his hands and backed away as if afraid she'd try to hug him. "Crazy females, always apologizing for things when there's no need," he muttered. When she made no move to wrap her dripping arms around him he finally met her gaze. "I have to admit I don't like stowaways, but I like men who threaten women even less." He stroked his beard, his frown bringing lines to his brow. "The danger don't bother me none. I just wished I'd been better prepared for them yahoos when they showed up. Instead they caught me unawares. It's a good thing they left my shotgun behind when they hightailed it, or I'd *really* be sore."

He lifted his arm to bring the weapon in question into view. "Couldn't find hide nor hair of your horse, though. The only other thing they left behind was this." He extended his left hand toward Darius, but Nicole snatched the object from his palm first.

442

"Jacob's knife." A wide grin stretched across her face. "Oh, thank you! I would have felt terrible to have lost it after he so selflessly lent it to me." Angling her side away from both men, she eased up the remains of her skirt and slid the blade into her garter sheath. A much easier task without all the petticoats in the way.

"Your woman carries a knife in her garter?" The freighter's shocked question brought a blush to her cheeks.

Nicole shot an apologetic glance to Darius, but he just smiled.

"My woman's a bit of a pirate."

My woman. The way he emphasized the phrase sent a flood of much needed warmth through her. She *was* his. And he was hers. Forever.

"Well, it looks like you both done walked the plank. Come on, then," the freighter said with a wave of his arm, "I got blankets in the wagon and some spare duds. It ain't much, but it'll keep you dry 'til we can get you home. We'll have to push the team to get to Oakhaven afore dark, but I reckon it's doable if your man, here, can help me get my team out of the trees without tanglin' the traces."

Darius winked at her as he took her hand in his, the love glowing in his eyes promising that together they could handle whatever the future threw at them. "I think I can manage."

After extricating the wagon, Holsten untied the tarpaulin and pried the lid open on one of his crates. "Help yourself. The loggers won't mind if you break in their new duds a bit for them. I'll grab the blankets."

Darius reached inside the crate and pulled out an assortment of denim trousers and flannel shirts. He unfolded them all, examined them, and then handed a set to Nicole. "These are the smallest ones of the bunch. You might have to tear off another strip from your dress to use as a belt, but they should keep you plenty warm."

Nicole accepted the gift without complaint. Propriety paled next to practicality in this instance. She'd wear a strand of fig leaves if it meant getting warm. What she wouldn't have given for a big tub of steaming water and a comb for her hair. But she'd settle for a drying blanket and a pair of denim britches.

Darius and Holsten turned their backs, and in minutes she'd peeled off what was left of her soggy garments and donned the masculine attire.

The shirt hung nearly to her knees, and she had to roll the trouser legs up to keep

444

from stepping on them, but with a makeshift belt at her waist, the clothes kept her decently covered.

Well, *decent* might be debatable. Maman would probably faint dead away if she knew her daughter was wearing trousers. But since stripping off her clothing and wrapping up in a blanket was the only alternative, she figured her mother wouldn't hold a pair of trousers against her.

CHAPTER 36

Once he got Nicole to finally quit fussing over the flesh wound he'd already cleaned with some water from Holsten's canteen, Darius handed her up into the wagon. He did his best not to pay attention to the way her borrowed britches accentuated the line of her legs and other . . . parts of her anatomy usually disguised by the bell shape of feminine skirts, but a man's imagination was a difficult thing to stifle. Especially when the britches and parts in question sat snugly against his side during the entire ride to Oakhaven.

He needed to get his family to Texas so he could take this woman to wife. He'd write the letter tonight.

A smile creased his face as Holsten turned the team up the drive. Darius could just picture the fuss his mother would kick up when she learned of his intention to marry. She'd likely have the entire Thornton household packed and ready to board the first available ship by the end of the day. He might have inherited his father's love of mechanics and business, but his tenacity came straight from his mother. If a mountain needed to be moved, everyone knew which Thornton to turn to. If he posted the letter tomorrow, his family could be in Galveston in a matter of weeks.

"What has you smiling so wide, Mr. Thornton?" Nicole asked in a prim voice at odds with the twinkle in her eye.

Darius leaned close, nudging her shoulder with his arm. "I was thinking about how much I'm looking forward to introducing you to my family."

Some of her lightheartedness dimmed. "Do you think they'll be angry that I'm forcing you to stay in Texas? They haven't seen you in nearly two years, and now I'm tying you to an enterprise that will keep you away even longer."

"First off," Darius said with a frown just dark enough to let her know how serious he was, "you're not *forcing* me to stay in Texas. I'm choosing to do so of my own free will. And second" — here he bent close to whisper in her ear so Holsten wouldn't overhear — "they will love you. It won't take them long to see what I see — a woman who is loyal, courageous, determined, and in possession of a soul so beautiful and wise she can draw a man out of his nightmares and restore his dreams."

Her eyes grew misty, shimmering with a joyous light. He wanted nothing more than to sweep her into his arms and kiss her until they both forgot where they were. Unfortunately, their companion remembered well enough for all of them.

"If you two lovebirds are done cooin' at each other," Holsten grouched, "you might wanna take a gander at those folks pourin' out of that fancy house up yonder. I think the boy's gonna run us down afore I can get to the barn."

Darius swiveled his head to see Jacob racing across the yard, leaving Wellborn and his wife to approach at a more sedate pace.

"You got her back!" Jacob sprinted up to the wagon, then gave a happy little half skip as he came alongside the driver's bench. "I knew you would. Yeehaw!" He slapped his palms together as he kept pace with Holsten's team.

Darius grinned at the boy, then turned to share a quieter smile with the woman at his side. Such affection and camaraderie radiated from her as their eyes met that his heart gave its own little half skip. *Yeehaw,* indeed.

When Holsten finally brought the wagon to a halt at the barn, Wellborn was there, his controlled demeanor the antithesis of Jacob's excited energy.

"Good to have you and Miss Nicole home, sir." A wealth of meaning passed between them as Wellborn dipped his chin. Worry, relief, and myriad questions shone in his eyes, barely restrained by the decorum necessitated by his position.

Darius climbed down from the bench seat and extended a hand to Nicole. "Good to be home, Wellborn. Though we won't be here for long." Darius squeezed Nicole's hand. "Miss Renard and I will leave first thing on the morrow for Galveston. It's time I asked her father for her hand." Among other things.

A lovely blush stole over Nicole's cheeks, but Darius wasn't given time to enjoy it, for his housekeeper swept in like a mother hen clucking over her chick. She wrapped a wing about Nicole's shoulders, cooing words like *poor dear* and *trying ordeal,* all while successfully ushering her away from the men with promises of a hot bath and warm tea. Darius didn't doubt Mrs. Wellborn's desire to nurture and pamper his fiancée, but

449

neither did he miss the way she tried to swirl her own skirts around Nicole's legs as they walked, as if trying to hide the fact that her future mistress was wearing trousers.

A chuckle rumbled deep in Darius's throat as he shook his head. One would think the woman would be used to people wearing unconventional attire after running his household for so long. Heaven knew *he* hardly ever dressed properly. She'd probably take him to task for corrupting Nicole and letting her run around in men's britches. But what did he care? As long as his little pirate was alive and well, she could run around in whatever she liked.

"How long will you be gone, sir?" Wellborn asked, breaking Darius away from the lovely image of Nicole romping around Oakhaven in her scandalous britches.

"I doubt we'll be coming back."

Jacob, who'd been helping Holsten water his horses, dropped his pail. The spilled water seeped into the hard ground at his feet. "Not c-coming back?"

Cursing his too-blunt tongue, Darius strode to Jacob's side and hunkered down to face him eye-to-eye. "You're coming with us, scamp. That is . . . if you want to." He slid a quick glance back to his butler before continuing. "I've got to take Nicole down to see her family right away, but Wellborn will bring you to meet us in Galveston once he and Mrs. Wellborn get the house packed up. If you're willing, Nicole and I would really like you to stay with us."

The boy's Adam's apple bobbed slowly up and down. He crossed his arms over his chest and peered off to the side. "I won't be takin' no charity, Mr. Thornton. If you ain't got work for me, I'll be movin' on."

Now it was Darius's turn to swallow hard. The kid had become like family to him, to all of them. He wasn't offering Jacob charity — he was offering him a home. But the boy wasn't ready for that yet. Maybe he never would be. If a job would keep the kid around, keep him safe and provided for, Darius would see to it that there was always a position open.

"Not got work for you? Have you seen how much stuff I've got laying around in that house up there?" Darius jutted a thumb toward Oakhaven. "Wellborn's going to need every extra hand he can get."

"Quite correct." His man nodded stiffly in confirmation.

"And when you get to Galveston, I'm going to need you more than ever. Nicole's father wants me to take over his shipping company, and I need someone I can trust to help me watch out for Nicole. Jenkins lives in Galveston, too, remember? Even if he has the dagger, he might not be above starting more trouble. How will I know who is safe to have working in my house and who will turn traitor if Jenkins stirs things up again? No, I need you more than ever, Jake. Please say you'll come with us."

The boy glanced to the north, a pained look slanting over his features, as if Darius were asking him to sever his right arm in order to follow him to Galveston. But then his jaw firmed and his eyes heated with determination. "All right, Mr. T." Jacob pivoted to face him squarely. "I'll go."

"Excellent." Darius ruffled the boy's hair and pushed to a standing position, doing his best not to allow the sigh of relief swelling in his chest to gush forth. He'd have to let Sheriff Davenport know about their move in case anyone came looking for the boy. Though, if no one had shown up by this time, the likelihood was slim that anyone would.

"Wellborn," he said, turning his attention to his butler. "Pack a bag for me, will you? Miss Renard and I will be leaving for Galveston in the morning."

His man nodded. "I'll see to it at once, sir."

"Oh, and Wellborn?" Darius called as the butler moved to leave. "Once your wife has Miss Renard situated, please ask her to put together a cold supper with plenty of hot coffee and cookies to go around. I have a rather adventurous tale to share. If anyone would be interested in hearing the details."

Jacob darted around Darius and grabbed his sleeve. "Can I come, too? 'Cause I want to hear *everything.*"

Darius grinned at him. "Of course, scamp. The whole family's invited. You, the Wellborns, Nicole. If Mrs. Graham hasn't already left for home, she can stay, too, though I figure she'll probably just pry the details out of Mrs. Wellborn tomorrow."

Darius couldn't be sure if the boy had caught the reference to family, but judging by the sharpness in Wellborn's gaze, his butler had. The man's mouth opened and closed as if he had no idea how to respond to such a radical statement.

Finally his butler managed to push a string of words past his lips. "Would you prefer the dining room or the kitchen, sir?"

The servant's domain or that of the master? Either had the potential for awkwardness. Darius met his butler's eye the same way he had on the day of the explosion. Man-to-man, not master-to-servant. "What would *you* prefer, Wellborn?"

"I . . . I believe the kitchen."

"Then the kitchen it will be. And speaking of kitchens . . ." Darius said, turning back to the freighter, who was watching the exchange with avid interest. "Jacob, why don't you escort Mr. Holsten up to the house and scrounge up some refreshments for him? He's traveled quite a distance out of his way to see Miss Renard and me safely home, and I'd like to express my gratitude. I'll stay and finish tending the horses myself."

Holsten began to protest, but Jacob grabbed his hand and started tugging him toward the house, chattering about the corn muffins and honey they'd had for breakfast as well as the leftover gingerbread no one had been in the mood to eat at noon. It wasn't long before the freighter picked up his pace enough that he was the one dragging Jake as Wellborn traipsed along behind.

When the trio disappeared into the house, Darius ducked into the barn and hefted two sacks of his best oats onto his shoulders. Holsten was too prickly to accept payment for the help he'd offered — he saw it strictly as his neighborly duty — but Darius wasn't about to let such a good deed go unappreciated. Without Holsten, he might never have found Nicole at all, and even if he had, without a horse or dry clothing for their return to Oakhaven, they both surely would have taken ill.

Darius slipped the sacks under the tarpaulin and pushed them back behind the crates Holsten was carting on to the logging camp. He'd not find the oats until he unloaded tomorrow, when it would be too late to protest. Darius grinned as he straightened the canvas covering and strode back up to the horses' heads.

He'd successfully navigated Jake's reluctance, Wellborn's deference, and even Holsten's pride. Now all he had to do was find a way to deflect an ambitious man's disappointment from his daughter onto himself without undermining his own credibility as a worthy heir for the Renard Shipping Company. Only the happiness of the woman he loved, and therefore his own heart, hung in the balance.

Darius groaned and rubbed a hand over his face. Why couldn't it be something easy like dodging scalding-hot water bursts and barrages of metal shards? At least then he could protect her with his body. But protecting her with words . . . ? He shook his head. God help them both.

CHAPTER 37

Nicole's legs bounced restlessly in the carriage as it rolled down Thirty-Fifth Street. Little more than two weeks ago she'd traveled this same road with a similar dread burning in her stomach — only this time it had nothing to do with her father's health and everything to do with his likely disappointment. She'd lost the Lafitte Dagger, the Renard family legacy. He'd forgive her for it, of that she was sure — he did love her, after all — but the idea of him looking upon her with crushing disappointment, and knowing she was the cause, nearly made her wish she'd met her end in that river.

Nearly . . . but not quite.

She turned from the view of familiar houses passing by to look at the man beside her, the one holding her hand and smiling at her in reassurance.

"Are we almost there?" He pulled her hand up to his lips to press a kiss upon her knuckles.

She managed a nod before turning back to the window, needing to watch their progress toward Renard House like a patient watching the approach of a doctor's suturing needle, knowing the end result would be painful but unwilling to let the jab take her by surprise.

Thank God she wasn't alone. Her grip tightened on Darius's hand, and his thumb immediately caressed her fingers in tender strokes. The knots in her abdomen eased slightly. She could do this. No matter what happened with her father, Darius would be there, supporting her, loving her.

Nicole inhaled a long quivering breath as the white columns of Renard House came into view. The rented carriage rolled to a stop. Any moment, the driver would arrive to open the door.

You can do this. She tried to believe the words, but her heart pounded so heavily, she could barely hear herself think them.

Her gaze was so focused on the window, she didn't see Darius's hand until it cupped her chin and forced her face around. "I love you," he whispered.

Then, before she could decipher his intentions, his lips brushed hers in a kiss so tender it stole her breath. She expected him to stop there, but he lingered, teasing each corner of her mouth until her eyes slid closed, the feelings he induced overwhelming her senses. Only then did he pull away.

And only then did she hear the hinges creak as the driver opened the door.

The scoundrel. They could have been caught in a compromising position. In front of her house, her parents! Yet she had to admit it'd been a rather successful distraction. And the blackguard knew it. Why, he looked downright pleased with himself, leaning back against the cushioned seat, arms crossed over his chest. She scowled at him, but it only earned her a grin in return. One she couldn't resist answering in kind.

Heavens, how she loved this man.

The driver reached his hand in to assist her down, only it wasn't the driver they'd hired at the docks. She recognized the thick fingers and the weathered skin of the man who'd been handing her out of carriages for as long as she could remember.

Swallowing down a resurgence of nerves, she slid her hand into his and lifted her head to meet the stoic features of her family's coachman. "Hello, John."

The man startled at her voice. His eyes flew wide and zeroed in on her face. "Can it be? Miss Nicki?" The man who'd never allowed her to tease a smile out of him broke into a full-blown grin, his cheeks retracting into wrinkled folds like gathered curtains about a window. "It *is* you. God be praised! Welcome home!" Then, as if the smile itself wasn't enough to knock her off-kilter, he grabbed her to him in a hug so full of joy, he bounced with it.

Tears moistened her lashes as she wrapped her arms about his shoulders and leaned into his embrace. *Home.* She was truly home.

Nicole felt Darius's presence behind her, and when John finally released her, she turned to introduce him, but the coachman had already spun toward the house.

"Mrs. Renard!" he shouted as he scuttled forward. "It's Nicki. She's come home to us!"

Nicole couldn't move, could barely breathe. The moment hung suspended. A foggy part of her brain registered Darius's hand at her back, but it was little more than a warm sensation, for all her attention narrowed in on the door standing between the front two columns.

Less than a heartbeat later, the door swung open and her mother ran through it. Apron flapping, sleeves rolled to her elbows, fingers covered in dough — a state in which her oh-so-proper mother would *never* greet a guest — she dashed down the front walk, her eyes frantically scanning the yard. "Nicole?"

All hesitancy fled Nicole's soul. With a sob, she sprinted forward. "Maman!"

The two fell together in a tearful embrace, both too overcome for words. Her mother pulled back to kiss Nicole's cheeks, then wrapped her again in her arms, as if she couldn't decide how best to show her affection.

"Nicki?" A deep, rasping voice reverberated across the air.

Her *maman* stepped back and swiped at her eyes with the back of her wrist. And there was her father, hunched in the doorway, grasping the wall for support.

"Anton!" Her mother instinctively took a step toward him before stopping. "John. Help him. Bring him to us."

"No, Maman." Nicole straightened her shoulders and stepped out of her mother's loving embrace. The time had come. "I will go to him."

"He has been out of his mind with worry these past weeks," her mother murmured softly as Nicole began moving toward the house. Her mother shadowed her. "He's not been able to get out of bed since the letter came from Monsieur Ackerman, informing us that you never arrived. I haven't seen him on his feet in days."

Yet somehow he'd managed to climb out of bed and make his way to the front door. Nicole's heart throbbed. If he could do all that for her, she could cross the yard for him. No matter what his reaction to her news might be, she owed him an accounting, and she'd not shirk her duty.

John reached him first and propped him up with an arm around his ribs, allowing him the dignity of standing straight. As Nicole moved to navigate the porch steps, Darius suddenly appeared at her elbow, offering his arm and his smile. Her fingers brushed his sleeve. The steely strength beneath her touch fortified her spirit.

Together. They would face this together.

She reached the porch landing and stepped away from Darius, toward her father. He looked so frail, yet his eyes locked on her as if she was all he could see.

"Nicki." His voice quavered over her name, and his hand reached for her cheek, his arm trembling from the effort.

She rushed forward and maneuvered her cheek against his palm, clutching his hand with her own to hold it firmly against her face. Her eyes slid closed and a tear slipped from between her lashes. "Papa."

"I thought you were lost to me, child." Somehow his head came to rest against hers. "Lost forever. And it was all my do-ing."

"No, Papa." Nicole lifted her head and looked him in the eye. "I went willingly. Knowing the risks." She'd not saddle him with that guilt. It wasn't his to carry. "Our plan may not have worked quite as we'd hoped, but it didn't fail, either." She paused to inhale a steadying breath. "I brought you an heir, Papa."

She glanced behind her and reached for Darius. His warm fingers surrounded hers with a firm grip. Assured. Strong. Then his thumb stroked the edge of her wrist. Lov-ing. Supportive. Everything she'd ever hoped for in a husband.

"Papa, I want you to meet the man I will marry." Her chin jutted up slightly at the pronouncement, announcing to both men that this part wasn't up for debate. "He has also agreed to act as your heir, should you wish it. Darius, this is my father, Mr. Anton Renard. Papa, this is Mr. Darius Thorn-ton . . . of the King Star Shipping Thorn-tons."

Darius sketched a quick bow. "An honor to meet you, s—"

"King Star?" her father interrupted. "Out of New York?" Gone was the regret, the sorrow from her father's gaze. A glow of triumph kindled there now, a triumph she'd given him. She prayed the rest of her story would not extinguish it.

A proud smile creased Darius's face as he answered. "Yes, sir. My father established the company, and my brother and I have shared in the running of it since we came of age."

"Nicki, my girl. You did it!" her father crowed. "Why did I ever doubt you would? You've never failed at anything you set out to do."

But she had.

"Papa, I-I took the dagger. I thought to protect you and Maman. But now . . . it's gone." She blurted out the truth before she could lose her courage.

"What?" Her father croaked the disbelieving syllable as he collapsed. John grunted at the sudden weight and struggled to maintain his grip.

Nicole flinched, her gaze dropping to the porch floor. "Fletcher Jenkins —"

"John, take him inside." Her mother bustled between, acting the buffer as she always did when tensions flared between father and daughter. "I refuse to be introduced to my future son-in-law with my hands and arms caked in crusty bread dough."

"I'll hear her explanation now, Pauline," her father rallied enough to growl.

Pauline Renard lifted her neck like a regal swan unperturbed by the wolf barking at the edge of her pond. "You'll hear her explanation in the parlor, Anton. Where we'll all be more comfortable." With that she swept past them, completely confident that her wish would be granted.

And of course it was.

Her father groused but ordered John to take him to his chair in the sitting room. By the time the coachman had her father settled, her mother reappeared, hands clean, hair repaired, and apron gone. She immediately went to Darius and clasped his hands. Leaning close, she placed a kiss on each of his cheeks. "Welcome to the family, *mon fils.*"

Then she turned a teasing smile on her daughter. "He's a handsome one, and he looks at you like your father looked at me when we were courting."

She glanced over to her husband, her face softening. "Anton still looks at me that way from time to time. I pray your man will do the same for you after two and a half decades of marriage."

"Pauline!" Papa grunted at her from his chair across the room.

Her mother smiled, the teasing light in her eyes only growing brighter as she patted Nicole's shoulder and moved to stand beside her husband's chair. She laid her hand on his shoulder, letting him feel her support. Nicole watched as her father sat a bit straighter, as if his wife's loyalty infused him with strength. As she and Darius took their seats on the sofa, Nicole couldn't resist reaching for the man at her side. He immediately wrapped her hand in his, and she felt her own infusion pour through her veins.

"Now," her father said. "Tell me about the dagger."

"Fletcher Jenkins has it."

She expected him to roar. To accuse her of being careless or weak or any of a hundred other things she'd already called herself. But he just slumped farther into his chair, his eyes slipping closed on a resigned sigh. Somehow that was even worse.

"I'm so sorry, Papa." Nicole slid off the couch to kneel at his feet. She raised her hand, intending to touch his arm, but she couldn't quite bring herself to do it, fearing the pain his rejection would send spiraling through her if he drew away from her touch.

"You were right. I never should have taken it. I did all I could to keep it safe, but in the end, I lost it. It's my fault, and —"

"No." The single word shot through the quiet room like a rifle crack.

Nicole watched her father's eyes open, and his gaze traveled to a point high above her head. Her mother, too, shifted her attention to the man who had risen to stand at her back. Nicole twisted to see Darius standing legs apart, as if braced for a fight. His expression dark, his eyes narrowed in on her father.

"It was *not* Nicole's fault." He enunciated each word as if forging it of gold and pressing his stamp into it. "Your daughter is the most courageous, clever, warm-hearted woman I have ever met. She escaped the Jenkins brothers time after time, uncaring of her own safety, wanting only to spare those in my household whom she had come to care about. She used herself as a decoy. She left the true dagger with me and asked me to bring it to you. But I refused. By the time I tracked her down, Fletcher Jenkins had her waist-deep in the Trinity and was attempting to drown the truth out of her."

Her mother whimpered at that, but Darius showed no mercy, just continued on with his blunt tale. Unable to watch, Nicole dropped her head and stared at the leaf pattern in the rug by her knees.

"I gave up the dagger, Mr. Renard. Willingly. Knowing all it meant to Nicole and to you, I gave it to Fletcher Jenkins. And I'd do it again in a heartbeat. I would forfeit anything to protect her. Even my life."

"Good." Was that her *father's* voice? "Then maybe you're worthy of her after all."

Nicole's head shot up.

"Nothing is more important to me than my daughter." Her father's gaze dipped down to meet hers. "Nothing."

Nicole's heart stuttered as she recognized the truth in his eyes.

"Every day after we learned of her improvised travel plans," he said, his attention never wavering from her face, "I prayed she'd send word she had made it safely to New Orleans. I considered sending my fastest steamer to fetch her but did not know if she was in Liberty or somewhere along the way. And I feared my efforts would lead Jenkins to her. So I just waited. Hoped."

He hung his head. "But word never came. And I began fearing the worst — fearing that in my desire to secure an heir, I'd sent my own child to her death."

"Oh, Papa." Silent tears streamed down Nicole's face. Her hand found his arm, all

467

hesitancy vanishing in an instant. The look that passed between them stripped away years of insecurity, of worrying that she'd never measure up. All this time she'd been using the wrong measuring stick. His longing for a son did not diminish his satisfaction with her as a daughter. It never had. She was the one who'd put that pressure on herself, the pressure to be something other than what she was meant to be.

Darius lowered himself to the floor beside her and wrapped his arm about her shoulders. "We notified the Rangers of the theft as well as the repeated attempts on Nicole's life."

"Repeated?" her mother interjected, her tone horrified.

Darius winced a bit and continued. "We also alerted the sheriff in Liberty as well as Sheriff Sparks here in Galveston once we docked. They each promised to do what they could to retrieve the Lafitte Dagger."

"My daughter has chosen well, Thornton." Anton Renard stretched a hand out to Darius. When he gave it a firm shake, a joy that she'd never known flooded Nicole's heart.

"Now, help my daughter back to the sofa. I want to hear all about this mess with Carson Jenkins's brood."

"And I want to hear how the two of you met," her mother said.

Darius grinned at Nicole as he tugged her to her feet. "It all started when she found an error in my calculations."

"Even the most brilliant of scientific minds make mistakes now and then," she teased as she took her seat on the sofa. "Especially when his handwriting is atrocious."

"Back to the beginning, girl." Her father's gravelly voice cut in. "What happened when you first landed in Liberty?"

The tale took the length of the afternoon to tell and continued on through dinner as her father grilled his soon-to-be son-in-law about his work with King Star Shipping, and her mother grilled him about his family. The discussion was still going strong when her mother's new cook served dessert.

A knock sounded on the front door, and the cook — Frannie, Nicole recalled — wiped her hands on her apron and bustled out to answer the summons. A moment later, Sheriff Sparks stepped into the dining room.

"Sorry to interrupt your supper, ma'am," he said with a tip of his hat toward Nicole's mother, "but I have some news to report regarding the dagger."

Her father's spoon clanked against his dish. "Well? Spit it out, Sparks."

The lawman shifted his weight from foot to foot and fiddled with his sleeve cuff, as if he wished he could be anywhere but there. "The dagger is nowhere to be found, sir. Jenkins claims he had no knowledge of his sons' actions and regrets any harm that may have befallen you or your family." He cast a quick, rueful glance at Nicole.

"Well, of course he claims that. The man's not going to simply admit his guilt and hand the Lafitte Dagger over to you because you asked him a few questions."

"I know that," the sheriff snapped. "That's why me and my deputies did a complete search of his residence as well as his shipping office. I also questioned men around the docks. Several witnesses reported seeing Fletcher and Will board one of their father's ships bound for Cuba yesterday."

Darius clenched his fist and pressed it into the tablecloth. "So they'll not pay for their crimes against Miss Renard?"

Nicole covered his fist with her hand and soothed away his anger. "God will hold them accountable, even if the law cannot reach them. They're gone, and they won't be causing any further trouble for us. Let's not waste time wishing for things that may never happen."

His fist loosened, then opened so that his fingers threaded through hers, and the lines across his forehead smoothed. "You're right. There are much more important things to focus on."

He was giving her that look again, the one that made her think of kissing.

"There are warrants out for their arrest," Sheriff Sparks assured them, "and I vow to see them carried out if either of them ever return."

"And the dagger?" Nicole asked.

"Never mind about the dagger, Nicki," her father said. "If it turns up, fine. If not, we will go on without it. Jenkins's lust for that dagger has stolen his children from him. Most likely he'll never see his boys again. He might not realize it yet, but one day he'll see that when a man loses his family, he loses everything. I thank God I escaped that fate."

"Me too, Papa," she whispered, then turned to look at the man who would be her husband, the father of her children, her family for the years to come, and thanked God for the providence that crossed her path with his. "Me too."

Epilogue

London, England
One month later

Darius Thornton extended his hand to assist his wife out of the hansom cab they'd taken from the hotel to Hyde Park. *His wife.* He still couldn't believe his good fortune. How a socially averse curmudgeon like him had managed to snare the elegant, sable-haired beauty stepping from the carriage was a miracle only God himself could fully explain. If it wasn't for the fact that he'd watched the same elegant beauty strap a blade to her stocking-clad thigh that morning before they'd left their suite, he might have been tempted to believe that Providence had made a mistake. But there could be no mistaking the intimate smile his sassy little pirate cocked at him as she emerged from the carriage. Nicole Renard Thornton belonged to him, and he'd thank the Lord for that blessing for as long as he lived.

As his beloved's gaze skittered past him, her eyes widened. "Oh, Darius. It's even grander than I imagined. Look at all that glass. It truly *is* a crystal palace."

He offered her his arm and led her up the wide path that wound past lush, manicured lawns and round pools with soaring fountains. Crowds of people from all walks of life milled about, slowing their progress, but Darius didn't mind. With Nicole's father regaining a bit of strength now that the stress of securing his daughter's future was behind him, they had the luxury of enjoying London at a leisurely pace, perhaps even for an entire fortnight. Plenty of time to see all the Great Exhibition had to offer.

"I understand that when Queen Victoria opened the exhibit to the public last month she declared it the greatest display of industry and manufacturing in the modern world." Darius tugged Nicole close to his side as they navigated around a group of gawking schoolchildren.

Nicole grinned at him, her excitement nearly as evident as that of the children they passed. "I can't wait to see what's inside."

"I hear there is a *raja*'s elephant draped in a jeweled *how-dah*." Darius bent his head to murmur in her ear, partly to make himself heard above the chattering children and partly to torture himself with the nearness of the delectable skin at her throat that he so loved to nuzzle. "And an upstairs gallery filled with stained glass that filters the sunlight in every color of the rainbow."

"And *I* hear they have steam engines of every possible variety and use." She arched her brow at him, not fooled at all by his mention of the more aesthetically appealing exhibits. He truly did long to dazzle her with the wonders of the World's Fair, but she knew him too well, knew he longed to dissect and digest all he could from the mechanical advances within the Crystal Palace. "And since this is as much *your* wedding trip as mine," she continued, "and since I fell in love with you fully aware of your addiction to boilers and steam mechanics, I suggest we investigate those first."

Darius chuckled. "You're too good to me, madam."

"Only as good as you are to me." She winked, and a soft laugh escaped her and warmed his blood. Yes, he would enjoy being good to this woman. For decades.

Once inside, the colorful displays demanded their attention. From a twenty-seven-foot-high pink glass fountain standing at the heart of the palace, to the steam hammer that could crush pounds of metal or gently crack an egg, to an envelope machine that could cut, fold, and gum thousands of envelopes an hour, to the largest diamond ever seen, the spectacle never ceased. After talking to nearly every steam engineer in the place, Darius steered Nicole toward the booths presented by France. It was past time to indulge her more feminine sensibilities. He dutifully smiled and nodded as she exclaimed over the rich tapestries, ornate furniture, and delicate porcelain, all while his mind processed the possible applications of the new designs for steam valves he'd seen. Or the submarine propeller for steamships. Or the —

"Darius, look at this."

"Hmm?" He turned, prepared to smile and nod again over whatever pretty thing had caught his wife's attention. So when she held up a metal gauge of some kind, it took him a minute to comprehend what he was seeing.

"The label declares it a New Metallic Manometer, and it's been awarded a Council Medal. Do you think it could be used to measure steam pressure? I spotted a small steam engine at the back of the booth." She pointed to a slit in the curtain behind the exhibit, where what appeared to be some kind of small boiler apparatus sat on a table.

Darius took the display gauge from Nicole's hand, his fingers trembling at the significance of what he could be holding. There was nothing heroic about its features, just a simple face containing a dial and hash marks to measure pressure levels. But when he turned the model over he encountered a design he'd never seen before. A curled tube followed the path of the circular frame, its sealed end attached to a linkage mechanism that would move the pointer on the front side. Darius lifted it to eye level to inspect it more closely while running a finger along the tube's edge. Fascinating. Not round as one would suspect, but flattened on the top and bottom.

"Would you like to see a demonstration, *monsieur*?"

Darius glanced up to find a dapper gentleman sporting a tailored suit and impressive chin whiskers.

"It is quite a marvel," the man continued, his French accent thick but not indecipherable. "It accurately measures pressure for steam, air, and water. I have every expectation that it will revolutionize the steam industry. No more exploding boilers to hold back our progress, *oui*?"

Or to steal lives.

Darius met the man's gaze, hope swelling

so full within him that he feared it would be his chest that exploded. "I'd very much like to see a demonstration, sir. I have a great interest in boiler safety, especially when it comes to steamboats. I've seen too much destruction, too many lives lost due to faulty handling of machinery that engineers don't know how to control with any consistency."

Nicole scooted closer, as if afraid she'd be excluded from the masculine conversation. She slipped her hand through the crook of Darius's arm. "My husband has gone so far as to conduct numerous scientific experiments to discover the causes of these explosions, working with the Franklin Institute of Pennsylvania. He has often commented on the need for a reliable mechanism to measure steam pressure."

"Ah, you are American." The Frenchman looked down his nose a bit as he said the word, but when he looked up at Darius again, interest and a glimmer of respect shone in his eyes. "I have heard of the Franklin Institute and have read their journal. A decent publication." He turned to wave to his assistant, signaling the man to bring the small steam engine out from behind the curtain.

"I think you will find that my New Metallic Manometer is just what you have been seeking. I have found it to be the most accurate gauge of steam pressure ever created." The man's boast smacked of overconfidence, but Darius reserved judgment. If the thing worked, he'd boast on the man's behalf to everyone who would listen.

"We are ready, Monsieur Bourdon," his assistant said. "The fire's been stoked and the heat is rising."

"Ah, *très bien.*" Bourdon tapped the gauge mounted on top of the boiler's water column. Darius's gaze never left it as the man went on to explain how the device worked. "As the pressure builds, the curled tube straightens slightly, moving the lever."

A familiar hiss developed in the boiler, signaling steam production. And just as the man predicted, the pointer on the gauge began to inch upward on the meter.

"It's working, Darius," Nicole whispered next to him, her quiet voice shivering with excitement. "It's truly working!"

Darius couldn't manage a reply. All he could do was watch the pointer continue to move as the hiss of steam grew louder. The lever had climbed nearly to the halfway point when the assistant popped the safety valve, releasing the steam.

"When the pressure decreases," Bourdon continued, "the tube relaxes back toward its original curved position, and the lever drops."

Darius tore his gaze away from the wonder before him long enough to nod to Bourdon. "I must congratulate you, sir. This shows great promise, indeed. I'd be very interested in bringing a model back home with me to study further."

"I'm afraid, *monsieur,* that I cannot allow such. This is a new patent, you understand, and I must protect my investment."

"Of course," Darius said politely, even as the muscles in his jaw tightened to the point that his teeth began to clench. America needed this device, needed it now. He might be able to replicate it if given enough time, but with his new responsibilities at Renard Shipping, time was an element in short supply. "Perhaps if I signed a document agreeing not to infringe on your patent . . . ? America needs a gauge like this desperately. Thousands of innocent lives are lost every year to riverboat explosions — explosions that could be avoided if we had an accurate way to measure steam pressure."

Bourdon raised a brow, his mouth straightening into a line of displeasure.

Blast it all. Darius hadn't intended to come across as threatening. He simply wished to convey the urgency of the situation.

Nicole's fingers wrapped around his hand, gently loosening the fist he hadn't even known he'd made. Darius glanced her way and found compassion glowing in her eyes, compassion tinged with warning. Forcing his muscles to relax, he gave her a tiny nod.

"My husband is passionate about this issue, *monsieur,*" she said by way of apology. "He experienced the deadly force of these explosions firsthand in New Orleans, aboard the steamship *Louisiana,* and longs to prevent such disasters from occurring in the future."

Bourdon's features immediately softened. "The *Louisiana?* My sympathies, *monsieur.* Even in France we heard of this tragedy. I'm afraid I cannot give you a model of my design to take with you, but I can tell you that another American approached me a few weeks ago when he saw my manometer. He wishes to buy the rights to my design in order to market it in your country. At the conclusion of the exhibition, we will begin negotiations. His name is Edward Ashcroft. I'd be happy to give you his direction."

Darius managed to choke out a thank-you through the thickness in his throat. As Bourdon disappeared behind his curtain to retrieve Ashcroft's address, Darius turned to the woman at his side.

"This is the answer, Nicole. I feel it in my bones. The Lord has answered our prayers."

Her smile washed over him with such joy, it was all he could do not to sweep her into his arms and kiss her senseless. He needed to celebrate. To share this moment with her in a way that this public hall would not permit.

"Would you mind terribly if we viewed the rest of the exhibits tomorrow?" he asked, his voice deepening to a husky timbre. "I don't think I could fully appreciate them in my current state of mind." He let his gaze rove over her in a way that communicated exactly what state of mind he was in. The blush that rose to her cheeks only added to the triumph surging through his veins. But she didn't look away. No, his little pirate met his gaze squarely.

"I find that suggestion quite agreeable, husband."

The moment Darius had Mr. Ashcroft's direction tucked safely in his pocket, he cut a path through the crowds swarming the grounds of the Crystal Palace with the efficiency of a jungle explorer on expedition. Only, the treasure he hunted was already on his arm. A priceless treasure whose value

was far above rubies, and one he would hold
tight to forever.

NOTE TO READER

Darius's gut proved correct. The Bourdon tube pressure gauge, invented by Eugene Bourdon in 1849 and debuted at the Great Exhibition in London in 1851 as the New Metallic Manometer, went on to revolutionize the steam industry. In fact, this design proved so efficient, it is still in use today. Edward Ashcroft successfully marketed the gauge in the United States, and with a viable way to measure boiler pressure, Congress was convinced to pass additional safety legislation. The Steamboat Act of 1852 not only called for inspections of vessels, boilers, and engines but mandated licensing of riverboat pilots. Higher standards for boiler construction could be regulated and enforced with penalties imposed by the federal government. Licenses could be revoked if a vessel or pilot failed to meet the code. Life preservers and lifeboats also became required equipment to have on board.

The reformation of the steam industry did not occur overnight, but progress steadily pushed the nation toward safer procedures, equipment, and personnel. As a result, fewer explosions stole innocent lives. Out of the 1852 Act, seeds were sown for the Steamboat Inspection Service, an entity solidified as an official government agency in 1871. This was the first regulatory agency of its kind and broke constitutional ground in giving our government the right to interfere with personal industry when public safety was at risk. It is because of this radical steamboat legislation that we are protected today by other agencies such as the Food and Drug Administration and the Federal Aviation Administration.

Darius and Nicole's journey may have been fictional, but the times and events surrounding it changed history.

ABOUT THE AUTHOR

Two-time RITA finalist and winner of the coveted HOLT Medallion and ACFW Carol Award, CBA bestselling author **Karen Witemeyer** writes historical romance because she believes the world needs more happily-ever-afters. She is an avid cross-stitcher and shower singer, and she bakes a mean apple cobbler. Karen makes her home in Abilene, Texas, with her husband and three children. Learn more about Karen and her books at www.karenwitemeyer.com.

The employees of Thorndike Press hope you have enjoyed this Large Print book. All our Thorndike, Wheeler, and Kennebec Large Print titles are designed for easy reading, and all our books are made to last. Other Thorndike Press Large Print books are available at your library, through selected bookstores, or directly from us.

For information about titles, please call:
(800) 223-1244

or visit our Web site at:
http://gale.cengage.com/thorndike

To share your comments, please write:
Publisher
Thorndike Press
10 Water St., Suite 310
Waterville, ME 04901